WITNESS BETRAYED

Books by Linda Ladd

Claire Morgan Homicide Thrillers
Head to Head
Dark Places
Die Smiling
Enter Evil
Remember Murder
Mostly Murder
Bad Bones

Claire Morgan Investigations Series
Devil Dead
Gone Black
Fatal Game

Will Novak Novels
Bad Road to Nowhere
Say Your Goodbyes
Witness Betrayed

WITNESS BETRAYED
A Will Novak Novel

Linda Ladd

LYRICAL PRESS
Kensington Publishing Corp.
www.kensingtonbooks.com

Lyrical Press books are published by
Kensington Publishing Corp. 119 West 40th Street New York, NY 10018

Copyright © 2018 by Linda Ladd

All rights reserved. No part of this book may be reproduced in any form or by any means without the prior written consent of the Publisher, excepting brief quotes used in reviews.

All Kensington titles, imprints, and distributed lines are available at special quantity discounts for bulk purchases for sales promotion, premiums, fund-raising, and educational or institutional use.

To the extent that the image or images on the cover of this book depict a person or persons, such person or persons are merely models, and are not intended to portray any character or characters featured in the book.

Special book excerpts or customized printings can also be created to fit specific needs. For details, write or phone the office of the Kensington Special Sales Manager:
Kensington Publishing Corp.
119 West 40th Street
New York, NY 10018
Attn. Special Sales Department. Phone: 1-800-221-2647.

Kensington and the K logo Reg. U.S. Pat. & TM Off.
LYRICAL PRESS Reg. U.S. Pat. & TM Off.
Lyrical Press and the L logo are trademarks of Kensington Publishing Corp.

First Electronic Edition: October 2018
eISBN-13: 978-1-5161-0739-1
eISBN-10: 1-5161-0739-X

First Print Edition: October 2018
ISBN-13: 978-1-5161-0742-1
ISBN-10: 1-5161-0742-X

Printed in the United States of America

Chapter 1

Below Will Novak's balcony, the final day of Mardi Gras was in full swing. Crowds walked along the narrow width of Bourbon Street, laughing and talking and enjoying the famous New Orleans celebration. The French Quarter was alive with excitement and good cheer, which put police on alert for inevitable drunken altercations. That's why Novak was watching. From where he sat in a chair drawn close to the wrought-iron rail, he could see several drunks stumbling around inside the crowd and others who looked well on their way to inebriation. His apartment was at the top end of Bourbon Street, so the riotous mass moved down the street in one direction like ants headed to a piece of pecan pie. Across the street, a jazz band was playing, filling the late night with the sounds of saxophone, piano, and bass fiddle.

Novak enjoyed the music, thinking the band was pretty good, as he swept his binoculars over the boisterous crowd as it moved along the ancient street with its old-fashioned lampposts and multitude of bars and novelty shops. The New Orleans Police Department had hired him on a temporary basis to spot probable troublemakers and report their locations to street cops. He'd been at it for a long time. Glancing at his watch, he found it was almost midnight. Eventually all the fun going on now would wane and the people would gradually disperse, but not yet. Maybe in another hour or two. He hoped so. He was dead tired.

Late February in south Louisiana was sometimes chilly; he had put on a leather jacket because of the nip in the air. The cold was not bothering anybody else, who kept warm by drinking beer and the sheer exhilaration of the moment. Unfortunately, nobody was calling it a night yet. Pushing, shoving, and hair-trigger, testosterone-fueled fistfights had been a regular occurrence all week long. At such occasions, Novak always watched first for the glint of steel. Knives were easily hidden under coats. This late hour was when either guns or knives were apt to be whipped out and innocent passersby hurt. Novak wasn't the only observer on the street. There were many others just like him with bird's-eye views of the action. He leaned back in his chair and adjusted his earpiece and microphone headset.

Loud shouts caught his attention, and he swung the glasses to a commotion starting up right across the street. A young woman stood high on a second-floor balcony opposite him. She looked as if she was smashed but didn't know it yet. She was having a good old time, giggling and waving at the men below her on the street. A crowd had already gathered, mainly because she kept pulling up her sweatshirt and showing her bare breasts. The guys below hooted and clapped and sent forth all manner of encouragement. She obliged their fervor by whipping the sweatshirt off over her head and shimmying for anybody inclined to take a look.

Skin shows were not unusual during Mardi Gras week. The guy standing on the balcony with her didn't appear to mind much, flinging off his own shirt in a show of support. His hairy chest didn't garner as much interest. Both leaned over the railing, blowing kisses and tossing strings of colorful beads to their drunken admirers, which immediately caused fights for possession. People were just damn stupid sometimes, but no real harm was done with something like that. He called in the incident. A two-team unit was dispatched to break up the crowd below, and then they'd have to climb the narrow interior stairs to the woman's apartment and order her to cover herself or go to jail. They had already warned the same woman earlier that evening. They might arrest her this time. Novak didn't care much, one way or the other. He riveted his attention back on the street. Many people carried red Solo cups so they could guzzle beer while they walked. Mardi Gras had always been a big drunken party and a giant headache for the NOPD. Tonight was no exception.

Novak was working solo. He hadn't been on a gig by himself in a while, not since he'd signed up with Claire Morgan's private investigation firm. His partner was unavailable, off to Italy with her husband, Nicholas Black. They had been tied up in Rome for days now, fighting Italian government red tape as they tried to adopt a ten-year-old boy named Rico. His parents had been murdered during a particularly bad case that Novak had been involved in, and since it had wrapped up, Claire and Black had given the kid a good home. They wanted him to stay there.

They were due back soon, though, and Novak was glad. He missed Claire. She was quite a woman, all things considered: tall, natural blond, athletic, good-looking, and sexy without knowing it. More important, she was a damn good detective and a damn good friend. He could count on her when things got sticky. Compared to most of their cases, tonight's gig was a breeze. Sitting in his own apartment watching people having fun was something he didn't usually mind.

Novak had lived in New Orleans since he was twenty-one and back from a childhood spent on his father's sheep ranch in Australia. He was well acquainted with the Fat Tuesday celebration. He didn't use his French Quarter apartment much, preferring his old plantation called Bonne Terre, down in Lafourche Parish. He'd inherited both properties the day he was born. In fact, he owned the entire building on Bourbon in which he sat, not to mention a fortune held in bank accounts that he rarely spent. His mother's wealthy Creole ancestors had owned the once-profitable sugar plantation since Napoleon Bonaparte reigned in France. Both properties were shabby now but worth millions in modern real estate markets. It was location, location, location. Novak would never sell either.

A shrill scream pierced the raucous noise. Novak instantly found the fight that was heating up. Two college-aged kids were circling each other, shoving and staggering, both drunk and confrontational. Their profane shouts escalated into swinging fists. Spectators circled them and cheered on the bloodletting.

"Got a fight starting up, just up from Red Fish Grill. Two young guys, both Caucasian. One in a red sweatshirt and a Toronto Blue Jays cap. Other guy is scruff bearded and wearing a light blue UNC parka and dark jeans. Crowd is starting to get into it. Better break it up fast."

A voice came back inside his ear. "On it. We see 'em."

"Red shirt just knocked the other guy down and is on top of him pummeling him with both fists. Crowd's trying to break it up."

Within minutes, two NOPD officers appeared and shoved their way through the eager onlookers. The two drunks were taken to the ground, handcuffed, and dragged off to a waiting paddy wagon. Novak lowered the glasses. NOLA jails were full to capacity tonight, just like most nights during Mardi Gras.

After sitting so long, his neck was starting to ache. Novak stretched his arms over his head and rolled his head back against his shoulders. His muscles were cramped. He hadn't eaten dinner and had stayed hunched over with the binoculars for the last five hours straight. He wasn't used to sitting around and doing nothing. He kept busy, either investigating cases, keeping up his properties, or out on the water in his boat. Truth was, that's where he wished he was now, out in the Gulf of Mexico sailing the seas in his forty-foot custom-built Jeanneau Sun Odyssey 379. Maybe he'd head there after this job wrapped up, head due south to the balmy climes and warm azure waters of the Caribbean Sea.

Novak leaned back and tried to relax. Once upon a time, this building had served his Creole ancestors in the St. Claire family as an elegant townhouse. Behind him, in the high-ceilinged, French-windowed rooms, antiques still sat in the original places. He had no desire to move them and rarely ever stayed at the apartment. He preferred his boat where it was moored behind his house on Bayou Bonne. Outrageous offers had been made for this building because of its prime location, but Novak's inheritance was sacrosanct. Most of that was tucked away in French and offshore bank accounts. His military retirement and private investigation pay was plenty to keep him in the red. But the once-lavish apartment behind him came in handy when enemies came sniffing around or Novak needed a safe house in which to hide endangered clients. Novak's stomach rumbled. All he wanted at the moment was to eat a steak, drink a beer, and get a good night's sleep.

Scanning the passersby, he homed in on a kid, maybe fourteen or so, as the boy grabbed a woman's purse and sprinted off. The thief headed straight for the intersection of Bourbon and Iberville, so Novak gave the cops a quick heads-up. Two mounted NOPD officers intercepted him near the Bourbon House. A stir of excitement ensued, but the crowd quickly lost interest and shuffled around the ongoing arrest like a lazy stream around a river island.

He poured himself more coffee from the thermos on the table beside him. His weapon of choice, a Kimber 1911 .45 caliber handgun, sat right beside it. He always kept his gun close. He'd learned to do that the hard way. He had enemies from his past, lots of them, some from his tenure with the NYPD but more from his military service as a Navy SEAL. Some of them wanted him dead. Some had tried and failed. But he stayed alert, even when sitting in the shadow of his balcony high above the street.

For fifteen minutes, Novak enjoyed a respite from trouble. The crowd was beginning to thin out but not enough to call it a night. Some people were peeling off onto the side streets, others heading back to hotel rooms. Novak had a knack for surveillance. He enjoyed people watching and learned plenty about human nature from that habit. He'd picked it up in the military, and it had kept him alive more than once. He could now pick out the bad guys nine times out of ten, by appearance and mannerisms and the bulge of concealed weapons.

Novak passed his glasses over the sidewalk on the other side of Bourbon. He stopped and moved his attention back to a woman standing there. Something was definitely off about her, so he pulled her focus in closer. She stood there alone, completely still, half hidden behind a support post. Novak felt at once that she was hiding from someone. She had on what looked like a man's raincoat, tan and belted tightly around her waist. It hung almost to the ground. He was startled to see that she was barefoot. A black New Orleans Saints ball cap was snugged down low over her face with most of her hair stuffed inside. Nobody seemed to notice her. More interesting, she was staring straight back at him.

Novak lowered the glasses. Their gazes locked for a few seconds. He was rarely spotted when on surveillance, and he was not advertising his presence. No way should she have noticed him sitting back in shadows, not with all the music and excitement surrounding her. Nobody else had, not one person all week long. He couldn't see her face well because of the cap's visor, but he was surprised that she didn't look away. She stared back, almost defiantly. Something about her made Novak uneasy. That didn't happen often, either.

Curious now, Novak watched her. She was looking from side to side as if searching for someone. Who and why? Then she riveted her attention back to him. He sensed she was worried, or maybe she was scared. His hunch told him it was the latter. She looked very young, early twenties, maybe a little younger or older, it was hard to judge. She had fair hair he thought, and she was not a particularly tall woman. He'd guess five feet four or five inches, at the most.

Novak picked up his cell phone and snapped a quick picture the next time she turned her face toward him. That's when he got a good look at her injuries. She had on a ton of black eye makeup that was smeared now but did not hide the deep and ugly bruise around her left eye. Her bottom lip was split wide open but no longer bleeding. From the looks of it, somebody had punched her hard in the face and more than once. He moved his attention to the people surrounding her. Nobody seemed aware that she was standing there alone, but she was interested in him, all right. She kept looking up at him, and then she'd resume searching the crowd moving down Bourbon. Then, suddenly, she spun away and pushed hard through the crowd on the sidewalk.

Novak focused the glasses on the people behind her. That's when he saw two men pushing hard in her direction, shoving people aside, with their eyes intent on the girl in the raincoat. Novak snapped photos of them. Both had short, scruffy beards. They were dressed like frat boys in town on spring break, but they were too old. They looked like guys with bad intentions. Worse, Novak was pretty sure they meant the girl bodily harm. He kept his focus on her pursuers. Both looked to be Hispanic, maybe, with dark skin and black hair and beards. He was fairly certain they were up to no good. His gut told him they had knocked around that woman before and were going to do it again. Why didn't matter to Novak. They were now within yards of grabbing her.

"Picked up a potential problem about to go down. Half a block up from Iberville. Two guys. Tall, Hispanic, shoving through people in pursuit of a woman in a long tan raincoat and black Saints cap. Female's roughed up, black eye and busted lip. She's short, five foot five. Taller suspect also has on black Saints ball cap. Number two has scruff and dark hair down to his shoulders, no hat. Both six feet, maybe a bit shorter; both likely concealed carrying. Woman's running, but they're almost to her. Better intercept in a hurry."

Alarmed for the woman's safety, Novak stood up and watched her fight her way through laughing revelers, out on the street now. Her pursuers were right behind her. One man lunged forward and grabbed the back of her raincoat. He swung her around to face him and punched her hard in the stomach. The blow bent her over forward, and she staggered, holding her stomach. She almost fell, but her assailant kept her upright with his grip on her coat. Then Novak glimpsed that telltale flash of steel in the woman's hand as she slashed a blade at him. He let go quick enough and about the time the cops showed up. They wasted no time taking the two assailants to the ground.

Novak watched the woman melt into the throngs of people. When he lost sight of her, he turned back to where the cops were frisking and cuffing her pursuers. Novak had been right about the weapons. Both guys were quickly relieved of handguns. Whoever the girl was, she was lucky Novak had noticed her. He attempted to locate her again as the men were hustled off to jail. If the young woman was smart, she'd get the hell out of town. Those guys wanted her dead, no question about it.

Maybe twenty minutes later, Novak picked the woman up again, right across the street in the exact same spot as before. She stared up at him, as if nothing had gone down. What the hell? He studied her face some more and was fairly certain he'd never laid eyes on her before tonight. Somebody screamed off to his left. Novak jerked the glasses in that direction. False alarm; the woman was laughing and horsing around with her girlfriends. Novak returned his interest to the mystery woman. She was gone again. He spent a few minutes trying to locate her but without luck.

Novak felt uneasy. He didn't like that feeling. That kind of visceral reaction rarely ended well for him. His danger detector was hitting alarm levels. When he got off duty, he was going out on the street and search for her. He was more curious than anything. Maybe he'd visit those guys in jail, too, if they hadn't been bailed out and released. He wanted to find out who they were and who she was. It didn't matter to him why they targeted her. They had abused a woman a whole lot smaller than they were; that just didn't cut it in Novak's book. He despised men who bullied women. It was a big trigger for him and a crime that angered him personally. Such men were cowards. Yeah, maybe he'd pay those guys a call. Maybe he'd bail them out and teach them a lesson in how to treat women.

As it turned out, Novak never got that opportunity. His muscles turned rigid as a woman's voice came softly from right behind him on the balcony. Novak was more concerned, however, with the gun barrel she jammed up against the base of his skull. Her voice was shaky.

"Don't you move, not an inch. Understand me? I will blow your head off if you do."

Novak didn't move. He understood, all right. He rapidly sorted through his options. There weren't all that many, so he played along, pretty sure he was dealing with the girl in the tan raincoat. He was damn annoyed she'd gotten the drop on him. It was embarrassing to be caught flat-footed in his apartment. He didn't like it much. He kept his words measured. "I'm not stupid enough to try something with a gun at my head. You got me cold, lady. Put the gun down. You're not gonna need it. Way I see it is you need my help. So let me help you."

Behind him, he could hear her rapid breathing. It was way off the normal range: quick, hoarse, raspy. Worse news, he could feel the slight trembling of the gun barrel now parting his hair, which meant her trigger finger was itchy, too.

Novak sucked in some fortifying air and steadied himself. He didn't want to make her nervous. She was nervous enough already. Slowly, he placed the binoculars down on the table beside him. "You're the woman I saw earlier, right? The one the two guys were after? I saw you watching me. I saw them attack you. I'm the one who put the cops on them." She said nothing. The gun was still shaking. "It looked like you were in big trouble down there. Why don't we talk about this? You need to put the gun down before it goes off. It's making me nervous."

"Are you Will Novak?"

Okay, now that surprised him. She knew his name, and she knew where to find him. Only a few close friends even knew that he owned this building. He was rarely ever there. Her knowledge of his business was not good news. Novak had been around the block a few times, had been hunted and had been the hunter. His enemies were hard-line criminals and didn't mess around when they wanted him dead. She could be one of them or she could be sent by one of them. His gut told him she wasn't there to kill him, or she would have pulled the trigger when he was unaware of her presence. The noise on the street probably would've drowned it out, and she'd have been home free.

On the other hand, no way would he take anything for granted. Maybe she was waiting to do it inside where nobody would see her. Whoever she was, she was pretty good. She had sneaked up behind him without him hearing a sound or sensing her presence. That rarely happened to Novak. He was well-trained, well-conditioned, and always aware of possible threats, but she had got him cold. Slowly, he raised his arms out to the side and spread his fingers. He did not want to spook her. She was edgy enough already.

"Take off the headset. Don't alert anyone or I will pull this trigger. Please don't make me kill you. That's not why I'm here."

Glad to hear that, Novak sure as the devil wouldn't give her reason to shoot him. He obeyed, considering whether he should take her down now or later. It wouldn't be hard. She was small, she was injured, and she was nervous.

"Place both hands on top of your head. Do it now."

Novak obliged her. She was stressed to the max, her voice weak and trembling. He had no doubt she was either scared of him, perhaps because of his size, or nervous holding a man at gunpoint. Maybe she'd never done it before. But she wasn't too frightened to confront him in his own apartment with a ton of people right below them, any one of whom could glance up and witness her accosting him. The gun barrel was shoved hard against his head and too unsteady to ignore. He could probably disarm her, and he might have already tried that if she'd had better control of the weapon. Even though she was standing behind him, he knew she was unstable, and that meant the outcome was unpredictable. It wouldn't take much for that weapon to discharge. It was better to play along until she calmed down enough to listen to reason, and then disarm her.

So he obeyed and said nothing. The woman reached around and snatched Novak's loaded Kimber off the table. That's when he saw the chrome handcuff dangling off her left wrist. The skin beneath the metal was bruised black. That shackle had been clamped on her wrist for a long time. She'd been somebody's captive. Novak stayed calm. Nothing much rattled him anymore. He'd been caught up in worse predicaments than this one. He sat still, just waited for her to tell him what to do next. She definitely had come to him for a specific reason. She wanted something, all right, but it probably wasn't his life. More than anything he was irked he'd been blindsided. He'd been caught like a novice. Claire Morgan would get a good gut laugh out of this story when she found out. He sat still and didn't make any sudden moves. A moment later, the gun pulled back a bit. Novak breathed easier.

"Okay." More heavy breathing; her pulse had to be racing. "Stand up slowly and walk backward into the house. Don't turn around. Don't try to alert anybody. Don't try to disarm me. Keep your hands on top of your head. I'm real shaky, I'm warning you."

No kidding, Novak thought. Her voice reeked of desperation. On the other hand, the woman appeared to know what she was doing. That could mean she had been trained in law enforcement. He hoped she was acting alone, but he couldn't be certain of that. There could be an accomplice inside the house behind her letting her do all the talking. There could be a second weapon trained on Novak's head. Below them, the crowd laughed and drank and moseyed along, unaware of the deadly takedown going on above them. Novak rose slowly to his feet, kept his hands tight atop his head, and stepped around the chair. He made his way backward until he stood just inside the tall louvered French doors. He kept his eyes focused straight ahead. The girl across the street had put her sweatshirt back on. She was not looking in his direction.

"Get down on your knees. Slow and steady now. Please don't try anything. I don't want trouble. I just want to talk to you."

"Then go ahead, talk to me."

Novak was not going down on his knees. Maybe she wanted to cuff him, maybe she just wanted to get him down before she shot him in the head, but it wasn't going to happen. He wasn't about to let her prod him with that gun, either. He took a couple of seconds to appraise the situation. She was frightened but knew what she was doing. Her nerves were shot to hell, so anything could happen. She could be in shock from the brutal beating and whatever else those two men had done to her. He had to gain control of the situation before one of them ended up dead. It was time to get answers. He ignored the order to kneel.

"Okay, lady, you said you wanted to talk. So go ahead. Tell me what you want. I saw you watching me. I saw those two guys come after you. I figure they gave you that black eye and busted lip, so I called in the cops to help you before they could hurt you again."

He heard the sound of metal clicking. She was messing around with the handcuffs. Then she said, "I need to cuff you. Please, just do what I say. I don't know if I can trust you yet. You might be one of them."

"Wrong. I don't know who *they* are. I don't know who you are."

Novak could see her now; her image was reflected in the antique gold mirror hanging across from them in the dining room. It had been in that spot for almost a hundred years, and the glass was dark and spotted, but he could still see that she was definitely the woman he'd seen across the street. "Listen, lady, I'm not working with those two guys. I'm not going to try anything, so no need to put cuffs on me. Tell me why they hurt you. Let me help you. That's why you came up here, right? So I could help you?"

Novak had been guessing at some of that, hoping she'd trust him. The gun barrel moved back a bit and then pressed hard into the hollow at the base of his skull. "Get down on your knees like I told you. Don't make me shoot. I don't want to kill you but I will."

Her voice was lower and steadier now. He could barely hear her. He was pretty sure she was alone. "Who beat you up?" he asked.

The pressure of the gun increased. Neither said anything. She was close to losing it; the tension in the room felt palpable. So Novak reconsidered. No way was he going to let her put handcuffs on him. He could spin around easy enough and snatch the weapon out of her hands. It'd be easier if he was already facing her, but he had disarmed plenty of people who stood behind him. He lunged to the side, spinning low and to his left, but she was ready for the maneuver. She stepped back out of his reach and redirected her weapon to his heart.

Novak stared at the Luger: chrome, German-made, 9mm, shiny bright with a carved ivory handle that she gripped tightly in her right hand. His .45 was in her left hand. The handcuff now dangled from her little finger. She was still barefoot. Her coat was slightly open in front. She was naked underneath. It looked as if she had been wounded. Blood was dripping down her leg and pooling on his carpet. The hat was gone, and there was a lot of blood soaking into some long and tangled wheat-colored blond hair. She was filthy, and she was trembling all over. Her heavy black eye makeup was smeared down on her cheeks, and her face was bruised worse than he'd thought. She looked in bad shape. She needed medical attention. Her gun hand was shaking back and forth like crazy.

"You need a doctor," he told her softly, not moving a muscle.

She swayed slightly. Her weapon did, too. Her finger was not alongside the trigger the way it should be; it was on the trigger and ready to tug it back if he looked at her wrong. Not good, that. Novak kept his eyes latched on the weapon and then moved his gaze up to her swollen eye. "Don't do anything you'll regret. Nobody needs to get hurt here."

"Then do what I say. Please, I'm tired, I'm just so tired."

Weak but determined, she meant it, all right. She looked tiny standing next to him. Novak stood six feet six inches; he towered over her. At around two hundred forty pounds, he was easily double her weight. Even if she hadn't suffered from abuse and exhaustion, she couldn't best him in a fight, not without some major ninja skills. They stared wordlessly at each other. Tension was building, slowly and steadily.

Then, without any warning, the hall door across from them burst wide open and slammed against the wall behind it. Both Novak and the girl went down into defensive crouches. One of the men chasing her earlier stood in the threshold holding a Glock 9mm with both hands. The intruder and the injured woman with Novak opened fire simultaneously. Novak lunged forward and tackled the woman around the waist and took her down to the ground behind the couch. He grabbed his Kimber out of her hand. She was hit in the arm and bleeding profusely, but the man at the doorway was dead, hit center mass with a double tap, right through his heart.

Novak didn't have time to think before the dead guy's partner showed up in the dining room archway and let loose with a barrage of fire. Novak rolled to the end of the couch and came up firing. He hit the guy in the head and throat, knocking him back into the dining room where he went down, choking on his own blood. Novak stayed low, behind the couch, and waited for number three. Nobody else showed. After a few moments, he took a knee beside the girl. She was on her back, moaning and already half-conscious. Her upper arm near the shoulder was a bloody mess.

Novak pulled a throw off his couch and wrapped it around her arm as tight as he could knot it, hoping to slow the bleeding until the paramedics showed up. The woman had already lapsed into unconsciousness. He got up and checked out his apartment for more gunmen but found no one. Both assailants were dead. Then he walked out onto the balcony and picked up his headset. The crowd below still moved blithely along, unaware of what had just gone down in his apartment. Either they hadn't heard the gunfire or thought it was fireworks.

"This is Will Novak. Requesting ambulance and homicide detectives. Home invasion. Two dead, one wounded. Come down the back alley between Bourbon and Royal. I'll be there to wave you in."

"Got it. What the hell's goin' on, Novak?"

Novak dropped the headset without answering. A siren shrieked on from somewhere down around Canal Street. He hurried back inside and searched through the pockets of the two dead men. He found wallets, keys, and cell phones. He stuffed all of them into his coat pockets. He left everything else in the apartment untouched. The evidence would clearly show that two men had burst inside and attacked them. It was all right there with enough forensic evidence to satisfy any practiced detective. He checked the girl's arm, realized the bleeding had not slowed down much, and tightened the tourniquet. Then he ran downstairs to the back alley and waited for the shrill sirens to find him.

Chapter 2

The ambulance skidded to a stop, spraying gravel on the two NOPD patrol cars coming right behind it. All three vehicles had their sirens shrieking like banshees. The EMTs scrambled out and jerked a gurney from the back. Novak led them quickly upstairs to his apartment, and the medical technicians immediately went to work on the wounded woman. Novak stood back, said nothing, and watched the police clear the house and string crime scene tape across the entrances. Two more patrol cars arrived with flashing lights, and those officers worked to keep Mardi Gras rubberneckers out of the alley. Novak hovered near the woman and answered questions, mostly with the truth: "I have no idea who she is. I don't know her. I've never seen her before."

After they were done grilling Novak, they made it clear they were not satisfied with his responses. So he sat down at the dining room table and waited for the homicide detectives to come on scene. That's when he would really get the third degree. He was the only witness to a double murder and had shot one victim dead himself. Lucky for him, he was acquainted with most of the NOPD detectives, at least by name, and knew several very well. That would work to his advantage and give him leeway with the truth. He knew better than to up and take off, even though he wanted to when the mystery woman was carefully loaded onto the gurney and rolled down to the waiting ambulance. He followed the EMTs, wanting information on her chances.

"How bad is it?" he asked the female paramedic as she slammed the rear door. She stopped briefly but was in a hurry.

"Her arm's chopped up pretty bad but doesn't look like much bone damage. She'll be going into surgery as soon as we can get her there."

As she walked away, Novak called out to her, "What hospital?"

She stopped with her hand on the driver's door. "Charity. We need to get her name. If you know it, you need to tell us. Somebody needs to be notified."

"I don't know, believe me. If I did, I'd tell you. I'd never laid eyes on her until tonight. She showed up here uninvited, and all hell broke loose. Those guys were gunning for her, not me, that's my take on it. Why, I haven't a clue. Get going, I'll come over later and talk to you."

Then they were gone, pulsating siren shattering the quiet night. The detectives assigned to the case showed up inside his apartment fifteen minutes later, one right after the other. Novak was pleased to see the lead investigator was Gabriel LeFevres. Gabe was an old friend of Claire Morgan's and a man that Novak knew fairly well. He would probably take Novak's word on what happened and trust him to be truthful.

Frowning, Gabe approached Novak, but he was looking at the blood spatter and the two victims sprawled on the floor in pools of their own blood. He stopped at the door and snapped on plastic gloves and paper booties. He was tall, maybe six feet three inches, Cajun-born in the bayou with black hair and dark skin to prove it. His eyes were big and brown and intelligent. Claire always said Gabe could see right through lies, and she was dead-on. That made him a hell of a good detective. He had started his career in ATF, and his last case there had not been a cakewalk. He had successfully infiltrated and worked undercover inside a notorious motorcycle gang called the Skulls. He had risen up fast to become their leader and survived inside for two years before he brought down every single member of that gang on drug charges. All were still in jail. When he reached Novak, he said, "What the holy hell went down in here, Novak? This looks like a damn war zone."

"Yeah, it pretty much was. The girl who got shot? Don't know her from Adam. She showed up here with a gun, and so did the victims. Never seen her before tonight, Gabe, I swear to God."

Gabe didn't even try to hide his skepticism. "Don't give me that shit. You know more than that."

Novak wouldn't have believed himself, either. "Not this time. The woman is a complete stranger. I have no idea who she is or where she came from or why she came up here to see me."

Gabe eyed him for a moment. "Okay, then tell me what you do know. Exactly what went down here, and don't leave anything out. We just talked to the hospital, and the woman's still in surgery. Preliminary call is she'll recover. The wound wasn't as bad as first thought."

"Her shoulder looked done for."

"Okay, let's get down to the facts. Your side of this thing. From the beginning."

"My side?"

"There are always two sides. We'll get hers when she wakes up. You know how this works. You're a detective."

So Novak told him exactly what happened. It didn't take long, but neither had the shootout. Gabe stood there and listened, hands on his hips, looking as if he didn't believe a word that came out of Novak's mouth. Then he did his job. He examined all the blood soaking into Novak's creaky hardwood floor and the blood spattered on the couch and doors. He looked at the bullet-pocked, blood-spattered wallpaper and gauged all the angles, and then he stood silently and watched the CSI techs gather up spent shell casings while the medical examiner searched through the pockets of the two dead intruders. They found nothing of interest—all of that was in Novak's possession because he wanted to know who they were before the cops did. Then Gabe came back to Novak and told him to repeat his story again.

Novak did so, almost verbatim, that being for show, but Gabe remained unconvinced. "So that's it in a nutshell, huh? Novak, cut the crap and tell me who these guys are and why you're smack-dab in the middle of another bloody crime scene."

"I know this all sounds crazy, but it's true this time, I swear. She just showed up here out of the blue and held a gun to my head. That's exactly what happened. No reason for me to lie about it. Why would I?"

"We both know why. You're protecting somebody."

"Not this time."

"So okay, you know nothing about a gun fight resulting in two gory deaths that happened inside your living room. Let me think, why doesn't that ring true to me? You tell me."

Novak agreed. That did sound worse than pathetic. He could make up a better story. "I know this doesn't add up. Sorry, man, but that's how it went down. I swear to God. That's the truth."

"Look, Novak, we go back a ways. I know what you do and how you do it. I know you cut corners at times, but you usually do the right thing in the end. You need to come clean and tell me everything. This is not a burglary; it's a double murder. Two guys are dead, and a woman is hurt bad."

"Okay, there might be one other thing. I did see these two men tailing the woman down Bourbon Street earlier tonight. It looked to me like she'd been held captive by them. See those handcuffs over there behind the couch? One was dangling off her wrist when she got here, and somebody had beaten her up pretty good. My take? I think they had her somewhere in town where they beat and abused her. Somehow she escaped, and they came up here trying to shut her up for good. They burst in here ready to put her in the ground; I have no doubt that's what they intended. They were shooting at her but would've killed me, if I'd gotten in their way. They thought I was helping her, I guess. I don't know, but that's what happened. Who knows if I'm right? I'm conjecturing."

"You've got no idea who they are or where they came from? If that's your story, it's weak, Novak."

Novak steadied his eye contact, tried to look his most earnest. "I was caught off guard. I've been working surveillance for you guys all week. This thing came out of the blue. You need to talk to the woman. They were following her, and I think they wanted her dead. My gut's telling me there's more to this than meets the eye, and I think there are other guys out there waiting to gun her down. Maybe you should think about putting an officer outside her hospital room."

"You need to come with me to the station and make a statement."

"I thought I just made one."

"An official statement. But it's late and this is going to take some time here, so I guess you can wait until tomorrow." He watched the forensic team a moment, as they snapped photographs and dusted the room for fingerprints. "This is a crime scene, Novak. You can't stay here, not until we release the scene, and that's not going to be any time soon. You can bunk over at my place, if you want, or get yourself a motel room."

"No problem. Once I know that woman's out of the woods, I'm heading down to Bonne Terre. I don't have a dog in this fight, and I don't want one, believe me."

"Well, you'll have to show up tomorrow for your statement."

"So I'm free to go now, right?"

"Yeah."

"I'm heading over to Charity. I'm pretty sure she came to me for help. She knew my name. I want to know why me before I bow out and leave it to you."

"Investigating this case is my job. Don't get involved. You got that, Novak? Don't do anything to get yourself in trouble."

"Who, me?"

Gabe just grimaced. "Damn, this scene is messy. This is gonna take all night. I doubt we'll get over to the hospital till tomorrow, and that's if the doctors will allow us to interview her. If she comes to tonight before

I get there and tells you anything, and I mean anything, you need to call me right away."

"Right. No problem. I'm here to help."

Gabriel side-eyed him as if he didn't believe him, and then he walked away to talk to his technicians. Novak took off in a hurry, wanting to get out before Gabe changed his mind and dragged him down to the station. In the garage, he tore down the crime scene tape and backed out his old dark green Ram pickup truck. Maneuvering around police cars blocking the narrow alleyway, he made it to the hospital in minutes. Traffic was light now, the crowds mostly dispersed. He parked outside the emergency room entrance. He knew where the surgery suite was because he'd spent some time there nursing various and sundry gunshot wounds he'd suffered. The surgical waiting room stood empty except for one intern in green scrubs who was lying across four attached seats, sound asleep. A nurse named Becky informed Novak that Jane Doe was still undergoing surgery. She wasn't sure how much longer it would take, either.

She walked off toward the nurses' station, and the first wave of weariness hit Novak. He needed to sleep, but he couldn't do that so he went searching for the vending machines. The coffee machine was well stocked and offered a variety of caffeine goodies, including cappuccino and latte, but he settled for two large black coffees and a plastic-wrapped ham and cheese sandwich. He carried the food back to the now-empty waiting room and chose a seat which kept his back to the wall behind the door because he was expecting company, the kind who carried big guns and hung around with the two dead guys now resting on a slab inside the police morgue. They had been hired by someone who meant business, and his gut told him there were plenty more of them and they weren't going to stop coming after that woman. She had to have something big and/or incriminating on them. So he kept his .45 loaded on the table beside him, and his right hand free. They were coming, no doubt about it, and they would do it before she got a chance to talk to detectives. Novak hoped they did show. He had some questions he wanted answered, too. He sat there alone in the silent room, downed one cup of coffee after another, and waited with the patience he'd learned while serving in the military where everything moved at a snail's pace.

It started raining about four thirty that morning. Everything was nice and calm except for a squad of solemn nurses moving about in crepe-soled sneakers. Novak sat alone and watched the rain trickle down the window in forked rivulets and paint the panes with silver drops that glowed from the halogen street lights. He was working on a new cup of caffeine. It no longer tasted good, but it kept him awake and halfway alert.

Jane Doe's operation had been declared successful a little over an hour ago. The nurse bringing the good news also emphasized that the injury to the arm was not something to be taken lightly. The bone had been nicked, and there had been bone splinters and damaged flesh and ligaments torn from bone. Surgeons had removed the bone fragments and thought they'd gotten them all. That said, the nurse apprised him that his friend's nasty wound would take time to heal but she'd been lucky that the bullet hadn't severed an artery or broken a bone. The patient was in recovery now, and just be patient, the surgeon will drop by to talk to you as soon as he can. They figured everything would heal nicely and her arm would be functional, given time and a bit of physical therapy. All that being said, it was still pretty much a lukewarm but hopeful prognosis. And she wasn't dead, which was always a good thing in Novak's world.

Novak had spent some of the wait going through the two dead men's wallets and cell phones, hoping to find out who they were and where he might find their buddies holed up before their next assassination attempt. It turned out to be a veritable treasure trove that he was just itching to explore. He had specific names and addresses now. That gave him a roadmap to find out who had hired these guys. He could hit them first and hit them hard. He liked that idea. All he needed was for the woman to illuminate why this stuff was happening so he could get on with it. He took offense to them shooting up and then dying in his living room. Gabe LeFevres would get the phones and wallets turned over soon but not quite yet. Not until he found out the why behind the bloody evening.

Novak grew increasingly impatient. Uncharacteristically, his mind was seething. Maybe it was with anger, or maybe it was simply annoyance. The girl's battered face kept coming to mind. He craved payback for that, and he didn't even know the woman. She needed to tell him what he was getting into. He had to find out who she was and what they wanted. Novak had a feeling that these guys liked to come at you in waves, like cowards always did. The attack could be mob connected, somehow. That's what it sounded like to Novak. He stood up when a doctor pushed through a swinging door. He still wore dark blue surgeon scrubs and had a surgical mask hanging loose around his neck. He looked tired. He held a Styrofoam cup of coffee that matched Novak's.

"Are you the man who's been asking about the Jane Doe gunshot victim?"

"That's right. The nurse told me she was going to be all right."

"Yes, we think so. I'm Dr. Palen. I performed the surgery. Your friend was lucky. A few inches to the right and she'd be dead. The operation went very well. It turned out to be a bit more complicated because of bone fragments, but she should fully recover, given time and a lot of rest. She's out of recovery now, and they'll be taking her down to her room any time. No need for her to stay in ICU. She'll be in Room 217. She's probably already there."

"What about other injuries? I saw signs that she was beaten before those guys shot her. I tried to stop the bleeding on that arm at the scene."

"She lost a lot of blood. We had to transfuse her. She'll be weak for a few days." He shook his head. "I hate to tell you this, but you probably already know. She was beaten, yes, but she was also tortured. We found cigarette burns on her breasts and thighs. There were bruises and lacerations on her face, arms and legs, and the bottoms of her feet." He hesitated and considered Novak. "I take it that you're not her husband?"

"No, I don't really know her at all. She was at my place when they got her. I'm trying to find out her name so I can contact her family. I've already talked to the detectives. They gave me permission to wait here and speak to you. Somehow I feel responsible."

"You shouldn't. You probably saved her life. Still, she has suffered major abuse. You can tell the detectives that she was repeatedly physically assaulted. I'm not sure if she was subjected to a sexual assault, but the bruising indicates that might be a possibility. She also sustained a minor stab wound to the abdomen, really more of a slash. The blade entered on her left side but didn't penetrate or hit any internal organs. I believe the knife wound occurred tonight sometime, but the other injuries look several days old, at least. She must have gone through something terrible at the hands of those men."

Novak nodded, well aware. He was going to find the rest of those guys and enjoy a little chat with them. "But she will survive and eventually be all right?"

"Physically, she will be fine if she takes care of herself. Emotionally, psychologically, that might be more difficult to predict. She's going to need therapy, I suspect. I'm glad the guys who did this can't hurt anybody else. They were brutal men."

"Yeah."

"I told the nurses that you can stay in the room with her tonight, if you like. Somebody should be there when she comes to. She'll probably wake up in a state of terror."

"I'll do that. Thank you, Doctor."

Novak watched him walk out and disappear down the corridor. Novak took the elevator to the second floor and had no trouble finding the room. There was no policeman on duty yet, which wasn't good. Inside, the woman lay on her side in the hospital bed, eyes closed, her breathing rapid and shallow. Her left arm and shoulder were bandaged and bound up to her body by a maroon sling. Her blond hair was smoothed back, but he could still see blood in it. The monitors were steady, blinking out her heartbeat and blood pressure, all of which looked stable. She had on a lightweight generic green hospital gown covered with tiny white squares that was tied in the back. There was absolutely zero color in her face. She was as white as a cloud against a snowbank and looked like a corpse left to rot on a battlefield. Novak pulled up a chair close to the bed and waited for her to wake up.

Outside in the corridor, he heard low murmurs of conversation between the nurses. Far away in the distance, yet another siren screamed like a wounded eagle until it died into echoes on the street right below him. Mardi Gras was over; he was done with that job. Now he had bigger fish to fry. He liked mysteries, and he had a doozy with this woman. He watched the corridor door because he was dead certain that a bevy of bad guys were incoming, all with deadly intent. His gut told him to be ready to react, and he always listened to his gut.

Chapter 3

An hour later, the woman shifted slightly under the sheet and attempted to open her eyes. Novak stood up and looked down at her. When she tried to move her bad arm, she groaned. Novak moved closer to the bed. He leaned down close so she could focus on his face. She made a valiant effort to see him but was so weak and groggy that her words were hard to understand.

"What...happened...?"

Novak glanced back at the door and then spoke softly, close to her ear. "You're in the hospital. The two men chasing you burst into my house and shot you. You killed one of them. I got the other one. Do you remember any of that?"

Her forehead furrowed, and Novak wasn't sure if she understood the question. She licked at parched lips sewn up with black surgical thread. Novak could see by her dilated eyes that she was still under the anesthetic and completely confused.

He tried again. "You were taken into surgery, and now you're in a private room. The doc says you're going to be all right."

She appeared to be trying to garner her thoughts but couldn't seem to make her mind work.

"Listen, I'm staying here with you, so don't worry about anything. I won't let anyone else hurt you. Just rest, and we can talk again when you feel better."

Her eyelids drifted down. She didn't open them again. Novak wasn't sure if she'd understood him. Her face looked terrible. They'd applied some kind of shiny clear salve on her bruised eyes. The left one was almost swollen shut. Her bottom lip had those three big, ugly, black sutures. Novak left her alone and walked out into the corridor to inform the nurses that she had awoken for a few minutes. The morning shift had showed up in a lot of bustle and hushed whispering, and two new nurses hurried in and busied about taking their patient's vitals. They entered their readings on a laptop and then tried their level best to get rid of him. Novak refused to leave, politely but resolutely. They gave in, but they didn't like it. Two hours later, the patient woke again. Her pain had intensified this time, and when she tried to sit up and realized her arm was bound, she panicked and tried to get out of bed. Novak held her down against her pillow as gently as he could.

"Let me go, I've got to get out of here! They want to kill me!"

Novak held on until she stopped struggling, which didn't take long. Then she lay still, exhausted. It was his turn to talk. "Okay, you need to listen up. I know they're after you. Do you understand? I know you probably came to me for help." She stared up at him, her injured eyes open now and locked on his face. "I want to know why. Who sent you to me? And why didn't you go to the police when you had the chance? They were patrolling everywhere on the streets last night."

"No! No cops!" She was becoming agitated again. Her plea was low but shrill, and she started pushing against his hold.

"They're already involved. It's a double homicide investigation now. I killed one of those men hunting you. I'm involved big-time, and I want to know why."

She squeezed her eyes closed, her breaths now low and labored. She didn't look or sound so hot.

Novak softened his tone. "Okay, you're safe here. I'm not going to let them hurt you. Understand? Just tell me what's going on. That's all I'm asking."

She looked small and battered and helpless, but somehow he knew she was stronger than that. She kept her eyes shut when she answered him. "I can't stay here. They'll get me."

"Sorry, but you're not up to going anywhere right now. You're too weak."

"Please, just can't you help me—"

"That's what I'm trying to do. Tell me who you are. What's your name?"

She turned away from him. Then she came out with it, so low that he could barely hear her. "Lori Garner, okay? But you can't tell anyone who I am, you can't, promise me."

Novak had never heard the name. "I won't. Who sent you to find me?"

"They'll kill me. They told me they were going to, but I got away."

Novak glanced at the closed door. He believed her, all right. "You can't be moved just yet. I'll stay here on guard and make sure they don't get in here."

"Please, just let me go—"

Her breathing was labored now, so much that her heart monitor went berserk: her pulse hammering, her blood pressure climbing rapidly. Novak laid his hand atop hers. "Shh, calm down. I'm not leaving you in here alone. Nobody's getting near you, trust me."

Before Novak could calm her down, an incensed young nurse pushed the door open and shooed Novak away from the bed. She went about her work efficiently, examining her patient, studying the chart, and then administering an injection that quickly sent Lori Garner to dreamland and dropped her vitals down to normal. She turned around, hands on hips, and eyed Novak with hostility. Her name was Juliet.

"I'm aware that Dr. Palen gave you permission to stay here, but if you continue to excite her like this, you'll have to go."

"I've got to stay here."

That got her attention. She bristled. "Why?"

"Because she doesn't have anybody else to look after her."

The nurse didn't roll her eyes, but she badly wanted to. "She has an entire staff of doctors and nurses here to look after her, if you'll recall. I can't force you to leave. I'd think you'd want to do what's best for her."

"I am."

"Do you understand that keeping her quiet and resting comfortably is our primary concern right now?"

"Yes, ma'am. I won't wake her up, and I won't get in your way."

She held eye contact for a long moment because she didn't believe him. Then she left in a huff, and Novak sank back into the chair. He needed sleep himself but was way too jacked up on adrenaline and caffeine. He dozed off a couple of times, however, but every little sound woke him. The nurses visited the room too often, or it seemed to Novak they did. A pair of doctors appeared once, hovered around Lori's bed, checking the wound and speaking in hushed tones. Then they disappeared, not to be seen again. No bad guys yet. Maybe Novak had been overreaching. Maybe there were just the two dead men working alone. Maybe they were inept assassins, and therefore lying cold and dead in metal drawers. He hoped that was the case because the threat would be over. It didn't compute. He was used to considering and preparing for the worst possible scenario. He hoped he was wrong. That would simplify everything.

The next time Lori Garner woke up, she appeared lucid. Novak moved to her bedside and was shocked by the first words out of her mouth. "Frank Caloroso sent me. He told me to come find you. He said you'd help us. He told me about that place you've got on Bourbon Street and the other one down in the bayou. He said I could trust you."

The name was all Novak needed to hear. Frank Caloroso was an old friend, an all-around good guy, maybe a bit complicated but a trusted partner with whom Novak worked at both the NYPD and in the Navy, all of which happened decades ago. Novak hadn't seen him recently, maybe five or six years ago, but they kept in touch. Frank was a good detective, a second-generation Italian American hailing originally from Kansas City. Last Novak heard, Frank was living in Galveston, Texas, where Frank worked as a private investigator. Frank had been with Novak the day he watched the World Trade Center crash down with Novak's entire family inside. Novak had lost his wife, Sarah, and their two little kids, all of them at once, on that terrible day. Caloroso was the man who had kept Novak up on his feet in the awful days that followed when all he wanted was to die along with them.

Unwillingly, Novak relived the moment, the cloying white dust, the rending of steel and shattering of glass. Then he blocked out the memory the way he always did. He owed Caloroso in a way that he could never pay back. He would lay down his life for him. Frank was probably the best friend Novak had ever had.

"Is Frank here in town?" he asked.

Lori Garner shook her head. Despite her swollen eyes, her gaze was focused on him. Her irises were big and the color of a summer sky. There were designs in the blue part that looked like tiny flowers. The whites of her eyes were bloodshot as hell. "He's hiding out in Galveston. They've got a bogus warrant out on him." She closed those flowery eyes and wet her lips, the tip of her tongue lingering to explore the stiff black suture thread. "I need to go now. Help me get out of here, and I swear I'll tell you everything. Take me somewhere safe until I can get back on my feet. I'll pay you anything you want. If you don't, they'll come here and they'll kill me." Her voice was much stronger now, strong enough to make him notice how full of fear it was.

"Nobody's going to kill you, not here or anywhere else. What kind of warrant is out on Frank? What do they say he did?"

"Frank didn't do anything. The judge is dirty. He took Lucy and told Frank he'd kill her if he interfered. Frank's in hiding, waiting for us to get back there and help him find her."

That took Novak aback. Lucy was Caloroso's daughter, the only family he had left since his wife had died five years ago. "Who took her? She's just a kid. What, eleven or twelve?"

"Just turned thirteen. She's leverage to make Frank back off his investigation into the judge's corruption. He says you'll help us. He says I should do what you say."

"You can trust me."

Lori's voice was hoarse, and she had trouble talking around the stitches, so Novak picked up the plastic pitcher of ice water and placed the straw up close to her mouth. "Don't drink too much at first."

She sipped a little and dropped her head back onto the pillow. Her eyes never left him. She was weak and becoming woozy again. She didn't trust him yet. But if those guys had taken Frank's little girl, Novak was going to help them get her back. If they hurt her, they were going to pay with their lives. Frank would kill them all.

"If Frank's a friend of yours, so am I," he told Lori.

She nodded a little. "They want me dead because I can recognize the guys who took me. If you get in the way, they'll kill you, too."

He pulled his chair closer. "You've got to tell me everything."

Lori didn't answer, succumbing to narcotic dreams. Impatient to know what had happened to Lucy, Novak sat there and stared at Lori's delicate profile. If those dead guys had Lucy Caloroso held captive someplace, they very well could be hurting that child just like they'd hurt Lori. The idea was enough to chill his blood. Lucy was a nice little kid, polite, well-mannered, sweet, and always had been. Novak was like an uncle to her. He loved her, so whatever was going down on Galveston Island, Novak wanted to get down there and end it. He was half-surprised Frank hadn't put all of them in the ground already. Frank was not a man you messed with, especially when it came to his family. Lucy was his whole world.

Impatient, growing antsier with each passing hour, Novak continued to sit and wait for something to happen. Nothing else he could do. More time passed. Lori came awake again. Novak leaned over her, and she started telling him the same things over again, her mind still muddled. "Frank said you'd help me. He said you were all we'd need." Color had come back into her face, infusing tinges of pink into the pallor. She squinted up at him, and then she got squeamish.

"Describe Frank to me. What does he look like?" It wasn't quite a demand, but it came close.

Novak couldn't blame her. He didn't trust people right off the bat, either, and he never trusted anybody completely. He always expected to see their bad side show up; that caution had kept him alive.

"Okay. How's this? Frank Joseph Anthony Caloroso has light brown hair, hazel eyes, closing in on six feet tall. He can shoot the eye out of a gnat at fifty feet. Damn fine detective. Great cook. His specialties are chicken parm, pizza with pepperoni, sausage, mushrooms, and black olives. Let me think, what else? He makes rigatoni broccoli with pink sauce for Lucy. That's her favorite. That enough or you want more?"

"Any scars?"

"He's got a quarter-inch-thick knife slash on the back of his left forearm. Got that in 2010 in Bangkok on a weekend pass out of Japan. Throws knives like a damn ninja. He's got a big tat on his back, had it done in Honolulu—crossed flags: Stars and Stripes and the Navy Flag."

Lori looked relieved. "Okay, you know him. Good."

"My turn to ask questions," Novak told her. "You've been well trained. My guess is you got that in law enforcement. So what was it? Police, military, or something else?"

"Military police before I opted out. I can hold my own." She opened her eyes and stared up at him. "Just so you know, I was up against four of those guys, and it was dark. They overpowered me."

Novak fought an urge to smile. That takedown had humiliated her. Novak could relate. She'd done the same thing to him when his guard was down. He had to give her points for that. "You caught me unaware and held me at gunpoint. Not too happy about that, to tell you the truth."

They both glanced away. Novak looked back before she did. She continually moistened the stitches in her lower lip with her tongue. Her mouth looked painful. He wanted more answers. "So what's your part in all this?"

Wariness showed up in her eyes; she wasn't exactly hiding her emotions.

Novak wasn't letting her get by with that, not anymore. "You really think they'll be stupid enough to come after you here?"

"They've got orders. They never go back until they've finished their tasks."

"On whose orders?"

"The judge nearly runs Galveston. He's got a lot of people working for him."

"So how are you involved? What'd you do to get on his bad side?"

Lori turned painfully onto her good side. She looked uncomfortable, but she tried to push herself up. She was a tough woman. That was obvious and something he liked.

"Tell me about these guys after you? Who are they? Where'd they hold you? Maybe I can put them down before they can come for you."

She sort of shrugged, but that hurt her arm, too. "They got me right outside Louis Armstrong airport. Pushed me into the car, slapped me around some, and then they blindfolded and cuffed me and put me in the trunk."

"Nobody saw them take you?"

"It was a red-eye flight. Nobody much around outside, not out in the parking garage, anyway. I wasn't expecting to be attacked outside Texas."

"Where'd they take you?"

"An old warehouse on the riverfront. I grew up in New Orleans, so I recognized the sounds of the French Quarter. I could hear the crowds and the music and the boat horns on the Mississippi. They chained me to a brick wall down in the basement and kept me there in the dark. It was cold and damp, and the windows were boarded up. They left me by myself for a long time. Then they came back." She shivered a little, remembering. He didn't ask her what they did to her. "I'm pretty sure they took me to the old King Cotton building a few streets off the end of Bourbon. Look, you need to get me out of here so I can check in with Frank. He's going to be worried. I was supposed to call him every day."

"How long have you been here?"

"Four days, I think."

A nurse chose that moment to intrude. This lady was older with very short gray hair in what looked like a buzz cut, late sixties, and all business. She informed Lori that she was going to give her a sponge bath, or a shower, if she was up to it, and that Novak was going to have to leave, no arguments. All was uttered in a neutral, polite voice that brooked zero complaints. Novak rarely antagonized crotchety old ladies, so he complied. Stepping outside the room, he leaned a shoulder against the wall opposite Lori's door and watched the elevator bank. Pulling out his cell phone, he punched in Frank Caloroso's home phone number. They hadn't spoken in a while, but that didn't matter. No answer. He tried Frank's cell and got a disconnected message. The elevator doors opened, and a lady stepped out and walked toward him with a clipboard balanced on one arm. She was from the admitting office and cornered him before he realized what she wanted. She asked maybe fifty questions in short order, none of which he could answer.

Novak denied knowing anything. He wasn't about to give her or anyone else Lori Garner's real name, not with thugs gunning for her. He didn't think they had given up, either, so he wasn't taking chances. He persuaded the lady that he was endeavoring to get information from a mutual friend, which was the truth, sort of. She mumbled on about insurance and fees and personal responsibility. He told her he'd pay for everything out of his own pocket. She smiled and took him at his word, which was always a mistake at times like this.

When he was eventually allowed back inside Lori's hospital room, the patient did look better, clean and fresh, in a new blue gown, her hair wet, with all the residual blood washed away. She looked as good as she could when all beaten up and just out of surgery. She had been given another strong sedative and was sleeping, at peace with the world, at least until she opened her eyes and recalled all those guys gunning for her.

The doctor who had entered while Novak was on the phone now stood at her bedside. He told Novak she was doing well and could possibly leave the hospital the following day, but only if she continued to improve and had somebody to take care of her. Novak volunteered his services and told the doctor he would nurse her diligently until she was back on her feet. That was true. Her connection to Caloroso was enough for him to go in full bore. He didn't know exactly how Lori Garner fit into his good friend's equation, but he'd soon find out.

She slept for a long time, giving Novak time to think things through. That's when he first became leery of her story. According to her, she'd been overpowered but somehow managed to escape from four armed captors while chained and blindfolded inside a dark basement. She might have been one hell of a good MP, but that kind of escape was Houdini caliber, military training or not. According to her, she had been shackled with cuffs but got away, found her way out of the building wearing nothing but a raincoat, figured out where Novak was, and sneaked into his apartment with a Luger nine and forced him to do her will. All on her own. All without help. Huh uh. Not likely.

On the other hand, she was in bad shape and she had mentioned Frank Caloroso's name. That earned her his help, albeit with some reserve. Once he got her down to Bonne Terre, he could deal with anybody sniffing around until he got hold of Frank. It stood to reason that Lori either had something the bad guys wanted or they were sick predators who hunted women in a pack. If she hadn't given up what they were after, they'd come back for seconds. He had to be ready.

The nursing staff sashayed in and out regularly. Hell, they woke her up to give her sleeping pills. He kept watch interspersed with light dozes. Lori slept well now, still and quiet, dead to the world. A nurse came in around two o'clock the following morning. Novak had reclined on the other bed, behind a drawn curtain that was parted just enough to see Lori's bed. This nurse was male and wearing the ever-popular dark blue scrubs with a stethoscope around his neck. He didn't acknowledge Novak's presence, probably didn't know he was there.

When he moved to Lori's bedside, Novak shut his eyes, used to the routine by now. He needed to catch some winks while he could. A moment later, he roused up when he didn't hear the soothing murmurs that all nurses everywhere used in the middle of the night when rudely disrupting a patient's peace. He opened his eyes in time to see the man take Lori's pillow out from beneath her head and push it forcefully down over her face.

Novak had always been quick on his feet for a big guy, and he was on top of that nurse in two seconds flat. He hit him the first time in the right ear, just about as hard as he'd ever thrown a punch. Stunned for a moment, the guy went down on his knees, before he grabbed for the rolling table and sent it skittering hard across the floor tiles. Novak jerked the pillow off Lori's face and went down on top of the guy. Straddling him, he clamped both hands around his throat. He glanced at the door. Nobody heard and nobody came. He pressed both thumbs down hard against the guy's Adam's apple, wanting answers before the guy lost full consciousness. The man struggled weakly under Novak's weight, but he was thin and slight and gasping for breath and bleeding from the ear and the side of his mouth. Novak pulled his head up by his hair and stared into a pair of dark unfocused eyes. So he slapped the guy hard in the face. Novak leaned down close to his good ear. "Who are you? What do you want with Lori Garner?"

The guy stared blearily up at him.

Novak pressed down harder until he couldn't draw breath. "Who ordered you to hit this girl? Why?"

The man tried to struggle.

Novak pressed harder. "Who hired you? How many more are coming?"

The guy wasn't the cooperative sort. Novak let up on his throat when the guy tried to moan out something that sounded like *lock,* but Novak couldn't be certain, and the word meant nothing to him. Then before he could regain his throttle hold, he sensed a presence close behind him. That's when the wire garrote came down in front of his face, and Novak jerked away and managed to get his forearm up between it and his gullet. It tightened hard against the back of his arm and drew blood. Novak struggled to throw the guy off his back as it twisted tighter. Then Novak feinted left and rolled back to his right and managed to shake the man's hold. He got in a good hard jab at his assailant's nose, and the strangle wire went slack. His attacker faltered a second, and Novak was on him, holding his arms down with his knees as he raised his fist to finish him. He jerked the smaller man up by his shirt, his intended blow faltering in midair as he recognized him. Shocked, he let go and staggered up to his feet.

"What the hell, Frank? Why'd you attack me?"

Frank Caloroso sat up, pinching his nostrils together. "I thought you were killing that nurse, for God's sake. Thanks for the bloody nose."

"He's no nurse. He's here to kill your friend." Novak glanced at the door, expecting a nurse to appear. Nobody came. They must all be handling some emergency on the floor or having a tea party in the breakroom. All remained quiet, so he extended his hand and pulled Frank to his feet. He stared at his old friend.

Frank Caloroso had always been a good-looking guy, usually in good spirits and wearing a big friendly smile. Any other time, he would be talkative and lovable and hell on wheels, especially on his downtime. They had worked Manhattan streets together for four years and locked up their share of street thugs. Novak would choose him first in any fight on any day of the week. He was glad to see the guy. Right now, his friend just looked angry.

"Well, shit, Novak, I think you broke my damn nose. Hell, I thought you were killing that guy."

"What the hell are you doing here? Lori said you were hiding out in Texas."

Frank grabbed a towel out of the bathroom and groaned as he pressed it against his bloody nose. "I came to find her. She hasn't picked up since the day she left. I was worried, and it looks like I had good cause to be."

"Well, they got her. Look at her face."

Frank stared down at the woman. "I should've come here instead of sending her. I didn't think they'd follow her out of town. I tried to call you first. You change your number, or what?"

"I change my number every six months. Hate to tell you this, but this is the second time they've tried to get her. We've got to get her out of here."

The towel muffled Frank's voice. "She doesn't look up to traveling to me. My God, look what they did to her. Poor Lori."

"She's lucky she's not dead. If I hadn't been here, she would be. So let's go. Go down to the parking lot and watch for them. Take out anybody you see coming for her. Then find my truck, and I'll meet you there."

"Okay, give me your keys. You still got that old junker green Ram truck?" Frank asked, and Novak nodded. Caloroso took off. Novak was glad he'd shown up. He would even the odds up a bit, but not all that much. Seemed their adversaries outnumbered them.

Novak knelt and dug through the thug's pockets and found nothing. The bad guys had learned a lesson with the first two guys: don't carry identification when you're out to murder people. Then he left him lying unconscious on the floor and pressed the button summoning the nurse. Nobody came quickly, so he stepped out in the hallway.

"We need help down here! Some guy stumbled in and collapsed. He's hurt bad."

Within seconds, two rattled nurses ran past him into the room. One knelt beside the unconscious man; the other checked Lori's vitals. The nurse taking care of the intruder looked back at Novak. "What happened here? Who is this man?"

"I don't know. He just staggered in here and fell down face first. When I saw he was bleeding, I called you."

Novak watched her push the guy's face to the side to clear his breathing passages. He wanted to know if the guy worked there. "Do you know him? He's wearing scrubs. Does he work on this floor?"

"I don't think so. I've never seen him up here. He might be a new orderly or something, but he's not wearing an ID badge."

There was no more time for chitchat. Novak moved back out of the way when two orderlies rushed in with a gurney. He watched them lift the guy, and then he followed them out into the corridor and watched them run their patient down the hall and into the staff elevator. The nurses' station was deserted, the other nurses checking out other patients for unconscious intruders. Another was on the phone trying to find out who the new patient was. They were all aflutter and discombobulated. Good, he wanted them distracted. He moved back to the bed. Lori had slept peacefully through the entire attack, dead to the world. Must be a heck of a sedative, but that was a good thing.

Novak wanted Lori Garner out of that room, out of the hospital, and then out of town. She was a sitting duck. They knew where she was, and they'd keep coming until she was no longer a threat to them. He didn't know exactly what the hell was going down, but he was involved now. This woman was number one on somebody's kill list. She had made it to the shower okay earlier, and now she had a pretty good incentive to leave. Outside, the nurses were back but still rushing around, the new shift arriving and being briefed in a staff room. So he grabbed a wheelchair parked down at the dead end of the hall. By the time he was back and had it next to her bed, Gabriel LeFevres showed up. Novak was not encouraged by the look on the detective's face. He made a quick decision that he hoped wasn't the wrong one. He had to tell LeFevres the truth, or at least a partial truth, and hope the detective believed him. They were friends, and Gabriel owed him a favor. Still, Gabe was no fool.

"Going somewhere with my witness, Novak?"

"Yeah, if you'll help me get her out of here."

"So let me get this straight, Novak. That unconscious guy downstairs in the ER? They told me he wandered into this very room and collapsed. And that's a coincidence? Don't think so. He's got a concussion from a serious blow to the head. Why does that make me think you might've hit him, Novak?"

"Okay, you want to know the truth? That guy waltzed in here in the middle of the night and tried to smother your witness with her pillow. I took offense. So naturally, I knocked the hell out of him before she ended up dead. That's try number two now by somebody. If they go to these lengths to get her, they'll keep coming. You know that, and I know that."

LeFevres stared at him. Novak knew the look. It wasn't always the good kind, but the detective hadn't slapped him in cuffs yet. He decided to embroider his story before that happened.

"Know what else? I'm taking her down to Bonne Terre where they can't find her. If I don't, they'll get her somewhere and somehow. They aren't going to stop. She told me that herself. You want her death on your conscience?"

"That's not going to happen. I'll put a uniform outside the door. She'll be safe here."

"How about after she's released and walks out that door? Your guys going home with her?"

Gabe frowned. "What is this, Novak? Fill me in. Give me the truth for a change, or I'm not letting you take this woman anywhere."

"You know the truth. When she came to, she gave me the name of a good friend of mine, a man that I trust with my life. Frank Caloroso. He sent her here to find me because he needs my help with a problem. So that's what I'm gonna do." He hesitated, considering whether to mention Frank was waiting downstairs, but decided against it because of the warrant. "I can't protect her here. I can do that in the bayou. You've been to my plantation. You know how hard it is to find."

Gabe was not buying what Novak was selling. "The chief will have my head if I let you take her out of town. She's a material witness in a double murder investigation. So are you, by the way."

"She's also one of the victims. These guys are organized criminals, Gabe. Three of them have already come after her. More will come, trust me. That's how these guys work. If they can't get her themselves, they'll hire an assassin who can."

Gabriel looked unconvinced so Novak kept talking.

"I'll keep you informed until you figure out what's going down. I'll send you her statement and anything else she knows about those guys. You can claim no knowledge that I took her. Tell them I sneaked her out, say you don't know what the hell's going on, but we need to get her out of here and somewhere they can't find her. Nobody can get to her once I get her on my boat out in the middle of the Gulf of Mexico. That's what I'm planning on."

Gabriel ran splayed fingers through his thick black hair, grumbled something under his breath, and stared down at Lori Garner's face. "Is she going to be all right? She looks pretty bad."

"Yeah. She's in a lot of pain, so they gave her painkillers and sedated her. She won't feel a thing on the ride down to the bayou."

"Damn it, Novak. I'm going to lose my badge one of these days, because of you. If Claire and Nick didn't vouch for you, you'd be on your way to a jail cell for assault right now. You put that man in a coma, for God's sake."

"He was murdering her, Gabe. So I reacted. I don't care what happens to that guy. He's probably the one who put out his cigarettes on her breasts."

Gabriel stared silently at Lori's bruised face. After that, he made his decision. "All right, damn it, Novak, let's get her into that wheelchair. I'll clear the way with my badge if the nurses give us trouble. And you better take my car. They've probably got a tail on that old truck of yours."

"Now you're talking, Gabe."

"You want me to assign a man to go with you?"

"No, I can handle it. I've got a friend who'll help me."

"Just keep in touch and answer my calls, you hear me? I need to know where she is at all times so I can vouch to my chief that she's safe and we can get her back here anytime we need her to testify or give her statement."

Wrong, Novak thought. "Done. I'll keep her comfortable and find out the details behind this thing and pass them along to you. That good enough?"

"I'm doing this because I do think they'll get her if she stays here, even under police guard. Sounds like a mob hit to me. So let's get going now while things are still quiet. They're going to have my ass if you screw me over."

"That's better than having a dead witness in your custody."

Lori Garner did not even stir when Novak slid his arms under her body and lifted her gently off the bed. He sat her up in the wheelchair, grabbed a pillow for her arm, and covered her with a blanket. If Gabe hadn't been there, Novak would've just carried her down the stairwell. It would have been faster and easier, but that would cause questions.

They made it fine down to the ER entrance with Gabe flashing his badge at any nurse who objected. A few argued with him, but the detective proved persuasive. He showed his credentials to the ER personnel and then walked outside to retrieve his car. When he drove up outside the entrance, Novak lifted Lori into the back seat, positioned her out flat, covered her, and settled her injured arm on a pillow. He wasn't sure it mattered; the woman was feeling no pain. They exchanged vehicle keys, and Gabe gave him a last warning about keeping in touch and then went back inside. Novak drove around the parking lot until he saw Frank standing beside Novak's truck.

"I'm taking her down there in this car. You got a rental you can use?"

"Yeah, that Toyota Camry over there."

"Remember where I live?"

"I've been there enough times to drive that road in my sleep."

"Follow me down now or find a motel room and get some sleep. You look too tired to drive anywhere. We'll be okay alone at Bonne Terre till tomorrow."

"I'll try to make it in tonight. A few hours of sleep at the side of the road will help if I have to."

"Just be careful they don't follow you. I'm taking her out in the boat by noon tomorrow. Be there or you're gonna get left behind."

"What do you take me for?"

"Now is not the time to ask that, Frank."

Novak slid up his window, drove to the Huey P. Long bridge over the Mississippi River, and headed west on Interstate 10 to US-90W, and they were on their way to Bonne Terre. Sixty miles down the road, he began to breathe easier. Nobody was following him, and Frank was not in sight. Novak wasn't worried about his friend. Frank knew what he was doing. He'd make it down there before noon the next day. Novak only hoped he didn't have a tail on him when he did show up.

Chapter 4

The drive to Bonne Terre took over an hour. Lori Garner slept in the back seat, limp-limbed and peaceful. The sun was a blinding blaze that flooded the car windows but didn't faze her. Neither did she stir when Novak carried her into his house and settled her in a butler's closet off the dining room that he'd made into a bedroom. He propped her on her side with pillows supporting her back, put another under her arm, and once she was settled, set the alarm system he'd installed.

Not so long ago, a different woman had recuperated in that same bed from horrific knife wounds. He had also brought Mariah Murray home in order to protect, but she had been murdered on his doorstep by a truly evil woman. He was guilt-ridden for allowing that to happen. His sister-in-law had been his responsibility, and now she was dead, lying outside his house near the empty graves of his family whose remains were dust in the rubble of 9/11. Lori Garner was not going to die on his watch. He would be more vigilant, and this time he knew her enemies would eventually show up. They could not linger long in the bayou. The vast waters of the Gulf of Mexico beckoned to him as a safe sanctuary, so that's where they were going. Tonight, they needed rest, and he wanted to talk to Frank before he made any kind of move. He already knew this thing was bad and getting worse; he needed to know just how bad it was going to get.

His house had been closed up for a time because he preferred living aboard his sailboat to staying inside this giant mausoleum. It was fairly warm inside against the February chill but had that stuffy, mildewed odor of any ancient house that had stood undisturbed for over two centuries. He rarely opened windows or aired the place out, and he wouldn't tonight. He was dead tired and still going strictly on adrenaline and caffeine at the moment. On top of that, he felt anxious about Frank's whereabouts and wished he would show up or call. Novak wanted to know everything that had already gone down in this thing, from beginning to end. Otherwise, he was going to take himself out of the picture. It was a dangerous game they were playing, and Lori Garner hadn't been particularly forthcoming. He was pretty sure there was a reason for her reticence. He was going to question her as soon as she awoke.

Novak walked down through the wide grand foyer to the back of the house where he had put in a large modern kitchen. His footsteps creaked on the original hardwood floor; the sound echoed slightly under the high ceiling hung with chandeliers that had been lit by candles at one time. He prepared a pot of coffee to help him stay awake, making it super strong, and then leaned back against his wide black granite bar and watched it brew. Before he shut his eyes, he wanted to do a search on the information he'd found on the cell phones he'd taken from the two dead guys who'd attacked his apartment. He had already disabled the GPS on those phones, so he was confident nobody had used them to track them to Bonne Terre. He poured a cup of the steaming coffee into a mug and sat down at his scarred farmhouse table. He opened his laptop and pulled up the law enforcement databases that Claire Morgan had downloaded for him. He had a feeling that wasn't exactly legal, but it had earned its weight in gold more than once of late. He was pretty sure it would bear fruit now.

Fishing the phones and IDs out of his pocket, he keyed in the names. Then he scanned the first driver's license picture and ran it through a facial recognition database. He picked up one of phones while the computer ticked through hundreds of felons, searching for a match. This phone was an old iPhone 5 and turned out a bust. No photos, no phone log, no history, all of which would have given him a wealth of info about the dead guy. Nothing gained but the basics on his driver's license. The two other phones were cheap burners. One hadn't been used long. It probably had belonged to a newbie, recently hired and unproven. The guy had been smart enough to leave his phone clean, though. Novak would give him that much, despite his ending up dead on his short career as a criminal.

Number three thug wasn't so circumspect. Whoever this guy had been, he'd either been stupid or overconfident. It appeared he'd already earned his gangster stripes and had been the man calling the shots. He hadn't been so good in that arena, either, since he was dead. The face on his Texas driver's license got a hit almost at once. His name was Emilio Starka. He appeared to be a ladies' man or at least thought he was. His machismo was readily apparent with all that gelled hair slicked straight back from his forehead and the wide, arrogant smile.

More concerning to Novak were the photographs of young women Starka had saved on his camera log. All of them looked prepubescent and all were posed suggestively wearing lingerie. All were much too young to be within a thousand miles of Starka's camera. Most looked around thirteen or fourteen, which would jibe with Lucy Caloroso's age. The idea of that sweet girl being held by a man like Starka turned Novak's stomach. Lucy's picture was not there, thank God. Some children appeared even younger, ten or eleven, maybe. Most of them were drugged, considering their empty eyes. A few looked terrified but had those same dull and confused eyes, pupils enormous. None appeared to have been beaten or injured, which was the only good thing Novak had seen yet.

These depraved perverts were peddling flesh, young innocent girls, but that would stop as soon as he got his hands on them. The sexy poses made his skin crawl. Angry, he pulled up Starka's phone contacts and found all the calls deleted. But there was a treasure trove of text messages. Some included directions to safe houses where they obviously were stashing the girls. Unfortunately, the texts didn't give the city involved, just the street addresses. All were probably quiet neighborhoods, the innocuous-looking houses acting as prisons for scared little girls. There was nothing lower in this world than what these guys were doing to children.

The knowledge made him more anxious to talk to Lori Garner. Maybe she had been one of those girls at one time and was out to get her revenge. Maybe that's why they wanted her dead. Once he had examined the phones, he forwarded the incriminating texts and Starka's name to Gabriel LeFevres and told him they were safe at Bonne Terre without incident. That should be enough to keep the detective happy for the moment.

"What is this place?"

Novak jerked around, his hand on his weapon. He left it in the holster when he saw Lori Garner standing in the doorway. She was leaning against the doorjamb for support. She didn't look well enough to be standing up and wary as hell. She still had on the same thin hospital gown but had pulled the white blanket from the hospital around her shoulders for warmth. She was barefoot.

"They sent a man after you at Charity, so I brought you down here. Do you remember anything that happened?"

"Where are we?" she asked again, looking around the kitchen.

"Deep in the bayous of Lafourche Parish. No way can those guys find us here, not for a while, anyway. I had to get you out of there fast, so I brought you to my place. You slept through everything."

Lori frowned. "I don't understand. The last thing I remember is those two guys bursting in on us at your apartment."

She didn't remember talking to him in her hospital room. It would be interesting to see if she told him the same story again. "You were shot and taken to the hospital. I called in the cops on the shooting, but whoever you have gunning for you aren't giving up. How about telling me why?"

"The police let you bring me down here? Are we on the run?"

"No, I happened to know the detective in charge. I can be persuasive when I want to be. He trusts me, sort of."

She eyed him for a moment, no doubt considering whether to believe him. Novak didn't blame her. She should be wary. "They came after me again while I was in the hospital?"

Novak nodded. She didn't say anything else but looked around some more, obviously trying to figure things out. Then she must've decided to give him the benefit of the doubt because she moved to the table, bracing her good arm on the wall for support. She held her injured shoulder in close to her. She was weak and probably shouldn't be on her feet yet at all. "How far are we from New Orleans?"

"Not far, but my place is difficult to find. Only a few people know where I live, and they know not to tell anything to nosy strangers. We aren't staying here long enough, anyway. Once we get out on the Gulf, we're home free. Time out on the water will give you time to recover and get your strength back."

"What?"

Nope, she wasn't tracking well. "I own a sailboat called the *Sweet Sarah*. We're taking her out tomorrow. Don't worry, you'll be safe out there."

"Who's Sarah?"

Her question surprised Novak. He didn't like anybody asking questions about his family. "She was my wife."

She considered him, and her expression didn't look particularly amenable to a sea voyage with a stranger. She scraped back a chair and sat down but kept a good distance between them. Her breathing was uneven. Her face looked pasty again. "I feel sick to my stomach. I need to eat something. Where's your bathroom?"

"The bathroom's right behind you. I don't think you'll be able to tolerate much. How about sipping a soda? Or dry toast, maybe?"

She nodded and hobbled to the bathroom, went inside, and shut the door. The lock clicked. She didn't trust him, all right, but she would eventually. He fetched a glass and poured her a Pepsi over ice. He put it down on the table where she'd been sitting and popped a slice of bread into the toaster. Then he splashed water on his face at the sink, trying to stay awake. Revived a bit but not much, he sorted through the medicine bottles in his cabinet, chose one, and spilled two tablets into his palm. He placed them beside the Pepsi, leaned against the kitchen counter, and waited. She wasn't going anywhere. There was no window in that bathroom.

A few minutes later, she came out. She had washed her face, and her color looked better, as if she'd pinched her cheeks. It looked like she'd used his brush on her tangled hair, too. She made her way back to the table.

"I could scramble some eggs, too, if that sounds good to you. It'd only take a few minutes."

She held up a palm toward him and stopped that idea in its tracks. "Oh, God, no. Just the toast. I feel so queasy. What did they give me to put me out like that?"

"Not sure. Most likely it was oxycodone for the pain and something else to help you sleep. How bad does your arm hurt right now? One to ten?"

"Fifteen."

"The drugs are wearing off. I put out two hydrocodone tablets. Take them. You're going to need to function in the coming hours. I've got more if you need them."

That brought a pair of big blue questioning eyes to his face. "Are you a dealer?"

"I'm a private detective. I've been known to have need of painkillers from time to time, so I keep a good supply around. Didn't Caloroso fill you in about me when he sent you here?"

"He didn't say much. So why don't you tell me?"

"Not much to tell."

She picked up the pills and downed them with a swig of Pepsi. He wasn't sure what she was thinking or what she already knew about him, but it didn't involve a whole lot of trust on her part. She was guarded and distrustful. The toast popped up, and he put it on a saucer and took it to her. He sat down where he'd been before. Neither of them said anything else, just sat there together in extreme and uncomfortable silence. She was smart not to trust him. If he were her, he wouldn't trust him, either. She didn't know much about him, it appeared, except what Frank had told her, if he'd told her anything. She had awoken out in the middle of nowhere with a big stranger she didn't know, weak and injured and alone. Apprehensive, oh yeah. She kept glancing around the room, studying escape routes, just like he would've done.

He watched her nibble the toast and sip at the soda. He wanted to go to bed, but that wasn't in the cards yet. They needed to set sail, but Frank hadn't shown up. She was still nervous as hell. Her hands had a slight tremor, either from drugs or nerves or fear, probably all three. She didn't have much reason to feel secure about anything. She had come to him, true, already injured and neck-deep in some ugly stuff. On the other hand, the two of them dancing around the subject wasn't going to help her much. She had to trust him, or she had to go it alone. She was in no shape to do the latter. She knew it; he knew it. Novak took the bull by the horns.

"Frank showed up at the hospital. He's on his way down here. Probably will get here soon."

That did the trick. Her relief was apparent. "He came in from Galveston?"

Novak nodded. "He said he got worried about you because you weren't answering your phone and figured you ran into trouble. He found us in the hospital."

"Good. I was afraid they had arrested him."

Novak waited for her to elaborate on the who, the why, and the when. She said nothing else, so he forced the issue.

"Way I see this? You've got two options right now, Lori. Number one: trust me and let me get you and Frank on my boat and the hell out of Louisiana in one piece. Two: go back to New Orleans on your own and hope to God they don't get you again. Because if they do, and in your present condition, you won't get a shot off and you'll end up dead."

Her chin rose just a trifle. "I know my choices, dude. You don't have to tell me what they are."

Dude? Painkillers must be taking effect. Her face had become slightly flushed and made her look better. Starka and his buddies hadn't beaten the spunk out of her. She still had an edge to her, all right. That was a good thing. He hadn't seen much of that when she'd held him at gunpoint with wobbly hands and a shaky voice. "Okay, then go ahead, lady, make your choice. Neither option is all that good for your health. If you want my help, fine. I'm good at what I do. I can protect you, and I'm available at the moment. If you don't believe me or think that's not such a good idea, that's fine, too. Wait for Frank to show up and you two can mosey off on your merry way. No skin off my nose. But you need to make that decision, right now."

Novak paused, but she just stared at him.

"Look, I didn't ask to get involved in this crap. You came to me, remember? They almost killed me in my own living room, and I don't know why, or who they are, or what they want, except for what Frank told me at the hospital, which didn't amount to squat. That's asking a lot of me if I'm going to have to put my life on the line. Then they tried to murder you again in your hospital bed, and I had to take another guy down. If I'd left you there alone in that room? He would've smothered you with your pillow, and guess what? You'd be dead right now. Guess I'm getting a pretty strong message so far. Being around you is hazardous to my health."

"They came for me at the hospital?"

He'd already told her that. Her mind wasn't exactly processing efficiently. So Novak explained again about the currently comatose guy wielding the pillow. Lori's flush faded to that death-mask white once more. She said nothing, attempting to fight through her drug daze and think things through.

Novak felt himself getting annoyed. Still, he gave it one more shot, but what little patience he still had was wearing a trifle thin. "Look, I'm tired of this intrigue, and I need some sleep before Frank shows up. So do you. I'm gonna bed down on that recliner beside your bed for a few hours with a gun in my lap, just in case they find us here. I don't think they can, not in a million years, but whoever these guys are, they seem to have a lot of men and a lot of resources, so I'm not selling them short."

She said nothing. Her reticence was grating on his nerves.

"After I get some sleep, I'm going to ready the boat to sail. After Frank gets here, I can drop you both off at any port along the Gulf coast where you think you'll be safe. Whoever's behind these guys, he's sending out his men in teams, one or two at a time, so far. They're halfway organized but not particularly well trained. Not pros, by any stretch of the imagination. Probably hoods, hired right off the mean streets. But they're gonna keep coming. That's not particularly good odds right now, especially with you hurt and refusing to tell me who the hell they are and what they want. I don't have a lot of patience with people who play games with me."

"I thought you said Frank was at the hospital. Why didn't he tell you?"

"He didn't have time. We just put down a guy, and we wanted you out of there. And yeah, you're welcome."

"Why are you so worried if this place is so secure?"

Novak shrugged. "Bad things happen all the time, in case you haven't noticed."

Lori watched his face closely and then exhaled a breath that told him how tired she really was. She took another tiny bite of toast and chewed it slowly and swallowed it about the time Novak's impatience hit a brick wall. Before he could explode, she looked him directly in the eyes. "I want your help. I need it, I do. I can pay you anything you want. I've got money. So does Frank. We're both ready to fight back, but you're right, we can't do it alone. We thought we could at first, but they're too powerful."

Holding his gaze, she didn't look like she could carry on in any fight. She looked small and feeble and alone and beaten up, with a bruised face, a shot-to-hell shoulder in a sling, and wearing that thin and flimsy hospital gown. Novak felt the first twinge of pity creeping in, and that tempered his annoyance. "I don't want your money. I don't want anything from you except information, like how Frank's involved. He's a good friend. I don't want to see him dead. Other than that, it's the underlying principle of the thing. A gang of cowards and bullies chained you up, beat you black and blue, and burst into my house with guns blazing. That kind of thing irks me. I don't like men who beat up women. Never have. So once I get you out of here and to a secure place, I can handle payback to these guys alone, especially if they've got Lucy. But not here, not on Bonne Terre."

He stopped a moment and contemplated her. "They're out there looking for us right now, Lori, believe me. You said there were four men in that warehouse. Three are out of the picture and shit out of luck. But if they somehow find out my name, they could possibly find out that I own this plantation, so we need to get the hell out of here as soon as Frank shows his face. But it's strictly up to you. I say we take our chances out in the Gulf where they'll never find us. Say the word, and as soon as Frank gets here, we'll cast off."

One beat. Two beats. She stared down at her plate a moment and said nothing. Only sound was the muted ticking of an eighteenth-century French grandfather clock sitting out in the foyer, where it had been placed almost two centuries ago. Then she looked up. Their eyes met and locked. Hers had a look of resolve.

"Okay. I've got to trust you. I've got no choice. I'll do whatever you say."

"You can trust me. First off, I want to know every single thing about whatever this is. I want to know the players and what they're after and how and why you fit in."

"It's ugly."

"You don't have to tell me that."

The barest hint of a smile at the corner of her swollen lip, maybe, but it was fleeting. She licked at the stitches and lapsed back into reluctant silence.

"Are you willing to listen to me, Lori, and do what I tell you?"

Novak got the feeling that Lori Garner was not a woman who let other people tell her what to do or make her decisions. She had to be tough to get through that kind of a beating. She showed that, too, when she surprised him in his own home at gunpoint. Her catching him napping still bothered him. He'd been in similar situations, where he'd been confined by enemies, with no control over what was being done to him. It was a terrible place to be, mentally, physically, and emotionally. It was humiliating and enraging and exhausting. Lori Garner had come through it. So far, anyway.

"I'll listen to you," she told him a moment later. "But this is my life and my problem. If I think you're screwing things up for me or Lucy or Frank, I'm gonna say so, and do it my own way. You got that, Novak? No negotiation. Don't think you can bully me. I've taken more of that than I can stomach."

Quite a polite ultimatum, but an ultimatum, nevertheless. Novak pegged her for having pride, and he was right. He admired her for it. "Fair enough. You come off as capable and well trained. First thing I want to know is exactly how this thing started, and I mean every single detail. Don't leave anything out. Lay it out straight in a simple timeline. We don't have much time."

"It's not simple."

"Make it simple."

"Ask me questions, and I will give you truthful answers."

Novak considered her. Lori Garner was nobody's fool, and she definitely still didn't trust him, not an inch, regardless of what she'd said. Her suggestion meant she was savvy and careful and clever. If he were her, he wouldn't tell everything pertinent to his own safety to someone he'd just met, either, and he wouldn't do that until he was certain they had his back. If Novak asked questions now, there were plenty of things he wouldn't know to ask and therefore she would have aces in the hole if things got sticky. Good thinking on her part.

"What's your real name?"

She hesitated a beat too long. "Lori Garner, just like I told you. I'm not dragging you, man."

"What?"

"Dragging you, dude. You know, like criticizing. It's slang. How old are you, anyway?"

Novak ignored that. He was a lot older than she was, that was for damn sure. "I think we're both liars when the need arises, and you know it. You lie to me about this, you're on your own."

"I'm not lying."

"Any way you can prove that? I'm working through a few trust issues myself at the moment."

"Why?" She sounded startled. He wondered if she really was.

"Would you trust a stranger that broke into your apartment and held you at gunpoint? Then caused a shootout that ended up with two men lying dead your floor?"

"No." Another silence. She was holding back, not wanting to tell him everything. "They took my ID and clothes and purse and backpack and everything else I brought with me. I barely got away from them. They were going to kill me; they were just having fun with me first. It was only a matter of time, so I did what I had to do."

He watched her face carefully. She looked maybe in her mid-twenties, maybe thirty, but that was pushing it. "So how did you get away from them? That couldn't have been easy."

"I can't see why you don't trust me."

Of course, she could see that. He rarely trusted anyone, anyway, unless they were an old friend like Frank Caloroso. They both knew that, and they both knew why. This conversation was becoming tedious fast. He wished Frank would get there and handle this woman.

"You were obviously chained up and beaten. How did you get away? Is that so hard to explain?"

Her answer came, but it was begrudging. "One of them took pity on me. He shouldn't have."

"You're saying you overpowered the guy? In your condition?"

"Hashtag, yeah, man."

"What?"

She scowled. "You're obviously not into SM, are you?"

"Sadomasochism? Hell no. What's that got to do with it?"

"No, social media." She frowned at him. "You know, Facebook, IG, Twitter. Social media."

"I don't have time to play on the internet. I work for a living."

"No kidding. Well, I do, and I'm good at it. That was part of my job in the army. Hacking and IT and other stuff."

She appeared to be perking up some now; maybe the pills and soda and toast had kicked in. Her youthful consciousness was showing, too.

"Okay, I'll use plain English. That guy? He unlocked one handcuff so he could take me to the bathroom. So I punched him in the throat with my fist. He went down choking, but it was long enough for me to grab his gun, hit him with it, grab his raincoat, and get the hell out of that basement."

"You killed him?"

"No, but he didn't wake up for a long time. I'm not cool with killing people or I would have. The other guys were down the hall somewhere. They would've heard the shot, anyway."

"Better adopt that killing habit. They sure as hell have. You're in a life-and-death situation here. What happened next?"

"I ran for my life."

"Nobody saw you? Where were the other guards?"

"I told you, down the hall in another room. I heard them talking, so I ran the other way and found a door that exited outside into a dark alley. I heard Mardi Gras crowds, so I ran toward them and came out on Bourbon Street. I mingled in with the crowd while I looked for your place. Frank told me where it was. Then I saw you up on that balcony and you met the description, but I wasn't sure if I could trust you, so I waited and watched you. I was a little out of it, you know, after all I'd been through, and not quite thinking straight. I didn't know what to do."

"Okay. Time to get down to brass tacks. Why all this?"

"It's complicated."

"Yeah, I figured."

She was hedging now, but Novak was tired of dancing around the facts. He wasn't sure about this woman. He hadn't quite pegged her as the good guy just yet. Frank had been known to mess it up with bad guys before, women and men alike. Maybe Frank didn't know her as well as he thought he did. Maybe she was playing him; maybe those men had a good reason for chaining her up. Maybe she was playing Novak, using her injuries and youth and good looks as a ruse. "What did they want from you? Be specific."

Her breathing was becoming more labored; she was getting excited. Not good. "Okay. They took a friend of mine. Her name's Judith Locke. They've got her now and her two little girls. They won't let her see her children. I'm trying to help her get away and find her kids."

"Who's got them and why?"

"Long story."

Her reticence was troubling. No innocent woman would be this unforthcoming. But Frank had sent her, and he trusted Frank implicitly.

"Her father's got them. Calvin Locke."

The name meant nothing to Novak.

"He's a terrible man, but he's a judge in Galveston. He's as crooked and corrupt as they come. So is Judith's big brother. You've probably heard of him. Stephen Locke? Both of them are rich and powerful; they're both as bad as they come."

Novak did recognize the second name. "Stephen Locke, the movie star?"

"Yeah, man. He does that action franchise thing. You know, Vince Hayden, the vigilante character. But in real life? He's mobbed up big-time with the judge's guys in Galveston and some even worse gangsters in Houston.

They all work together, laundering money, racketeering, running women, and all kinds of illegal stuff. Frank thinks the Hollywood crowd might be involved somehow, too."

"How?"

"That's what we're trying to find out. The only sure thing is Judge Locke. He's as dirty as river bottom mud, and his men were the ones who grabbed me at the airport. They spoke Spanish together, but I heard his name."

"And this judge is mobbed up, too? You're certain about that?"

"He might as well be, but he comes off totes legit because of his position. He's corrupt as they come and has a handle on what goes on in Galveston. We think the guy in Houston furnishes most of the muscle. Frank can tell you more when he gets here. He is coming, right? You're telling me the truth?"

Well, the floodgates had certainly opened, and she was just pouring out information. But was it true? "He's coming, all right. And this actor is actively involved in criminal activities? Can you prove that?"

She nodded. She was absently rubbing her wounded arm now. "That's right. He's Judge Locke's son and Judith's brother, like I just said. Judith hates them both. We've been best friends since college, and I know all of them well."

"Why is the judge threatening her?"

"He wants to control her. She thinks he had her husband murdered, so she told him she was taking her girls and leaving Texas. That's when he used his judicial power to get custody of Susie and Sammi. I think Stephen reported Judith to child protective services. They've got other local judges and some of the Galveston cops on their payroll. It's hard to get them on anything. After that, Judith never had a chance because of the kids."

"What part does Stephen Locke play in all this?"

"We don't know, just that he's involved. He's on location most of the time, so he's not in Galveston much anymore, but he does show up at times. You've heard about him. He's got this bad boy/woman killer reputation, and he likes to flaunt his fame." She took a deep breath. She had been animated for the last few minutes, but now her burst of pep was eroding, exhausting her from all the talking. "He gropes women and threatens them or pays them off if they complain. Judith says he's bragged about forcing sex on every actress in every movie he makes. But she's nothing like them. She wants her kids out from under his influence before it's too late. Her family's too powerful for her to get out alone, and now they've got her somewhere under lock and key."

"From what I've heard about Stephen Locke, he's a jerk."

"He's an egotistical sexaholic. Hollywood's full of those kinds of guys. Judith told me about them. I don't know Stephen all that well. He's a good bit older than Judith. I know I can't stand him."

"How do you know they took the kids away from her?"

"She called and begged me to come help her find them. Asked me to hack into her dad's computer and see if I could find out where they were keeping them. I haven't found them yet, but I think he's got them in his mansion in Galveston. She's collecting proof that he's into illegal stuff."

"All this is going on in Galveston?"

"And Houston. Stephen stays at his father's estate when he's in town, but he's filming out in Arizona, Scottsdale, I think. We found out that his father and the mob boss over in Houston fund his movies. It's one big criminal cartel. Get one of them, and they'll all fall. That's what Frank says. We just can't prove everything yet."

"Okay, so Judith found out about their illegal activities and threatened to burn them to the authorities, that's what you're telling me, right? And now they're holding her prisoner in her own house?"

She nodded. "Her father loves her more than anything, or she'd probably already be dead. According to her, everybody who crosses him ends up dead. That's why they came after me. They know I'm helping her."

"That's a strange way to treat someone you love. So what exactly do you want me to do?"

Lori looked uncomfortable. Novak knew he wasn't going to like her answer. "She wants us to contact the FBI and set up witness protection for her and the kids. She says she's got the goods on Stephen, enough to indict him, her father, and the other guy in Houston as well as the guy they work with out in Los Angeles."

Novak scoffed. "No wonder he's got her under lock and key. Who's the guy in L.A.?"

"We found out his name is Mike Mickey. You've heard of him, right?"

Novak had heard the name. Mike Mickey was in the news a lot. He was one of those handsome, charismatic producers, usually seen on *Hollywood Happenings* and other entertainment shows touting his next smash action film. Novak wasn't into movies much, but he'd seen both Mike Mickey's and Stephen Locke's pictures on magazine covers at the supermarket. Both were Hollywood elites and powerful in the industry. Bringing them down would not be so easy. But it sure as the devil would be gratifying. Novak hated Hollywood types.

"Mike Mickey's a big name out there. You have proof he's dirty? You better have the goods, if you're going after him."

She laughed but with no trace of humor. "They're all dirty out there, don't kid yourself."

"It's not going to be easy bringing these guys down. She better have concrete proof, or nobody in the FBI's gonna touch it."

"Judith says she does, and I believe her. She's been collecting evidence since her husband died and her father forced her to bring the kids back and live at his estate. We need to get her out of that house, because I think she's still in there. I believe her. I believe everything she told me."

"What kind of evidence?"

"Documents and tapes, I think. Whatever it is, she said it would hold up in court. They're using her kids against her now, that's the only reason she hasn't come forward. When they found out I was snooping around, some of his cops stopped me and took me in for questioning. Then they issued a warrant on Frank after I went to him for help. Some jacked up charge. They want to know why I was looking for Judith."

"So they don't know yet that Judith's planning on going to the Feds?" Novak hesitated as she nodded, and then he said, "Did the guys at the warehouse make you tell them anything?"

"No. I held on, but I wouldn't have much longer." She looked away from his concerned eyes. Novak didn't push it.

"Are you sure Judge Locke is on the take? Judith can prove it?"

"He's disgusting. He's a genius at public relations, and his son has a huge fanbase. They both have a lot to lose if Judith turns them in. Locke considers Judith and his granddaughters as his personal possessions. He's obsessed with them. He considers everything in his orbit as his possessions."

"There's no way she can get away from her father without working with the Feds?"

"He's got control of her children! Dude, you aren't listening. He told her she'd never see them again if she tries to leave." Now she was openly agitated in the telling of her tale of woe. Her next words came more reluctantly. "Calvin Locke's been molesting Judith since she was eleven years old. He totally controlled her even when her husband was alive and after her kids were born. Judith's afraid he'll abuse them, too. She tried to leave once before. She was planning to pick up the kids at school and disappear, but Stephen found out somehow. She hasn't been allowed to see them since."

"Tell me about the guy they're associated with in Houston. Who is he? I know something about the mob down there."

"Hennessey is his name. Timothy Hennessey. He's Irish and about as sadistic as they come, according to Judith and Frank."

"Never heard of him."

"Everybody in south Houston is scared of him. His M.O.? He shows up at his victims' houses, and when they answer the door, he throws acid in their faces to subdue them. Once they're down on the ground, he beheads them with a machete, right in front of their family. That's how he warns people not to cross him. Sometimes he goes after their family members, even little kids, just to make his point."

"He's sadistic, all right. Worse than that. Is Judge Locke in Galveston now?"

"That's his turf. He's got two places there; one's a big estate in Houston, the other's a beach house on Galveston Island. He's got a big stake in the oil industry, too. Most of it's inherited from his grandfather, who was a big oil baron. He's got half the Galveston police officers on his payroll, we think." She stopped and took a drink of the soda. She was really spilling her guts now. "They took me down to the station as soon as I showed up at the Locke estate demanding to see Judith. My military background spooked them, I think, so they let me go. I asked Frank for help, so that warrant that's out on him is my fault. He kept coming at them, so they took Lucy and threatened to kill her. That's when he gave me your name and sent me here to ask you to help us. They grabbed me at the airport just like I said." She stopped, out of breath and shut her eyes. She looked like she was on her last legs now. Too much talking and too much excitement, plus the hydrocodone was kicking in.

"They made a serious mistake when they took Lucy."

"Frank's going crazy."

"I understand that."

Novak wasn't sure she was telling him everything, but now he had the full picture. It was ugly, all right. Frank could fill in the blanks if she'd left anything out, but he didn't think so. Lori Garner had shown some guts. He'd give her that, and it was a good thing she had. She needed his help, because not just one but two crime bosses were now probably gunning for her.

"You got any whiskey, Novak? I need to feel no pain."

"Liquor and painkillers don't mix."

"You're not my daddy. I'm past that point."

She had earned herself a drink, no doubt about it. It wouldn't kill her. He got up and opened the cabinet. He pulled out a bottle of Jameson and poured two short glasses, hers only a swallow or two. He slid it across the table to her. "Go ahead. You've earned it."

Lori picked up the glass. "Here's to you and me and Frank bringing down those bastards." She tilted her head, downed the booze in one swallow, and plunked the glass down on the table. Bravado, that's exactly what it was. It wouldn't last long, not with whiskey and painkillers.

"Go back to bed before you collapse. I've gotta check out the weather maps out on the Gulf and chart a course to Galveston. That's where we need to go, and we need to get out of here as soon as I can get the boat ready. A few days out at sea will help you get your strength back."

"I need to know what you're going to do."

"I'm getting your friend's children out of that house, and then I'm going to track down Lucy Caloroso and put down anybody who stands in my way. That okay with you?"

For the first time, Lori smiled. She looked good.

He watched her wobble off down the foyer and disappear into the makeshift bedroom and close the door. Okay, now she would pass out for a while. He wished Frank would get himself in gear. Despite all she'd told him, he had more questions, including a few about Lori Garner herself. He turned back to the laptop and pulled up a map of the Gulf of Mexico.

Galveston was maybe a three-day sail if the weather held, but it didn't look like it would. They should make it there, but they were going to face rain and maybe even some squalls. He'd chart the course, find protective anchorages in case they ran into any major storm fronts, and then he'd stock the boat in the morning. He needed to get both of them the hell out of Louisiana. He worked on voyage preparation for about an hour, and then he walked down the hall to check on the woman. She was asleep again, on her back this time, her arm resting on a pillow. He sat down on the recliner, levered it back, put the loaded Kimber in his lap, and shut his eyes.

Sleep did not come easy. He kept thinking about what had happened and what was probably to come. Neither was good. The men after the woman could not know exactly where he was or that he had a sailboat, but they could probably guess where he was heading. That was common sense, not that men like them had much of that. Novak had put down two of their ranks himself. They would not let that affront pass. There would be big trouble waiting for Novak on the coast of south Texas, and Novak wasn't sure how bad it was going to get. After lying awake and thinking of how best to handle the situation, he finally shut his eyes. It took him a long time to drift off.

Chapter 5

Novak woke up to the sound of tires crunching over the white shells lining his driveway. Snatching up his gun, he peered out the front shutters. Frank Caloroso was climbing out of his white rental car. Novak met him at the top of the veranda steps, glad he was there. Frank wanted to see Lori, so they peeked in. She hadn't moved, so the two men set off together down the sloping back lawn to the banks of Bayou Bonne. They didn't say much about what they were facing. There would be plenty of time to talk after they got Lori out of Louisiana.

Frank had accompanied Novak on more than a few ocean voyages. He knew the drill for embarkation. The bayou moved slowly along, the muddy water sluggish but with swirling eddies and undercurrents. The sky was dark, threatening an impending storm, clouds pressed low against the horizon like piles of black thumbprints. There was no wind, no rain, no sun, just a dreary day to match everything else about what they were facing.

The *Sweet Sarah* was battened down tight, ropes tied off securing her at berth. Novak set the gangplank and told Frank to top off the fuel tanks while he opened the boat and checked out the food and water provisions. The latter was hardly necessary. Novak always kept the boat fully stocked and ready to sail. That penchant had saved his life on a couple of tense occasions. His weather inquiries worried him a bit. He didn't want to run into a violent electrical storm. It looked as if they'd miss the incoming rain once they headed west. The weather would be a little chilly with some predicted squalls, but there were no high winds in the forecast. The sail to Galveston looked routine, maybe three days at sea with a couple of nights at anchor. He already had chosen sheltered stops that he'd used before, and those evenings would give them time to sit down and work out some kind of plan, because they were going to need one.

At any other time, Novak would choose to sail the Intercostal Waterway, but its heavy traffic of barges and pleasure craft meant a greater danger of being spotted. He had to be overly cautious on this crossing, even though he planned to head out to the open waters of the Gulf. He didn't think the men he'd encountered in New Orleans had the smarts to figure out Novak's mindset, but he couldn't take that chance. It depended on who was calling the shots and how bad they wanted Frank and Lori dead and buried. It appeared they wanted that quite a bit, enough to keep trying. So he meant to stay alert and hold his weapon close.

The voyage to Texas was no problem; he could make it blindfolded. He'd sailed there and back countless times, sometimes to visit Frank and Lucy. They were good to go, the only danger being land stops here and there to refuel. Novak liked to use the same ones each time, and most of those were not heavily trafficked. Right now, they were wasting valuable time. Lucy was Novak's first and foremost priority. She was too young and too vulnerable and too alone, and he wanted her out of those men's hands. He feared for her and what they were doing to her, just like her father did. Frank looked terrible, haggard and tense and unshaven, but all that was understandable.

Within the hour, Novak was at the helm and steering the *Sarah* down the bayou toward the vast reaches of the Gulf of Mexico. Lori and Frank sat together under a blue awning and watched him maneuver the boat. About the time they reached open water, the sun eased out from under those inky clouds and sparkled a carpet of diamond chips across the sea. Novak's spirits lifted considerably. The smell of salt air and sting of whipping wind and the feel of rough chop beneath his feet told him he'd been landlocked far too long. He stood at the wheel and lifted his face to the warm sun and let the cool wind caress his face. Such peace was not going to last long.

Once far enough out to sea, he and Frank worked together, and it wasn't long before the sails filled and billowed out with the familiar rush of air and flap of white canvas and jingling lines growing taut. The boat skimmed over the water, and Novak stayed at the controls while the other two rested. Later Frank joined him at the helm and spilled out his heartrending story. It wasn't easy to listen to. The man was distraught over the capture of his daughter. He blamed himself, of course, as all fathers would.

Novak listened and felt his pain and let him get the torment out of his system. Frank needed that burn of tears and tremble of voice and pain of heartbreak. This was the time to be emotional and let his weakness show. Later on, he had too much to lose to break down. After a tearful catharsis in the telling, Frank went down below to check on Lori. Novak manned the wheel and headed west. Not a single boat crossed his path along the way, except for the occasional glimpse of the giant cruise ships silhouetted on the southern horizon. Novak pushed hard under obliging gusts, hoping to get a good ten-hour sail before they dropped anchor. He knew the cove where he was headed well, had stopped there often on his travels. They would be safe there, out of sight, out of bad weather, and with little chance of trouble.

It took nine hours, but the small isle was deserted, and he moved into the leeward side and secured the *Sarah* as he'd done countless times before. He usually sailed alone, so he needed no help and got her settled at berth, double-checking the riggings and lines. After all was secure for the night, Novak descended to the main cabin. Frank was standing at the galley counter making tuna fish salad sandwiches and pouring Lay's potato chips onto three paper plates. He uncapped a beer for himself and Novak. Novak had settled Lori in a fore cabin. He could see her door from the galley. It was shut with no sounds inside. The painkillers he'd given her when he'd carried her down to the boat had kicked in.

The two men sat down and ate dinner at the dining table. Frank had gotten control of his emotions now, probably better off for getting all his concerns and worries off his chest. Maybe not the debilitating anger eating him alive inside his gut, but he could use that to fuel his determination. Now he looked ready to fight, his eyes intense, his features set in hard lines.

Not long after they finished eating, Lori came out and joined them in the main cabin. She appeared to be in a lot of pain, but was trying to hide it. She sat down between the two men and nibbled at a sandwich. She didn't look so hot. Her face was drawn, her movements weak, and her arm cradled protectively. She would be no help, if and when they met the enemy. For a moment, he contemplated dropping her off at an island clinic where she could recuperate from the gunshot wound in a nice safe haven. He suggested the idea to her but did not receive a receptive audience.

"No way in hell are you dropping me off anywhere," she told him. Her narrowed eyes dared him to insist. Novak didn't touch that argument.

"I'm with Lori on this," Frank agreed. "She's got a bone to pick with those guys now. And she can help us, Novak. She's well trained and a good shot. She's also a miracle worker when it comes to the internet. Anything you need via computer, she can pull it off. Give her a chance. You'll see."

"Yeah, I know, but training only goes so far when you can't move one arm."

"Hey, I know, Novak, why don't you just back the hell off? You can't order me around. You've got concerns, granted, I understand them, but I'll be fine as soon as I sleep off all those damn pills you've been forcing on me." She pushed her plate away. "Maybe you think I'm a liability, but I'm not. After what those men did to me, I think I deserve to get my revenge. Don't even think about leaving me behind."

All that was true, but so was the fact that she was a definite liability in the kind of fight they faced. "You're not up to par. You could get yourself killed. You could get all of us killed."

Frank was not having it, either. "Like I said before, Novak. You don't know her that well yet. Just wait and see. She'll show you what she's made of." He grinned at Lori for about two seconds before he remembered Lucy and the look faded. Nothing was going to help him until Lucy was in his arms, safe and sound.

"How bad is your arm? Did the nurse give you any word about how long a recovery you had?" Novak watched the way she was massaging her upper arm. She did that a lot. She was wearing the sling because she couldn't raise her arm.

"Not anything definite. I'm not a hundred percent, but so what. I don't need both hands to shoot a weapon. What? You have some kind of problem with a woman coming along?"

Novak studied her face a moment. "I don't have a problem with you or any other woman. I have a problem with hotshots who think they're invincible even when they're seriously wounded. You came to me for help. How about shaking off the attitude?"

Unabashed, Lori gave him a dead-eye stare. Frank frowned, not liking the friction. Novak's two companions were not thinking rationally because they both harbored personal grudges and had loved ones in serious jeopardy. They were in way too deep, mentally and emotionally. That could get them killed.

Novak's bottle of painkillers was sitting on the table. Novak picked it up and read the label. Then he slid it over to her. "It's not going to do you any good to sit there and hurt like hell while we're at sea. It's unlikely we'll be boarded out here or they even have boats. These guys are urban dwellers and street scum. I picked a safe place to anchor. Take enough of those to do the trick while you still can. You need to sleep and hold that arm immobile and let Frank and I take care of things until you're up to task."

"Taking a bunch of drugs won't cut it if they do show up out here."

Novak was done arguing with her. It was her pain, her decision, and none of his business. He was pretty sure she could hold her own if need be, whether she had taken painkillers or not. She was an adult, albeit a young one, and could make her own decisions. He wasn't her daddy, for God's sake. Frank seemed to trust her abilities, and he had always displayed good judgment. Well, almost always.

After she finished nibbling at her food, she downed a couple of pain pills and chased it with some bottled water. Then she looked at him. "Know what I'd really go for, Novak? A nice hot shower."

"There's a head right next to your cabin. You need help?"

She gave him a look. So did Frank. "Thanks, but I think I can handle it."

"I'm not coming on to you."

"Good thing."

Novak was amused. "You're still a wee shaky. Wouldn't want you to fall down."

"Thanks, but I'm good. The sleep helped. All I need is to get cleaned up and put on some clean clothes. This stupid hospital gown is nasty. You got anything on board that I could wear?"

"Yeah, I've got some women's stuff that you could probably make do with. It's all in the drawers under your bunk."

"Thanks." She stood up, paused there, and looked at him. "I mean it, Novak. Thanks for what you're doing for us. I didn't mean to snap at you."

Novak acknowledged the apology with a nod, glad she'd dropped some of her weird slang. He watched her move across the cabin. She was definitely not up to snuff. She would go down in any fight in this condition. He hoped she wasn't forced into anything she couldn't handle.

"You got a girlfriend, Novak? That why you got women's clothes?" Frank asked him.

"Nope. Worse than that. I fished a young woman out of the sea a few months back, one who put me in the direct sights of a serial killer. She left some of her stuff aboard. Okay, let's get down to business now and figure out what we need to do once we land at your place."

"Let's talk up top so we can keep an eye out, just in case we get incoming."

"We're safe here, but whatever makes you feel better. Grab us some more beer and take it on up. I've got to do something. I'll be there in a few minutes."

Novak cleared the table, stowed food in the fridge, and threw away the paper plates. About the time he was done wiping the counter, Lori Garner showed up again. She looked a hell of a lot better now. Her blond hair was still wet and looked darker. She had it combed straight back off her forehead. It accentuated her high cheekbones and made her look even younger, almost like a kid. He wondered how old she was. Her face was scrubbed clean and flushed pink from the hot water. She was definitely a good-looking woman under all that makeup and bravado. She had on a short pink nightgown now that reached mid-thigh. He couldn't remember ever seeing the garment before. It was made of fine silk and showed a lot of bare skin. Her legs were long and tanned. He could see the bruises there, too, but no cigarette burns. He was glad he couldn't see that. Just thinking about what they'd done to her started a ripple of rage inside him. She was barefoot and sans the sling this time, but she cradled her bum arm close to her side. Despite the ordeal she'd suffered, she looked fine.

"Where's Frank?"

"Up top having a beer."

Uncomfortable at being left alone together, they just stared wordlessly at one another for a moment. They were caught up in a bad situation. Literally, they were two strangers passing in the night and forced to believe in each other. There were no second choices. Good thing Frank had showed up earlier to help break the ice. "Want to come up and join us?" he offered.

Lori looked straight into his eyes without answering. He was finding that she was the bold type and didn't mind offending someone when need be. This time, it was not so much that. "I didn't mean to come at you earlier. You helped me when I needed somebody to step in. I appreciate that and everything you've done for me."

"No problem. You already apologized, no need to say anything else. I was just telling you the way it is. No offense meant. You've been through a lot. It's going to take some time to get over it."

She gave a slight nod. "Frank was right about you. You're up for the job. But so am I. You'll find that out."

"Good." More awkward silence followed, in which Novak avoided looking at her. "We'll get your friend out, and we'll find Lucy. We won't stop until we do."

"I hope you're right, Novak. But you don't know these people, not the way we do."

She didn't wait for him to answer, just turned and walked back to her cabin, went inside, and slid the door closed. The painkillers must have kicked in. She clearly felt better and looked better, but she would conk out any minute. He climbed to the stern and did a quick 360-degree search of the horizon with high-powered binoculars. Nothing in sight. Sea was nice and calm. The moon was rising high and full and bright and white, dangling above them in the night sky. It looked like a perfect round diamond on rich black velvet. Billions of stars were visible and beautiful and shining the way they only could be seen so far out at sea. Waves, calm and gentle, just barely rocked the boat at anchor. The wind felt soft against his face. Nothing in sight, and Novak could see for miles in every direction. He took a cold Dixie longneck from Frank and sprawled out on the couch across from him. He was tired.

"When Lori contacted me to help her get Judith away from her father, I didn't know it was gonna go south like this. It was just another case for me. Lori was a good MP when we worked together in Iraq. She's young and eager and computer savvy and definitely has a knack for law enforcement. I thought we could wrest Judith away from the judge with a little persuasion and persistence but without serious complications. I never expected him to go after Lucy; the possibility never even entered my mind. Good God, Novak, when I think about her, wonder where she is, I can't bear it. They could be hurting her right now while I'm out here doing nothing." His voice broke, and he dropped his face into his palms.

Novak said nothing. Nothing would comfort him. Frank had to learn to deal with it until they found her. It got quiet; the only sound was waves breaking against the hull on their way to shore. Frank didn't move, didn't speak again. Maybe he did need to talk about it instead of suffering in silence.

"You can't know that she's being mistreated, Frank. If she's their ace in the hole meant to stop us from helping Judith Locke, and that's why they took her, right? If they're holding her to control you from going at them, they're going to take good care of her. You did get proof of life?"

"Of course." Frank sat up and sighed. "They put her on FaceTime and let me talk to her but only for a few minutes. She looked okay, but I could tell she was scared to death but trying to be brave. She's like that, Novak. She wants to be brave and make me proud. That's the only way I'm surviving this thing because I think they're leaving her alone. Now, after the way they treated Lori, I'm not sure anymore. That scares the hell out of me."

"But she was okay when you saw her. We need to believe she still is. We're on our way to get her, and we will get her, Frank. You just gotta hold on. You've got to stay focused on the mission."

Novak wasn't at all sure his friend could manage any kind of calm acceptance, but Frank needed to believe. Novak was going to give it to him. Frank had been there for him on 9/11 and been Novak's rock when he was mired so deep in despair he couldn't function. He owed the guy in every way.

"You'll be fine, Frank, and so will Lucy. You know what you're doing, and instinct always kicks in when the going gets tough. Lori Garner? She's the unknown quantity."

"I told you that Lori's okay. You don't have to worry about her. She'll do her part, and she'll back off when she can't pull it off."

"So how good is she?"

"I trained her. She's a genius working comms and a whiz at all that social media crap that I don't have a clue about. She's good at tactical decisions, and the best shot in our company, hands down."

"Better than you?"

Frank gave a little grin. "Hell no, but she's not far off me."

"What exactly is her connection to this judge's family? She said the Locke girl was her best friend. That true?"

"Yeah, they were college roommates at Tulane, up until Lori enlisted and Judith got married to some guy named Poole. She knows the Locke family as well as anyone can. She can map out the locations and floorplans in both their homes or hack into the architect's blueprints or pull out the family legal documents. She knows their habits and personal relationships. If they've got Judith and Lucy inside either one of those houses, that alone makes her invaluable. She persuaded me to come aboard on this case. I wish I hadn't, but I didn't know then how serious this would get."

"You're under a lot of emotional stress, Frank. You're trying to get a grip on things, and that's good. It's not gonna be easy, but you're going to have to do it or we won't get them back. These are heavy odds against us."

Even in the pale light of the moon, Novak saw Frank's expression change, saw the angry tilt of his jaw and tension in his body. "I want revenge, Novak. That's what I want. I want to mow them down, cut them to ribbons. That's the only thing that's keeping me going. I want Lucy back safe and unhurt, and then I'm going to kill anybody who took her or laid a hand on her."

"I understand. I feel the same way, and I suspect Lori does, too, since she got you into this. We will find Lucy, and we'll make them sorry for taking her. Just like we always have. We're a good team. We can do this. Trust me, Frank. What we need is a good plan before we dock in Galveston."

Frank took a swig of beer and leaned back, propping his foot on his opposite knee. "What did they do to Lori? She wouldn't tell me."

"You saw her face. They punched her around some. Gunshot to the arm that did some damage to her shoulder. It happened at my place, but the wound wasn't as bad as I first thought. Surgery went well, and the doctor said she should recuperate well enough if she takes it easy for the first few weeks, which she isn't doing. I tried to make her take care of herself, but she isn't hearing me. So I'm going to let you handle her. She's waiting for me to prove myself before she fully trusts me, and I'm pretty much doing the same thing with her."

Frank was silent for a moment, and then he said, "Did they rape her?"

Novak shook his head. "I don't think so, but they put out cigarettes on her skin. Doc said there was bruising but no conclusive evidence of sexual assault. I'm pretty sure they were going to get their jollies before they killed her. They came after her hard once she could identify them and tie them to Judge Locke. She knows too much now for them to let her go. Kidnapping, forced imprisonment, torture. It's a damn good thing she got away and showed up at my apartment when she did, or she wouldn't have made it."

"They tried to get me, too, but put me out of commission with that warrant. You're in their sights now, too, Novak. They've got a lot of dirt under their fingernails."

Novak wasn't sure any of them would end up in one piece. These men had been out to kill Lori because she knew too much. Lucy could identify her captors, too. They had to kill her if she could finger them. That meant they had to find her fast. "All right, Frank. You need to tell me your part of the story. I need to know everything I can about this judge and his operation."

"Okay, but first, tell me how many men were there in New Orleans? Do you know?"

"Lori said four, but there could be more that she didn't see. Two guys attacked us inside my apartment, and we put them both down. Another guy showed up at the hospital after she came out of surgery. You saw him. He's not going to be a problem for a long time. You're ankle-deep in some serious shit, Frank. These guys aren't gonna let up until they find us."

"I know. I'm sorry I involved you. I didn't know where else to turn. I tried to call you, but your number's changed. So I made the mistake of sending Lori. I sure as hell didn't think they'd follow her all the way to New Orleans. I didn't expect that at all. I should've gone myself but couldn't bear to stop looking for Lucy. When I realized Lori was in trouble, I had to come."

"So where are we going once we get to Texas? They're looking for both of you. You got a safe house somewhere?"

"We're both holed up at my fish camp. You know how isolated the cabin is out there. My wife inherited the place when her father died, and it's still in his name. We never got around to changing it. They can't find us there."

"It's isolated and off the beaten path, so I'd say there's little chance of it."

"Look, Calvin Locke is a terrible man. He and his son are both batshit crazy. Worse, they've pretty much got Galveston locked up under their control. Lori said she told you the cops were paid off, and he's got some city judges, too. He's got enforcers out of Houston for the rough stuff. There's no one in that city that I feel I can go to without it getting back to him. I can't and don't trust anybody. That's another reason I sent Lori to you. I wanted to get her out of town. These guys don't stop, even with women and children, they take down anybody who gets in their way. Thank God you're going to help me. I hate like hell that I brought all this down on you, but I'm glad to have you on my six."

"If Lucy's in trouble, I'm in, no question. We'll get her back, Frank, no matter what it takes. And we'll get Judith out and make the deal Judith wants out of the Feds. If we involve the FBI, they'll put their resources into finding Lucy."

Agitated, Frank stood up and started pacing. Novak remained where he was and watched him. He needed to move and talk and do whatever it took to keep himself calm. He had to relax or he wouldn't be any good to anybody. But Novak needed to know everything, and he didn't, not yet.

"How'd they get Lucy, Frank?"

Frank stopped in front of him and blew out a long breath. "I'm not exactly sure. I think they might've just knocked on the front door. I was with Lori working out how to find Judith. The judge must have found out that I was involved. One thing's for certain, Lucy put up one hell of a fight, just like I taught her to do if anyone ever tried to abduct her. The living room was destroyed, lamps broken and on the floor." His voice trailed off, and he lost his words.

They were silent after that. Novak was worried now that Lucy had been mistreated but didn't want to say so.

"I never expected them to target her, Will, I swear to God. I should've known, though. She's my one vulnerability. Locke doesn't care who he hurts. It's all a big game to him. I've got to find her. Too much time has gone by already."

"When did they take her?"

"Six days ago."

That was a long time for a kid to be held captive. Novak didn't like to think about it, either. "Did they contact you? Or threaten to kill her? How'd that go down?"

"The first guy called me from her phone and said they'd kill her if I didn't back off Judge Locke's business. That's when I demanded to see her." He swallowed hard. "They said they'd butcher Lucy and send her to me piece by piece if I moved against Locke. I saw her face when they said that. Oh my God, Novak. Another guy called once and said I better stop Lori Garner from snooping around or they'd send me her finger. He told me to stay away from Lori."

"That's when you sent her after me."

Frank leaned up against the bulwark. "Yeah. I've been online trying to find word of Lucy. But Locke's never heard of you. You can do things and show up places where we can't."

Silence descended, both thinking about the mess they were in.

"Okay, Frank, show me what you've got off the internet so far. Let me study it. We both need to get some sleep tonight. We cast off at first light."

Frank nodded. They went below and talked a bit longer. Lori remained closeted inside her cabin. After Frank went to bed, Novak glanced over the papers Frank had downloaded and found exactly nothing to indicate where either woman was being held. They were all guesses and stabs in the dark. Things did not look good, and they hadn't even stepped foot on land yet. Now that he knew the odds they were up against, he didn't get much sleep. He kept thinking about what had already gone down and that some truly terrible things were probably waiting for all three of them down the pike.

Good news? Locke didn't know where Lori Garner or Frank Caloroso was. They didn't know Novak was involved or that he owned a sailboat. They'd be staking out the airport and train stations and bus depots. Chances were they could probably guess they were headed back to Galveston. Another plus for Novak was the ineptitude and downright stupidity of Locke's crew. Novak put down two of their ranks himself within hours. Lori had gotten another one. That rapid a depletion of enemy forces would make the judge shorthanded. It should also tell the boss man that he was dealing with people who knew how to fight back. They'd had time to get ready. They'd have a big welcoming party on hand. Oh yeah, they were heading into a buzz saw, all right.

Chapter 6

The squalls had found them, and the rain intensified as Novak showered and dressed in sweatpants and a white T-shirt. He was glad he'd made it to the sheltered cove before the downpour hit them. The weather had changed abruptly, the front coming in fast with buffeting winds. That would delay their departure and complicate the voyage. He sat down at his bedroom desk and rechecked the weather reports and redrew his chart. Hopefully the thunderstorms wouldn't last long, but a long line of weather disturbances down along the Texas coast did not look good, nor did the fact that it would probably last several days. He hoped to God the gusts would stop soon so they could be on their way.

When the smell of frying bacon drifted in to him, his stomach actually growled. Frank was up and cooking breakfast. Frank was a hell of a good cook, and Novak was hungry. He left the master cabin, but it was Lori Garner standing at the stove, already up and dressed in a pair of boot-cut jeans that fit her fairly well and his black sweatshirt, which did not. It hung to her knees and looked like a dress. Her sling was gone again, which was a bad idea. As usual, she protected her arm close against her body as she busied around the galley. She was turning the bacon. A carton of eggs was out, and she had bread in the toaster.

When she saw him watching her, she smiled at him. "Hey, man, don't look so shocked. I can cook as well as anybody. You and Frank don't have to nursemaid me. I can fend for myself. Besides I already owe you enough."

Novak wondered why she felt it necessary to say all that. "You don't owe me anything. It's fine with me if you want to cook us breakfast. I just figured that Frank would insist. You know him and the way he is in the kitchen."

Lori lifted out a strip of bacon to drain on a paper towel, and then she glanced back at him. "If Frank cooks breakfast, it would be sausage pizza. My stomach isn't up for that much Italian yet. At least, not this early in the morning." Then she smiled again. The pleasant look reconfigured her normally serious face. She looked better without all the lipstick and black eye makeup, too. Despite the black eye and ugly bruises, she looked younger today. She was trying to be sociable; that was obvious. She was still talking.

"I learned a lot about Cajun cuisine from my grandmama in Terrebonne Parish. But this is good old country Southern cooking straight from my Mississippi daddy's cookbook. I could win prizes, if I was idiotic enough to enter cook-offs."

Her background took Novak by surprise. He helped himself to coffee and sat down at the dining table. "You're bayou born?"

"Yep, born and raised to raise hell, as they like to say in my neck of the woods. But you're not, are you? You live in that creepy old plantation house down in Lafourche, that's true, but you're no native. I detected this odd inflection in your accent the first time you opened your mouth. What is that, anyway, Novak? You an Australian masquerading as a Ragin' Cajun, that it?"

Well, he had to say that she was up on her dialects and in a pretty good mood after having a recent beating and gunshot wound. Those pills were either working like gangbusters, or she was faking her good mood. Novak assumed the last was more likely. He ignored her question, never one to willingly give out his backstory. He still wasn't sure he could trust her; probably could, but he wasn't up to sharing confidences yet. She was growing on him, though. He glanced at the fore cabins. "Frank's still asleep?"

She nodded as she wiped her hands on a towel. "Yeah, but he didn't shut his eyes until after dawn. I could hear him next door mumbling to himself. He's real shaky, Novak. I understand why, I really do, but he's got to get a grip before we hit land."

"Yeah, I know." Novak watched her for a moment. "So you feel better, do you? You look better."

"What's this? A compliment? This early in the morning?"

"You do look like you feel better today. I'm not coming on to you. You're too young and immature for me."

She knew he was joking. "Yeah, right, don't kid yourself. I'm older than I look. Going out with you would be iffy in my book, though. You're too clueless about social networking. We'd need a translator. Maybe I could teach you a few things, given time."

Novak wasn't quite sure how to take that. "I can use the internet. Not much into hacking, though."

"Too bad. You can learn a lot from hacking. Anybody who lives out in the boonies like you do has to be a hermit or antisocial, maybe. You look like a guy who needs to have some fun. I could show you a good time."

Novak wasn't sure how to take that.

"OMG, dude, c'mon already, not that kind of good time."

Novak felt relieved. He didn't get her or her lingo and had a feeling that went both ways. "Maybe you should lay off the hydrocodone, after all, kid." He smiled a little, but she came back, not liking the kid reference.

"How old do you think I am? Fifteen?"

"Twenty-one or two."

"Try soon-to-be thirty-one. Next week, in fact. How old are you?"

"Older than that. You look younger."

That brought a frown. "How could I even be that young? I was graduated at Tulane and in the military for eight years."

"I don't know your background. I know nothing about you. Why don't you tell me all about yourself?"

She ignored that request. "Well, as for looking better, I do feel better, especially now that we've got ocean between us and our enemies. Better than yesterday, for sure, and better than any other day since I got Judith's text asking for my help. My arm can actually move on its own this morning." She moved it up and down to demonstrate but only a couple of inches. "My face doesn't feel like somebody just slammed it with a two by four. Tender mercies, true, but appreciated. How about you?"

"Fine, I guess." Novak wondered if her high spirits was bravado or if she just felt better and her true personality was emerging from the hell she'd endured the last couple of weeks. "Glad to hear you've got movement in that arm. You've been through a lot. Those guys worked you over pretty good."

"Understatement of the year, man."

After that exchange, she sobered and said nothing else. Novak sat there and watched her crack eggs into the bacon grease. Not long after that, she forked bacon onto their plates, followed by fried eggs and grits. Toast and orange juice and a second cup of black coffee followed. He offered to help, but she waved him off. Instead, she juggled through it using one hand and did an okay job. Novak knew what she was doing. She was showing him that she could still function physically and that her mental state was not compromised by fear or stress from being held captive under horrible conditions. The sudden good cheer, the joking, the lightheartedness, all of it was out of place at the moment but intended to show him that she could hold her own and be helpful to them in the coming days. He wished she didn't feel the need to prove herself to him.

Truth was, however, she wasn't a hundred percent; maybe thirty percent at the most. Give her a few more days of rest and recuperation and she might get halfway back to full capacity. Food preparation did not equate with handling a loaded 9mm in life-and-death situations. She was forcing the happy mood, but good for her. That was a damn sight better than groveling in self-pity or nurturing internal rage. Lori Garner had guts, all right. Maybe she could convince herself that no harm had been done to her psyche, but it definitely had and would exhibit someday. She needed to talk to somebody about what those men had done to her, but Novak wasn't sure he was the best person to help in that capacity. Frank probably wasn't, either, not in his present state of mind.

When she sat down across from him, he watched her surreptitiously while they ate. Neither said anything. Seen from up close, her black eye was fading a bit and most of the swelling around her mouth had gone down but still had the stitches. She actually had some natural color in her face. His intuition told him she could be tough as nails when she had to be, and she was going to have to be. She dined with good manners and gusto and enjoyment and no self-consciousness. Before he was half-finished, she pushed back her plate, blotted her mouth with a paper napkin, and began to tell him about Judith Locke.

"You may think I'm not necessary for this mission and don't need to tag along with you guys, but guess what? You do need me. Just like Frank told you, I know all the dope about this family. Judith Locke and I were college roommates, all four years. She's my bestie. I know her family big-time. I've stayed at both their houses. I know the floor plans and where everything is. I know pretty much when and where he posts his guards. I know how much grief Judith suffered because her daddy and her big jerk of a brother are sicko perverts. Her mom died when she was six. After that, the judge only had eyes for her. Judith says it's because she looks exactly like her mom did. Cringy, I know, but she meant it. He bought her affection with gifts and money." She stared into his eyes. Now that the swelling was down, hers were big and brilliant and a beautiful shade of blue. "You can imagine what that kind of affection that turned into."

"I'm surprised Judith told you all this."

She nodded. "She trusts me. That's why she came to me for help. And probably also because I never lived in Galveston or been under his influence. Everybody else in her world is under his thumb. People are scared to death to cross him. So I headed straight to Galveston because she sounded so desperate."

Novak listened to all that and watched her face. "What happened when you got there? Did you get to talk to her?"

"I made a beeline straight to the mansion and demanded to see her. The snotty butler told me she wasn't home and he didn't know when she'd be back. So I sat out on the street in my car and watched the front gate all day long but she never came. Then I drove down to their beach house on Galveston Island. Judith loves it out there the best. I jumped the wall and got inside the grounds but nobody was home. It was all closed up. So she could be anywhere. She's in big trouble, Novak. We need to get a move on. She's in danger."

"You've got no idea where he's got her stashed?"

"I think she's still inside the mansion. He likes to keep her close at hand, for obvious reasons. He totes obsesses about her. He's as sick as they come. She said he acts like she's his wife sometimes. I've seen him do it. She hates him, and she hates Stephen."

"You think he ordered her husband killed?"

She shrugged. "Maybe. Danny died in a car crash. It wasn't deemed a homicide by the Texas Highway Patrol, but Calvin's got his tentacles good and tight around lots of people in local law enforcement. Maybe the fix went in. Timothy Hennessey's mob is more dangerous than Locke's people but not as clever or as cautious. He's pretty much just a sick and sadistic bastard. He likes to kill people. Up close and personal so he can see the fear in their eyes before he throws acid in their faces. That's what Judith says, anyway. She's got the goods on him, too, and I believe her. She wants to bring them both down but only with a guarantee of witness protection for her and her girls. She's scared, Novak. She's thinks he'll kill her if he finds out she wants to betray him."

"You think the children are with her?"

"I hope so. She's terrified her father's gonna take them for good and she'll never see them again. I don't think he'll do that. Judith's the one he wants to keep close. Her kids are just an incentive to make her stay."

"How old are they?"

"Samantha's three. Sammi's what we call her. Susie's a year older. Judith almost died when she had her."

"How far is Frank's fish camp from the Locke mansion?"

"Locke's big estate is in Houston. In River Oaks, which is real hoity-toity, believe it. Frank's cabin's about an hour or so away, maybe more.

It's on an inlet behind a big wildlife preserve on the coast. Pretty hard to access by road, you know, narrow and graveled and remote, but you can sail this boat right up to his dock easy peasy."

"Yeah, I know. I've been there lots of times. Has the area built up in the last few years? Are neighbors gonna notice us coming in?"

"Next to nobody lives out there. Way too isolated. I haven't seen a single soul since he took me out there."

Novak hoped the judge hadn't found it. It was a good place to hide and an even better base of operations. "Look, I'm sorry about your friend, Lori. But Lucy Caloroso's my main concern right now. There are things I can't ask Frank because his emotions are all over the place, so I'm asking you. Will these guys kill her?" He watched Lori's face react and knew her answer before she spoke it aloud.

"Yes. They are killers. The men who had me liked me being at their mercy." She looked down and kept her eyes latched on the tabletop. "They were going to kill me once they got done playing with me. They joked about how I'd die and smiled when they hurt me. They're all sadists. Every one of them."

"I'm sorry you had to go through that. But you survived, and that means you're tough. You're going to be all right. It'll take some time, though."

She wouldn't look at him, so he asked her another question. "How many men does the judge have on his payroll?"

"Too many for the three of us to put down. Two personal bodyguards travel with him, or they used to. Sometimes they're in his car; sometimes they follow him in a different car. His driver is armed. All of them are armed. He's got enforcers that go after anybody who gets out of line or causes trouble. Some Galveston cops are paid off. I don't know who or how many. Getting Judith and Lucy away from him won't be easy."

"What about his routine? Is it predictable?"

Lori looked at him again. "I followed him around for two days. He's as good as clockwork. He leaves the Locke estate at eight sharp every morning and is driven down to Galveston Island to the courthouse. He stays there until the docket's done but is usually back home around six."

"But he lives in River Oaks?"

"Yes, where else? It's one of the wealthiest communities in Texas. Maybe in the entire country. You know, motorized security gates, perfect lawns, high walls, and top-of-the-line alarm systems. He's got a weak spot, though."

Novak took interest. "What's that?"

"His hobbies. He's got the hots for orchids, believe it or not, you know, those exotic kinds of flowers. I mean, he acts like some kind of nutcase about them. He's got his own hothouse on the estate worth a small fortune. He loves those stupid flowers, dude, you just wouldn't believe how he acts about them. He babies them and talks to them and waters them with little squirt bottles. It's nuts, man. He likes collecting guns, too, which I can understand. You know what kinds: antique muskets, black powder, rare dueling pistols, and he loves derringers. All those weapons are worth tons of money. He brags that he's got Wyatt Earp's legit six-shooter from the O.K. Corral."

"He attends court every day?"

"Most days, I guess, but not on weekends. They shut down, I think."

"So we can usually pinpoint his whereabouts by the time of day?"

She nodded. "I guess so."

"Who's the easier target? Locke or Hennessey?"

"Neither."

That wasn't an answer. Novak waited. She seemed a little hyper now.

"I guess Locke might be easier. Hennessey's mobbed up in the rough stuff. Drugs, prostitution, sex trafficking, you name it. I heard he's into white slavery, too. He's as dirty as they come. I've never met him, but Judith told me he's huge, maybe even bigger than you. What are you, anyway? Six feet seven, eight?"

"Something like that."

"She says his head's the size of a basketball and completely bald. She told me his eyes are awful: cold and black as midnight, and they look right through you. She said he sent a shiver down her back when she first saw him. He grins all the time but nothing ever reaches his eyes."

"How does Frank fit in with these guys?"

"I don't know. I don't think he is any kind of pal to them. Other than knowing what he does about the criminal element in the Houston area. Frank's been a PI around here a long time. That makes him savvy to the undercurrents."

"Frank's savvy in lots of ways."

"He's in bad shape. That's one reason I came looking for you. He's not acting rational. Sometimes he's dead-on, but then he goes off when he starts thinking about what's happening to Lucy. She's his only kid, and she's just so young. He can't stand the thought of her being with those men. I can't, either."

Novak didn't say anything. What father wouldn't feel helpless and angry? Lucy was such a sweet little kid, a tomboy with all that thick curly red hair and freckles, and usually wearing a baseball cap turned backward. She had always been Frank's pride and joy, good at sports, running track, and the goalie on her soccer team. Fear rose inside Novak, too, just thinking about what they could be doing to her. The men Lori had tangled with in NOLA could hurt that kid in ways she would never recover from. Frank had been teetering on the edge of panic ever since Novak had been with him, and a frantic, desperate Frank Caloroso with a deadly weapon was not someone you ever wanted to meet up with. He would be hard to talk down or take down.

"Okay, when we get to Galveston, we'll figure out where to hit them first. You need to come up with the most likely spot where they're holding Judith and Lucy. You're right, you have a good feel for these people, and we've got to use it. Try to remember everything your friend's told you about her family, her other friends, any vacation homes, anything where they might be holding them. A cabin in the woods, or maybe he's got a private apartment in Houston. He's got them locked up somewhere, but I'd guess his mansion would be the most secure place to keep them. It'll be easier if we go in after Judith first. Then hopefully she might know where Lucy is. We will get both of them back. I promise you that."

Lori didn't believe him. "You can't promise that."

She was right, but he didn't want her to think that way. "I said we'll get them back, and we will."

Her eyes told him that she still didn't believe him.

Chapter 7

Due to the bad weather, the voyage took four full days at sea, which equated with four full days of wasted time. The winds that blew in did give them time to rest up, recuperate, and double down on what they had to do. Novak felt uneasy as the delay dragged on and grew more so as he uncovered more information about the criminal element they were about to face. It was readily apparent that the three of them were outnumbered, outgunned, and out everything else. All they did have was the element of surprise, and even that was now questionable. He did not want to give the judge time to gather allies or call in favors. His worst fear was they'd run into a lethal welcoming party at Frank's fish camp.

When the coast of Texas finally loomed up in the distance, Novak navigated the boat north of Galveston to the Texas Point National Wildlife Refuge and took the inlet off the Gulf that led to Sabine Lake. Frank's fish camp was just north of the refuge boundary on an offshoot of the lake. He'd been there before, but the course looked a bit different. Once they got off the main channel and into the waterway leading into Frank's place, they passed no other boats nor saw any people. Thick woods and tangled vegetation lined both banks, and the distance from Houston and inaccessibility would give them good cover. He no longer expected a welcoming party.

The river was shallow but navigable with muddy water which made it unpopular with swimmers and ski boats. The alligators didn't help, either. Only serious fishermen enjoyed its bounty. They passed a couple of deserted docks and one uninhabited cabin that looked like its roof had been blown off by hurricane winds. This was indeed a good hiding place that would give them the sanctuary they needed, and the deed was not in Frank's name. No paper trail to follow ownership to Frank.

Novak motored along, sails furled, watching the riverbanks. The first thing he glimpsed was the widow's walk Frank had built atop his two-story cabin for some unknown reason. That was Frank and one of his whims. The log cabin was rustic and raw but snug and comfortable. The two of them had spent a lot of good times in that house, fishing and drinking beer around a campfire. That probably was not going to happen this time.

A fine drizzle wet their windbreakers and obscured the bank in a thick gray mist by the time they chugged up alongside Frank's property. A grove of oak and hickory trees surrounded the cabin, and as they slid alongside the long dock, the rain drummed itself to a downpour, plastering Novak's hair to his scalp. Frank jumped down onto the planks and expertly secured the lines. Thunder rumbled up slowly from somewhere downstream and sounded like the battle drums of shogun warriors. Novak helped Lori off the deck and across the gangplank, and Frank lifted her down onto the slippery dock. Novak followed them as they took off for the house. A jagged fork of lightning split the sky, and the ground shook under Novak's feet as it struck somewhere in the woods behind the cabin. The bad omens just kept on coming.

Frank ran up the steps to the screened porch. Although Frank and Lucy had a nice home on Galveston Island, he loved this place and vowed never to sell it. Novak felt the same way about Bonne Terre, which boasted the same hushed quiet and slow ebb and flow of the bayou out back. More than that, he liked the complete separation from all things deemed civilized, like crowds and malls and traffic jams. Locke wouldn't be able to find this place, not without a lot of time and effort. Novak climbed to the porch and thought about time he'd spent sitting out there. But that was a long time ago. Things were different now. Evil was closing in on them. Frank ushered them into the living room and then went into the linen closet to fetch them towels.

"You still got vehicles out here, Frank? The ones that nobody knows are yours?"

"Got two now. Both locked up in the barn."

"What kind?"

"You know good and well what kind. One is my blue 1969 Mustang Mach 1 that I drove down here from New York. I've kept it out there under a tarp for sentimental reasons. My wife and I had some good times in that car. The other vehicle's a used 2012 black Jeep Cherokee that I picked up a few years ago. Only time I drive either is to the gas station about a mile down the road or up to Port Arthur. Never have gone into Galveston, Houston, or even Sabine Pass in them. My Audi's still sitting in my driveway in Galveston. I took an Uber to the airport when I headed to New Orleans. Nobody can link either of these to me. They're a safe bet to take into Houston, if that's what you're thinking."

"They'll be watching your place. Where are you staying, Lori?"

"I got a motel room in north Houston. My car's still in long-term parking at the airport."

"Well, you can't go anywhere near them, just to be on the safe side." Novak was eager to get a move on, take off now to look for Lucy, but he knew better. "There's got to be more going on here than meets the eye. Lori, they followed you out of state to capture you and rough you up, maybe even kill you. Why? Just because you're asking questions about an old friend? I think there's more to this. Hell, Frank, what if you just had gone straight to the FBI about Lucy's abduction instead of backing off trying to find Judith? They didn't know you wouldn't do that. They're taking a chance threatening you and going after Lori."

"Hennessey's probably involved now and worried Judith has dirt that would blow back on him," Lori suggested. "He'll be suspicious about the judge locking her up at his estate. He's paranoid to the extreme, that's why he kills anyone who looks at him wrong. If he figures out she's turning evidence, he'll murder her and start a mob war with the judge."

"That doesn't sound like a bad idea, a mob war between them. Let them kill each other off, that's fine with me," Novak said.

"We've got to find Lucy before we do anything else. She comes first." Frank's face looked flushed and angry.

"Look, Frank, we will find Lucy, but we've got to lie low for a few days. I understand how worried you are, I'm worried, too, but we've got to be smart or we won't have a chance against those guys. We can't jump the gun and do something rash that'll get your kid killed."

Frank glared at him and turned away.

Novak let him stew. He didn't blame him for being pissed off, but he was going to have to use his head and not his heart. "All right, Frank, we'll do something now. Let's drive into town and see what we can find out. The rain's still coming down hard. That'll be a good cover for us, especially since they won't recognize either of your cars."

Lori stood up. "I'm going, too, and don't try to talk me of it. I can't sit out here by myself and do nothing. Frank and I have waited long enough to do something."

"Did I say you couldn't come?"

They couldn't take the blue Mustang, way too noteworthy. It would stick out like a New Yorker inside a Cracker Barrel restaurant. So they piled into the Jeep Cherokee. It was filthy, inside and out. Both the fenders and wheel wells were covered with dried mud. That wouldn't last long under the pelting rain. The Jeep would be spotless by the time they reached the city. The dust caked on the windows turned to mud smears, and then the wipers did their job and washed it clean enough to see.

The drive took a long time. They drove over narrow wooded gravel for a time and then got on some blacktopped state highways, all of which had seen better days. Potholes and cracks in the tarmac made for a rough ride as the storm grew fierce and raged on. Novak didn't mind the bad weather. At least they were on the move now. They finally hit Interstate 10 that would take them into Houston proper. Not much traffic because of the late hour and downpour, and not much conversation inside the Jeep. Novak drove, and the other two sat in the back seat hidden behind smoked glass windows. When they reached the giant outside sprawl of Houston, Frank and Lori slouched down. Both their names were written in blood on Calvin Locke's hit list. That meant Novak was pretty much on his own, but that's the way he liked it. He'd been a loner since he'd lost his family.

Lori keyed in Calvin Locke's address on her cell phone, which gave him precise directions to the mansion inside River Oaks. Novak felt certain it was the guy's palatial nerve center for rampant criminal operations. Novak had been in Houston lots of times, but it hadn't been for a while. He remembered the Loop with all the hotels and the murderous traffic. Logistically, he was going to need the other two for guidance. "Exactly where is this place, Lori?"

"It's on the main drag called River Oaks Boulevard, where money grows on trees. This is a fancy-ass place. John Connolly lived in here—I guess he still does if he's still alive—and Joel Osteen, that cute evangelist. The real estate prices are gargantuan, most estates inherited. Calvin Locke's is. His daddy and granddaddy were big oil tycoons back in the day."

"I think we should burn down the entire place," Frank suggested from the back seat, still in a bad way.

"Maybe we will, or parts of it. Let's just see how it all shakes out before we inflict undue damage."

When they turned onto the aforementioned boulevard, it was wide and lovely with neat sidewalks and green grass and nice bright streetlights. The rain even let up as if in awe and unwilling to shower upon rich folks' homes. Lots of mansions and estates lined both sides, some sitting back off the street inside privacy walls. Calvin Locke's property turned out to be the biggest diamond in this crown jewel of communities. Glimpses of the resplendent red-bricked Georgian mansion showed them perfection with symmetrical white pillars and huge wings stretching out on either side. There were balconies outside giant Palladian windows, lots of chimneys, and a ton of Disney World–worthy landscaping. The house sat deep into the acreage and was just barely perceptible from the street. Yes, the rich and famous and powerful cowboys of Houston wanted their fellow citizens to know who they were and that they were to be coveted for their wealth.

"His place is bigger than the other estates," Novak commented as they drove along a six-foot-high white brick wall that followed the property lines down the street and around the corner to a private alley at the rear of the back gardens. "How did Locke manage to accumulate this much real estate in a neighborhood like this?"

"He's rich as Bill Gates, is why," Lori told him. "His original property was huge, because it was one of the first in here, and then he gradually bought up every house around his as they came up for sale and then demolished them. Judith said some of those places were beautiful and historic. Any homeowner who balked at selling eventually gave in or disappeared mysteriously. He did the same thing out at the beach. He likes to enclose himself in a compound for obvious reasons. Calvin's well-known around here for getting exactly what he wants when he wants it, one way or another. Judith calls him the Emperor of Houston."

"What about that beach house? Easier to get into than this one?"

"Yes, but he's got guards posted out there, too. Most of his men are stationed inside these walls, though. Judith says not as many are around as there used to be. I guess he wants to feel invincible, and he's bribing half the cops in this town."

"He's a judge in Galveston, and he lives up here?"

"The beach house takes care of the residency requirements. He calls it his main house and shows up there a lot, but he lives here."

"I think Judith and Lucy are both inside this place. It looks like a freaking prison." That was Frank.

"You saw the kind of guys who held me in New Orleans," Lori said to Novak, leaning up and bracing her good arm on the back of the front seat. "Armed and deadly but not exactly mental giants. They shoot first and don't care who goes down. Neither does Judge Locke. Bodies just disappear, never to be found. Probably dumped at sea. Locke doesn't answer to anybody anymore. Not in this city, anyway."

"They can't shoot first if they're dead," Novak said. "Everybody answers to somebody. That goes for Locke, too. He's got a weakness. I'm going to find it and exploit it."

"Novak knows what he's doing, Lori. You can trust him."

"How many men patrol inside this estate?" Novak asked Lori. "Give me a guess, if you don't know for sure."

Lori thought it over but not for long. "When I was here on spring breaks, I'd say there were, maybe, fifteen to twenty, all armed with handguns. Maybe more, I think they worked in shifts. At the time, I didn't pay much attention to them. They kept a low profile, but they were always there. Judith called them bodyguards. I didn't question that, him being a judge and all. They wore those headphones to communicate, I remember that because I told Judith they looked like FBI agents."

"How many were posted inside the house?"

"A few, maybe. They kept in the background. Judith knew most of them by name and acted like it was no big deal for them to hang around. They're posted outside, I think. I don't know their routine. Wish I could tell you more."

"The perimeter wall, does it have other outside gates?"

"They use that big front gate between the pillars most of the time. It's got a talk box and a security camera. You've got to swipe a special card the guards wear on lanyards to spring the gate. There's another gate out back that comes out in their private drive behind the house. It opens from his rose garden and that's near the hothouse where he has his orchids."

"Does he let Judith and the kids spend time outside on the grounds?"

"He used to, back then. Pretty much whenever they wanted to go anywhere they could just get in the car and tell the chauffeur where to take them. When Judith contacted me, she said he doesn't trust her anymore so he keeps her inside. I don't know if that goes for the little kids, too. There's a nanny for them now. She emigrated from Nicaragua but doesn't speak much English. She's an older lady and seems scared of everybody." Lori paused. "Judith is terrified he's going to molest her girls, Novak, either now or in the future. It's hell on earth for women who live in that place."

"She really thinks he'll molest his own grandchildren?" The idea was so abhorrent that Novak had trouble stomaching the thought. If that were true, Novak had no qualms in cutting this guy down. No man who did something like that deserved to walk the streets.

"Judge Locke's a bastard, all right," Frank said. "But Hennessey's the real monster. I've seen photos of a couple of his acid attack victims, and it's not pretty. The kind of acid he uses totally disfigures the face, especially the eyes, just burns them out. But he usually kills them afterward, anyway. He likes to leave disfigured heads lying around as warnings, too."

"Tell me everything you know about him, Frank."

The rain had let up some, but the wipers were still slapping hard against the windshield. Novak pulled over on an adjacent street. No one would notice. The houses were too far back and too far apart. "Hennessey heads his own mob, but they're not the ones who call the shots here in Houston. But he's cut out his own little territory, and the big guys don't mess with him unless he steps out of line."

"Then who is in control of the crime syndicate?"

"Jonathan Wagner. His family owns the streets, and they have since the 1950s. They keep their noses clean and launder their money and don't get caught with their pants down. Hennessey's not so careful, and his gang is more violent. They do crazy things and act as enforcers for Wagner and the judge. My buddies in the police department tell me they recruit the crazies. They deal with the Mexican cartels and use acid and decapitation as deterrents."

"What's Hennessey's first name?"

"Timothy, and he's one sadistic son of a bitch. I met him once. At some kind of church bazaar, believe it or not. He's Irish Catholic and a violent SOB. Word is, he enjoys killing with a distinct penchant for torture by blade. Nobody rubs him the wrong way, believe me, and I mean nobody."

"How tight are Hennessey and Locke?"

"They work hand in hand. Are they good buddies? I can't say that. They both like power and intimidation, and pretty much get away with it by buying off cops and politicians. I think Hennessey provides Locke with extra muscle when he needs it. They're tight in a business sense."

"That sounds like I need to take out Hennessey first."

"Either way. I just pray that Lucy's nowhere near Hennessey." Frank's voice broke. At thirteen, Lucy was still a child and possibly in the control of a sadistic madman. Novak didn't like that visual image. He thrust it out of his mind and tried to memorize the names of streets and shortcuts to use, if and when he was being pursued.

They drove around the affluent community for a time, and then moved further out into the city, Lori and Frank pointing out to Novak other properties owned by Locke, and there were plenty. The beach house was located in Galveston, down south of Houston on the coast and the last place on their list. They couldn't get to it easily because it was isolated and built down at the end of a narrow sandy road. There were other houses along the beach, but none in sight of Locke's place. Locke also owned some warehouses and seedy bars here and there, which doubled as hangouts for his men. "I need to decide which guy to take down first. So let's head back to the cabin. I think I've got everything straight in my mind. Now I believe that Locke should be our primary target. We need to rattle him, make him a nervous wreck, if we can. Hit him hard and make him wonder who we are and why we're targeting him. I intend to come back out here and cause Locke some major headaches. You two can stay at the cabin and out of sight."

Unsurprisingly, Lori didn't go for that. "You can't face these guys by yourself. Don't be a hero or they'll kill you."

"Yeah? So who's going to help me? You got a bum arm that you can barely raise above your waist. Caloroso's got a warrant out on him, and his description's probably in the hands of every cop in the state. Right now, you're both distractions and useless to me. Maybe you can tag along in case I need to get the hell out fast. But that's it. No arguments. I go it alone."

Neither said anything. They could be helpful in other ways, but Novak liked missions better when nobody slowed him down or got hurt or killed because of him. If he stepped the wrong way, only he was going to pay the price. He knew what he was doing. So that's the way it had to be. Now he needed to eat something, get some sleep, gather up what he'd need, and then tomorrow he'd throw down a gauntlet on the playing field and see how tough these guys really were.

Chapter 8

The next morning when Novak got up, Caloroso was gone, probably off on his early-morning run. Any other time, Novak would have joined him. He did that at Bonne Terre because it cleared his head and got his blood pumping. Frank needed physical activity right now to even out his nerves. Lori Garner was standing at the living room windows, massaging her injured arm as was her habit now and staring down at the mist cloaking the *Sweet Sarah*. She was wearing the sling. Novak stopped in the doorway.

"Is your pain worse?"

Lori hadn't heard him come into the room. She spun low in a defensive crouch. She was jumpy as hell, just like the rest of them. She was dressed in those same boot-cut jeans with a man's white T-shirt knotted at the waist. She wore her Glock in a black leather belt holster riding on her right hip. She didn't answer his question.

"You're lazy this morning. I've been ready to go for an hour."

"You're not coming with me."

"Where are we headed first?"

They stared at each other. Novak decided this woman was in the running for the most bullheaded, stubborn female he had ever known. Worse than Claire Morgan, and that was saying something. "I've got to see somebody before we can move on this thing. I do it alone, or I don't do it."

"I'm legit, Novak, with a spotless military background. You need to trust me and let me help you. We are facing a veritable army out there."

Novak was tired of talking about it. "Look, Lori, I've known you for a few days. You have done okay. Right now, I'm not sure what's going down around here. I go it alone when I set up the groundwork. Always have. Always will. No offense intended."

"So I've got to earn your trust. Or is it your respect?"

"I respect you, damn straight, I do. You've gone through hell at the hands of those men. I don't know you well enough to put blind trust in you. I don't put blind trust in anyone, to be honest. That's just the way I am. I'm tired of arguing about this."

They locked stares. That wound had to be painful. She just wouldn't admit it. "Frank was awake all night expecting Hennessey or Locke to show up."

"Frank's not himself and won't be until Lucy's back home. Wouldn't you worry if they had your daughter?"

She didn't answer.

"Lucy's his only child. She's the only family he's got left in the world. He loses her? He loses himself."

"I know that. He's losing himself right now. And I can't seem to help him."

"Nothing's gonna help him until he's got her back."

Novak contemplated her. She had reapplied the black goop on her eyes. It took away her youth and painted her as older and tougher. Maybe that's why she did it. He fought the urge to tell her to wash it off. What Lori Garner did was none of his business, and he needed to remember that. Her next question told him she'd acquiesced to his decision. "How about I fix you a cup of coffee before you leave? I made it extra strong. Figured we'd need it to be."

Novak felt relieved that she wasn't forcing an argument. He was tired of bickering and having to explain himself. He wasn't used to that. "Yeah, sure, thanks. Make it black and give me plenty of it."

"I'll fill up a thermos to take with you." Lori moved into the kitchen, reached up with her good arm and retrieved a mug from the cabinet. Novak sat down at the table, and she brought it over to him and sat down with her own cup. "Will you at least tell me where you're going today?"

"The less you know about what I do from here on out, the better it is for you. That goes double for Frank."

"Have you even considered that something could go wrong? That's when you'll need us. We've got to know where to start looking. You need a backup plan."

Okay, maybe she hadn't given up. That didn't surprise Novak. "You're not going, so give it a rest, kid. You never listen to me, and you're beginning to get on my nerves."

"I'm not a kid. How long's this super-secret mission going take? When should we start worrying that you might be dead and lying in a ditch?"

Novak ignored her sarcasm. "Don't know yet. Depends on how things shake out."

"You would be better off telling me. You better believe I wished someone knew where I was when I was chained up in that basement."

"You were outnumbered and caught by surprise. I won't be. I'm meeting a friend, if you've got to know."

Lori shook her head. "Who? At least tell me that much."

Novak took another hard look at her. Her intense interest made him wonder about her motives. She read his expression correctly and explained away his doubt without him having to ask the hard questions.

"When Frank comes back, he's going to ask me where you are and what you're doing. What should I tell him?"

Novak looked past her face and put his gaze outside. The mists were not clearing up. It was going to be a dark and dreary day, but it wasn't raining. No sign of Frank out there. He wondered where he ran when he was at the cabin. Maybe Novak should take a look around and make sure he was okay. He took a sip of the coffee. It was too hot and burned his lips, but it was so strong he could barely drink it. Next time, he'd make the coffee. Fact was, he just didn't trust Lori yet, not the way he trusted Frank. He wasn't quite sure why. She was definitely competent and a victim, but that didn't always matter in his book. He rarely trusted anyone right off, or ever. He decided she'd earned the benefit of the doubt. "Okay. You told me Judith wants a deal with the Feds, right? She wants to set herself up in witness protection in return for turning state's evidence against her father. Somebody's got to reach out and set up the deal. I know people who might be able to get that done quickly. I don't need your help with that. Satisfied?"

"Who are you reaching out to?"

She was too pushy, which intensified his trust issues. She should understand why he wasn't telling her more and back the hell off. Still, she wouldn't let up trying to pry details out of him. Why would she do that? He wanted to trust her and thought he could, but still, he wasn't stupid, and she was being too obvious. "Let's go with need to know here, how about that?"

"Is this person trustworthy? Our lives are on the line here, too. Frank's and mine. We have a right to know who you're bringing in with us."

Novak frowned. "I trust this person. I'll decide if I still can after I have a chat with her."

"Oh, for God's sake, Novak. Let me come along. I'll stay in the car and watch your back. That's all I'm asking."

Novak wasn't going to discuss it anymore. He stood up and choked down the rest of the coffee. "Stay here. Rest your arm. If I need you or Frank, I'll call you on the numbers you gave me. Don't go anywhere and keep your head down until I get back."

That did it. Lori finally gave up the argument, glanced away, and stared out the window. Novak didn't say anything else, either. Yep, she was definitely getting on his nerves. He left out the back door, glancing around for Frank again before heading to the barn. He decided to take the Jeep. It was identical to a thousand other Jeeps in the Houston area. Nothing flamboyant that anyone would notice. The keys hung on a pegboard just inside the door, all labeled with the make and model. Frank was anal that way. He was anal about anything dealing with motor vehicles.

Novak took off and kept to county roads that he'd traced out on a Google map, using different roads than they'd used on their way into Houston. He went around Port Arthur and finally merged onto Interstate 10, after which he made good time. Frank had chosen the fish camp's location because of its inaccessibility, and he'd done a good job. It was difficult to find and difficult to get to once you knew where it was. Traffic was light, so he stepped on the gas. Now that he was on his way, he was eager to see his old friend. He knew her from his NYPD days when he was just starting out in law enforcement, and he was certain that she could set up a hastily signed witness protection order as well as any other special agent.

Leslie Ann Taylor was not a woman you could count on every time without some worry. She was not a woman easy to figure out, either, or know what went on inside her pretty little head. She was a firecracker, small and dark and tough and sexy as hell in a dangerous sort of way. All were attributes he enjoyed in a woman, especially the latter. Now that he was on his way, he was eager to see her again. It had been years since they'd been together romantically, but he had kept track of her through passing time. They'd met on and off in official capacities but not recently. He drove at a speed that ate up the miles but not too much over the speed limit. After about an hour, he pulled out his cell phone and put in a call in to Claire Morgan. She picked up at her end in a hurry.

"Hey, Novak. You in trouble again? That's the only time you ever call me anymore."

"Where are you?"

"Rome, you know, the one in Italy. So I hope you're not calling me to bail you out like you usually do."

"I need your help, but you can do from there, if you will. How's it going with Rico's adoption?"

"Black's working everything out slowly and surely in the most ridiculous iron-clad detail but with his usual abundant charm, not to mention making sure everything is legal and aboveboard and won't come back on us. Yep, all i's are dotted and all t's are crossed and all Roman palms are greased, I guess. You know how Black is. On top of everything, all the time, every time. I'm going to keep him. He makes things happen."

"Yeah, I've seen him in action. I figured it would go okay for you guys."

"So how's Mardi Gras going? You still putting drunks in NOPD lockup?"

"No, that's done. Things got a little dicey the last night, so now I'm in Houston looking to screw over some bad guys."

"Same old, same old, huh? But what the hell's going on, Novak?"

"I'll tell you all about it later. It's complicated. Right now, I want you to find out everything you can on a Houston mobster by the name of Timothy Hennessey and a dirty judge in Galveston named Calvin Locke. Hennessey's operation is small, but it sounds like he's up to his eyeballs in every crime you can think of. Is Harve available to research this stuff for me? I know you've got your hands full over there."

"Sure. Harve's lonely without Rico to go fishing with. What'd these guys do to you?"

"Nothing much yet, except try to kill a woman I just met and kidnap the daughter of an old friend."

There was a moment of silence. "Is that all?"

"One's a dirty politician; the other's a sadistic bastard. You know, the usual types. They're both said to be ruthless and deadly, and half the Galveston police force and judicial system is working on Locke's payroll, not to mention a gang of inept thugs acting as enforcers. Locke's a pompous elitist who sexually abuses his daughter, and Hennessey's probably sex trafficking underage girls. Hopefully not the girl we're looking for."

"I declare, Novak, the criminals you take down. Well, good for you. I'll ask Black about Hennessey. See if his big bro hangs with any mob associates in Houston. You know, crime boss fraternity kind of stuff. Harve's gonna have to dig up the dirt on them. I'll send it along the minute I get it. Right now, I've got to sit through all these court proceedings where guys in fancy robes drone on for hours, and in Italian, mind you. Boring, don't you know it. Black is fluent in Italian, but of course he is."

Novak had to smile. Claire wasn't one to sit around and do nothing. She was Type A on steroids. But she'd go through anything to adopt Rico. Her husband, Nicholas Black, was a crack psychiatrist and a savvy businessman who could hold his own with any lawyer or judge anywhere at any time. More important to Novak, Black's older brother was a well-connected crime boss in New Orleans, an underworld organization of which Black had no part but had used his brother's connections to get Novak out of hot water more than once. Black was a good guy to know. "Thanks, Claire. I owe you."

"Need me to fly back there and get you out of trouble again?"

"Not yet, but stand by. I'll tell you all about it when you get home."

"All right, just be careful. I want you alive and kicking when I get back. I've picked up an interesting case over here."

"I'll tread lightly. I want to make sure these guys are as bad as they're purported to be before I do something to them I can't take back. So when are you and Black slated to leave?"

"Soon, maybe in a couple of weeks. Maybe sooner. Cross your fingers."

"Big Easy or Lake of the Ozarks?"

"The lake. We're decorating the nursery up there."

Novak smiled again. He was not a smiley person, but Claire did that to him. "So how's the future daddy handling all this?"

"Ever heard of cloud nine? Black's been spending a lot of time floating around up there."

Novak laughed. "I am not surprised. How about you? You feel okay? Any morning sickness?"

"I feel a hundred percent wonderful—no, two hundred percent. Black treats me like I'm made out of crystal. Like a fragile little figurine that he's got to hold on to so I don't trip over my own two feet. But it's sweet. He's so excited that it's reached the ridiculous point. He's buying all kinds of stuff for Rico and the baby. He'll need to buy another plane just to fit in all his presents. He's got something for you, too."

They spoke about the coming baby for a few minutes longer and then hung up. Claire sounded good, even better than usual, but she had good reason. Novak was glad to see her happy. She and Black had been through some terrible things when she worked homicide at Lake of the Ozarks in Missouri. He'd worked a few of those cases with her, and they'd faced some hair-raising stuff. Claire deserved time off with her family. She probably wouldn't have taken it, however, if Rico's adoption hadn't been hanging in the balance.

After the call to his partner, Novak concentrated on driving. When he hit the outskirts of Houston with its masses of intersecting highways, he headed for the Northwest Freeway that would take him close to the FBI offices on Justice Park Drive. When he was almost there, he put in a call to her office to make sure she wasn't out of state on assignment. The receptionist informed him that Special Agent Taylor had taken the day off. So Novak continued northwest to her home in The Woodlands. He hoped she still lived in the same place. She probably did; she loved her house out there. It was still early, the morning sun glinting fire into his eyes. He poked on his sunglasses, hoping she was sleeping in since she didn't have to work.

Leslie Ann Taylor's home was in a quiet neighborhood with broad avenues lined with oaks and elms and lots of expensive suburban homes. Her house was a modern facsimile of the Victorian era, painted a soft sky-blue with double white verandas and about a thousand yards of fancy curlicues. Leslie was a woman who required all the modern conveniences, including the kidney-shaped grotto pool in her backyard. Maybe he'd get lucky and she'd be making breakfast. She could cook just about anything to perfection. She hailed from Birmingham, Alabama, and preferred Southern cooking, just like him, including the ever-present pitcher of sweet tea. They had gotten along famously for a time, in bed and otherwise.

After about fifteen minutes of waiting and watching her house, he strolled up Leslie's front sidewalk and tapped a knuckle on her cut-glass door. He hadn't expected anybody to be following him or even know who he was, and he'd been right. He had not picked up a tail; he'd made sure of that. He would take advantage of his unknown persona while it lasted, which probably wouldn't be very long. Nobody answered the door. He pressed the doorbell a couple more times, heard the muted tinkling of chimes inside, and a few seconds later glimpsed a movement through the milky glass cut with floral designs. He readied himself because he was pretty sure she wouldn't be thrilled to see him. The door opened a bare crack, and there she stood. She had on a short black silk kimono with red and yellow Chinese dragons and no shoes. Her long black hair was piled atop her head and held in place with some kind of silver clip shaped in the form of a conch shell. She looked shocked to see him standing there, and then she shut the door in his face. Novak stopped it with his foot.

"Just give me a chance, Les. I just want to talk to you for a minute."

"I don't want to talk to you. This is my day off. I've got plans, and they don't include you."

"This won't take long, I swear."

"Let me guess. You need my help."

She knew him well. "Yeah, I do, but not like last time. Nobody's going to get hurt." That was probably not true. In fact, it might be the understatement of the year, but she probably already knew that. "C'mon, Leslie, talk to me. I won't stay long. This'll probably get you a nice promotion if we handle it the right way."

Staring at him a moment, she eventually heaved out a heavy fake sigh and let him in. She did not look pleased, but he hadn't expected her to. Novak walked inside the front hall, and she shut the door behind him. It didn't look much different than the last time he'd been there. The hallway stretched back all the way to a rear porch. The ceiling was high and chandeliered, and impressionist paintings lined the crisp white walls like inside an art gallery. Each painting had its own little brass spotlight. She couldn't afford the real things on her salary, of course, but she enjoyed these priceless paintings anyway, a lucrative inheritance bequeathed to her by her wealthy grandmother. Thus, she had installed an extremely formidable home alarm system that Novak knew enough not to trip.

"I'm having coffee out back this morning. I guess you can join me. But you're not staying long, understand me, Will? You're going to make this fast, whatever it is. Is that clear?"

"No problem. Let me have my say and then I'm gone."

He followed her through a spacious navy and white kitchen and out through a tall set of white French doors to the glassed-in portion of the back gallery. A wicker table had been set up with a silver coffee urn, also bequeathed by said rich granny. A Blue Willow platter was filled with giant cinnamon rolls, displayed artistically as if for a summer brunch at a ritzy seaside hotel. That was Leslie in a nutshell. Even when alone, she made things look like a million bucks. He remembered those rolls. They dripped with white icing and smelled fabulous. The coffee smelled good, too. It was hazelnut, and its faint and pleasant scent hung in the air. There was an antique creamer and sugar bowl made of silver. The chairs were fancy white wicker but had wide seats and arms. Novak hated wicker furniture with a passion. He always feared it would collapse or crunch to kindling under his 240 pounds. All of it should be burned.

Fortunately the chair held him. Leslie allowed a small smile at the gingerly way he took his seat. "My, Will, aren't you looking old and haggard," she said to him, sipping from her Blue Willow cup. Her Alabama drawl sounded like music to him, and she held the saucer in her other hand because she was a Southern lady and former debutante who had been taught correct etiquette for every occasion. "Maybe you should get more sleep," she added.

"Thanks. You're looking as lovely as ever." For some reason, Leslie Ann Taylor did not age like normal people.

"Stop already, Novak. Flattery's not going to work on me this time. It played out its course last time and is dead as a doornail now. I know you only too well. Please don't try to play me; it doesn't suit you."

Novak recalled their problems, all right. They'd been lovers when he was stationed at Brownsville for a couple of years. It had been a long time ago, and they'd had one hell of a good time until he brought her in on a private case and got her in some serious hot water with her SAC. Everything went sour after that and in about fifteen seconds. "I'm sorry about your demotion. I had no idea things would go south as fast as they did."

"Not just a demotion, Novak, you got me a three-month suspension and a desk job for a year. I'm just now back on track in my career, and here you are, returned to destroy me again. At least, that's why I assume you're here. Can't think of any other reason you'd drop by."

"I'm not here to cause you trouble. Like I said, maybe this will settle that score in your favor this time."

Leslie glanced up from pouring coffee into his delicate blue and white china cup. Two gulps and it would be gone. Novak felt idiotic picking it up by the tiny little handle and sipping it as if he were some burly extra in *Gone with the Wind*. It held ten tablespoons, maybe, at the most.

His companion was observing him, well aware of his discomfiture. "You're saying you can get me back to where I was in the Bureau's pecking order. Well, I'll listen to that speech. Go ahead, get yourself a cinnamon roll. I can see you're drooling over them."

Novak shrugged. "I skipped breakfast. They smell good." He picked up the biggest one on the plate and took a bite. "It is good. You made them, right? I remember your buttermilk biscuits, too."

"Yes, of course I made them. So tell me, how exactly do you plan to get me a promotion?"

"Ever heard of Calvin Locke?"

She arched a brow, interested. "The esteemed judge from Galveston, the one who's as dirty as a three-dollar bill in a dumpster? Oh yeah, he's been on our radar for years. Can't seem to pin anything on him. Too rich, too tough, too smart, and too connected."

"Maybe I can help you bring him down."

Leslie observed him over the rim of her cup some more and then handed him a white napkin with small pink rosebuds embroidered all over it. Novak felt as if he was in some *Alice in Wonderland* tea party bad dream. Leslie smirked as if she could read his thoughts. But her cinnamon rolls were worth it. He took a second one.

"Pray tell, how are you going to make me a hero to my superiors? Not an easy task."

"Locke's holding his own daughter and her two small children against their will. Most likely at his River Oaks estate or the beach house he owns down on Galveston Island. His daughter has informed a trusted friend that she's ready to hand over incriminating evidence against him to the FBI in exchange for witness protection. Evidence that will put him away forever. I thought maybe it would be a good idea if she handed it over to you, and you set the whole thing up and made the arrest and got yourself some serious kudos from your higher ups. My way of making up for what happened last time."

"Horseshit."

"It's not."

"What kind of evidence?"

"Ever heard of Timothy Hennessey?"

"That man is certifiable but also crafty enough to stay out of prison. Acid attacks and beheading is what he does for fun. Usually he chooses Mexican illegals that have no way to fight back."

"According to Judith Locke, he works with her daddy dearest. Thick as thieves, they are. She can get us proof of that and only wants witness protection for her and the two kids in return. So? You interested? Or do I have to go to someone else in your office with my offer?"

"Hell, yes, I'm interested. Why wouldn't I be?"

"Tell me what you know about Hennessey. He's sort of the wild card here. This friend of Judith's? She claims to know the judge intimately and has passed me information about his homes and his business dealings. She doesn't know Hennessey all that well. So he's my blind spot."

"Intimately, as in intimately? Wife? Lover?"

"Not sexually. She's Judith's best friend and has spent time with the family. She knows them better than most and has been allowed inside their inner circle for years."

"Hennessey's based here in Houston. He's as criminally insane as you would think, but he doesn't run with the big boys. That would be Jonathan Wagner's syndicate. We've got Wagner under constant surveillance for drugs and prostitution and gambling, but he's a smart and savvy modern businessman who runs a tight ship and kills anybody he even suspects of betraying him. We haven't been able to infiltrate his operation, either. Hennessey's just the opposite. We think he's mostly into sex trafficking of young girls, twelve to fourteen usually. The way we've seen it is he finds good-looking young guys to woo and seduce the girls with free drugs and flattery, and then they drug the girls, kidnap them, and move them from state to state so frequently that nobody can ever find them again. That makes it hard to crack down and put them behind bars. We've heard rumors of white slavery going on, too. Mostly in Middle East countries."

"I was afraid of that."

"They put their girls up in quiet suburban neighborhoods and make sure everything looks normal to neighbors. Sometimes we're lucky enough to get wind of some poor child who's managed to escape. She's usually too terrified to name names or tell us anything about her captors. They just want to go home and hide out in their bedrooms and never come out again. Besides that, Hennessey threatens to behead family members if they ever contact the cops. One girl told us he brought her little brother's disfigured severed head in a bowling bag and dumped it out in front of her. As a warning. It worked. She shook like a leaf the whole time I was interviewing her."

"Get ready. He's about to go down as hard as I can make it happen. He made the mistake of taking the kid of a friend of mine."

"What friend?"

"Frank Caloroso."

"Oh my God, you're not talking about little Lucy?"

Novak nodded. "Frank's going nuts. Thinking the worst, of course."

"He has good cause, Novak. What is she now? Twelve, maybe?"

"Thirteen. She's an important pawn in this case, so I don't think they'll hurt her. Frank was helping the girl I told you about, Judith's friend. He's good at what he does, knows this city inside and out. They knew he'd be trouble and how tenacious he is. So they took Lucy to warn him off. On top of that, Judge Locke signed a bogus warrant on Frank so he has to lie low. I want Lucy back, and I want Judith out, and I want to bring both those guys down and make them suffer." Novak stared hard at Leslie. "Can you help me make any or all of that happen?"

She took a sip of coffee and watched him from over the rim of her cup. "I'd move heaven and earth to get Lucy away from those sickos. She's such a sweet little thing, just beautiful with all those red ringlets. It sickens me to think of her anywhere near that Hennessey creep. He's as cruel as they come. I hope the judge is holding her. He's an evil son of a bitch but he's not crazy."

"Okay, if we're on the same page, let's get this thing going. How fast can you set up negotiations for witness protection? Think you'll run into problems with your SAC?"

"No, I think my SAC will be in hog heaven if he gets the dope on either of those rotten criminals. He's as much a jerk as the last one. But he cuts me slack when I need it to get a job done. Sometimes more than he should. I don't trust him entirely, but he'll go for this, I think, because it's going to win him kudos at Quantico. But I'm going to need more information before I lay it out in writing and get his stamp of approval. Do you have any idea where Lucy is? Maybe we can get a Federal warrant and go in and get her first? I want her home with Frank."

"Me, too. It's my top priority. I'll find that out today, if I can. Tonight at the latest. My gut's telling me that Lucy's somewhere under Locke's control. Same goes for Judith. I think he's got them both at one of his houses, which are set up like fortresses, by the way. Another option is a stash house that he uses for the girls he traffics. I've got to take time to set up surveillance and hope I get lucky and find them fast."

"Do you need our help with that?"

"Not now, but I may later."

"When you bring us in, I hope I don't have to clean up a lot of dead bodies, Novak. You know, like before."

That's probably exactly what she'd find, but she didn't need to know that until it happened. "I just want those two women out of danger and somewhere safe. Can you arrange protection, or not?"

"Of course I can, but I can't go in and take them out of a sitting judge's house without cause."

"I know. I'm bringing Lucy to you, and Judith and her kids. Can I trust the Feds to protect them? Will they put them in a secure place? I don't want any screw-ups."

"Of course. You know better than to ask that."

Novak rose, ready to go. He stared down at her. "I'll keep you posted by phone. It's going to take some time to find them, but I've got a plan. You know how that goes. I'm going to need some luck on my side."

"I do, indeed. Suspension, demotion, embarrassment, humiliation. Not going to happen again, trust me. I'm going to watch you like a hawk."

"This is on the up and up. We need to get Judith out before Frank and I can come down hard on them about Lucy. Lucy's their ace in the hole. I don't want you involved in that. Maybe we'll get lucky and find Lucy when we go in after Judith Locke."

"If Hennessey's got Lucy, she's probably long gone, already far away in some other state. If they've got her, with her red hair and white skin, she'll be a prized piece in the overseas sex trade." She shook her head. "Is Frank going to get through this okay? He dotes on that child."

"Frank's trying to keep himself centered, but you know how emotional he is. If he loses it, he'll take a lot of them out before they can put him down. You think your guys can understand a father's grief, if it comes to a murder or two."

"A murder or two, you say? Wow, Novak, just wow. That depends on the circumstances, and you know it. Make sure you whitewash anything you two do that's illegal. I'm not throwing everything away for you again, huh uh, not this time."

"No problem. I understand. I appreciate what you did last time. You saved lives and you saved my hide."

"Yeah, I know. My hide took a severe flogging, though. I haven't forgiven you, so don't think I have."

It got quiet. Novak knew she hadn't and probably never would. He broke the silence. "Okay, I get it. I'll be in touch. You got a new number?"

She told him her private cell phone number, and Novak committed it to memory, then turned and left her sitting alone on the sunny gallery. The birds continued to sing, the ornate iron fountain down in the grass continued to tinkle, and the cinnamon rolls still smelled good. He left by the front door and crossed the street and got into the Jeep. Despite her snarky attitude, Leslie Taylor would come through for him. She always did.

Chapter 9

"Where the hell have you been, Novak?"

Frank was furious. He sat hunched over at the kitchen table, his face set in hard lines, hands clasped around an empty glass. A whiskey bottle sat nearby, only half full. Lori Garner stood at the kitchen sink, holding her bad arm. She said nothing. They both stared at Novak.

Novak ignored his demanding tone. Frank was not himself. He wouldn't be until they found his daughter. "Stand down, Frank, I took the time I needed to set up a witness protection agreement for Judith Locke and her children. An FBI friend of mine works in Houston, and I trust her to get it done."

Frank gave him a stony look.

"You don't want me here, that it, Frank? If you'd rather spout off and blame me for those guys taking Lucy, fine, do it. If you want me to forget about Judith and her kids, that's fine, too. I'd rather spend my time looking for Lucy. I don't know Judith Locke from a hole in the ground."

"I want my daughter back. I don't give a damn about Locke's daughter. She's a Locke and one of them as far as I know. Lucy comes first. I want her found. That's why you're here."

Frank was a highly intelligent guy, always had been. Novak had never seen him this enraged except a couple of times when the guy was drunk. This time it was all internal, which made it worse. His expression was deadly, and his muscles were tensed hard and coiled as if he would spring out at Novak any minute, but he wasn't drunk. He was hovering on the brink of losing his cool, and he was acting unreasonably. Novak wasn't about to fight with him.

He stared back at Frank. "All right. Go ahead, tell me where Lucy is, and I'll go get her right now. She comes first with me, too, and you know it. I love that kid."

Frank shot to his feet, overturning his chair behind him. He took a step toward Novak before he regained his senses. The anger on his face drained away. He hung his head, so full of pain that it was hard to look at him. "Oh, God, Novak. I can't do this anymore. I can't handle it. I've got to find her!"

"You got to get hold of yourself because I need you. I told you I would find your daughter, and I will find her. I won't stop until I do, I swear to God, Frank. You've got no choice but to pull yourself together and get your head on straight. Sitting here doing nothing is better than getting caught and sitting in jail on a trumped-up charge. You are no good to me locked in a cage."

Frank's hands shook. He clasped them together to make it stop. His voice came low. "They traffic young girls, Novak. They force them to do things. They addict them to drugs...." His voice faded and he turned away but swung back around. He seemed calmer but nowhere close to okay. "I cannot sit here and do nothing. Better keep me with you so you can talk me down. Right now, I want to kill somebody. I want to kill all of them. My gut is all twisted up with it."

Novak knew better than to let his own mind linger on what they were doing with Lucy. Mental pictures of her with adult men made him sick to his stomach. The fact that it was happening to lots of other young girls made it even worse. There was nothing bad enough for men who forced children into sexual acts. He was pretty sure Lucy was alive, but she was going through an ordeal that would affect her forever. Disassociation from negative images had come hard for Novak when he was younger, but he'd mastered it. Frank had better learn to do it, too, and soon. Lucy was the target age and type for those perverts. Lucy would never again be the young, innocent, and joyous girl she had been before she was taken, not in a million years.

"You know me, Frank. You've worked with me. You've got to trust me now and give me some time and space to get this done. I can't and won't go after these guys blindfolded. Let me figure out their M.O. and see how they're organized and how they move the girls around. Then we might know where they stash them. This is new territory. I don't know this area well or Texas statutes. I don't know the major players. We will take them down. We can make them pay. You can make them pay, I'm all for that, trust me. I'll stand back and you can take your vengeance any way you want."

Slowly, Frank was coming down. Novak could see his muscles starting to relax. The tic in his cheek faded. The distraught father shifted his gaze outside. The trees were tossing wildly in gusting wind. The temperature had dropped significantly during the night. Rain had moved into the interior of the state, heading for Dallas.

"All right, Novak," Frank said, refusing to look at him. "Sorry I jumped your case like that. God help me, I can't think straight anymore. I'm irrational, and I know it. Lucy's in the seventh grade, the seventh grade, for God's sake. How can they do this to kids like her?"

"We don't know they're doing anything bad to her. She's valuable to them, more than the other girls." Taking action was the only thing that would pull Frank out of his mental torment. "So let's get going. First thing now is to take my boat out on the water so I can watch Locke's beach house. I've thought this through, and I think it's possible he might be keeping them down there. We need to eliminate it, in any case. It's also a place where he can move girls in and out, either by car or boat, with nobody any wiser. We saw few neighbors close enough to see what he does in there. It's isolated and easier to penetrate than the estate. I can watch, and if I see Lucy or Judith, I can go in under cover of night and take them out."

"Novak's right," Lori agreed, on his side for a change. "He'll keep Lucy close to him. I'm sure of it. She's what's keeping you from doing your job, Frank. It isn't in his best interest to hurt her. He's afraid of you and your contacts."

"He better be afraid of me."

Novak wasn't sure Frank should be involved, but he needed him. "So we'll check it out. See if he's got guards posted. Prisoners would be harder to keep concealed out there, especially from the water. If I'm wrong, we'll come back and concentrate on getting inside the River Oaks house. We've got to take this thing one step at a time. There are three of us, and he's got men everywhere."

"I'm going with you." Frank's voice was adamant.

"Frank, you're smarter than this. You can do more good here. Do some research on these guys so I can figure out what's coming next. See if you can get me the blueprints of Locke's mansion so I know where the security cameras are. Find me the judge's itinerary and court docket for the next few weeks. That's what you can do, research that will help us. You show your face on the streets, you'll be dead or locked up. Use your head or you're going to screw things up. When that happens, I'm out. Sorry, Frank, but you need to pull it together."

"I agree. So I'll go with Novak. Don't say no. You need backup. You are not invincible."

Novak didn't like Lori's attitude. He turned to her. "Better if you keep Frank company. You're the hacker. Help Frank get me the information I need."

"Ever wonder how you're going to find Locke's beach house from the water? There are lots of them up and down that coast that look exactly the same."

Novak was damn sick and tired of arguing with these two. He wished they'd just back off and let him do what they brought him here to do. "You describe it, give me directions, and I can find it myself. They see you out there? You're right back in the hands of those guys who hurt you, or dead, and they'll find out about me. I know what I'm doing. I've done this kind of thing before. I can handle it. You stay here, and quit complicating my life."

"Did Frank tell you that I'm a trained army sniper? I can shoot any rifle with this bum arm. You're not Superman. If you're as smart as I think you are, you'll admit you need help and take off that stupid red cape."

Damn her. Worse, she was right on. Once again, Lori Garner reminded him of Claire Morgan: feisty but reckless. Lori knew what she was doing and would have his back. He planned to lay anchor a good ways out in the water and watch the house through his rifle's high-power night scope. Locke's guys probably assumed Frank was out of the picture and Lori still hiding out somewhere in New Orleans. They would not be expecting a rescue attempt or a bold offensive attack on Locke's property. Having Lori's eyes on his back could definitely be helpful.

"Okay, you're right. You can come as long as you stay out of sight. They know you, but you can identify Judith if he's holding her out there. I've seen her photo, but that doesn't mean I'd recognize her."

"Good call. Just know that I can take orders. Not that I like to, you understand."

"Just remember that I call the shots. Frank, stay out of sight and find me something I can use. Claire's working on it, too. If Lucy's inside that beach house, I'll bring her home to you tonight. I swear to God, I will. You've got to hang on until I do."

Frank's expression became a little more hopeful. "Keep me posted or I'll go crazy waiting out here by myself."

"I will. It might take all night, maybe even tomorrow night. Just sit tight."

"We're wasting time. Let's get her out of there," Lori said, moving to the back door.

"Get your gear and put on something warmer than that shirt. We may have to watch that house all night."

"The beach house has a wall of windows that face the ocean. No drapes," she told him. "If they're in there, we should be able to see them if we watch the house long enough."

Not long after, they were on the dock. Novak cast off the mooring lines while Lori climbed aboard. Looking self-satisfied, she sat down in the stern and watched him maneuver the boat off the dock. They made it down the outlet to sea, and when they left the river's mouth and entered the Gulf, the ocean was as smooth as a glass window, and that heralded easy sailing. The sun put on a spectacular show that reflected sunlight off the waves in flames of fiery gold. It was beautiful. Novak wished he was setting sail with Lori Garner on a leisurely cruise instead of waltzing into a nightmare What they were facing in the next few days was not going to be pleasant.

Novak felt edgy, a rare state for him. He was a calm person, able to make himself relax because he knew how to face personal danger and what to do and how to do it. This time out, he felt blind to the enemy he faced. He had to rely on Lori and Frank for background, and he wasn't certain they had all the facts down pat. Novak worked fast to hoist the sails because the winds were brisk as they headed south along the coast. According to Lori, the beach house was on the south end of the island. It wouldn't take long to get there. He was anxious to drop anchor, more anxious to get back in one piece, anxious about everything about to go down.

Lucy's image kept plaguing him. Lucy was a pretty little thing, very much like her mother with that beautiful russet hair. Last time he'd seen her, it had been long and she'd worn it in a ponytail that reached almost to her waist. Lots of freckles that she hated with a passion and said she looked like she had the measles. She was small and sweet and young and innocent. She would make traffickers a lot of money. A point in her favor was that she was strong willed, and she was street-smart. Frank had taught her to be and how to defend herself. He prayed she was all right.

Lori's directions were right on target, and they found a place to anchor, maybe two hundred yards out from the beach. Binoculars brought the big house into clear view. Somebody was home this time. Lights lit the vast expanse of windows facing the sea. Other lampposts were positioned along the beach, looked like solar lamps maybe, considering the dim light they cast off. A red blinking light indicated a dock, and that indicated boats. He turned off all the lights aboard and stationed himself beside Lori at the port windows. Both zeroed their binoculars in on the windows.

Locke had quite the seaside paradise, all bought and paid for by illicit sex trade and legal decisions sold to the highest bidder. The house was ultra-modern, long and sleek, two stories high with plenty of glass that gave next to zero privacy. Built from sturdy white stucco, the walls looked thick enough to withstand battering hurricane winds; the windows, not so much. Better yet, the windows were clean and undraped, as Lori had reported. A ton of sliding glass doors led onto upper and lower concrete patios. Thank you for easy access, judge.

The patios were dotted with several umbrella tables, and there was a large rectangular infinity pool replete with a tumbling rock waterfall. The place looked like a posh Tahitian resort plopped down in south Texas, a honey of a place with towering palms whose trunks had been wrapped with twinkling white lights. To one side of the house was a double attached garage with a small guesthouse beside it, both of which interested Novak. It looked like a good place to house prisoners, but so were any number of bedrooms the beach house boasted.

On the down side, there were bodyguards milling about all over the place. Some smoked cigarettes and huddled up against the seawall, their backs turned against the cold wind sweeping off the ocean. Nobody paid a bit of attention to the water or the fact that a sailboat was anchored in sight of the house. Nobody expected attack from the water, especially in the dark. Probably weren't expecting anything to happen because it had never happened before. Corrupt judges with an army of enforcers were rarely attacked head-on in their own homes. That kind of confidence made them careless.

Novak searched the shoreline for a place to put in with his Zodiac rubber boat. He knew where to enter the grounds with the least amount of trouble. And now he had backup for the job, thanks to Lori's stubborn streak. He hoped she was as good a shot as she bragged about. More important, he hoped she had no qualms about putting somebody down if the need arose.

He turned to her. "Do you recognize any of those guys?"

She was beside him on her knees on the dining banquette, her binoculars propped on the porthole's edge. She kept swiveling the glasses back and forth. "Not yet. Maybe a couple of them look vaguely familiar. I don't see the judge, though, and I don't see Judith or Lucy or the children. The house looks unoccupied."

"Does Locke come out here only on weekends? Does he have some kind of routine?'

"He used to spend every weekend here out here. That was when Judith and Stephen were both in college. I've been here lots of times with Judith.

I don't know how often he comes now. He loves this place, so I suspect he shows up a lot. Otherwise, it would be closed up with the shutters locked. He used to meet hookers out here. Judith told me that, too."

"You've been inside this house recently?"

"Yeah, but they've added on and remodeled since then. The guesthouse wasn't here when I visited. Or that garage. They didn't have the tennis court. It's been five or six years, I guess."

Novak lowered his glasses and sank down on the padded banquette bench. "Will he kill Judith? Is he really that coldblooded? Not many men could kill their own daughter."

Lori didn't look at him. "Oh, he wouldn't do it. He'd have it done so his hands stayed clean. He used to worship the ground she walked on. You can guess why." She was still watching the beach house. "She said he molested her nearly every night. I couldn't believe it at first. Later, she took that back and told me she'd been lying because she was mad that he wouldn't buy her a new convertible."

"But you do believe it?"

"I saw how he looked at her and how he touched her inappropriately. He liked to pull both of us down onto his lap and tried to make it look like innocent affection. He made me sick with all those unwanted tight hugs and wet kisses. I remember how uncomfortable I felt. I always kept my distance. He stank of cigars and was heavy, so he always started breathing hard and getting all excited, you know, panting when he had us sitting on his lap. He kept brushing against my breasts and pretending he hadn't meant to. I knew what he was doing. And when he was holding her, I felt like I was watching a nasty film. And the embarrassed look Judith got on her face was just awful. He's always so creepy when she's around."

"Did he come on to you other than the lap thing?"

"No, I never liked that dude even before I knew what he was. I stayed away from their homes sometimes because of him. He never tried anything else with me."

"Is Timothy Hennessey like that, too?"

"I don't know him. I know from Frank that he's small potatoes as far as mob bosses go. That could be why he hooked up with Judge Locke down here in Galveston. All I know is that he's a real bad man that nobody ever wants to cross." She sat down beside Novak, sighed heavily, and searched his face. The floor lights were on but gave only faint illumination inside the main cabin. Novak could barely make out her features. "You think Hennessey's got Lucy, don't you, Novak?"

That was exactly what Novak thought, but he didn't want it to be true. "I hope not. That's the worst-case scenario."

"Yeah. Me either. I hope she's over there in that beach house right now, locked up in some bedroom watching television and reading magazines and painting her toenails."

"Guess we'll find out soon enough. If we see her, I'm going in tonight."

"You see how many men he's got out here? Frank says you're good, but you're only one guy."

Novak could take down the guards. That would no problem. "Right now, we keep watching and bide our time. I think they've got somebody in there, or why so many guards at an empty house? We'll watch tomorrow when it gets light, and then I'll pay them a visit tomorrow night and check the place out."

"I'll have your back. Don't worry."

"You better. Did you see how many guards he's got?"

Lori smiled at him. The first real one he'd seen from her.

Chapter 10

The rain beat steadily on the roof of the cabin, and they could hear the jingling and jangling of the riggings blown around. They had not lucked out with the weather. Novak and Lori took turns on surveillance all night long, one of them dozing on the couch, the other watching the beach house. Dawn valiantly tried to smuggle a glimpse of the sun out of clouds the look and color of fireplace soot but didn't have the energy to get it done. As hours passed, the light remained drab and dull and dingy, the clouds forming a distinct line of demarcation just above the sea horizon. Wet fog hung in wisps atop the surface of the water, and the beach was barely visible. There had been no movement inside the house.

Novak knew they were wasting time that Lucy and Judith did not have. Sitting there watching was getting them nowhere. Even when the sun finally bludgeoned its way, kicking and screaming, out from under the cloud cover and light blazed alive across the land, nobody showed. Locke's hired henchmen walked their assigned posts, AR-15 rifles slung over their shoulders, clueless they were being watched. They were armed for trouble but not expecting it. He turned his focus onto the dock that stretched maybe thirty yards out past the surf. Two fast and sleek speedboats were tied up on either side. Nobody seemed to notice or care about the forty-foot sailboat that lay at anchor just off the beach. So that was one good thing.

Lori's arm appeared to be killing her at the moment, but she had stubbornly refused to take her meds until they finished what they'd come to do and weighed anchor for home. She was good at surveilling, had more patience than he had, so Novak felt better about bringing her along. She hadn't started an argument, either, which was even more to his liking. He glanced back at her. She lay on the opposite couch. The sling was tight against her torso. She was lying on her back, fully dressed, holding up pretty well despite some shallow, restless breathing. She groaned and twisted around and muttered in her sleep, locked inside her subconscious mind with something terrible. Novak could pretty much figure what she was reliving. He had nightmare problems himself. He turned back and refocused his concentration on the house.

Oversized sliding doors opened out of a giant living area, all seen up close as if he stood inside. A kitchen had been built against the back wall, separated by a long white marble counter with six matching stools. Lots of couches and chairs and tables were sitting around in conversation areas. There was a fireplace set with logs ready to be lit and a wet bar with glass shelves holding every kind of liquor made by man. The bottle of bourbon looked pretty good to Novak at the moment. That open room encompassed the entire ground floor. He could see everything, but had yet to see anyone inside.

The guards remained outside. It appeared that was one of Locke's idiosyncrasies—keeping his bodyguards outside—and not a particularly smart move on his part but good for Novak's intentions. He noted when and if the guard duties shifted, mentally filing back any unpatrolled areas. Tired, Novak put down the binoculars, leaned back, and rubbed his eyes with his fingers. He was fighting serious mental fatigue and inner frustration. They couldn't waste much more time. Lucy's days were numbered; he felt it in his gut. He had counted on finding one of the women there, but it was a dead end. He decided to give it another night.

His perseverance paid off two hours later when a vehicle appeared on the road leading up to a rear gate. A long black limousine drove toward the beach, all sleek and shiny and expensive, the kind of car that carried self-important people. Novak perked up, fairly certain this one belonged to the corrupt judge he had been waiting for. Novak hungered to get that guy alone and enjoy some violent chitchat. He was not calm and collected anymore. He had a personal stake this time. So an encounter with the judge was going to go down, he just didn't know when. It was Saturday, so he assumed the judge was following his old habit of weekends at the beach. That was good news. Habits set in stone always helped a pursuer.

The limo slowed and drove through the iron spiked gate when a man ran to open it. Novak watched it proceed around to the south side of the house and disappear into the garage. Novak waited, interested to see who stepped out of that car. Nobody appeared, so they had entered through an interior door. Swiveling his glasses back to the stretch of windows, he caught sight of someone moving around inside.

Minutes later, the center slider pushed back, and who should step out but Calvin Locke himself. The sun was gone again, huddled behind a hump of storm clouds, and the judge glared up at the sky as if it had disobeyed his command. In the flesh, the notorious judge didn't look so threatening. He was overweight but tidy with a protruding paunch and had on attire similar to some 1930s film star. He wore a white silk ascot around his throat, a tan blazer, navy pants, and a brown felt fedora pushed down on his head. Hell, all he needed was a twelve-inch white cigarette holder. Instead, he preferred a fat cigar that he held between his thumb and forefinger. Minutes later, a woman walked outside. She was older than the judge, late sixties, graying and stocky and dressed in a plain black dress that almost reached her ankles. More important to Novak, she held the hands of two little girls. She looked as if she was scared to death of anyone and everyone. He felt a sense of elation. Those kids had to be Judith Locke's daughters, had to be. Novak smiled to himself. *Gotcha, Locke.*

Novak called out to Lori, and she joined him at the porthole. The sun came back out as if a token of good luck, and the day brightened as if a switch had been thrown. The surface glittered and shone and so did the windows. Both children looked hangdog and unhappy, totally unlike most kids arriving at a beach. They were cute girls, with the same unusual shade of platinum-blond hair as their mother. Both pressed in close to the nanny's legs. They looked very little.

"Oh my God, that's Sammi and Susie! We found them, Novak!"

Novak nodded. "You're positive it's them?"

"Damn right. I'd know them anywhere. God, they look so scared, don't they? We got to get them out of there now."

"Not now. Tonight."

"Oh, they look so sad."

"You see anyone else in the house?"

Lori scanned her glasses back and forth. "No, but they might have them locked up in the bedroom wing over on the side of the house. Or the garage or guesthouse."

Novak stiffened when Locke sat down in one of the cushioned patio chairs and motioned the children to be brought to him. They hung back, clinging to the woman's hands. The nanny bent down and spoke to them and then nervously pushed them toward their sleazebag grandfather. After that, she disappeared inside the house. They walked over to the big man, holding hands, and the judge scooped both up onto his lap and started kissing them on the face.

"That bastard," Lori said viciously. "I can still smell his tobacco."

Novak wanted those little girls out of that house and as far away from that perv as he could get them. If Calvin Locke had molested his daughter and separated those children from their mother, the reason was obvious. The idea of what he might be planning ate at Novak. He focused in closer on the older girl's face. Both of them looked small for their ages and somehow delicate. Locke kept caressing their cheeks with his fingers and pressing them up tight against his chest. Roiling emotion inside Novak's chest kindled quickly to rage. He let himself feel the fire of it race through his blood, and then he shut it down by force of will. "Look at how he's holding those kids."

"He's an animal. Please let me help you take that monster down."

"Maybe."

"You think Judith's in there, too?"

"Maybe. The guards seem to hang around the guesthouse more than is necessary."

"It could be Lucy."

They sat there and watched the judge cuddle and tickle his unwilling granddaughters for almost an hour. The girls kept trying to squirm out of his grasp, especially Susie. Novak was happy when the nanny returned and hurried the children inside. Once he was alone, the judge shed his blazer, rolled up his shirtsleeves, and took a swig out of a silver flask. He stretched out, relaxed back on a double chaise longue, and closed his eyes. Novak lowered the binoculars. He had already decided what he was going to do.

Lori knew, too. "We've got to move in tonight. He's already touching them inappropriately. We've got to get them out before he goes further."

Judging by the way the girls shied away from him, Novak was afraid that might have already happened. "I need to check out that guesthouse and garage for Judith and Lucy. How many bedrooms does this place have?"

"Four. I can't see him having a prisoner in the house without the girls asking him questions. Especially if it was Judith, he wouldn't want her around to interfere now that he has control of the girls. If anyone's in there, it's probably Lucy."

"I think you're right. He's got a live-in nanny. Did they have that before?"

"He hired her not long ago, but before that, Judith always took care of them herself. She's a hands-on mom. She loves those girls more than anything. He needed a nanny once he decided to lock Judith up. And she doesn't understand much English, so she won't know exactly what's going on."

"Okay, I go in tonight. You stay here and cover my back."

"I'll do whatever you say. I want them out of there."

"Were you really a sniper?"

"Why would I lie about it?"

"Just how good are you?"

"I was based in Mosul for a year. That's all I did."

"How good are you?" he repeated.

"Wanna see my medals?"

Novak wanted to smile. She looked so smug and self-satisfied. She should be. You had to be damn good to qualify as a sniper in a battle zone; they chose the best of the best. "Glad to hear it. You have to cover me as soon as I hit the beach. I've got a rifle with the best silencer I could find. It's a good one, so you shouldn't have a problem. Night scope's the best you can buy. If anybody gets in my way when I've got those kids in my arms, you have to blow them away. No hesitation. Can you do that?"

"I'll kill every one of them to get those kids away from that pedophile." Her eyes were hard and did not waver.

"Just don't get too carried away. You may not have to shoot anybody. I should be able to get past them without being seen unless something goes wrong. You are strictly backup in case I run into trouble. Just don't let them kill me."

"No worries."

That was easy for her to say. She might be the best sniper in the history of the United States Army, but she had gone through a traumatic nightmare and only days ago. She could be triggered by emotions and freeze. Then he'd end up dead. "Just keep me in your sights the whole time, okay? Especially on the way out with those little girls. That's when I'll be most vulnerable."

"I know. I'm good with it."

"How's your arm?"

"Better. I can sight in and pull the trigger. No problem, Novak."

"Once inside, I'm going to check out the grounds first, and then I'm taking the girls out of the house. No way I'm leaving them out here."

"They're scared of him. Did you see the way they were pulling away?"

"Maybe they can tell me where he's got their mom locked up. If she is in that compound somewhere, I'm bringing her out, too."

"How? They can't swim yet. And his guards are everywhere."

"Did you see the Zodiac boat at the stern?"

"I did. We used the same boats in training."

"I'll paddle to shore, extract the kids, and bring them out here in that boat. I've done this kind of thing under worse conditions. I can get past the guards without being seen. But I've got to be able to depend on you if I get in trouble."

"Dude, this convo's getting old." Lori scowled up at him. "Let me tell you something about your extraction. Those kids are not going to want to come with you. Know why? Cause you're a big, scary guy showing up in their bedrooms in the dead of night. They'll be scared to death of you."

"Yeah? So? You'd rather me to leave them in there with Locke?"

"What if they scream and cry?"

"They won't if you tell me something I can say to them that'll put them at ease. You know, something or someplace you've been, a pet name you've got for them, anything to prove you're out here waiting and that's where I'm taking them." A thought occurred to him. "Did Judith give them a safe word?"

"Probably, but I don't know what it is. They know me pretty well." Lori suddenly smiled. "Tell them Bunny. That's what they called me when they were toddlers because I gave them both a bunny stuffed animal. Tell them that and they'll go with you. We had lots of fun on that visit."

"I'm going in as soon as it gets dark."

"You're certain you can get past all those guards?"

"I'm not absolutely certain that the sun's coming up every day. But yeah, I can do it, and I won't get caught. You think he's already molesting them?"

"Judith was older when it started. God, it makes me sick to even think about it."

"We'll get them out."

"Did you see those boats at the dock? Even if you get them out, they'll come after us."

"If things go according to plan, we'll be long gone by then. But I'll sabotage the boats. Just do your part and trust me."

"You got it, Novak."

He and Lori Garner went together like oil and water. Still, he sort of liked the woman. She was holding up better than most. "You keep watching. I'm gonna get my gear ready and then get some shut-eye. Call me if anything happens."

"Yes, sir. Can you really sleep now?"

"I can sleep anywhere."

"I'll wake you up if anything shakes."

Novak's instincts were telling him he could trust this young woman, but his past experiences were dragging the idea down. He left her on watch, went into his cabin, and lay down on the bed. In minutes, he was asleep. Three hours later, he was up again and pulling on black sweatpants, T-shirt, and nylon windbreaker. He quickly packed a waterproof bag with the tools and weapons he'd need, and then he pulled the long gun out of the rack bolted beside his bed. He slung the bag over his shoulder and carried the rifle up to the stern, checked out the beach, and found no guards watching the ocean approach. They were really stupid. Then he set about lowering the Zodiac on the starboard side, out of sight of the house. The judge was in residence, so they should be on their toes. They no doubt felt safe inside that walled compound with no close neighbors and no easy access, but they shouldn't. They'd find that out the hard way, as soon as the sun came out tomorrow morning.

Chapter 11

Inky and impenetrable, night fell like a black hood dropped over Novak's head. That was good. He wanted to be invisible. Periodic rain persisted and so did his case of nerves. Novak felt an unfamiliar but innate sense of doom. He wasn't sure why. This extraction was not far afield from many others he'd successfully completed while with his SEAL team. He usually felt something akin to exhilaration and high expectations, a keen sharpening of purpose right before he walked into danger. He had to go in and rescue those little girls. Still, something nagged at him, held him back.

Maybe he was afraid of what he'd find inside that beach house. Maybe Lucy and Judith were there, injured or hurt. Maybe they were already dead and buried. He lay on his bed in the dark, his body totally relaxed, his mind, not so much. Although he'd mastered the art of patience a long time ago, waiting for the perfect moment had never been his thing. He liked to prepare and then get things done. This time he needed to wait. The guards were terrible, but he wanted them drowsy and tired, because he was going in alone with only Lori Garner for backup.

Despite the inexplicable reserve, he had managed to get some sleep. Lori had not. Last time he checked, she was still surveilling at the port but she had yet to see Judith or Lucy show up in the house. She reported the guards worked in two-hour shifts and had since they'd dropped anchor. Each man had specified posts they worked every time and mostly along the perimeter wall. Unfortunately for Novak, they were more alert and efficient with the boss in the house. Since the judge had arrived, the hanging out together while smoking and laughing had ended. Still, he could zero in on areas to avoid or how he could evade their notice.

They were heavily armed, with both rifles and 9mm handguns. All now wore desert camouflage, the pants legs tucked inside heavy black leather boots. Their uniforms were too hot and too formal for this kind of beach patrol. The judge was a pompous fool who wanted matching toy soldiers in his own little private army. Too bad their wardrobe was better than their fight skills.

On the other hand, there was the nanny to worry about. She would fight for her charges. She was too old, too short, too stout, and no problem. That is, unless she screamed bloody murder when he stepped out of the dark in her bedroom. He would be better off to avoid her. If she slept in the same room as the girls, that's when she'd become a problem. He hoped she didn't interfere. He didn't relish tussling with a little old lady in the dark.

For most of the evening, she'd been sitting at an outdoor table shaded by a red-striped umbrella while watching the two little girls sit cross-legged and play with Barbie dolls. She looked nervous. Maybe she already sensed that her employer was a damn disgusting pedophile. Maybe she didn't know. Maybe she would protect the little ones if Locke tried to molest them. He didn't think so. She looked more frightened of him than the children did. He had to get those kids out tonight. No way was he leaving them in there alone.

When the house finally went completely dark inside, and the night guards got lazy again, Novak stepped down into Zodiac and picked up a paddle. He glanced up at the roof of the main cabin. Lori was lying on her stomach, hidden inside the soft and velvety darkness only found when alone on the ocean. His high-powered rifle was propped on a tripod in front of her, and he had watched her zero it in and fix it on the beach house. He had watched her check out the weapon, load it, and adjust the settings on the scope. She knew what she was doing, all right. She was motionless up there now, bad shoulder resting on a pillow, both hands steady on the weapon. If she had the guts to put down any guard who tried to stop him, Novak might make it out of that house with those kids still breathing. They would know soon enough.

Thrusting the paddle deep into the water, he started stroking toward shore with long hard strokes. The momentum propelled him swiftly away from the hull until he skimmed swiftly out over the dark water. He didn't have to fight against the wild chop driven in to shore by the massive thunderstorm raging miles out at sea. The currents helped increase his speed. Unfortunately, it would be a fight to reach the boat on the way back.

For several hours he'd sat out on deck in the dark, waiting to move and watching nature's fireworks flitting and flaming across the horizon. Jags of horizontal lightning had flared and died, backlighting the silvery clouds, and then faded away, only to appear again in psychedelic bursts of energy. It had been almost hypnotic to him watching the jittery strobe effect. The smell of ozone was thick in the wind driving in behind him, and he could feel the restlessness of the ocean beneath his feet. That furious storm onslaught was headed his way. He glanced behind him at the *Sweet Sarah*. She was barely visible now. A second later the sailboat was silhouetted as a bolt of blinding lightning forked down with a golden stab into the sea. Faraway thunder promised more to come and then faded away.

Novak hunched lower. If he could see the sailboat in the lightning flashes, the men on shore could see him. He increased his labor with the paddle; he wanted to get in and out fast. Violence in the sky would complicate that. It was already raining, but only a drizzle that stippled the water around him. A downpour could be a good thing. Every sound, every crack of thunder and gust of wind would distract the guards and make Novak harder to spot. Only dim solar lights were affixed atop the seawall but at wide intervals that enabled him to pick out the shadows of men on patrol. There weren't many about. The ones who were stood under palm trees or under the dock overhang, afraid they'd get wet, no doubt. They had to be young thugs out of Houston, nowhere near tried and trained bodyguards. Novak wondered why the judge felt the need to hire inferior protection when he could pay trained mercenaries who would be a thousand times more competent.

Once Novak got closer, he tried to hit the beach around a forty-degree angle away from the long dock. He lifted the paddle about twenty yards offshore, kept low and allowed the surf to push the Zodiac up onto on the sand. When it scraped the beach, he eased out and pulled it all the way up. He estimated about thirty yards separated him from the dock, but he had come in at the far corner of the perimeter wall. Dragging the boat up, he took cover behind the wall. He left the boat there and waded back to the water. When he was chest-deep, he used a breaststroke to pass through the breakers and swam toward Locke's speedboats moored to the dock. They were guarded, two men, but they were standing out on the sand a good distance away. These guys were laughable. Bits of their conversation drifted out to him over the low rush of the waves. It sounded as if they were debating pros and cons of Dallas Cowboys football. When he reached the end of the dock, he lifted himself up into the first boat, found the gas tanks, pulled out his Ka-Bar, and punched several huge gashes that let the fuel drain into the water. Then he moved to the other boat and sabotaged it. Nobody noticed him; nobody watching. It was an effective deterrent. They weren't going anywhere on empty tanks. Once that was done, he swam to deeper water and floated closer on the incoming surf where he was less visible. The guards sauntered down the beach, still clueless.

They were talking animatedly and weren't worried about intruders. Once they got far enough away, Novak let the waves push him the rest of the way in. When his feet touched bottom, he crawled up on the sand. He made it to the seawall undetected and flattened his back against the thick stucco. He waited there to catch his breath and listen for alarms. All he heard was the rhythmic ebb and crash of salt water against sand, and the cold raindrops spattering his sodden clothes. The rain was intensifying.

Novak squinted out over the water but couldn't spot the boat. That was good. If he couldn't see it, they couldn't see it. If Lori was on the ball, she'd be under a protective tarp now and have the night scope beaded in on every move he made. He hoped to hell she did. The idea of her out there gave him a sense of security. She wasn't a badass SEAL but she could shoot.

Once the guards were far enough down the beach, he backed off a few feet, took a run at the wall, and managed to climb up enough to grab a handhold. He swung himself up and lay flat for a moment. He pulled out his weapon and broke the nearest solar light. Still no alarm. He dropped down inside the compound. The lawn felt soggy under his feet. There was thick shrubbery planted along the wall, and the tall palm trees were swaying, the fronds rustling in the wind, but the twinkling lights glittering around their trunks had been turned off. The house and grounds were dark enough to provide cover. He skirted the wall and found the wide boardwalk that would take him up to the pool and then the house just beyond.

He squatted down behind an outdoor shower at the bottom of the walkway. He sat there a moment, watching and waiting, fearing someone would unknowingly blunder upon him. Nobody showed, but there was a guard on the rear patio close to where the judge had sat earlier. It was quiet inside the wall, the sounds of the sea muted slightly. He crept up the incline, but he was in no man's land and hoped Lori could still pick up his movements with the scope.

The house was now twenty yards above his position, and the shimmering pool shone turquoise in the darkness, painting the white stucco on the back of the house with reflections off the windblown water. He skirted it, but the night-lights set at the base of the exterior wall were a problem. Still, there were deep shadows, and he kept to them. Wind and swaying palms and steady rain drumming on the surface of the pool concealed any sounds he made. Everything was going okay so far, but he didn't expect that to last. He made his way around to the garage, slipped inside and found no guards, and then checked it for prisoners. Nothing. The attached guesthouse turned out to be housing for the guards. Most of them were inside there, asleep, he hoped. Judith and Lucy were not there.

Returning to the house, he stood behind a thick palm and searched the windows facing the sea. The living room and kitchen he'd observed from the boat were now pitch black. He moved around the side of the house where Lori had told him there were four bedrooms on the second floor. He knew she couldn't sight him in there so he was in no man's land. Two windows right above him were dark, but the second two had dim lights burning inside, most likely night-lights. His gut told him the children were probably in one or both rooms, so he made his way beneath them and took a knee. That's when a guard stepped around the corner of the house, smack-dab in front of him.

Face to face, both of them were shocked standstill for the first seconds. Novak moved first. He rocketed up out of his crouch, hit the guy with an undercut to the jaw, and grabbed the guy before he could hit the ground. He got behind him with one hand over his mouth and the other around the neck and started squeezing off his air. The guy struggled, but he was skinny and weak and half Novak's size and nowhere near as strong. Novak kept him in the blood chokehold until he lost consciousness. Within seconds, he turned slack and hung limp. Novak dragged him into some bushes hugging the house, pulled out the duct tape, and bound him up, wrists, ankles, and mouth. Nobody showed up to help the guy.

The Spanish architecture of the house included black wrought-iron private balconies outside each bedroom, a definite siren call to burglars or any other intruder. The balconies were bolted nice and tight to the thick stucco walls with perfect footholds for scaling to the top floor. Novak never understood why people would build such open invitations for trouble. He took a running jump, caught hold of the bottom of the upper balcony, and pulled himself up until he could swing over the railing onto the small balcony outside the glass sliding door.

Seconds later, he was up there and watching for guards. The slider was undraped. He took a quick peek inside. It was the nanny's room. She was sound asleep in her bed, a hardback book facedown atop her chest and a small reading lamp burning on the bedside table. He climbed over the side railing and jumped to the next balcony. There, he hit pay dirt. Inside, both children were snuggled together under the covers of one of the twin beds. A night-light burned on the table between the beds, the kind that rotated while playing lullabies and casting moving pictures of animals dancing and cavorting on the ceiling and walls.

The balcony door was locked, but he slipped it with no trouble. He inched it open wide enough to step inside. Closing it behind him, he knelt down and listened. No sound except the soft soothing music of the night-light. This was all going way too easy. He wasn't used to easy extractions; there was always a snag. He stood back against the wall and searched each corner of the room for a security camera. He didn't see any. That surprised him, too. He figured the judge was a sleazy voyeur, the kind of man who liked to watch people in their bedrooms. But it could be hidden. He'd have to take that chance. The room was painted white and looked utterly austere. It looked nothing like most child nurseries. It looked more like a sterile room in a sanitarium. There was a big-screen TV on the wall right across from the beds, but Novak saw no toys, no children's books, no cute posters depicting Disney princesses or Mickey Mouse or Dora the Explorer, nothing.

Still hesitant, Novak stood there without moving and watched them a moment. No way would he not scare the hell out of those two little girls. He was dressed in black clothes and a black watch cap, his face blackened to blend into the night. He would be a huge dark monster looming up unexpectedly in the night, a bogeyman come to get them. They were going to be terrified. That didn't sit well, but he had no choice. He had to get them out of there. Inching closer to the bed, he got a better look at the children and froze in his tracks. The four-year-old was wide awake. What was her name? Susie? Big brown eyes were glued on him, huge and horrified and reflecting the night-light. Stiff with dread, she stared mutely at him. Novak immediately dropped down on his haunches, trying to look less intimidating. He softened his voice. "Hi, Susie, don't be afraid of me. I'm not gonna hurt you, I promise."

Susie pulled the blanket up and hid her face. Novak wouldn't have believed him, either. Under the covers, her body was shaking. Novak glanced at the door leading out into the hall. "Listen to me, sweetie, I know you're scared. But you remember that lady you call Bunny. The one who knows your mommy?" The child did not move a muscle. "Well, I know her, too. She's awfully worried about you, so she sent me in here to get you and your sister so we can go find your mommy. If you'll stay real quiet and come with me now, I'll take you to her, but you gotta be very quiet. Okay, Susie, okay? Will you come with me?"

It took her a few minutes to garner her courage, minutes that Novak didn't have. She finally peeked out from under the quilt. Her eyes were wide but wary.

"I'm not going to hurt you. I promise you, Susie. Okay? Bunny wants you to come and see her. You remember her, don't you? Her real name's Lori."

Susie's eyes were locked on Novak's face, and her voice finally came, low and hesitant, a mere whisper. "Are you gonna take us away from Grandfather?"

Novak swallowed hard. He wasn't sure if she wanted him to say yes or no. "I've got to, baby. Your mommy doesn't want you and Sammi to stay here with him, not anymore. She wants you to come be with her, okay? That's why I've got to sneak in your room like this, so your grandfather won't know. And that's why you've got to be real quiet when I take you out." He looked at the smaller girl. She was still asleep. "You think you can make Sammi be quiet, too?" Because he didn't think she could, and he didn't think a three-year-old was going to understand anything, no matter what he said. "Is there anybody else here in the house, Susie? Is your mommy here or a girl with red hair? Her name's Lucy?"

She shook her head and squeezed her eyes shut. "Just me and Sammi and Nanny. And Grandfather. He took us away from our mommy."

"I know. We're going to find her, I promise. Come with me and we'll look for her, okay?"

"You promise, cross your heart?"

Novak didn't have time to cajole the kids. "Yes, I do. What about the girl named Lucy? Have you seen her anywhere? Up here in the bedrooms, maybe?"

She shook her head again. She had the most enormous brown eyes, so dark they glittered in the dim illumination. "Just Grandfather and those men he has around."

"I'm gonna find your mommy, I promise, but we've got to get you out of this house, okay? Remember, you can't make noises or scream or cry. If you do, they'll make you stay here."

"I won't cry." Susie wasn't exactly convincing.

"Okay, then wake up Sammi and tell her I'm not going to hurt her, okay? She's got to be quiet, too, or your grandfather's gonna hear us."

She nodded again.

Novak left her and moved back to the door that led into the hall. Susie shook her sister awake, and they started whispering. He cracked the door. Nobody was in the hallway. Not a sound. He shut and locked it and then returned to the bed. Sammi looked as if he was there to kill her. He knelt down. "Okay, I'm gonna pick you up, and we're going out through your balcony over there. Your grandfather and Nanny won't hear us if we leave that way. That means you both have to hang on tight and not let go of my neck, no matter what. Your friend, Bunny? She's out there in a boat waiting for you to come and help her find your mommy. You've got to be brave. I won't drop you, but you have to hold on tight. Okay?"

Susie nodded, but Sammi turned over and hid her face in the pillow. Susie pushed down the covers and climbed out of bed. Then she pulled her sister out from under the covers. They both stared at him. Novak had a bad feeling this would turn into a disaster.

"Let's go. Bunny's waiting out on the boat."

Sammi was the tiniest little thing. They both seemed small for their ages. Novak looked at them, fighting an overwhelming impulse to surprise Calvin Locke in his bed and end him while he slept, quick and efficient and forever. But he couldn't do that yet. He needed to get these kids somewhere safe, and fast.

Novak led them to the balcony door and knelt, putting his forefinger to his lips. Mute and docile, the little girls stood silently, staring at him. He wondered what they'd been through alone with Locke all this time and then wished he hadn't. "Okay, here's the deal. Susie, I'm putting you on my back, and you've got to hold on as tight as you can around my neck while I take you down. You can't let go, no matter what, okay?"

She nodded, and Novak looked at the little one. "I'm going to hold you in front of me, Sammi, is that okay? Remember, you have to be quiet. We don't want anyone to hear us before we get out there to your friend, Bunny. Okay, it's going to be all right, I promise. I'm not going to let you fall. I'll be holding on to you too tight."

Susie nodded. Sammi just stared. They didn't act like normal kids would when awakened by a big stranger in the middle of the night. Most children would scream their heads off if he showed up, dressed in all black. These children seemed used to it, and that did not bode well. He told them not to let go, no matter what, and they both immediately locked their arms in strangleholds around his neck. He stood up, taking them with him, one arm around the baby, the other holding Susie on his back. It felt as if they weighed nothing. It would not be hard taking them down to the ground. They didn't move, but they were breathing hard, scared to death. He held onto Sammi tight with one arm as he swung his leg over the rail. Susie had a tighter hold. He turned and quickly climbed down with them until he was hanging by one hand off the balcony. Then he let go and held both girls in place as he dropped down to the ground.

When his feet hit, it shook Susie halfway off. He caught her by her nightgown and thrust her back in place. Sammi lay against his chest, her arms clasped around his neck and her face buried in his jacket. Neither made a sound. He was both relieved and surprised. He knelt and lowered them to the ground, and then he drew his weapon, fearing a guard might have heard them. Nothing stirred. The first guard was still lying prostrate in the bushes. But Novak's pulse was jumping as he waited to be attacked.

After a moment, he scooped both girls up on his left arm. They both grabbed his neck again. Now came the hard part, the part where they could get hurt. His experience was telling him to beware, tread softly, but his heart was screaming to hurry up and get them the hell out of there. Both girls were breathing hard; he could actually feel their rapid heartbeats. They were going to need a lot of love and attention after this scary night, maybe even a good child psychologist. Lori better have some magic up her sleeve to calm them down. He stayed as low as he could, clutching them tight, keeping to the shadows but moving as fast as he safely could. He kept his eyes alert and ears open, listening to any sound. Short palms and thick, manicured vegetation grew along the boardwalk. He didn't step up on it but followed it down to the wall. Sammi sounded like she was gasping for breath now, absolutely scared out of her wits, maybe on the verge of screaming. He could not let her do that, or they were done for. He had to calm her down.

"It's okay, Sammi, I promise. I've got you, you're okay," he breathed his words into her pale hair, out of breath himself. She smelled like baby powder, but she was too scared to listen to anything he said. She started out with a little sob, soft at first, but then she let go with it. When Sammi started crying, Susie gave her first little whimper. Novak didn't waste any more words; they were much too scared. Watching for guards, he headed hard for the beach.

About the time Novak came up level with the shower stall, a burly guard showed up where the wall opened onto the beach. When he glimpsed Novak, he stopped in his tracks then went for his rifle. Novak dropped the girls to the sand and lunged at him, grabbing for the weapon. His forward momentum sent both of them to the ground and rolling out onto the deep sand on the beach. They grappled there for possession of the rifle until the guard got his arm loose and punched Novak in the head. He ducked to the side, but the blow sent his mind spinning. Then the guard crawled desperately for the rifle a few feet away. Novak grabbed the guy's legs and jerked him back, struggling to get on top of him and force him on his back.

The guy was as strong as Novak and struggled until Novak got a good hard blow to his throat followed by a quick jab to the nose. Blood pumped, and the guard recoiled a bit, groaning. That gave Novak time to punch him again. He got him hard in the bridge of his nose this time and felt cartilage crunch under his fist. The other man stopped fighting and rolled over onto his back. Novak jumped atop him and pressed his thumbs hard against his windpipe. Choking for air, the guard clawed desperately at Novak's locked wrists. Novak increased the pressure, using his weight to hold him still until the guy passed out.

On his knees, panting from exertion and tasting his own blood, Novak turned back to grab the two girls. They were not there. Panic set in, and he pushed himself up, pressed back against the wall, pretty sure another guard could have heard the fight. It hadn't been exactly quiet, but all he could hear was the pounding in his eardrums and the roar of the surf. Novak backed through the gate, rifle in one hand, and scanned the lawn. The little girls had not gone far. They were huddled inside the shower stall, hiding their eyes and clutching each other tightly. When Susie saw him, she ran into his arms.

Novak wasted no more time. He grabbed both kids, made sure the beach was deserted, and sprinted along the outside wall toward his boat. He ran into a second guard about six feet from the hidden Zodiac. He skidded to a stop, tightening his hold on the little girls because this time the guard had him dead to rights. He thrust them both behind him as the guard pointed his rifle at Novak's chest.

"Don't you move, you son—"

That's all the guard got out before a bullet hit him square in the mouth and blew most of the back of his head off. The impact knocked him off his feet; he was dead before he hit the ground. Despite the silencer, Novak heard the muffled crack of the high-powered rifle that died quickly under the wind and rain. Novak picked up the kids again and took off to the boat. Lori Garner was a hell of a good shot, all right. He was in love. He dropped both kids into the boat, dragged it down to the water, and ran it a few steps out into the surf. Pushing off, he jumped in and paddled like hell for the *Sweet Sarah*. He kept glancing behind him and could see lights coming on inside the house. They'd sounded the alarms. Armed men were rushing around with flashlights, their beams swinging around in arcs through the darkness looking for him. He could hear them shouting. They hadn't pinpointed the beach yet. Next time he looked back, four men burst through the opening in the wall and headed for the speedboats. Novak paddled harder. They weren't going anywhere.

The sailboat lay anchored in utter darkness. He could barely make out its silhouette against the night sky. Rain was drumming the water all around them, drenching them and plastering hair in their eyes. Behind him, the little girls were clutching each other and crying. Then he picked out Lori at the stern, God bless her, where she stood waiting to pull them in. She still had the sniper rifle in one hand. She put it down when the Zodiac bumped up against the landing platform. He tossed her the rope and she tied it up. He grabbed the little one and handed her out to Lori, and then he picked up Susie and climbed up to the deck.

Once they had the children safely inside the main cabin, Novak ran back up top, pulled anchor, got the engines going, and headed straight out to sea. He had to put as much distance between his boat and that beach as he possibly could. They could not pursue them unless they had other boats nearby. Even then, he would have a good head start. So far, so good. They had the children, and all four of them were still alive. That was saying something.

After he was satisfied they weren't being pursued, Novak went down to check on the girls. Lori had them dried off and wrapped in warm blankets. They were sitting beside Lori on the couch, one child on each side. She had her arms around them and was talking softly. The girls no longer looked afraid. Neither was crying. Sammi looked half-asleep.

"That was lit," was all Lori said to him, but then she smiled. "That's Twitter talk for good job, Novak."

Novak nodded, picked up the sniper rifle, and quickly headed back to the helm. It was going to be a long night spent trying to avoid the worst of the storm heading inland, and probably just as tense as everything else he'd faced since he'd first laid eyes on Lori Garner below his balcony on Bourbon Street.

Chapter 12

The adaptability of small children never failed to astonish Novak. His own twins had been that way, and now Judith Locke's little girls were holding up better than he'd expected. Truth was, though, they were definitely affected by all that had gone down: skittish and worried and easily upset. Their quiet reserve and the wariness with which they looked at him were proof enough. Thank God for Lori Garner. She was their anchor in the middle of a sick and messy situation, and somehow made them feel protected and safe. Novak was glad she'd come along. Somehow he was surprised she was so good with kids. She hadn't seemed the type, but she was. Once they had embarked on the sail back to Frank's fish camp, she had hushed and shushed and patted and soothed the girls on her bed in the fore cabin. After a while, she climbed up to the stern where Novak steered the boat through a dark, gloomy night. The rain had stopped, the stars had come out, but there was a definite chill in the air. She sat near him, drawing a blanket tight around her.

"Well, they both finally went to sleep. You do know they think they're going straight home to see their mother. Since that's not true, what should I tell them?"

"Tell them we're looking for her and we'll find her soon and then we'll bring her home. You're good with them. I'm impressed. They'll believe you. You make them feel secure."

"They're so little and seem so lost." She pulled her knees up to her chest and leaned back on the banquette. The night had grown still, and the moon had come out in all its white glory. Good news was that they weren't being pursued by killers. That was always a plus. Not yet, anyhow.

They were well on their way back home, but that didn't mean holy hell couldn't break out any minute. If the judge reported the children's abduction with an Amber Alert, if he called in his dirty cops and caught them at sea, Novak and Lori would find themselves sitting behind bars. Locke was their grandfather and legal guardian, and they had no proof that he had abused them. Instinct told Novak the judge wouldn't involve legitimate law enforcement. Not without a ton of adverse publicity and TV cameras pushed into his face as reporters asked him pointed questions about the whereabouts of the girls' mother and why the children had been taken if no ransom had been demanded. Nope, the police and media would not be involved. One concern Novak could check off.

Calvin Locke was the sort of man who would handle the sticky stuff by himself. He would come after them, all right, Novak had no doubt. He was still raging around inside that beach house, punishing his men for the abduction and calling in his buddy, Timothy Hennessey. Novak felt a certain vindictive pleasure thinking he'd tied his enemy's hands. Rattling one's enemies put them on the defensive. Make them run around in circles, panicky and blind to exactly what was going. That's when they got careless and did stupid things.

Lori had been sitting there, quiet and pensive, but now she spoke, pretty much echoing Novak's thoughts. "Locke's coming after us himself, right, Novak? He can't call the cops or they might find all those nasty skeletons in his closet."

"He doesn't need cops to find us, not with mob contacts. By the sound of it, he's already paid off enough dirty police officers to feel safe on his home turf. If they get lucky and figure out who I am, they'll conjure up a phony warrant on me. I don't think the guys I put down on that beach can identify me. They might remember my size, maybe, but it was dark and everything happened fast. The one you put down will never say another word."

"Locke won't stop until he's got those kids back. You know it; I know it. It's going to get intense now."

Novak shifted his attention to her. She had her head resting on the back of the seat, gazing at a blanket of stars. He didn't blame her; it had turned out to be a beautiful night. "You think those little girls are going to come out of this thing okay?"

"God, I hope so. All they want right now is to have their mother back, but they trust me. I'm pretty sure they'll believe that we'll find her and they can be together again. They miss her terribly. They said the nanny was nice, but they didn't like Locke and his men."

"Do they have any idea where their mom is?"

"Susie said the judge locked her mom in her bedroom at the mansion and wouldn't let them see her." Sighing, she sat up. "It's sad, you know. She and Sammi used to lie on the hall floor and talk to Judith under her door when the judge was in court. The nanny let them, but she wasn't supposed to. They're scared to death of Locke, too. They definitely do not want to live with him."

"You think he's hurt them?"

"I think he's still wooing and earning their love. You know, pampering and spoiling them and getting them ready. That's the way it's done. You saw how he was kissing and tickling them. I'm so relieved we got them out of there."

"I guess I owe you a thank you. That guy had me dead to rights when I was holding those kids. You hit him dead-on."

"No problem. Did the girls see it?"

Novak shook his head. "They hid their eyes against me."

She was quiet for a time. "I recognized him, the one I shot. He's one of those bastards who got me at the airport. He's the one who..." Her words trailed off. A moment later, she finished. "He deserved to be shot. He would've killed you without a second thought."

"You got him in the head. That's good shooting from that distance in the dark and rain."

"Not that good. I aimed between his eyes."

She dropped the subject after that, and Novak didn't pursue it. That guy had done something awful to her, something she didn't want to talk about. He didn't want to hear about it, either.

After that exchange they said nothing, just sat and listened to the prow cut through the waves. They were headed north up the coast, and the cold wind felt good on his skin.

A long time later, she spoke again. "Judith was in the sixth grade when he started messing with her. She told me all of it once when we were still at Tulane. She wept the whole time. She said she'd never told anybody before because after her mother died, the judge wouldn't let her have any friends. I keep thinking if she'd had somebody, anybody, to report him to back then, if her mom had lived, if she wasn't so scared of him, maybe that pedophile would be rotting in jail instead of wearing judicial robes."

"We'll find her, Lori, but until then I guess we keep the kids with us. It's not the best option, but we've got little choice." He thought about it for a moment. "Maybe I can persuade Leslie to take them into protective custody now, before we find Judith. We've got a clue where to look for her."

"If she's still in that bedroom. He could have moved her."

"I think she might still be there. If he loves her, he'll keep her close."

"You think the Feds will take them without her? I mean, we just broke into the house of a state judge and kidnapped them. They're not going to want to get involved in that."

"Leslie's different. She doesn't always go by the books, so I think we've got a chance to convince her. I can't promise you a deal, though. We do have an ace in the hole. My partner? Claire and her husband are influential in some circles. If push comes to shove, they might be able to pull some strings. Can't count on it."

"We can't count on anything right now." She stared at him. "You've got a woman for a partner? Awesome. I read you as a man's man, all macho and no women allowed."

Novak wanted to smile. "You're aboard my boat, aren't you?"

"Yes sir, I am. Despite all that kicking and screaming you did."

"You exaggerate. I noticed that's a bad habit of yours."

"Get real. You haven't begun to see my bad habits yet." She stopped there and watched him a moment. "Frank told me about your wife and children, you know, that they died on 9/11 when the World Trade Center came down. I just want you to know I'm sorry that happened. That's the worst thing that could happen to anybody."

Novak stiffened where he stood and kept his eyes straight ahead. Few people ever mentioned his lost family to him, and he immediately felt defensive and uncomfortable. "Sorry but I don't talk about that."

"Maybe you should. Maybe it would help you cope."

"Maybe it's none of your business."

"You're right about that."

Novak leaned back in the swivel chair and propped his foot on his opposite knee. He was glad she was willing to drop the subject. He was wrung out. He wanted to go below and collapse on his bunk, but that wasn't going to happen any time soon. "Just so you know, I don't hate women, with a few exceptions."

"What about me? You like me?"

Novak could barely see her face in the moonlight, but he knew she was smiling.

"You saved my ass tonight. I look for that in women."

Lori gave a little laugh and stood up. "I'm going down to check on the kids and get some sleep. Call me if you need me to spell you or save your ass again."

With that, she disappeared below. Lori Garner was turning out to be something else. What that was, he hadn't pinned down yet. He was beginning to like her. That didn't mean he wanted her up in his business 24/7. He believed now that he could trust her. They had been thrown together in a dangerous situation, the kind that he worked better on his own. As long as Lori listened and didn't go off half-cocked, they'd get along fine. One thing for certain, she was a crack shot.

They made good time back. The cabin was still there, not burned to the ground by the bad guys. No gang charged the boat with guns firing. The night was quiet and dark, and Frank met them out on the dock with a flashlight. He caught the lines Novak tossed to him, and Novak shut off the ignition and drifted into berth. Once the boat was secure, he set the gangplank and stepped down onto the dock where he filled his friend in on how things had gone down.

"But Lucy wasn't there?"

"No, and we watched the house for hours. Judith wasn't, either. I checked out the property and didn't find any prisoners. Now we think Judith's still in his house in River Oaks, so maybe Lucy is, too. It's secure there, and they can control who comes in and out."

Frank's face appeared disappointed, and his anger was coming back. Novak told him about the little girls, and Frank wanted to see them. They went below and found Lori and both kids asleep. The sliding door had been left open, and Novak pushed it together. He wanted them to sleep as long as they could. All three had been through a lot. They sat down in the main cabin, and Novak related everything that had happened. Frank listened but had lapsed into a brooding silence. After a while, he walked back up to the house. Still nervous about possible retribution, Novak stretched out on his bed, fully dressed, his .45 right beside him. There was a lot he needed to find out before he ventured inside Locke's estate, but he was definitely ready to go in and leave behind a good bit of havoc and hellfire.

When he slept, his repose was patchy and troubled. At one point, he heard a sound and came awake with his weapon clutched in his hand. No bad guys, just the quiet lapping of the current against the hull. Then he sensed a presence and switched on the bedside lamp. Susie was sitting cross-legged on the floor in the doorway. Novak quickly hid the gun. The child said nothing to him but stared at him with her big, haunted eyes. She did not seem afraid anymore.

Novak glanced around. Not a sound. Nobody else was awake. He swung his legs off the bed and looked at her. "You okay, Susie? You need something?"

She answered in a whisper. "I'm real hungry."

Novak stood up. "Okay, no problem. I can find you something to eat." He stopped and squatted down beside her. He found that put little kids at ease. Get down to their level when you talk to them. "How about some chocolate milk? You like that?"

She nodded. Funny that she sought him out, instead of waking Lori. He wouldn't have expected her to come to him. If they got friendly, maybe she'd talk to him. Maybe she knew stuff she hadn't said yet, like which room her mother was held in and the best way to get to it.

In the galley, he got out a gallon jug of milk and poured some in a mug while she sat at the galley table.

"I like marshmallows in mine," she told him in the same barely audible voice.

Novak did like kids, always had. He got along just fine with them. "Well, I think I just might have some. Let me see what I can find."

Susie just sat and waited, as if she hadn't been taken out of her house in the dead of night by a complete stranger. She was a brave kid for four years old. She was not afraid of him. Neither of them said much else as Novak took the milk out of the microwave and stirred in a couple of spoons of Nesquik. Susie watched without a word. She was so small that her feet didn't touch the floor. Novak rummaged around in the cupboards until he found a package of miniature marshmallows and a bag of Chips Ahoy! cookies. What kid didn't like chocolate chip cookies? As far as that went, what adult didn't? He popped some marshmallows into the cocoa and carried the mug and cookies to the table.

"It's pretty hot. Don't burn your tongue."

"Okay."

He watched her pick up the mug and blow on the hot milk. But she didn't take her eyes off Novak's face, not for a single second. Now she looked wary. Novak easily read the change in her mood. So he said nothing else, just sat down across from her and watched her pick up a cookie. She ate four of them in short order. Then she finished the cocoa, which left a milk mustache on her upper lip, which she dabbed off with a paper napkin. Susie was a polite little kid. He hoped she would start talking and tell him something he needed to know.

Finished with her snack, she sat back in the chair and waited, as if she expected him to do something. Novak couldn't think what else she wanted. He had a feeling the child was done with her end of the conversation, so he ventured a subject that had been bothering him. "I hope you and your sister feel okay. Nobody's hurt you, have they?"

She shook her head but didn't expound.

"Good. I'm glad. So how about your mom? Lori said you miss her pretty bad."

She nodded.

"How long has it been since you've seen her?"

She gave a little shrug. "A long time."

"How long? A week, maybe, or more than that?"

"He took her away so we couldn't see her."

"Your grandfather did that?"

She nodded again.

"Do you know where she is now?"

She shook her head. "He took us to this big hotel place and made us stay there with the nanny for a long time, and then he came and got us and took us to the beach."

"Did he leave your mom at your house?"

"He locked her up in her room. Sometimes we sneaked out in the hall and talked to her under the door, but he wasn't there or we'd be scared to do that. She'd hold our fingers under the door, but then Grandfather caught us talking to her and took us to the hotel."

"Did this happen in the big house with the white wall around it?"

She nodded.

"Where's your mommy's bedroom?"

"Upstairs. Down the next hall from me and Sammi."

"But you haven't been there for a while?"

"When we went back to get our swimsuits, we saw her. She was waving at us from her window. She blew us kisses."

Tears welled up inside those dark eyes and shone in the overhead light. That's when Novak felt another urge to kill Calvin Locke. The world would be a better place without him. "Well, that's good. You got to see her for a little bit."

She wiped at her tears. "She was crying, and that made us cry, too."

"Listen, Susie. We're going to get your mom out of there. You know how I came in and got you tonight at the beach house? I'm going to do that with her, too. That okay with you?"

"Pinky promise?" A hopeful expression had come into her face, and she held out her little finger to him.

Novak vowed to get her mother out of that house, if it killed him. He hooked his with hers. "Pinky promise. I'm going to get her as soon as I can, okay?"

For the first time, the child smiled, but it faded quickly. "Yes sir."

"Want another cookie?"

Silence descended as she took one from the package. She chewed it awhile, and then she looked back at him. "He hits my mommy sometimes. We saw him do it. You know, like this." She demonstrated a pretty accurate backhand slap.

Then the child's remarkable courage cracked a bit, and Novak clearly glimpsed her pain. Her words spilled out in a hurry. "He said Sammi and me has got to do what he says, or he'll never let us see Mommy again. So Sammi and me are being real good. He said he wouldn't let her out of her room, if we were naughty and didn't mind Nanny." Tears welled up again, and this time rolled down her cheeks.

"You're safe now, sweetie, okay? I'm gonna get your mommy for you. It might take me a little while but not very long. Think you can be brave and wait just a little bit longer to see her?"

"Couldn't you just maybe go out there and get her right now?"

He shook his head. "No, not tonight. I'm sorry, but I'll bring her here soon, I promise."

"We act bad sometimes and get in trouble with Nanny. Is that why he took Mommy away from us, cause we're bad?"

"No, it's got nothing to do with you. Your mother loves you and wants to be with you. Just keep thinking about how she'll be home soon. Right now, you've got Lori here to take care of you. She's okay, right?"

She nodded. "Do you think Grandfather can find us?"

"No, nobody knows we're out here."

"Can we stay here and live with you and Lori until Mommy comes?"

"Sure you can, for a little while anyway, until we find a safe place for you to stay."

"Sammi gets scared. But I'll be brave."

"I know you are. How about we let your sister and Lori sleep some more? When Sammi wakes up, you can give her some cookies. How about that?"

She nodded, more comfortable with him now.

"Okay, let's get you back to bed. Maybe we can talk some more later."

She nodded, rose obediently, and walked back toward Lori's cabin. She turned around at the sliding door. "Is my mommy really okay? He didn't hurt her again, did he?"

"I think she's just fine." Novak paused. "Did you ever see anyone else locked up in your house, Susie? Maybe that other girl named Lucy?"

"Sometimes girls get locked up in the garage. Sammi and me peek out the windows and see them and then Uncle Stephen takes them away."

So the famous actor was neck-deep in this thing, too. Good to know. "Did you see any girls with long red hair, maybe pulled up in a ponytail?"

"I saw one girl who looked like that. They took her in Grandfather's office and shut the door. Then they took her down to the garage with some other girls."

"Was she okay? Did they hurt her or anything?"

"I don't think so. But she was real mad at them."

"How do you know that?"

"Because she kept trying to kick them."

That sounded like Lucy Caloroso, all right. He hoped she hadn't gotten hurt trying to defend herself. But that meant he could tell Frank that it was a pretty good bet she was alive and well inside Locke's garage. Unfortunately, it didn't mean she was safe now or that she was on the estate. "Did they hit her or anything?"

"One of them did this." She mimed grabbing somebody by the shoulders and shaking them. "That's when we ran away and hid under the bed."

"When did you see her, sweetie? Was it a long time ago?"

"I don't know, but it was before we went to the hotel."

"You are a brave little girl, Susie. So is Sammi."

Suddenly Susie ran back to him and pressed her little body against his chest. He circled her inside his arms and gave her a tight hug. She felt small and defenseless and like Novak's little daughter felt a long time ago. His throat burned at the memory, but he shook off the emotion. Susie's words were muffled when she spoke. "I'm glad you came to get us. We didn't like it there."

After that, Susie let go and scampered back to bed. Novak sat where he was and thought about what she'd told him. Now he was sure the judge had Lucy somewhere, maybe not at the mansion but somewhere nearby. Locke was into some ugly stuff, most likely child pornography or worse. They had to find her.

Good news was Lucy had been seen alive and hopefully was still somewhere in Galveston. If she was inside that mansion, Novak could find her. Frank desperately needed some good news, and now Novak could give it to him. Novak had to get in touch with Leslie and persuade her to take the children off his hands until he found their mother. He wanted to bring down Calvin Locke and his criminal empire about as much as anything he'd ever wanted. He wanted to make sure nobody involved ever walked the streets of Houston or Galveston again.

Novak headed up to the cabin and found his friend in the kitchen nursing a bottle of whiskey. Novak told him the good news, and Frank seemed to deflate like a punctured basketball.

He stared up at Novak out of bleary, bloodshot eyes. "I'm going to kill them," he told him, words slurred. "I'm going to kill every single last one of them."

"Sounds good," Novak said.

Then Frank put his head down atop folded arms and sobbed. Novak sat down beside him and placed a hand on his back, but there was little else he could say. Nothing in the world would comfort Frank's despair until Lucy was safe at home. They had better find her soon or the judge might retaliate on Lucy for what Novak had done that night. Novak couldn't bear to think about that. They had to find her—fast.

Chapter 13

As tough as Lori had shown herself to be under pressure, she was every bit as soft and gentle with Susie and Sammi. She kept the children close to her, murmuring reassurances and doling out Reese's Pieces and M&M's that she'd found in Frank's pantry. The children were playing quietly with a Chutes and Ladders game and an old baby doll that Lori had dragged out of Lucy's closet. The three adults sat around the kitchen table, watching them.

Lori broke the silence. "Okay, we know Judith was at the mansion the last time the girls saw her. Doesn't mean she's still there, though. She could be anywhere by now."

"There's a good shot she's in there. It sounds to me like he's controlling her through threats against her daughters. I say we go in and find out, the sooner the better." That was Frank, a lot more hopeful now that he'd learned Lucy had been seen alive and well. "They had Lucy there, and she fought back. She still might be there. So I'm with Novak. We go in. We get lucky and maybe we'll find them both."

Novak felt better about Frank. He had really settled down and was thinking clearly. He appeared calm and focused and ready to roll. Novak needed him that way. "We've got to all be on the same page, because it's going to take teamwork to pull this off. I want these kids in a safe place before we do anything. I don't want to worry about them, and it might take the three of us to get inside. No way can they stay out here alone. So I'm for handing them over to Leslie for protection. After that, we go in for Judith. I think Lucy's somewhere in Houston, too. Or if we're lucky, Judith can tell us where they're holding her."

Frank's gaze was intense. "Then let's do it. Waiting isn't going to help anybody. If we don't move, we'll miss our window."

Lori was in agreement. Novak wanted to move in, too. He pushed back his chair and stood up. "Hang tight while I make the call."

Outside in the yard, the grass was still soggy from rain and the dirt road had turned to mud. He walked out under a gnarled oak tree and punched in Leslie's private number.

She picked up on the first ring. "Yeah, Novak? You got Judith Locke?"

"There's a problem."

Her sigh was exaggerated and tinged with annoyance. "Oh, Lord, of course there is. Please don't tell me Judith's dead or has changed her mind and all my prep work is for nothing."

"Don't jump to conclusions. I don't have her yet, but I will soon. I'm talking about her kids, Susie and Sammi. I grabbed them last night."

"Grabbed them? What the hell's that supposed to mean?"

"I took them out of Judge Locke's beach house, so don't be surprised if he's turning over every rock in south Texas to find them."

"You did what? Never mind, I heard you. Where are you? Are those kids with you now?"

"For the moment. That's where you come in, Les. I want you to take them into protective custody until I can deliver their mother to you."

"Oh, is that all?"

Novak said nothing.

She came back with incredulity. "You kidnapped a sitting judge's grandchildren out of his home? Have you lost your mind, Novak?"

"Not exactly kidnapped. I'm calling it rescued. He was going to molest them sooner or later, and I wasn't going to let that happen."

A few beats of silence and then: "Okay, okay, let me think. Good God, I can't believe this. Please tell me you had some kind of admissible and legal proof of molestation?"

"No, but it was going to happen, trust me."

"Know what you've got, Novak? You've got yourself one hell of a dilemma here. He's probably got the entire Galveston police force out looking for you. Where are you?"

"He won't call the cops."

"No? Tell me why. Please tell me something that I can use."

"Because cops will want to know where the mother is and why the oldest kid says the judge locked Judith up and wouldn't let her see her own children. I've got that much proof. The kids are talking, and what they're saying is incriminating."

"But he hasn't abused the children yet?"

"We don't think so. We haven't questioned them much about that. They're traumatized. They're scared and confused and want their mom back. Judith was molested by her father at age eleven, and it's still going on. He's been locking her up, forcing sex, and using her children as leverage. A jury won't view any of that too kindly, judge or not. The kids say a young girl who sounds a lot like Lucy was also held prisoner inside his estate."

"Not enough for a Federal warrant. Not without proof. A toddler's account won't stand up in court."

"She's four and really bright, so I believe her. It all fits and explains some things I couldn't quite figure."

"Where's Judith now? She's our primary interest. I've got to get her in custody to make this work."

"I'll get her, don't worry about it. I want these little girls in your hands where they'll be safe and secure. I need you to come through for me on this, Leslie."

"Novak, you are unbelievable. You're lucky I even talk to you."

She was right. They both knew it.

"Oh, all right. I'll take the girls and get them settled in a safe house, and then we'll wait for you to deliver Judith Locke. I need her under my control, Novak. My SAC is not going to go for any of this until Judith's signature is on her statement."

Leslie instructed him to text photos of the little girls for verification. Novak hung up, walked inside, and had Lori snap some pictures. After he texted them to Leslie, he felt better. He'd been expecting a flat refusal. It was asking a lot of the agent, especially without hard evidence of judicial corruption or child abuse. If all went well, Leslie would come out of this thing as a rock star. Now Lori was reading a book to the girls in Lucy's bedroom, some story about a brown-spotted pony and a sick little girl who loved him. He hoped it ended well. He hoped what they were doing ended well.

Frank was edgy again. "Lucy could be in another state by now. She could be anywhere."

"Yeah, she could, but the girls put her in Houston. We're gonna make them pay for taking her. You've done the right thing by staying out of sight. Locke doesn't know who I am or where to find me. I can show up anywhere in plain sight, and they'll never be the wiser. All they know is that somebody's putting the screws to them. I want to go inside that estate, but I'm gonna need help. That's where you and Lori come in. Once we get the kids to Leslie, we need to find out everything we can about Locke's operations. Not going in until I know what we're facing."

It took twenty minutes before Leslie's call came back. "Okay, it's a go, Novak. There's nothing on the news or in the papers about the kidnapping, and no Amber Alert or reward. You're right. Locke's going to handle this on his own. Which is worse for the three of you, believe me. They do not play nice. So good luck. You're going to need it. No way that you don't know that."

"Just take care of the little girls and let me worry about myself."

"I'd be better off if I learned to say no to you years ago."

"Oh, you've said no plenty of times." They had been together for a while, but they hadn't been compatible enough for a long-term relationship, more on her part than his. That kind of reconciliation was not in the cards. No bridges had been left intact.

"I'll let you know when we're coming. Have those kids ready." She hung up.

Novak looked at the others. "Okay, she's agreed to take the girls and get them into a safe house."

So they waited. Lori fixed lunch, and they sat down with the children and ate bologna sandwiches and potato chips and drank Cokes. Novak's phone vibrated again before they finished.

"I'm on my way with a four-man team. Be ready. Where are you?"

"I've reconsidered. I want to meet at a neutral location."

"Why?"

"Doesn't matter why."

"Good God, Novak, now you don't trust *me*?" She gave a heavy sigh. "Oh, all right, just give me a time and place so we can get this over with. Being around you makes me nervous."

"Meet us at the Love's Travel Stop on Interstate 10 west of Lynchburg. Do you know the place?"

"Hell, no. Why would I? Houston's a big place, Novak."

"There's a strip mall right before you get to the Love's. It's got a cleaners called One Day Clean. Next to that, there's a Subway restaurant and a big Goodwill store that's been closed down. Park in the Goodwill's side parking lot, and we'll find you. Three o'clock this afternoon."

"We'll be coming in two black Chevy Suburbans."

Novak laughed. "Yeah, tell me something I don't know. You Feds are nothing if not predictable. Don't forget your dark suits and sunshades."

"Just don't be late," she snapped and hung up.

Novak walked back inside, nodded affirmation to the adults, and moved into the room where the kids were now watching a Disney movie. The princess one that had a mermaid named Ariel. They were sitting together on the floor, and Novak lounged down beside them. "Hey, guys, you like this movie?"

Both the girls looked at him. The distraction of the movie fled their faces and was replaced by wariness. Always the spokesperson but this time with a frightened expression, Susie answered. "We love Ariel. She's pretty. Are you taking us away?"

Novak was reluctant to tell them they had to go off with a bunch of complete strangers. "She is pretty. And yeah, we're going to move you somewhere else, a place where you'll be safe, okay? A nice lady named Leslie is going to take care of you for a little while. That okay with you?"

Sammi looked terrified at the idea. Susie watched his face. "Will you be with us, too?"

"No, I've got to go find your mom."

"Is Lori coming?"

"She's got to help me, honey. But when we find your mom, we'll bring her there and you'll all be together again. The important thing is that you're safe with Leslie and nobody can find you."

"You promise that Mommy's coming back?"

Susie was a bright and perceptive little kid. Novak attempted to stick to the truth. "We're going to look for her as soon as you're safe. I think we'll find her pretty soon."

For good reason, Susie looked unconvinced. Sammi stared, wide-eyed. She'd said next to nothing since he'd taken her out of the house.

"You promise?" Susie asked again.

Novak considered a moment. He didn't want to promise, but he didn't want to lie, either. "I promise you that I'm not going to stop looking until I find your mommy."

Susie seemed okay with that assurance. Her furrowed brow relaxed, and she got up and hugged Novak. Sammi immediately followed suit, because she did everything her big sis did. Novak hugged them both in tight for a moment. They felt so damn small and vulnerable. He hoped he was doing the right thing putting them in Leslie's hands.

Later that day, the exchange went off without a hitch. Lori and Frank insisted on coming along, and Novak didn't try to dissuade them. If they kept a low profile, there would be no problem that far out of the city proper. He needed them close at hand, anyway, to show him where the bad guys lived and worked. They parked at Love's where they could see the strip mall. The children were happily eating Happy Meals from a nearby McDonald's while they waited. They told Lori they'd never had Chicken McNuggets before, which was surprising to Novak. He assumed every child in the country had eaten them.

As soon as he spotted the twin black SUVs approaching the Goodwill, he started the Jeep. When he was satisfied nobody was following the Feds, he pulled out and drove to the designated meeting spot. When they got there, he and Lori got out of the Jeep. Frank stayed slumped down in the back seat. Not many people were around. The children kept their boxes of food when they got out of the car. Lori knelt down and reassured them everything was going to be all right.

To Novak's surprise, when Leslie Taylor walked over, she was surprisingly gentle with the children. He had not pegged her as maternal. He had pegged her as anything but maternal. Smiling, she bent down and gave each of them a stuffed teddy bear she'd been hiding behind her back. Then she told them her name and smiled and said she was taking them somewhere safe. She told them there were lots of toys there to play with and lots of good stuff to eat and that nobody would hurt them. Susie rewarded her with a tentative smile. Novak watched them but kept an eye on the Interstate and the parking lots. He was being cautious, to say the least, and both Locke and Hennessey had long and deadly tentacles. They were wasting time standing out in the open. Lori kissed both children, and the kids surprised Novak by running over and hugging him around the legs. He squatted down and told them he'd see them soon. After that, they obediently climbed into the back seat of the first Suburban, the one Leslie was driving. The Feds took off in a rush. When they were out of sight, Novak started the Jeep and headed back into Houston.

Traffic was god-awful but Novak eventually got them on the 610 Loop between downtown and uptown. Frank stayed alert in back, watching the road behind them for tails, a loaded double-barrel shotgun lying across his lap. Lori sat in the passenger's seat wearing large black sunglasses with her hair stuffed inside a Houston Astros ball cap. She had it tipped low over her face. Novak wore shades and one of Frank's Texas Oilers caps. He followed her directions until they finally turned onto River Oaks Boulevard and entered Locke's ritzy subdivision. The lush grounds were planted with every flowering shrub and flower imaginable, including azaleas and crepe myrtle, with driveways lined with giant oak trees. The big ostentatious houses looked even better in the daylight.

Yep, it was indeed a snooty suburb, all right, one that harbored politicos, doctors, CEOs, and other wealthy tycoons, each and every one rolling in a ton of money and just as much prestige, as they ruled over their private fiefdoms. Calvin Locke was disguised as an honorable man, with the most despicable crimes hidden underneath his long black judicial robe. Novak hungered to bring him to his knees in a way that would pretty much end his privileged facade. The real Judge Locke would soon be exposed to all of Galveston and Houston and his fellow phony River Oaks friends, as his business relationship with the underbelly filth of the city would be placed on public display, but first things first. Novak was fairly certain that Judith was imprisoned inside that big impressive estate, and that meant hours of watching and waiting and wasting time they did not have.

Lori knew all that, too. She was antsy and impatient and demanding and didn't mind showing it. She wasn't favorable concerning their chances of pulling off a second extraction, either, not one without consequences. "This place is a damn armed fortress. Judith used to call it the Locke Castle. It's unreal inside those walls, so you better listen to me. When Judith was little, she wanted a castle with a moat, and her father actually built one."

Novak glanced at her.

Frank said, "You're kidding."

"Nope. He had a lake dug out back and left a tiny island in the middle for Judith's playhouse, and an architect came in and designed a miniature castle. There was even a fancy little drawbridge. It's still in there for Susie and Sammi."

Frank scoffed. "Well, that was indulgent."

"Judith paid dearly for that indulgence." Lori's tone was hard-edged.

Novak said nothing.

Frank propped his arms on the back of Novak's seat. "You really think he's got Lucy in there? He'd have to know that if the Feds got a warrant, how could he ever explain holding prisoners on his property?"

"He's overconfident and doesn't worry. No warrants against him will be written unless the Feds do it, and he doesn't think they'll have cause. Even then, he'd have time to stash her elsewhere."

Frank choked up when he spoke again. "He told me if I didn't back off, he'll cut off her toes one by one and mail them to me, and then he'd start on her fingers."

"That's not going to happen," Novak told him. "We'll get her out. You've got to keep believing that."

Now Lori was incensed. "He's a monster hiding in plain sight. Out here with all this. It's sickening."

"Any ideas how I can get in there? That's problem number one," Novak said.

"We could use demolition and blow a hole in the wall the size of New Jersey." Unsurprisingly, that had come from Lori Garner.

"Yeah, that sounds stealthy," Novak replied.

"You asked. I answered."

"They'll kill Lucy if we storm the place," Frank told them.

Novak thought for a moment. "My partner, Claire? She went undercover as a waitress once. Sexed herself up to get our target's attention."

Lori gave him a look. "I take it that's not aimed at Frank."

Novak grinned. "Think you can distract a guard at the front gate long enough for me to slip inside?"

"I've done worse things."

"Like what?"

"Like seducing a suspect in a bar so I could get into his apartment."

"Really? You did that?" asked Frank.

Lori looked at each of them in turn. "Problem is, some of Locke's guys know me on sight. It'll work if it's a new guy. Otherwise, I'll need a disguise."

"It could be dangerous."

"I'm sure."

"You'll have to be able to get his interest."

Lori frowned at Novak. "Are you implying that I'm incapable of looking hot?"

"Not for a minute."

Lori smiled.

"You got a low-cut top, something like that?" Novak suggested.

"I'm not going to wear a sleazy top or a sleazy anything else. What's the matter with you? I don't need to do that to distract a man. A short skirt might be in the offing. Not sleazy, short."

She was underestimating the effect of a plunging neckline, but she had nice legs, so she was probably right. Problem he had with Lori Garner was her unpredictability, a trait he didn't approve of in anybody working with him. One wrong step with these guys, one impetuous word could get her shot again, or worse. He couldn't trust Frank to keep his cool if things went south, either. Both were too close emotionally to the victims. Novak would be better off acting alone. He'd much prefer that, but unfortunately, he couldn't.

"You'll have to put makeup on those bruises."

"They're hardly visible anymore."

"They're visible, Lori."

She didn't argue. "I've got makeup and lipstick."

They canvassed the classy area for a time, driving past one elaborate manor after another, all sporting those giant emerald lawns, and all with glimpses of sparkling blue pools and manicured flowerbeds. Most were separated by concrete walls or shrubbery hedges but none had walls as high as Calvin Locke's estate. Infiltrating adjacent properties to scale the wall was not a good option, either, considering all the homes had well-placed security signs posted, warning intruders to back off. Novak was certain that Locke would have men patrolling the grounds and watching the outer walls, probably ones better trained than the inept ones at the beach house.

Not much traffic, though, all quiet everywhere, just an occasional jogger or dog walker. Frank's mud-spattered Jeep did not exactly fit in but probably could pass as that of a hired gardener or pool boy working for the elite few. They found a place to park under some shade trees with a clear view of Locke's front gate and where they wouldn't stand out. There was no guard standing watch there, not yet, anyway. Lori said there sometimes was. There was an intercom box, though, and a security camera atop the pillar aimed down at cars entering the paved driveway. The wall was about six to seven feet tall, it looked like, but that would not be a problem for Novak to scale unless they had sensors on top. On closer look, that turned out to be the case. Locke did not want any uninvited guests.

They sat surveillance, waiting, watching, and positioning the Jeep at different locations so as not to raise suspicions. Nobody seemed to be paying attention to them. The houses were too far back off the streets and the inhabitants too self-absorbed. Lori clicked photos of the vehicles entering or leaving Locke's estate, making sure to scribble down the license plate numbers. They pulled away and parked elsewhere at times, not wanting to be noticed. They ate lunch at a nearby Denny's restaurant. By seven o'clock that evening, they were back parked under the shadows of three oak trees when a familiar black limousine pulled up to the front gate. The big guy himself was inside that car; there was no doubt in Novak's mind.

"He's late," Lori told them. "He usually gets home between five and six. Usually closer to six."

"He just had his grandchildren snatched out from under his nose. I'm surprised he showed up at court today at all. I'm pretty sure he's raging around behind the scenes, which will make him do stupid stuff and accuse all the wrong people. No reason for him to suspect another attack. He probably thinks it's impossible for anyone to get inside this estate."

"He'll figure that it's me or Lori screwing him up," Frank said. "He might make Lucy pay for it."

Novak didn't like to think that way. "I don't think so. She's not his priority at the moment. He'll be too worried about the children. If anything, we've given him something else to think about. Lucy's his leverage over you, and he knows you'll ask for proof of life before you move in. Guys like him like to swagger through life, but they're nervous as hell the whole time and expecting to be knifed in the back."

Lori turned in her seat to look at them. "If he's buddy-buddy with Hennessey, he'll probably get that blade in his back sooner rather than later. That's who Hennessey is. The judge probably thinks Hennessey took those girls for his own leverage. I wouldn't put it past him. He'll think that nobody else has the guts or stupidity to kidnap them."

"He needs to keep thinking that way. We want him nervous and unsure of himself. Maybe we should disrupt his other businesses. You got any ideas where we can hit him where it will hurt the most, Frank?"

"I know he's got warehouses and storage units and rental houses all over the city. I say we raid them and burn them to the ground."

"We can do that. If I make it onto the grounds, how can I get Judith out without getting shot?"

"You'll need me to find your way around, so I'll go with you. I proved myself out on that boat." It was not a statement but a demand.

"C'mon, Lori, using a sniper rifle is one thing. Scaling a wall or fighting hand to hand is something else. You're no good to me in a fight until you're a hundred percent. Besides, I need you as a distraction at the gate. Frank, I need you to stay home and keep out of my way. Agreed?"

For once, Lori didn't argue. Instead, she answered his question. "Best way to get her out is through the back gate. The lawn is huge with lots of trees you can use for cover. The swimming pool's behind the house, and the lake is out in the middle of the back lawn, so you can avoid them, both are lit up at night. There's a big rose garden all along the back wall with lots of bricked paths and Greek statues. Down around there is where he keeps his prize-winning orchids. They have their own hothouse. That's his one passion, other than Judith. He's totally obsessive when it comes to those stupid flowers. Hell, he's got a whole room in his house dedicated to the trophies and ribbons he wins at flower shows."

Novak smiled. "Maybe I should burn down that hothouse and everything in it on my way out. Make him cry like a baby."

Lori laughed out loud. "I'd love to see his face if he sees his precious orchids turned to ashes. You'll have to get past the Dobermans first."

"Shit. How many dogs?"

"Six, I think. You good with big salivating monster canines, Novak?"

Novak didn't answer. He wasn't, but he knew some pepper spray that was.

Chapter 14

The following evening Novak and Lori drove Frank's prized 1969 blue Mustang slowly alongside Locke's tall white wall. They'd left Frank at the cabin, but he hadn't liked it much, not until Novak pointed out that if the two of them got captured or killed, somebody needed to be left behind to find Lucy. Still reluctant, he agreed to stay as a backup. Lori would act as the lure and the getaway driver.

The wall was well secured. Along the street side, it was lined with decorative evergreens spotted by solar lights, positioned every ten yards or so. They were searching for a good place that was not in the direct line of periodic security cameras mounted atop the wall. The thorough security setup had nixed any hope of going over the wall as he had done at the beach. So they were going to Plan B.

Novak pulled the Mustang over about sixty feet from the main entrance. Switching on emergency flashers, he glanced up and down the dark street. It was late: no traffic, no pedestrians. So far, so good. Novak shoved the gearshift into park and glanced over at Lori where she sat in the passenger's seat. "You sure you're okay doing this? It's a risk. You've been in their hands once. I'm not forcing you, and I don't want you hurt."

"Hell, everything we do is a risk right now."

"You sure you can drive with that arm?"

"My arm's cool. I can drive. Quit worrying about me. You've got enough to worry about."

Earlier that afternoon, Lori had gone off alone in the Jeep on a shopping spree up in Port Arthur. She had on her new purchases. The black skirt was so short and tight that it should be declared illegal. So should her long bare legs. The white silk blouse was unbuttoned far enough down to draw the eye of any man with red blood circulating through his veins. He was pretty sure she wore nothing under either garment. She had not gone too far, but she was pushing that fine line big-time. The blousy sleeves hid her bandaged arm, and she'd ditched the sling again. She kept saying it was healing and getting stronger every day, but Novak wasn't sure that was true. She still cradled it. She cradled it now. "Now that we're here, I'm not so sure this is a good idea, Lori."

"It was your idea. Be cool, it's dope. I've suckered men before. I'm not exactly a novice at seduction, dude. You're just not interested in sex anymore. Frank told me."

"That's not exactly true."

She turned and looked at him. "So this outfit's working on you, admit it. Awesome. That's a good sign. Rest your fears, buddy. I'm good at this sort of sexy lady thing."

"Don't make it look too good, or you'll overplay your hand and end up chained in a basement again."

"These guys? All I've gotta do is stand there and look like a damsel in distress. Men like them think ladies buy into bad guys are hot. If I smile, they'll congratulate themselves for being so handsome. So what would you do, Novak? You drive by me, minding your own business, you gonna stop your car and help me or not?"

Lori looked sexy, all right, which she knew only too well. The makeup did cover the residual bruises, and the lipstick was fire-engine red. Her blond hair was loose and long and curled down her back. She had on red high heels. The guy would stop and help her, all right. Novak was more worried about what that guy would try next.

"I'd skid to a stop. You bet I would."

That brought out a smile on that scarlet mouth. Her eyes were darkened all around. She called it smoky eyes. "Wow, now I'm triggered for sure. Don't know you all that well yet, but way I see it? You'd stop for anybody having car trouble, especially some poor clueless girl who doesn't know how to change tires. You're a knight in shining armor. Look what you did for me, right after I held a gun to your head, too." She grew serious. "You saved my life, Novak, when I was in a hell of a lot of trouble. I appreciate that. You're a standup guy. I owe you, and I know it."

Novak didn't want to talk about that. "You don't owe me anything. More like, we owe each other to still be breathing, and we just met. Only thing I'm saying is just be careful with this guy. They're not exactly brainiacs, but they're armed and dangerous and don't have any compunction about killing anybody who gets in their way."

They stared at each other. She was smiling, and she really did look pretty. The woman was growing on him. He didn't want her to grow on him. She was interesting and unpredictable and skilled, but she was too young and too much a pain in the ass for her own good. He got back down to business.

"Okay, all you've got to do is fake a story about your car not starting. Get the guy to sit down in the driver's seat. After I take him out, you drive the car around back and wait for me. You ready?"

"Yes sir, I am raring to go. Don't you forget that the judge keeps a night crew up around the house, but they usually patrol with the dogs. You worry about yourself. I'll be fine. Time to make yourself scarce. But please, take this guy down fast. Like you love to harp on, my arm's not quite up to fighting off a grabby guy, not yet anyway."

"He'll go down quick. Don't worry."

"I believe you. You give no quarter. I like that in a man."

Novak checked out the street for cars. The coast was clear. It was long after midnight. Apparently, the old fogies in this kind of affluent neighborhood rolled up the streets at ten o'clock. The place looked as dead as Arlington Cemetery after dark. He climbed out, rounded the car, and squatted down behind the rear fender. He had already checked out the wall for surveillance cameras and motion sensors and made sure none were pointed in his direction. Locke was doing something highly illegal inside that wall, something they wanted no one to know about. Novak had one opportunity to get through that gate undetected. Their plan was risky as hell and not particularly unique as clever plans went, but still worth a try. If Lucy and Judith were in there, they were coming out with him. He watched Lori walk around and lean up against the trunk. She did look good in that little scrap of a skirt. "Don't fail me, Novak," she said, not looking at him. "I don't want to mess up my new clothes. I like the way you look at me when I'm wearing them."

Novak ignored that. Neither of them spoke again, just waited in the quiet street for somebody to show up. It was past time for the night guard. At twelve twenty, a pair of blinding headlights swung around a curve a good distance up the street. Novak backed farther out of sight. If all went down as they hoped, the driver in that car would be a six-foot-one guy by the name of Charlie Henson. They'd watched his movements the night before. Lori had heard the name but never met him. Judith had once told her that he was a jerk and to stay away from him. Judith based that opinion on the way Charlie treated her children. Novak hoped he was a Good Samaritan jerk.

The black Lexus they were waiting for sped down the street toward them but slowed when the driver caught sight of Lori. He drove past her but hit the brakes a bit while he gave her a long hard look. She waved, after which he proceeded on, turned into the front drive, and braked in front of the motorized gate. Hidden in the shadows, Novak held his breath and hoped the man would nibble on Lori's hook. Henson climbed out of his vehicle and leaned both arms on the top of the Lexus and stared down the road at Lori. He had on a black leather jacket and a black ball cap, Locke's official hoodlum uniform. Lori wasted no time. She started strolling toward him. She had that sexy walk down pat. Novak hadn't noticed that before because she hadn't walked that way before. She was a whole different persona in her new outfit. Tonight was indeed a revelation.

"Hey, mister," she called out to Henson. "How about helping me out over here? My car just died on me, and now the engine's flooded, I guess, or I'm out of gas. I can't get it to start."

Novak tensed up as she neared the Lexus. Henson should be suspicious of her, out this late in this kind of neighborhood, dressed like that. Novak would've approached her with caution. Apparently her legs won Henson's internal debate on whether or not to help her, because he rounded the back of the car and strode quickly to meet her. He was grinning stupidly, as if lady luck had found him. Halfway there, he called out, "You need me to call a wrecker for you?"

Lori stopped and waited for him to come to her. She didn't want to appear too anxious, Novak assumed. "I've been trying to call for help but everybody's closed till tomorrow morning. Now my stupid cell phone's gone dead. Maybe my car's got a low battery or something? I don't know anything about cars. Maybe you could jump it with cables, isn't that what you're supposed to do?"

Henson suddenly decided he was her father. "You shouldn't be out so late at night all alone, you know that, right? Something bad might happen to you."

Novak grimaced. Something bad like him.

"I know. I was cutting through here to get home because I'm running so late. I went bar-hopping with my besties and time got past me."

"Does your husband know where you are?"

This guy was clumsy in the come-on department. Lori was not going to have trouble enticing him to step into her car.

She smiled up at him, quite the little flirt when she wasn't shot up and bleeding or holding Novak at gunpoint. "I don't have a husband anymore. I divorced him because he was always so jealous."

That was such a blatant female green light that the guy had to know he could pass Go and collect $200. Henson appeared pleased about her marital status. He stepped up close to her. She reached almost to his shoulder, hooker heels and all. "That's too bad."

"No, that's too good."

Henson and Lori laughed softly. Novak wished she'd cut the coquettish chatter and get on with it.

"I hate to bother you, but I sure do wish you'd try to start my car. I just can't seem to get it to turn over."

Henson just couldn't seem to take his eyes off her naked legs. "No problem. I'll take a look, but I'm not much of a mechanic, I warn you."

They walked back to the Mustang together, and Lori stood back when he opened the door and got into the driver's seat. She stepped back out of the way as he turned the key. By the time the motor fired in a smooth purr, Novak was right beside him. He sent his doubled fist slamming into the guy's temple before Henson even knew he was there. The force of the blow knocked him across the console and halfway into the passenger's seat. He didn't move, knocked out cold.

"Good God, Novak, you're gonna kill somebody with those fists."

"You wanted him out, so he's out. He needs to stay that way for a while. He'll probably be all right." He jerked Henson out of the car, peeled off his black jacket and cap, and pulled the lanyard with the employer card key off around his neck. Then he dragged him back to the trunk. Lori opened it, and Novak dumped the guy inside, grabbed a roll of duct tape he'd left there, and put a double layer over his mouth then secured his wrists and ankles together. "Okay, Lori, you know where to wait for me, right?"

"Drive out back to the private alley and park halfway down just past the rear gate with my lights off. If you find Judith and Lucy, you'll bring them out through the rose garden."

"If I don't show up in, say, thirty or forty minutes, an hour at the most, or you hear gunshots, just take off and go back to Frank's and stay there. He'll help you ditch Henson. Understand? Don't come in there after me, no matter what happens. You got that?"

"Got it." Lori climbed into the driver's seat and drove off.

Novak snugged the hat down low over his face and tugged on the jacket. He picked up his backpack full of tools and walked quickly back to Henson's Lexus. Keeping his face averted, he waved at the camera as he got in and swiped the card key he'd taken off Henson. A voice came back in a static buzz, "You're late, Charlie. Quit messing around. Get in here."

"Right," Novak muttered.

The gate parted slowly, and Novak drove into the inner sanctuary. The road wound its way through a grassy, tree-dotted front lawn until it rolled out into the open and forked at the front of the house. There, one arm circled around to the pillared front portico, the other road veering off left and around the side of the house. Novak took the second one. Out back, he found a triple-car garage with a paved parking area on one side, just as Lori had described. Novak pulled in next to a Toyota van. Maybe that meant only a few guards were pulling night duty or maybe they carpooled.

Lori had mentioned that the night shift was small but well armed. No guards stood about ready to shoot him. Good thing. Problem was, Novak wasn't sure where or how many men he would eventually run into. He parked the car and got out. That's when he picked up the sound of a dog baying somewhere in the distance. Maybe they only let them out of the pens when intruders were spotted. That would be nice. He wasn't counting on it. A couple of animals howled along with the first one for a few minutes then shut their mouths and the night settled back into silence.

The house was completely dark except for a couple of windows up on the second floor. No lights on the third floor. Novak took a moment to check out the garage for prisoners, hoping to find Lucy there. There was nobody inside, but he found the locked stalls in the back. All were empty. If Lucy had been there, she was gone now. After that, he headed for the servants' door that Lori had described as his best bet for getting inside the house unseen. She also told him how the servants hated the judge's guts and liked to spit in the food they served him. Maybe he could find some allies on staff, if things got out of hand. Still, nobody was around and the servants' door was locked up good and tight. He swiped Henson's card key, hoping it worked everywhere on the property. It did. The lock clicked open, and the handle turned.

Inside, he found a long shadowy hall lined with metal lockers and coat hooks. It stretched out before him like an oversized school coat closet with a few umbrellas and jackets hanging here and there. Cautiously, he moved forward, deeper into the house. He heard no sounds and encountered no one. At the first cross corridor, he glanced quickly in both directions. Silver sconces lit the way every ten feet, but they threw off dim light. No sound. Novak was surprised the house was not guarded better than this. Maybe Henson was the sole guard posted at night. That would be lovely, but soon proved not to be the case.

A man suddenly appeared at the far end of the hall and strode straight toward Novak. He was looking down at something in his hand. Novak ducked back into an alcove that led into what looked like a closet and hoped the guy didn't see him. The door was locked, of course. He pushed back against the wall and rose onto the balls of his feet, ready to come out fighting if he was discovered. Unfortunately, the guard turned right into the alcove with Novak. The guy's initial shock worked to Novak's advantage. He grabbed the smaller man, wrestled him around, and got his arm around his neck. He had to go down quietly. Chokeholds came in so handy, and he was good at them.

The guard was wiry and stronger than he looked, but Novak held on as the guy dropped to his knees and tried to knock Novak off balance with his feet. Novak went down with him and hung on, cutting off his air until the guy stopped struggling. Seconds later, he was unconscious on the floor. Novak dragged him up against the closet door and taped him up. Then he inched back out into the hallway. As long as he had the element of surprise, the takedowns would keep on coming.

The house was huge, with spacious rooms and wide halls, but fairly dark except for the wall sconces. The judge must figure no one had the internal fortitude to break into Locke Castle. Novak moved along quickly, following Lori's directions until he reached the magnificent marble staircase that led up to a furnished mezzanine where an eight-foot-tall Palladian window faced the rear lawn.

Novak caught a glimpse of the night sky outside, full of stars with the moon partly obscured by silver gray clouds. He moved on, searching for the back servant staircase Lori had described. Palatial houses were not his thing, but they always had a servant's staircase so the wealthy owners wouldn't have to look at the peons unless they were groveling over their masters. Lori said it rose out of the kitchen. He passed through one room after another, all big and rectangular and posh and furnished with priceless antiques. He counted twenty white leather chairs around a black marble dining table.

He took his time as he walked through, looking in closets and recesses but found no imprisoned women. He found steps leading down to the cellar behind a door but found nothing down there except rack after rack of expensive aged wine. Where the hell were the guards? The lack of security didn't make sense to him.

Back upstairs, he entered a kitchen that gleamed and smelled like a grove of pine trees and oranges, with shiny stainless-steel appliances, white marble floors that were all mopped and waxed to a singular and spectacular glow. He discovered the steps he sought behind a white bi-fold door and crept up them, the Kimber .45 out with his finger near the trigger. Wary about the dearth of guards so far, he moved stealthily, eyes wide open, ears pricked for sounds. He should have seen another guard by now, sitting around the kitchen bar, drinking coffee to stay awake the rest of the night. Hell, even one guy was asleep on a couch. That's just the way night shifts worked, in the military, in business, and anywhere else. That went double if Locke was holding prisoners inside his house. Calvin Locke was careless with his own security. Maybe he thought the superb setup on the outer walls did the trick. Wrong. The steps rose to the second-floor landing, and more steps led up farther, probably to an attic. Still nothing, no talking, no footsteps, nothing. Novak stood still, undecided. It all seemed a bit too easy. That's when he started fearing a major trap.

Novak ventured a peek into the dark wing of the second floor where the family's bedrooms were located. Also quiet and deserted. Same sconces, same ambient light, same muted hush. Where was everybody? He stepped out onto the wide tan-carpeted corridor and eased open the first door on his right. It was a bedroom with no one inside. Empty. The next two bedrooms were designed to please little girls, with lots of princess posters and white queen-size canopy beds and plenty of stuffed animals: Sammi and Susie's rooms, no doubt about it.

After a quick check of the other bedrooms, Novak found nothing amiss and no one about. He turned the corner and moved into the adjacent wing. At the far end, a door stood ajar. A narrow shaft of light spilled out onto the dark hall. Somebody was at home. Novak edged up close and darted a quick look inside. It was a big room, a combination sitting room and bedchamber, the largest Novak had seen thus far. It also proved to be the jackpot.

Calvin Locke sat at the elaborate mahogany desk at the far end of the room across from a fireplace and underneath another giant Palladian window. The judge was smoking a slender cheroot, and gray smoke and the pleasant smell of expensive tobacco hung in the air. He appeared to be studying a sheaf of papers that he held in one hand. A green-shaded lamp burned atop the desk; the rest of the room lay in darkness. Gas fire logs flamed in front of him. He wore a crimson velvet robe like some lord in King Henry the Eighth's court. Locke didn't move, didn't look up, didn't have a clue Novak was anywhere around.

Novak felt the urge to step inside and bludgeon the judge right then and there, but it wasn't the time. He wasn't going anywhere in that stupid bathrobe. He stepped away from Locke's bedroom and tried the door handles of the other bedrooms. It didn't take him long to find the one affixed with a big sturdy bracket and padlock. It looked incompatible to the spotless condition of the rest of the house and the rich wood of the mahogany doors. This guy was a devil. No key was in the lock. Novak's gut told him Judith Locke was trapped inside that room just as Susie had told him. Hopefully, Lucy was in there, too. That would make Novak's job so much easier, but it was already too easy to take anything for granted. The house was so utterly silent that he could hear his own breathing, soft and regular.

    Novak wanted to know where everybody was and what they were doing before he even thought about rescuing whoever was locked up inside that room. He entered the back stairs again and ran lightly up to the third floor. There, he finally found signs of life. Two young girls, most likely housemaids, stood in an open doorway at the far end of the hall, whispering together. The servants' quarters, not a place Locke would deposit his daughter or any other valuable prisoner, not with the way most household staffs gossiped. He searched the door handles for padlocks, didn't see any slide bolts, either, but hadn't expected to. This was where Locke's servants lived. Locke seemed fairly nonchalant about his criminal activities, but he sure as hell couldn't hide from employees when he was holding a family member prisoner. They probably knew but were too scared to alert the police. Novak would bet Judith was inside that room. Locking up one's recalcitrant daughter was not the same thing as imprisoning an abducted thirteen-year-old. Novak felt good to go. Now for the fun part: paying the judge a nice little visit that he would not enjoy.

Chapter 15

Novak had to take care of Locke first; in fact, he'd been looking forward to getting his hands on that pervert. Once he put him down and searched his office, he'd take whoever was in the room out through the back gate. He was almost positive it was Judith and hoped Lucy was in there, too. The unexpected ease of infiltrating the house wore on him. Way too easy in too many ways. Only one man had stood in his way so far. On the other hand, this wasn't a SEAL mission, either, with the dangers involved in one. This was a private home that was not expecting trouble inside the grounds. It was understandable they were careless, but it was a big mistake on their part.

Moving cautiously down the hallway, Novak headed toward Locke's bedchamber. It was dark inside except for the desk lamp, and Locke still sat at his desk absorbed in work, the perfect unsuspecting victim. Pulling down the ski mask over his head, he slipped into the room and couched himself in the deep shadows along the wall. Hopefully, and if all went well, Calvin Locke would never enjoy another peaceful moment inside his own home.

Novak continually searched for security cameras, didn't see any, and hoped they weren't hidden in the bookshelves of legal tomes lining three walls in the office alcove. He kept expecting to hear an alarm or step on a creaky floorboard. Like a shadow out of hell, he moved slowly, which went against his impulse to go in, get it done, and get out. He wanted the judge to feel like a helpless fool.

Locke was so intent in his work that Novak had no trouble easing up right behind him. Surprise was a wonderful thing when it worked. Novak was in place and not a man who wasted time, so he didn't hesitate. He darted up quickly behind the man, hooked his left arm around his neck, right hand clamped on his left wrist in a hard and sustained chokehold. He'd always attacked full force so they didn't have a chance to resist. He flexed his biceps tight against Locke's Adam's apple. The force of the strangulation lifted the judge completely off his swivel desk chair. It rolled away to the side as Locke kicked and struggled to throw Novak off, but the judge was out of shape and his bodyguards were not there to fight his battles. Novak was too strong for him.

The judge looked like an impressive figure in his robe, but he wasn't strong and he wasn't agile. When push came to shove with a man Novak's size, he didn't have a chance. He was a tub of belly flab and soft white skin, a lazy, pampered, disgusting excuse of a male. With the life slowly being choked out of him, he panicked and clawed at Novak's arm with manicured fingernails and reared up like a cornered stallion in a stall. He made no sounds but grunts, his screams cut off as Novak applied relentless pressure. Novak knew how long he could hold him without killing him, and just before the judge lost consciousness, Novak spoke low words against his ear. "Nobody crosses Timothy Hennessey and gets away with it."

Seconds later Locke's body went slack, unconscious. Novak let go of him, and he fell into the desk and crumpled to the floor at Novak's feet. He knelt down beside his victim and shrugged off his backpack. He pulled out a roll of silver duct tape and stripped the judge naked. Novak slapped two pieces of the tape over his mouth and quickly taped his hands and feet together. Then he rolled the guy over onto his stomach and bent his knees back and taped wrists and ankles together. The idea of a servant finding him trussed up like a pig appealed to Novak and should do serious damage to the judge's sense of superiority and security. It would give his staff something to whisper and laugh about upstairs in the servant wing. Novak pulled out his phone and snapped a picture, just in case he ever needed that kind of leverage.

Novak moved back to the door and checked out the hall. All was quiet. The next few minutes were spent methodically tossing the desk and credenza. Gathering up the papers Locke had dropped to the floor, he stuffed them into the backpack and quickly rifled through the desk drawers, hoping to find a key to the bedroom's padlock and anything else he could use as blackmail. Anything he could do to trigger Locke's distrust of Hennessey would work. If they turned on each other, it would even up the odds for Novak. He jimmied open a locked drawer and found several bound blue ledgers inside and a bunch of DVD discs. He stuffed them in, too, deeming them important, and also found a key he suspected opened the lock on that bedroom door. Lying beside that key was a beautiful little antique derringer with an ivory handle held inside an ornate, hand-stitched red leather holster that looked handcrafted, probably centuries ago in Spain or Mexico. The gun looked like something Locke would prize, so he took it. He snapped Locke's Apple laptop shut and stuck it in the backpack with the other goodies. Then he trashed the room a bit, destroyed the desk with a fireplace poker, stomped a couple of Locke's prize orchids to death under his boot, and moved back out into the hallway. Still nobody. It was unexplainable, but Novak always took good luck where he found it. Calvin Locke was overconfident. Good for Novak; bad for the judge.

Back at the locked bedroom, he inserted the key. It turned easily. He quietly lifted the lock off the bracket. He pushed down the door handle and found it secured from inside. He fished out his lock pick and had the door open in seconds. He pushed it open and waited a moment, then cautiously entered the darkened room, feeling along the wall for the light switch, not quite sure what he'd find inside. That's when something hurtled out of the dark right at him. He sensed it and tried to duck, but the lamp glanced off his shoulder and crashed to the floor. Then an all-out attack came at him. He knew at once it was a woman; he could smell her perfume, spicy and exotic. But she meant business and had her sharp claws out, so he grabbed her shoulders, spun her back against him, and clamped one arm around her waist and the other over her mouth.

"Stop, stop fighting," he gritted into her ear. "I'm here to get you out."

The woman did not stop. She was definitely giving it everything she had and caused him a lot more trouble than the judge had. Those sharp nails scraped down the side of his face, drawing blood. Novak had had enough. He shook the woman hard enough to stop her fight. It worked. "Lori Garner sent me, damn it. Shut the hell up or you're gonna get us both killed."

Lori's name did the trick. She collapsed in front of him like a punctured balloon. He let go and let her fall to her knees in front of him. Novak checked the hall and shut the door. He jerked her back up to standing and switched on his pen light. It was Judith Locke, all right. She looked older than her photograph and haggard but little change otherwise. Her ultra-short white hair was gelled to stand straight up, and her huge brown eyes were unmistakable. She was incredibly thin, her face pinched. He was pretty sure she was anorexic or maybe her father was starving her to death. "Come on, let's go."

"No, no, I can't leave my girls here with him, I won't!" She started struggling again.

Novak pulled her close and spoke harshly against her ear. "Listen good, lady. Do what I say or I'm leaving you here. Your girls aren't here. I've got them. I took them out of your beach house last night. They're in a safe place. Either you shut up and come quietly or I'm leaving you in here."

She sagged on her feet and would have fallen if he didn't have a good grip on her arms. "He told me they were here."

"Well, they aren't. They're fine, trust me. Where are the guards?"

She turned and searched his face. "Who are you?"

"That doesn't matter. Why aren't there guards in the house?"

That's when she decided to trust him. "Daddy keeps them outside. He doesn't like them up here in the bedroom wing."

Yeah, I'll bet, and for obvious reasons, Novak thought.

"They're outside with the dogs. But Daddy's in his office right down the hall, I think. He's got a gun in his desk."

"Not anymore."

"What do you mean?"

"I mean he's not gonna cause anybody trouble at the moment."

"Is he dead? Did you kill him?" She sounded half worried and half excited.

"I'll just say he's indisposed at the moment."

"How do I know you're telling me the truth?"

"He locked you in here. I found the key and got you out. Proof enough? C'mon, I don't have time to argue with you." She continued to hesitate, and Novak got mad. "Look, lady, Lori Garner's out back in the alley waiting for you. She's driving a blue Mustang. The Feds are ready to take you and your kids into witness protection. Do you still have the evidence that'll nail your father?"

"I've got more than enough."

"If it's here in the house, we've got to get it and get out. We can't come back."

"It's out in the yard in the playhouse."

"Okay, let's go."

After that exchange, she ran back to a dresser and stuffed a few things into a backpack while Novak waited at the door. "Not a word, understand," he told her. "Stay close to me and do what I say."

She nodded, but she was scared.

They made it downstairs without getting killed and crossed the big shadowy kitchen to a back door before Judith Locke decided she wanted more answers. "Who are you? Why are you helping me?"

"I told you, so hold off, okay? We aren't in the clear yet."

Novak inched back the bottom of the back door blinds and peered outside. It led out onto a flagstone patio surrounded by trees. A fancy swimming pool was adjacent to the patio. Nobody in sight. Locke's guards were shit, all right. He unlocked the door and stepped outside into cool night air. That's when he came face to face with one giant, salivating Doberman Pinscher. The dog took an instant disliking to him. It hunched down, hackles rising in a stiff ridge down its spine. His growl came low and threatening. Novak pointed his silenced .45 at him. He'd been attacked by a ferocious guard dog once before in Iraq and still had bite scars on his calf to prove it. He would never let it happen again.

Judith grabbed his arm. "No, wait, don't shoot her. Come Daisy, heel," she whispered softly.

The big dog immediately relaxed those dripping jaws and bounded over to lie at her feet, like some kind of friggin' puppy. Judith knelt and scratched her ears and stroked her head. The dog lay down, docile and sweet as apple pie. Probably knew how to tear him apart on the right command, too.

"Stay," Judith ordered the dog in her firm voice. The dog cocked his head and did not move. She looked up at Novak. "She's sweet when you get to know her."

"Yeah, right. No thanks." Novak grabbed her arm, and the dog growled deep in its throat. He let go of her, better safe than sorry. "Which way to the playhouse?"

Judith pointed down at an area beyond the pool. He waited for her to shut the dog inside the kitchen, and they took off at a run. She kept up fairly well, and they kept inside the dark cover under the trees. Still no guards in sight. Novak was beginning to think somebody was playing with him, watching everything he did, wanting him to feel safe before he walked headfirst into a well-laid ambush.

It didn't take long for him to spot the ring of solar spotlights illuminating the banks of the manmade lake Lori had described. It did have a little humpback bridge crossing over to it. All fairytale like and everything. Novak pulled Judith down onto her knees and visually searched the sidewalk circling the water. That's when he spotted the first armed guard, down there protecting an empty playhouse. These guys were a joke.

The man appeared to be on patrol, but he wasn't looking in their direction, or any other direction, truth be told. He was gazing down at his cell phone, its dim glow illuminating his face in the darkness. Novak could hear the faint bangs and explosions that pretty much identified a video game. The man had his back to the bridge. Locke's guards ought to be shot for dereliction of duty. They would've been if they were in the military. They probably would tomorrow once they found the judge all trussed up and helpless.

"Where'd you put it on the island?"

"I hid it inside the castle under a floorboard."

"Where exactly?"

"It's hard to explain. I'll have to go and show you."

Novak grimaced. This was getting absurd. He wanted to get out of that compound. Time was wasting, and it was a matter of minutes before somebody saw them. But he had to have that evidence. "We can't use the bridge. How deep is the water?"

"Knee-deep on you, probably. It's a koi pond. We weren't allowed to swim in it because of the fish."

"Then we'll have to wade out there."

She pointed out the best way to circumvent the guard's notice, and they crossed through the water together, Novak gripping tight to her elbow. If he made it out of this compound without being shot, it would be a miracle, especially if even one guard woke up and did his job. The little castle was not so little. It was about the size of a starter home for newlyweds, with turrets and ramparts and a retractable drawbridge, the whole works. Judith led him up to a back door, and Novak stood outside and watched the incompetent guard play his game while she went inside. It took her too long for his comfort. A full five minutes later, she reappeared, holding a brown leather briefcase.

"How'd you get the dope on him?" he asked her.

"I memorized the combination to Daddy's safe. He opened it in front of me a couple of times."

"He didn't miss what you took out?"

"Not yet."

They waded back down into the moat, waking a ton of fish that darted here and there as they sloshed their way across to the lawn. They were pushing their luck, big-time.

"Listen, Judith, here's what you're going to do. See the path there. Run down it to the back gate and find Lori. Don't stop, no matter what. I'll put down that guard if he sees you."

"You're not coming with us?"

"I've got a few things to do first. Go now. Tell Lori to wait for me as long as she can. If she sees a guard, take off. She'll know where to go. Go on, you've got a clear path to the gate right now."

Judith took off running, without further argument, but the guy with the phone heard her and turned around. Novak moved up behind him, and for a few seconds, the guard looked stunned to see an armed intruder coming at him out of the dark. Then he got over the surprise, dropped the phone, and clawed desperately at his holster, but it was too late. Novak tackled him around the waist and took him down hard. The guy fought back, and they rolled on the ground, grappling for advantage, but Novak was bigger and stronger and managed to wrest the weapon out of his hand. He clubbed the guy hard with the pistol and hit him again in the forehead. The second blow did it; the guy didn't move. Panting, down on his knees, Novak crouched low for a moment, expecting reinforcements because the altercation hadn't been exactly quiet. Nothing moved.

Peering down the sidewalk, he couldn't see Judith. He breathed easier that she was already out in the alley, but there was one more special surprise he wanted to leave to make the judge crazy. Nobody shouted alarms, so he got up and dragged the unconscious guard off the path and into the bushes and then headed out to look for the prized hothouse. It wasn't difficult to find. The glass building was lit up like a Hollywood marquee on opening night. He moved inside, duck-walked below the windows. He figured the gardener would have supplies stowed somewhere nearby, and he was right. And then, there it was, voila, a big red can of gasoline with a handy pouring spout.

Grabbing it, he quickly drenched all the orchids sitting around in their fancy clay pots and splashed it on tables and down between the aisles. It wasn't a sturdy structure. It'd go up like a bottle rocket on New Year's Eve. He wanted the judge to freak out, and this should do it in spades. He trickled a stream of gasoline through the main door and about ten feet down the sidewalk. Then he pulled a Zippo lighter out of his pocket and tossed it down on the flammable fluid. He didn't hang around but took off at a hard run for the back gate.

Moments later, a terrific whoosh filled the air, followed by a big explosion. That would be the chemical fertilizer stored all over the place. He looked back, and the hothouse was a flaming inferno. Licking flames reached high into the sky, and glass and debris were raining down, crackling and hissing and sprinkling the grass, a nice little distraction to give him time to get to the Mustang. The gate was standing wide open. So thank you for that, Judith. He burst out onto the alley, home free, except for one thing. The Mustang was gone. Shit.

Of more concern at the moment were the three armed men rushing down the alley toward him, guns out and blasting. He'd finally found the guards. Novak raced back through the gate, heading up into the tree cover, arms pumping, trampling rose bushes to give insult to injury. He kicked down the solar lights as he ran, hoping the night would hide his flight. He had to make it over the front wall before they set the dogs loose; then he might have a chance. He could hear men shouting, the sleeping bodyguards all waking up at once. He made it to the garage in under a minute and found Henson's car gone.

No good options left, he sprinted down the winding drive, cutting through the loops of pavement to reach the front gate. It was closed up tight, but he increased his speed, hit the wall with his feet, climbing up it far enough to jump, grab the top, and pull himself over. Alarm sensors immediately went wild, and he kicked one of the cameras loose as a bullet ricocheted off the wall near his foot, sending shards of stucco out like torpedoes. He hoisted himself the rest of the way over and dropped down to the street. Scanning in both directions, he saw nothing, but he could hear a vehicle gunning somewhere nearby. That's when the Mustang squealed around a corner at the next intersection and barreled toward him, pedal to the metal. Henson's black car swerved out right behind it.

Novak waved Lori on past him and stood out in the middle of the road, holding his weapon steady with both hands, beaded on the Lexus's windshield as it sped straight at him. He fired three shots in rapid succession. The first two hit the windshield, and the third smashed it and got the driver in the chest. The vehicle careened wildly and ended up slamming into the brick wall head-on with enough force to throw the driver out onto the hood. The other man in the car slumped down in the passenger's seat. He didn't move.

Novak wasted no time sprinting for the Mustang, where it sat twenty yards up the street, motor idling. He was there in seconds. He jumped into the back seat, and Lori stomped on the accelerator and took off with a screech of the tires. Novak turned around and watched out the back window, but nobody came after them. Three streets over, Lori popped the trunk, and Novak pulled Henson out and dragged him to the side of the road. Somebody would find the guy, sooner or later. After that, they drove at a more leisurely speed that wouldn't cause attention. Nobody said a word as they drove through dark and deserted streets. Judith was huddled in the front seat, holding the briefcase of evidence clamped tightly against her chest.

"Well, that didn't exactly go according to plan," Novak finally said.

"Judith's out of that house, and she's got the evidence to hang her dad. We're all still alive. Can't argue with that kind of success."

True, but Novak was not happy. It had ended up a sloppy raid. He just hoped nobody had seen him long enough to describe him. He did not want to be identified. He needed Locke to wonder who he was and who had sent him. Hopefully, he would think it was Hennessey double-crossing him. Time would tell. Judith Locke was free and would soon be reunited with her children under FBI protection. He could live with that.

Chapter 16

"Are you sure Susie and Sammi are all right?" Judith was upset and worried about her children. "Who is this FBI agent you gave them to? Can you trust her with my children?"

"Her name is Leslie Taylor. She's an old friend. Like I told you, you don't have to worry. You can trust her. Nothing's going to happen to those kids while they're in her care, I promise you."

Judith did not look reassured. She wasn't comfortable that her children had been sent off with complete strangers. Once she saw them and knew they were all right, she would be okay. She sat on the couch in Frank's living room, wringing her hands and watching the door. Leslie had phoned and was on her way. Problem was, after the raid on Locke's estate, nobody felt safe holed up at the cabin, and that went double for Judith Locke. She was so nervous that her anxiety was transferring to the rest of them. Novak didn't want to let Judith out in the public, so he'd asked Leslie to pick her up on the river. She said she'd arrive as soon as she could get there. That had been over three hours ago. As minutes ticked by, Novak worried more that the judge might find them before Judith and her children were in FBI custody. He stood at the kitchen windows, staring out at the road and wondering which group would show up first.

Novak turned and looked at Judith. "We need to talk."

Startled at his tone, she rose, but she looked totally spent and unable to think coherently. Sleep deprivation did that to a person. Who could blame her? She was putting her trust in a lot of people she didn't know from a hole in the ground.

"I can't help worrying. I want my girls here where I can hold them."

"We understand that." Lori had been soothing her friend ever since she'd arrived at the river. She glanced over at Frank. He said nothing. When they'd returned without Lucy, he'd grown silent and introspective again. Not a good sign.

Judith had been taking turns fretting about her children and praising them for getting her out of the house. She wasn't finished, either. "I don't know how to thank you. I mean that. You risked your lives to get me out of that house. I'll never, ever forget that. I thought I'd never see my children again, that he would kill me first."

Lori sat down beside Judith and placed her hand on her friend's back. "You and the girls are free now. You're doing the right thing handing over the proof of his corruption. He has hurt so many people. He still is."

Judith nodded, but she apparently needed to talk. "He's a monster. I hated every minute my children had to be around him. They were babies when my husband was killed in a car accident. They never knew him at all, so Daddy took his place. After Danny's funeral, he just took over my life again, forced me to change my name back to Locke and live in that house with him. He wanted my girls to bear his name, too. He has to have control of everybody in his life. Stephen's okay with that. I'm not. I just want to be free of both of them."

"Stephen's involved in the judge's crimes, right?" Novak asked.

She nodded. "He's turned out just like Daddy. Bad to the core. Actually, in some ways, he's even worse than Daddy." She shook her head and clasped her hands together. "He inherited Daddy's..." She paused a moment. "...perversions. They both get by with unthinkable crimes because of Daddy's wealth and political connections."

Novak wanted to know more. He needed to dissect these guys, know them inside and out. Judith was the best source to get that information. "How about some specifics about how they do things?"

Judith met his eyes. "Stephen's into drugs and pornography, and God only knows what else. I don't trust him alone with my children, either, if that tells you anything. Stephen's nothing like the heroic image he projects on screen. He wouldn't be in films at all, if it weren't for Daddy's money and influence. He bought Stephen's way into Hollywood. They both know all the big names out there, you know, movie producers and directors and other A-list actors. Most of Stephen's roles are simply payments for favors that Daddy provides them."

"Has Stephen been in trouble with the law?"

"More than anyone knows. Daddy bails him out and hires crack lawyers to keep everything confidential and expunge his records. Stephen's always been into sleazy women, gold digger types, and especially porn stars, and the younger they are the better. He likes to call them his personal sex slaves. He's a terrible man, really, mean and hateful and cruel. I think down deep, he must hate women. I was a handy victim when we were little." She paused and looked away from Novak. "He liked to hurt animals. One time he taped my little Yorkie's mouth shut and shot her with his BB gun. He killed that poor dog. Daddy made him see a child psychologist after that. I think I hate Stephen even more than I detest Daddy. But I despise them both. I hope I never have to see them again."

After hearing that, Novak decided that Stephen Locke was a stone-cold sociopath. If he had Lucy, no telling what he'd do to her.

"Where's Stephen now?" Lori asked Judith.

"Last I heard he was on location out in Arizona. Scottsdale, I believe. But he's into all kinds of illegal stuff. He's just awful. I can't say that enough."

Frank had heard all he wanted to hear. "And that guy's got his hands on my daughter. We need to quit hanging around here and see if he's got her, Novak. She just said he likes young girls. We've got to stop him before he hurts her. You should have killed Calvin Locke when you had the chance."

Novak swiveled his gaze to his friend. "I'm not an assassin, Frank. There are other ways to bring him down. When I get them, I want to get them all."

"You should've killed him. I would have."

Novak didn't doubt that. "Be patient a bit longer, Frank. We going to get her," Novak told him.

Judith commiserated with Frank's fears. "I'm so sorry about your little girl. I know how you feel, I do. Complete helplessness and frustration. I was scared to death when Daddy took them away from me. And Stephen, he is capable of the most terrible things. I'm ashamed to be part of this family."

"What exactly does he do to women?" Frank was not going to be consoled. Not ever. Judith's talk was only intensifying his pain.

Judith's expression told Novak that she didn't want to answer. So she skirted his question. "She may be in Houston and not with Stephen. I used to hear vans and trucks coming into the estate late at night, usually well after midnight. The maids told me they could hear girls crying sometimes out in the garage. I never saw them myself, but maybe Lucy is out there."

"She's not out there. I checked. But we'll find her." Novak's impatience was growing. Where the devil was Leslie? What was taking her so long? "I searched the whole place, Judith. Lucy's not there. Tell me about the dirty stuff the judge is into? What kind of evidence do you have in that briefcase?"

"The kind that will put him away for good. When I decided I had to get away, I started documenting what he did, you know, I eavesdropped on people who came to the house and listened in on phone conversations. I recorded some of it, and I took some pictures of people coming and going. I got logs and files out of his safe. I have all the proof I need. Daddy and Stephen are into prostitution. I've got some dirt on Timothy Hennessey, too. I'm not sure what it all entails, but he's definitely involved with Daddy's business. He provides men when Daddy needs them, I think. Hennessey is so brutal; he scares me."

Novak wanted concrete facts, and he wasn't getting any. "Think, Judith. I need to know everything you can remember, especially about Hennessey's operations. Any detail you can think of. He might be holding Lucy for the judge."

"I don't know that much about him. Daddy never let me come around when he was at the house. He was born in Ireland, I believe, and he's still got a thick Irish brogue. I remember hearing that he came to Houston in the 1990s and set up a business he called King Cotton. I know he's utterly ruthless and most of his guys are Irish nationals. He doesn't trust Americans. The things they do to their victims are worse than what the Mexican cartels do." Her voice dropped to a whisper. "He beheads people, sometimes just as a warning. I heard he left a decapitated head on the front stoop of the victim's mother." She shivered a little.

"Have you met him?" Lori asked her.

"No, and I don't want to. You don't, either, believe me. Really, Lori, stay as far away from him as you can get. He's unpredictable; even Daddy complained about that. I got the impression that Stephen and Daddy might be a little afraid of him."

Frank stood up. Novak recognized the look in his eyes. He was going to murder somebody before this thing ended. Novak wasn't sure if he could or would stop him. At the moment, he leaned toward helping him take anybody down who stood in their way.

Novak glanced at a picture of Lucy Caloroso, where it was propped on the fireplace mantel. She looked to be around ten when it was taken, young and innocent and happy with that wide smile and shining eyes. Her hair had been plaited back then with her long russet pigtails hanging over her shoulders.

"Lucy's going to be all right." Novak stated that again, but he was tired of saying it and not sure it was true. He wanted to find that kid and get her out of the hands of those animals before something terrible happened to her.

Frank turned away and walked out onto the front porch and sat down on the swing. He needed to breathe some fresh air. Novak hoped he stayed out there awhile because there were questions he needed to ask, the kind Frank didn't need to hear.

He turned back to Judith. "Okay, there's something else I need to know. Where does Hennessey operate? Tell me what building he's based in and the products or businesses he runs. Anything you can give us will help us hit him where it'll hurt him the most. Because Locke has already enlisted his help to track down you and your daughters, trust me."

"His legit business is the King Cotton thing. Daddy says they manufacture mattresses and pillows and the like. I guess he bought it out when he came over from Ireland. It's his center of operations, I think, the legit one. There's a big warehouse in Galveston down near the ocean, close to where the cruise ships dock. That's probably where he runs his criminal activities. I don't know that for sure, though. He's got other properties, too, rental houses and some storage units, places like that. He works out of King Cotton for the most part, but I don't think he'd keep Lucy there. But who knows? He's crazy."

"Have you been inside either of those warehouses?"

"No, but Daddy took me to the King Cotton place once when I was in junior high. I remember because he made me wait out in the limo with his driver. We had to sit out there for hours. Our driver back then was Bobby Hondo. He would get in the back seat with me and taught me to play checkers on a little travel game." She smiled a little but then grew serious. Whatever came next seemed difficult for her to share. "When Daddy came back, he told Bobby to go inside and help them load the trucks. He told him not to come out again until he called him." Judith kept her eyes focused on her lap. "That was the first time that he raped me. The last time was night before last."

Nobody said anything, but Lori put her arm around Judith's shoulders. Judith shed no tears over the memory. Probably didn't have any left, not after years of fighting off her disgusting excuse of a father. Novak felt his chest constrict. It was getting harder to contain his anger. He wanted a piece of those guys, all of them. He wanted to bring them down, the harder the better. Maybe Frank had been right. Maybe he should have finished off Calvin Locke when he had the chance.

Judith kept talking, as if dammed-up floodgates had finally burst open. "I've known for a long time that Daddy's been into sex trafficking. I don't know all the details, but I think Hennessey is involved in it, too, somehow. I guess they're business partners. I heard Hennessey telling him how they groomed young girls before they snatched them." She paused. "They'd find good-looking young college guys to sweet talk them, you know, win their trust, and then introduce them to drugs. They want them to be docile, so they addict them." She glanced outside at Frank and took a deep breath, not liking to tell them what was going on any more than they liked to hear it. "We had a maid at the house once. She told me they'd done that to her. Daddy took a liking to her looks and brought her out to live at the mansion. He's got several girls upstairs that he uses that way. I feel sorry for them. Most of them don't understand English."

Lori's face looked flushed. Novak was pretty sure it was anger. "I wish you would've killed him, Novak. He doesn't deserve to live another day." As usual, Lori had stated her feelings concisely. She never minced her words.

Novak stared at her. "He'll get what's coming to him, one way or another."

Novak pitied Judith Locke. Incest victims sometimes loved their parents even if they were abusers, no matter how they suffered at their hands. He couldn't understand how they could, but he'd seen it happen. Not the case with Judge Locke's daughter. Her next words proved him correct.

"I hope you do kill him. I hope you take a long time doing it and make him beg and crawl and weep. He told me..." She paused there for a moment before continuing. "He told me that he was waiting for Susie and Sammi to reach the age he liked best. I told him I'd die before I let him touch them. He laughed at me and wished me good luck with that. That's when he locked me in my bedroom and wouldn't let me see them. I'm so worried that something's gone wrong with these FBI people. What's taking so long? Do you think he's got my girls again? Can't you call them or something?"

"They should be showing up any minute," Novak said. "They'll protect you and the children. You'll have around-the-clock protection as long as you hold up your end of the bargain and provide those documents. The information in that briefcase is pertinent, right? Big enough to bring them both down?"

"I think so. I took a lot of his private papers."

"Just trust Leslie and do what she tells you. She'll make sure you stay safe while they build their case."

Judith didn't look impressed. "I don't trust anybody, not anymore. I probably never will again. I'll wait and see what she does, and if it's acceptable, then I might trust her."

"She's going to want to comb through all the evidence before they set you up somewhere in a new life with a new name."

Judith got quiet. "I need to tell you something. I do trust the three of you. I didn't at first, but I do now. You've proved yourselves. I've got a safe deposit box down at a small bank in Corpus Christi. There are copies of the proof I'm handing over to the FBI inside. Just in case anything happens to me and that briefcase."

"Do you think he suspects you're turning on him?"

"Maybe now, but he didn't when I was gathering the goods on him. I made copies of every single thing. There are two identical folders, one here in the briefcase, the other in that safe deposit box. If he gets to me somehow, I want you to get it and put him away with it."

"Leslie's got this. You can count on her. Your father doesn't have a clue you've got this stuff?"

"I was careful." She opened the briefcase sitting at her feet and brought out a small key and a signed form giving him permission to get into her safe deposit box. "They're aware I might send somebody to pick up the contents."

"Did you use your real name?"

"No." She looked at Lori. "I used Lori's name and her social security number. Hope you don't mind. I knew Daddy would find out if I used my own."

"Of course, I understand."

Novak was pleased about the duplicate copies. He backed up everything he did, and had never regretted the habit. "Everything's going to turn out okay, Judith. In an hour, you'll be far away from here and anybody who wants to do you harm."

"I know, but this is just a bit of added insurance if anything should go wrong."

The sound of approaching vehicles brought them all up to their feet. Either the Feds or Locke's thugs had found them. Novak pulled his weapon, and Frank was back inside now and holding a rifle. They stood at the back door, weapons held ready. Novak pulled back the blinds. It was dark outside, but the dusk-to-dawn lamp lit up most of Frank's backyard. Three black Suburbans pulled up and stopped right outside the back door. Leslie stepped out of the first one and headed to the porch. A female agent followed her. Four other agents stood waiting outside the car doors.

Novak let her in. The other woman waited on the porch. Leslie glanced around the room then looked up at him. "So I hear you guys had some fun at the judge's house."

"Not so much, but we got Judith out, so you're welcome," Lori said, frowning. It appeared she already didn't care for Leslie Taylor.

"From what I could ascertain from my undercover guy in Hennessey's employ, Locke called him and also alerted his buddies at Galveston PD.

My man said Locke's keeping your little home invasion quiet so he can kill you himself. They know somebody broke in and took his daughter and his granddaughters. He said his dirty cops were scouring the city as we speak. They don't know your name yet, but they do know you're big and tall and grabbed some of the judge's confidential papers. He's most upset about his orchids. Want to tell me what the hell you're thinking before you end up dead, Novak?"

"I don't know what you're talking about."

"Don't you?" Then she looked at Judith. "I'm FBI Special Agent Leslie Taylor. Your children are fine and waiting for you in a safe place. I understand you have some information that will put your father behind bars. Is that correct?"

"More than enough."

"Good. We'll go over those documents when we get you to the safe house, and then you and your little girls will effectively disappear off the face of the earth. That will happen before we go in and arrest Judge Locke. Any questions you'd like to ask me?"

"Where are they? Didn't you bring them with you?"

"I thought it safer not to. They are waiting anxiously for you, believe me." She turned to Novak. "If you've got incriminating evidence you filched tonight and want to donate it to our case, please don't hesitate. Meanwhile, my advice? Watch your back and don't do anything that reckless and stupid again or you'll probably end up in a morgue, or best-case scenario, I'll be forced to arrest you. Hope you have a Plan B in the works."

"We're going after Frank's daughter. We're going to find her and bring down Timothy Hennessey and the judge any way we have to. Just so you know."

Leslie's eyes were hard. Then she laughed, the cold, mocking one that he remembered so well. "Okay, best of luck with that. We've been trying to take Hennessey down for years. Anybody brave enough to work for that sadistic, psycho maniac is too scared to turn evidence on him. And Hennessey's clever enough not to make stupid mistakes. We've tried to infiltrate his organization before and ended up with three dead agents whose bodies have yet to be discovered. We've got one man in there, so don't think you can blow his cover and get by with it. Just so you know."

"So if we need help, you will come through for us, right?"

"C'mon, Novak, you know good and well that there's no way in hell I can promise you that, or anything else. Your handing over a material witness against a crooked judge won't hurt your chances of our cooperation, but I can't make any guarantees that you won't be charged if you commit crimes. Which you've already done, by the way. Sorry, but that's just the way it is."

"Good enough. We mean to take them down. I wanted to give you fair warning."

"Better to keep incriminating threats like that to yourself."

"I'm going to kill the bastard who's got my daughter," Frank told her. His face was quite calm, but his voice betrayed him.

"If he doesn't, I will," Lori added.

Leslie looked at each of them in turn. "I think you three need to get yourselves under control. I do not want to arrest you and send you to prison. Get your acts together now. Understand me?"

Novak said, "Don't worry about us. Worry about keeping Judith and the kids alive."

"You won't be on my mind, not after what you've done. I've got plenty else on my hands to worry about. Are you ready to go, Ms. Locke?"

Judith nodded. "Can you assure me that my children will be safe with you?"

"Of course. This is what's going to happen. We will transport you to the safe house where you'll reunite with your girls. Once there, I'll need to interview you on tape, and you'll have to look over and sign legal documents and subject yourself to an in-depth interrogation. Are you willing to do that?"

"I am ready to do whatever it takes to keep my father away from my children."

"I understand. Do you have luggage?"

"Only the clothes in my backpack and this briefcase."

"Anything you need, we can provide for you and your children. We need to go, though, right now."

Judith hugged Lori tightly and thanked them profusely. Then they all walked outside and watched Leslie settle Judith in the back seat of the middle car between two armed agents. Novak took hold of Leslie's arm and pulled her aside. He spoke quietly. "How about sending me a list of Hennessey's real estate holdings in Houston? You've probably already got that on file. And a list of his and Locke's known associates? Sure would help me out."

"How soon do you need it?"

"Tonight. Within the hour?"

"What exactly are you planning to do?"

"I told you. We're going to go get Lucy, no matter what it takes."

"How?"

"You don't want to know the details, Leslie."

"I understand how you feel about that kid, Novak, believe me. I've been investigating these two bastards for three years. But you gotta know that I'll come after you if you break the law, right?" She stared at him until he answered.

"Take good care of Judith and those little girls. They've been through a lot. Locke's going to come after them with everything he's got, and when he finds them, he'll probably kill Judith, along with you and anyone else around you. He's a vindictive man. Judith's terrified he'll find her."

"Not on my watch. We can protect them."

"You gonna send me those lists, or not? I've got another possible source if you can't."

"Who?"

"That's classified." The source was Claire, but he hadn't heard from her or Harve yet.

"Right. Okay, I'll think about it. I'm not making any promises."

Novak watched her climb into the front seat of Judith's vehicle. The caravan took off in a crunch of gravel, and Novak watched them until the last vehicle was out of sight. Okay, first problem solved. Time to move on. Finding Lucy wasn't going to be easy. There was a distinct possibility that they'd never find her, and he knew it. She might already be out of the country. Frank was hanging on by a thread as it was. If they didn't find the teenager soon, he was going off the deep end. Their odds were not so good, all things considered. He turned and walked back into the house, ready to get answers. He didn't really care how. Not anymore.

Chapter 17

They talked late into the night, all of them concerned about Judith, even more worried now about Lucy, not sure how anything was going to turn out. Novak rose at first light; the others slept in, exhausted. Fine with him, they needed to rest; the going was about to get tough. He could function on a few hours, had never required much sleep. He put on a pot of strong coffee to keep him alert. He had research to do and a lot to think about.

He retrieved the papers he'd taken out of Locke's home office and opened the first manila folder. He flipped through quickly and found it held photographs of teenage girls, some preteens, probably. Some extremely sick sadists and pedophiles had Lucy in their clutches. He had to get her out before she sustained irreparable damage to her body, mind, and mental stability. Sorting quickly through the other files, he was terrified he'd find her among those pitiful photographs. He could never let Caloroso see them. That would be too much for him to bear. He'd go to pieces; his own imagined fears were enough. After a few minutes sorting through them, he did find a file with Lucy's name and photograph. She had her own individual folder. The tab was labeled *Lucy C. – Special Case.* Lucy did not appear under the influence of drugs. She had been separated out and treated differently, and that was the only good news to date.

Instead, she looked defiant. Scowling, her jaw jutted, she glared into the camera with both hands planted on her hips. There was an ugly bruise on her left cheekbone that somebody had attempted to disguise with flesh-colored makeup. It was obvious that she was not giving her captors an easy time. Novak realized he was clenching his teeth. His jaw ached from it. She was resisting, that was obvious. Novak wasn't surprised. She was a sweet, lovely child, but also had a deep-rooted independent streak and a mind of her own. That propensity had shown itself even when she was a small child. She'd inherited that from Frank. He had raised her to be spunky and self-reliant and street-smart. That could mean she might manage to escape, but it was unlikely.

Novak removed Lucy's picture and placed the others back inside the folder. He kept it on the table in front of him. He leaned back in the kitchen chair and sat there staring at Lucy's face, letting his anger fuel his determination. He was ready to do anything it took to get her back unharmed. He had to take Locke and Hennessey down before Frank found them and murdered them. In that moment, Novak couldn't think of a reason he shouldn't be allowed to do it. He inhaled deeply and then blew it out. After that, he folded up the photo of his friend's child and placed it inside his wallet.

By the time Frank shuffled into the kitchen and sat down at the table, looking haggard and bewhiskered, Novak had conquered his emotion. He got up and poured his friend a cup of coffee. He placed it down in front of the exhausted man and said, "You get any sleep this time?"

"Not much. You find anything about Lucy in those files you took?"

Novak avoided answering that question. "I think Hennessey's behind the sex trafficking and Locke's a customer as well as a partner."

Frank's eyes found Novak's face. "Did you find Lucy in there?"

"She's leverage. They'll handle her with kid gloves."

"I feel sick to my stomach."

So did Novak. "Yeah, I know."

"I feel like shit."

"You aren't sleeping. You aren't eating. You need to lay off the booze and take better care of yourself. You need a clear mind to do what comes next."

Frank just stared at him, silent.

So Novak got up and started fixing breakfast, just to have something to do. When the bacon was sizzling, he got out the eggs, but he kept his attention on Frank, who sat at the table with his face buried inside his open palms. He was on the edge of a complete breakdown. "You want to know what's going to happen next, Frank? We're going out there, and we're going to kick ass, and then we're going to rescue Lucy and every other girl, every single one of them, and then we're going to take them home."

Frank turned around in his chair. He looked more interested now.

"We've wasted enough time. Tonight, we go in after Hennessey and mess him up in ways he won't expect. Claire Morgan texted me the locations of his properties in Houston late last night. I think that's where they keep these girls. Leslie didn't come through. So we are going in and taking them out."

"How the hell did Claire get that kind of info? Isn't she in Italy?"

"You know her. She's got contacts and she uses them." The food smelled good. Novak was hungry. He poured the eggs into the skillet. "She's got friends everywhere. Including Jacques Montenegro."

"Montenegro is a New Orleans mobster."

"He's also Claire's brother-in-law and has helped us before."

"You shittin' me? Your partner is part of a NOLA crime family."

Novak laughed. Even the idea was ludicrous. "Not Claire. Her husband. Both of them are on the right side and totally legit. Jacques intercedes if we bump up against his mob friends. He's a good ally to have if you're a PI. He's trying to go legitimate; at least that's what Nick Black keeps telling me."

"I think I want to meet that partner of yours. She sounds like somebody I need to know. Way I see it? Hennessey's gonna be hard pressed to get to. He's a ruthless SOB and so are his men. I've tangled with some of them, and they don't play fair."

"I say we hit them tonight and cost him some serious cash flow problems and give his business a severe setback. Get his attention where it hurts him most. Find the girls he's running and get them back to their families." He stirred the eggs and pushed down the toast. "Good news is: Locke didn't report my little visit. I left him thinking it was Hennessey who messed him up. Don't know if he'll buy that without proof, but Judith already told us he's paranoid about the guy. Maybe we'll get lucky. The fact that he's holding our raid so close to his vest is a good sign. That might mean he wants to exact payback for the insult himself. Hopefully, that will come down on Hennessey's head. If he doesn't do that, we will. I want to turn them against each other. So we'll keep hitting them both in their bottom lines until they declare war. If Lucy's being held in one of Hennessey's houses, we could have her back tonight."

"Then I'm all in. Just tell me what you want me to do." For the first time, Frank looked hopeful.

"So am I. I'm ready to go now." That came from Lori, who now stood in the hall doorway.

"Good. I need you both. So let's eat something and prepare to move out tonight. I'm counting on you having enough weapons and ammo to pull this off, Frank. It just might turn into a war before it's over."

Caloroso actually grinned. First time Novak had seen that since he'd shown up. "I've got everything we need, plus some. All locked up down in the cellar and out in the barn. I've got two Kevlar vests and some hand grenades if we're getting serious."

"You expecting a war, or what?" Lori asked him, joining Frank at the table.

"It is war. I'm always prepared for emergencies. Never know who might show up with a long memory."

Novak nodded. "I'm thinking we're going to need plenty of that ammo."

"Got it stockpiled. All calibers. Never know when you need it."

"We have to plan out how to hit his houses and in what order. We'll go in fast and get out fast and take everybody down. We can't let them get ahead of us and be waiting when we show up at the next place. We're outnumbered, to say the least. But we're better trained, which just might even the odds."

"Just so we find Lucy, that's all I care about."

"There's no guarantee that's happening tonight, Frank, but my gut tells me she's still in Houston or maybe down in Galveston, most likely under heavy guard. She's an important pawn, and they might threaten her life if we strike this hard. So we need to find her tonight at all costs."

"If we don't, I'll make them tell me where she is."

As far as Novak was concerned, Frank could do that and with any method he chose. He was fully capable of making somebody talk.

They discussed how it would go down as they ate, and then they got quiet, preparing mentally for the night to come. Novak got a few more hours of sleep, but Caloroso and Lori stayed up, neither able to relax. They were both on edge and wired up on caffeine, which could be good or bad. Caloroso had laid off the whiskey, so that was a good sign. Novak was hoping their nerves would act to keep their minds keen.

Later that afternoon, they spread out a map of the greater Houston area. Novak pointed to the locations that he'd marked off earlier with a red circle. "You familiar with any of these towns, Frank?"

Frank studied the markings. "Yeah, I've worked in some of them. Which one are we hitting tonight?"

"All of them."

Lori wasn't so sure about that. "We can't hit that many houses in one night. We don't have the manpower, and the minute they get out the word of an attack, they'll be waiting for us. It would be suicide."

"It's gotta be all or nothing. We're going for surprise, so we have to go in fast, destroy everything we see, and hopefully find Lucy and get her and the other girls out. She's bound to be at one of his properties, because she wasn't at Locke's." He leveled his eyes on Caloroso. "You need to prepare yourself, Frank, because they may have already moved her out of state. From what I've seen and heard, they constantly keep these girls in transit and don't let them know where they are or where they've been. They've got stash houses throughout Texas and the surrounding states."

"Well, I don't think they'll take her very far," Lori said. "She's their bargaining chip. So far, Frank's been staying out of sight. They think their threat of hurting her is working."

"Hopefully, they'll turn on each other."

"To depend on that is risky. If Locke accuses Hennessey, he might expect to be hit. They'll be ready for us, and they'll pull Lucy out or use her to stop us."

"We'll move too fast for that," Novak said.

"No matter what else, we have to find her before they move her," Frank said.

Novak needed to make something clear. He wasn't particularly worried about Lori going off half-cocked, but Frank could. "Listen to me, Frank. You cannot go crazy and screw things up tonight. If you can't control that rage eating you up inside, you need to stay here and let Lori and me handle it. More important, if you lose your cool, it could cost Lucy her life. So are you still in? Can you do that?"

Frank was incensed at the affront. Angry, his face flushed hot under tanned skin. "I'm not going to do anything stupid. My daughter's life is at stake. I'm good to go, and you can count on me. When have you ever seen me lose it?"

"You know the answer to that. Lucy's never been at stake before. That's the difference."

Frank said nothing, just sat there, sullen and silent. Novak and Lori exchanged glances, but neither could blame the guy. Lori's expression told him she was worried about Frank, too.

"We've got a good plan and a strong element of surprise. But it's going to be one step at a time, knocking those houses down like dominoes and so fast the next target doesn't have time to be on the defensive."

As the day dragged on, Novak fought impatience. Frank was the wild card and wouldn't listen if things got dicey. He had murder in his eyes. After an evening spent combating jittery nerves and perfecting strategy, they loaded their gear into the Jeep and left just after two o'clock in the morning. The county roads proved to be dark and deserted, and traffic on the Interstate was light. Heavy rain had moved back into the Houston area, which would help them launch surprise attacks. Most people were at home, sleeping, unaware of the ugly underbelly of the city and what went on in houses imprisoning helpless, exploited girls. They were children in big trouble that they'd probably never get out of without help. Far from home, separated from anyone who loved them, tricked, drugged, and used, with little recourse to escape the awful things they were forced to do. If all went well, their nightmare would end tonight.

All the properties were located south of Buffalo Bayou and west of the south Loop. They had plotted the best course to take down the properties fast, one by one from east to west. Hennessey had chosen the houses fairly close together but in separate neighborhoods in separate towns, quiet and unassuming, where probably nobody had a clue what was going on inside. The first place on their list was located in a suburb called La Pointe, not far from Sylvan Beach Park. They found it easily, the property being the last house on a dead-end street, thereby making it perfect for their purposes.

Nearby residences had well-maintained yards, small street frontage but deep lots full of old trees and only a few fences. The house they sought had one, a five-foot-high chain-link fence that would be no impediment to entry. No dogs were in sight, and no guards loitered around, either, which was surprising but didn't mean they weren't inside the house toting handguns. The homes they passed were dark except for a couple here and there. Hennessey had chosen the site well, setting up in a nice, private, innocuous-looking little hellhole for abducted girls. No one would guess what went on inside that house. Novak wasn't sure, either. He hoped he found girls to rescue instead of sleeping quarters for a dozen heavily armed thugs.

Novak pulled the Jeep up beside the opposite curb about thirty yards down the street from the target driveway. There were cars parked along both sides of the street, so their vehicle would not draw undue attention. Treetops tossed in the wind, but the rain had slackened. Novak turned off the motor, and they sat silently in the shadows watching the place. Nothing moved, inside or out. After a few minutes, they climbed out and headed down the sidewalk, light drizzle spattering their jackets. Novak and Frank took one side of the street because Novak wanted to stay close to Caloroso in case something triggered him and he went batshit berserk.

Lori crept down the opposite side of the street on her own. Novak didn't worry about her; she was calm and collected now that the mission was in play. Novak carried his .45 in his belt holster, a sawed-off shotgun, and a baseball bat. Frank had a SIG 9 mm and an AR rifle that could do some serious damage anywhere at any time. He'd also stuck his favorite Ruger inside his back waistband. He'd come to make waste, all right. All their weapons were attached with silencers.

Lori Garner had chosen well, too. She carried a sweet little Springfield rifle and a weighted sap and had a loaded grenade belt strapped around her waist. She carried a gasoline can with her good arm. She had grown quiet on the drive over, hardening her resolve as she had probably done not so long ago in Iraq. Her training showed in the way she walked and held herself. She looked as relaxed as anybody could be under the circumstances. She would not screw things up. Any other time, Frank wouldn't, either. He was a battle-hardened warrior and conditioned for any fight, but not when it came to his daughter. That made him a particularly well trained, violent time bomb with a hair trigger. Not always the best person to have your back.

They approached from the side yard, crouching low and using the bushes growing along the fence as cover. There were two cars in the driveway, a white panel van and a black Lexus. As planned, Novak vaulted the fence first and headed out back with Frank close behind him. Lori headed straight for the front door. The house had no basement, only a crawl space. The back door had a low stoop, but the kitchen window blinds had been left open. Nobody was inside the kitchen or could be seen in the living room beyond. He could see the flickering light of a television set. Lori would be out front waiting for him to go in first. In a house this small that meant most of the people inside were in the bedrooms, hopefully sound asleep. That would be nice.

Once in place, Novak wasted no time. He took a step back, kicked the door as hard as he could. It slammed wide open and banged against the interior wall. He went in first, hard and low, with Frank at his heels. Lori would be coming in the front when she heard them force the door. First thing Novak heard was a female scream coming from the back of the house followed by heavy footsteps thudding down the hall to his left.

Novak took cover behind the kitchen wall, and when the first guy showed in the doorway, he swung the baseball bat as hard as he could against the man's chest. The guy went backward hard, hit the wall, and crumpled to the floor, the breath knocked out of him. Frank clubbed him in the head with the butt of his rifle and went into the hallway with Novak behind him. Two guys burst out of bedrooms down at the far end. One got off a shot at Frank but missed him, so Frank shot him dead and then did the same to the other man, both put down with double taps to body mass. Frank was a good shot, fast on the draw and clean, always had been. He never wasted a bullet. Now they could hear multiple women screaming their heads off. Maybe they'd found the girls. Only seconds had passed, and Novak rushed down the hall toward the female voices, stepping over bodies as he went. The first door on his right was locked. Frank moved around him to the next door. Lori yelled all clear from the front of the house. Novak stepped back and kicked the door open. Caloroso did the same at the next bedroom.

Four women were inside, all screaming and cowering in a corner just across from him. All of them were naked except for underwear and plastic gloves on their hands. Novak had heard of this practice before. It was done so they wouldn't steal the cocaine and hide it in their clothing. There were four card tables set up, covered with black plastic tablecloths. Large bags of the white powder sat atop them, alongside boxes of baggies and small weighing scales. One man was inside the room. He sat in the far corner at a table containing stacks of bundled money. He was on his feet, a phone in his hand, but he dropped it and ducked down behind the table and got off a shot at Novak. Novak hit the floor, too, and stayed down as he fired back. His first slug hit the guy in the shoulder, spattering a swath of blood on the wall behind him. The second one hit his upper thigh. The man screamed in agony and dropped his weapon, clutching his bleeding leg as he groaned and writhed.

"Clear," Frank yelled from the hall.

The women had stopped yelling now, huddling together and hiding their faces and attempting to cover themselves with their hands. The odor of gunpowder and smoke hung in the air, thick and caustic. Novak walked over to the wounded man and shoved him onto his back with his foot. He picked up the phone and made sure he hadn't gotten off a call for help. He hadn't.

The man on the floor was middle-aged, somewhere in his late forties perhaps, heavyset with a beer belly and a bushy, unkempt black beard. He had not been there to stand up against armed intruders. He was a money counter and overseer. He looked terrified and clutched his bleeding wounds. He started pleading for his life in a heavy Irish accent. Novak kept his weapon centered on his chest and motioned the women outside where Lori was waiting in the hallway. Novak looked down at the money counter. A leather-pronged whip was hanging off his belt.

"Where are the girls you traffic? Tell me where you keep them, and I won't kill you."

The man kept shaking his head, but Novak was pretty sure his fear had more to do with what Hennessey would do to him if he revealed anything to Novak. When he answered Novak, he was breathless, his words coming out between groans of pain. "You just...made a big mistake, man. Timmy's gonna come after you.... He's gonna cut off your head."

Frank appeared in the doorway. "The other bedrooms are empty. Sleeping quarters, it looks like."

Novak frowned. This guy wasn't going to tell them anything. He let Frank hold the man at gunpoint while he returned to the hall. The guy he'd put down with the bat was having trouble breathing, but Lori had prodded him up onto his feet. Novak pushed him against the wall and jabbed him in the stomach with the end of the bat. The man doubled over, gasping and holding his belly, and collapsed down on his knees. "You tell Hennessey that Judge Locke didn't appreciate his visit the other night. You got that?"

The man groveled on the floor, holding his stomach and retching.

"Tape him up," Novak told Lori. He walked back inside the bedroom and looked down at the wounded bean counter. "What's that whip for?"

No answer. Now he was weeping like a woman and begging for mercy.

"He beats us with it!" cried one of the girls. She had an accent, too, but hers sounded Chinese or Korean.

That did it for Novak. He clubbed him in the back of the head with the bat and put him down. He was still breathing.

Frank was already herding the women down the hall. Novak followed them and watched as they cowered together against the wall. "These guys traffic women. Are you part of that? Do they sell you?"

That brought a bunch of frightened sniveling and weeping and shaking of heads. They were all Asian, young and fresh-faced, probably shipped to the States from China and Hong Kong. They kept their eyes averted, terrified to look at him. Finally the boldest one peeked out at him and garnered enough courage to speak. "We bag...powder for man. He make us." Her words were hard to understand. The others continued to tremble and moan and press together under the threat of their guns.

"They don't make you go with men for sex?" Lori asked the girl, not one to beat around the bush.

The frightened girl shook her head but still wouldn't meet their eyes. "We not good. We not pretty."

"You got clothes to put on in here somewhere?"

Timid and shaking, she pointed a finger at a bedroom down the hall, eyes downcast, still afraid to look at him.

"Lori, take them in there and get them dressed." Then he spoke again to the frightened women. "Listen up, all of you, you need to get the hell out of here and never come back. You got that? Understand? Get out of this town as fast as you can, or they'll find you. Do you understand what I'm saying?"

The woman who had spoken before nodded and spoke rapidly to the others in what sounded more like Cantonese than Mandarin. He understood enough to know she had translated what he'd said. After that, Lori hastily herded them off down the hall.

"Frank, we're taking that product off their hands; the cash, too."

Novak followed Frank inside the money room. The guy on the floor was unconscious. Novak found his car keys in his pants pocket. He gathered up the bundles of hundred-dollar bills and headed back to the bedroom. The girls were getting dressed, and he tossed a bundle to each girl. "Take this cash and get out of town as fast as you can. Don't stop driving until you reach the next state. Don't ever come back here." He turned to the girl who'd spoken before. "These are the keys to the black car sitting on the front driveway. Can you drive?"

She nodded her head vigorously.

Novak wasn't so sure she was telling the truth, but he hoped she was. "Take the car and get the hell out of here right now."

Shocked into silence, they all just stood there and stared at the money in their hands.

"Go on, get out of here! You're free! Don't come back. Go!"

That did the trick. They sprinted down the hall and fled out the front door.

Frank came out of the bedroom. "There's probably a hundred thousand dollars in here, maybe more. I got those guys' billfolds and the keys to that panel van out front."

"Good, we'll take it with us. It might come in handy down the line. Gather up the rest of the money and all the cocaine you find. Lori, you search for business records or tally sheets or anything else we can hand over to Leslie. I'm going to tape up the guys who're still alive. Make it quick. We've already been here too long."

Novak left them searching through the bedrooms and walked through the living room to the front door. It was standing wide open. He searched the street. Their shots had been muffled, but the thugs' gunfire was not. If somebody had heard them, he'd have to deal with that. The neighborhood was dark and quiet. One porch light had come on a good distance down the street, but moments later it went off. Nobody came outside to investigate, but that didn't mean they hadn't called the cops. The four women had piled into the Lexus and were backing out of the driveway. The driver kept hitting the brakes and jerking the car to a stop. She hadn't driven much, if at all, but was getting the job done. They finally took off, the car weaving around at first but gaining better control as they rounded the far corner a good distance down the street and went out of sight. Novak picked up the can of gasoline Lori had left on the front porch. He walked back inside, and he and Frank dragged all of Hennessey's thugs out into the grass and dropped them back a good distance from the house. Two were dead, and two were wounded but would live. He wanted them left alive to tell Hennessey what had gone down.

If Novak got lucky, Hennessey would take the bait and pin the drug heist on Locke. If they turned on each other, Novak's job taking them down would get a hell of a lot easier. Back inside, they gathered up the cocaine in a duffel bag, splashed gasoline around the living room, and trailed it out a good distance to the backyard. Throwing the can aside, he struck a match, dropped it, and watched the fire streak through the kitchen door, wanting the house to burn to the ground in a nice little pile of ashes for Hennessey to pick through. It was their first volley over the bow, and there would be plenty more to come.

They stole the white van. They backed it out and dropped Lori off beside the Jeep. At the first intersection, Novak called the fire department and an ambulance on a burner phone and then tossed it out the window. By the time they were a mile from the burning house, several sirens were shrieking toward the fire. Novak turned the van and headed for the next house on his list with Lori following right behind them. The raids had just begun but had started out in spectacular fashion.

Chapter 18

They wreaked havoc for the rest of the night. The second house they burned to the ground was right off Fairmont Parkway near San Jacinto College Central, followed by one in Golden Acres off Vista Road. All turned out to be drug houses, much like the first one; so were Novak's fast brutal takedowns. All had girls forced to measure and package Hennessey's drugs, mainly cocaine and weed; another house handled only pills, including oxycodone, crystal meth, uppers, downers, you name it. Hennessey had a big operation going on in east Houston and was raking in a ton of money with his illicit drug trade. A nice chunk of that money was now in Novak's hands. Apparently shocked that anyone had guts enough to attack them on their home turf, guards were almost too easy to take out. Most came out wounded but still alive. Hennessey might be a bad dude, but the people manning his workforce were no better than the judge's flunkies. They had grown complacent, no doubt believing their own violent reputations. Their hired guns did well against poor and helpless victims, but put them up against three trained military veterans and it didn't turn out so well.

House by house, guards ended up bound and gagged and laid out in nice neat rows behind blazing houses, just like their heads would be lined up once Hennessey found out he was now missing his ill-begotten cash and product. They had one place left to smash up, and Novak hoped to God they would find Lucy Caloroso there, because they hadn't found her or any other preteen girls yet. This next place was on West Harris Avenue in Pasadena. It turned out to be larger, better guarded, and more isolated. Maybe they had found the crown jewel of Hennessey's criminal empire.

They parked the van a good way down the street and proceeded up on foot through a wooded area. This place turned out to be a warehouse, small but surrounded by parking lots on all four sides. The structure was set apart from a couple of smaller buildings that could possibly house offices, but most of them were dark and boarded up. Lori told Novak it looked like the place she'd been held captive in New Orleans. Now she was getting some payback for the abuse she suffered at these guys' hands, and that payback was about to get a little sweeter. Hennessey's operations were going downhill as fast as a runaway stagecoach on an icy slope.

Two white panel vans identical to the one they'd stolen were parked outside the front near a well-lit exterior door. There were three additional street doors, one on each side of the warehouse, so there were four altogether, plus several truck doors to unload cargo. The property was more secure than the houses they'd destroyed, enclosed all around by a twenty-foot-high fence topped with razor wire. The gate was held together with a heavy steel chain and industrial lock.

Before they moved out to the fence, they searched for surveillance cameras along the roof but didn't see any kind of security other than the locked gate. Novak found that hard to believe. No guards posted on the outer perimeter made little sense to him, not in Hennessey's line of work. The judge had better security at the mansion, and it had been piss-poor. Novak took a giant mental step backward and appraised the situation. Maybe Hennessey really was overconfident, considering he murdered all competitors and scared off everyone else with body mutilations and bloody decapitations. Hennessey probably had a good part of the Houston police officers paid off. Possibly Jonathan Wagner's organization backed him up with men and business connections. This last place could be a trap. Even so, Lucy might be inside, so they had to go in.

Once they were in place behind the complex, Lori stood lookout while Novak ran to the base of the fence and climbed to the top. He threw a quilt over the razor wire, pulled himself over, and jumped down to the ground inside. Frank came up and over right behind him. Nobody appeared to challenge them. He ran across to the back side of the building. He could see dim lights in some high windows, indicating somebody could be inside or it could be night-lights. The question was: How many men were in there? The back door was locked.

Novak waited for Frank to reach him and then took a couple of bracing breaths, fully aware odds were against them this time. His gut told him they were about to run into a fight. It didn't appear that any alarms had been set off. He was almost positive that nobody escaped their previous raids that night in time to call a warning in to the boss. Hopefully, Hennessey thought all was well in his world and was sleeping peacefully in his bed.

Novak retrieved a short crowbar from his backpack and used it to knock the lock off the door. Inside, he found only darkness. He and Frank stepped inside, weapons ready. Down to one side, a ceiling spotlight faintly illuminated the corridor, maybe twenty feet distant. The door at the end stood open. No lights there, either. Novak used hand signals to point Frank down an adjacent hallway to check out the rest of the rooms in the office wing while he moved cautiously down to the door that led out into the open floor of the main building. Inside, the overhead lights were off, but there were a few lit on the perimeter, enough for him to see a man running straight at him with an AR rifle. When he saw Novak, he stopped in his tracks and fired a barrage at him. Novak ducked as the bullets started pinging off the wall behind him. He took cover behind the steel door and waited for the guy to reload. When the gunfire ended, he was closer to Novak's position. Novak glanced down the hall. Frank was nowhere to be seen.

Seconds later, he heard a distant burst of answering fire, followed by a back and forth series of shots. When that firefight died away, he darted a quick look and found Frank standing just outside a door at the other end of the office hallway. Two men were sprawled out in the middle of the warehouse floor. Novak breathed easier until he caught movement high above them on a catwalk. He opened fire, and when Frank followed suit, the third guard went down. Novak and Frank kept behind cover, waiting for the second wave, but no shouts echoed in the distance. No footsteps came running. No gunshots. All quiet.

Novak stepped back out onto the warehouse floor. He signaled Frank to separate and approach from the opposite side. When he found a light switch panel on the wall, he started flipping on the overhead lights. One by one they flashed on and illuminated the interior. It was not a packaging operation like the others had been. It appeared to be empty, just a big empty room with nothing in it. Afraid to take that for granted, he eased up to the heavy gray plastic curtain hanging across what appeared to be a truck alcove. He lifted the side edge with his rifle barrel and shined a flashlight inside. He found another big empty room, but this one had three truck doors, all of which were closed. Then he spotted the large shipping container positioned on the side adjacent the doors. His hope took a giant leap. Maybe they'd finally hit pay dirt. Frank had come to the same conclusion and was already running toward it. Novak followed him more slowly, covering him and watching the doors and the catwalk. When he got there, Frank had already thrown the bolt and was pulling open the doors. That's when the foul odor hit them.

They both staggered back, gagging on a thick stench of urine and human feces and vomit and unwashed bodies and cold sweat of fear. He swept his flashlight around the interior and stopped on a group of young girls sitting together in one corner. Trembling, they were hiding their faces like all the other women they'd set free that night. They were all in terrible condition, starvation-thin and wearing dirty, ragged nightgowns. They darted quick looks over their shoulders at him and moaned when he focused the light on their faces. None of them looked older than fourteen or fifteen.

"Lucy's not in here, damn it, she's not here!" Frank paced several steps away, cursing and shaking his head.

Novak kept his eyes on the frightened girls. He gentled his voice as much he could. Judging by their looks alone, these girls had been through hell. "It's okay, don't be afraid," he said to them. "We're not going to hurt you. We're here to help get you back home to your family. Come on out. I'll help you. You're free now. Your guards are dead."

They didn't believe him. They just huddled there together, embracing one another and making these low pitiful moans. They were listening, though, and they were beginning to have hope. They didn't trust him; they probably wouldn't trust any male ever again. When he heard running footsteps out on the floor, he spun around, but it was Lori.

She stopped in front of him and peered into the shipping crate. "Is Lucy in there? Did you find her?"

"No, not Lucy, but these girls need help. Think you can get them to come out of there?"

"I can try."

Novak turned to Frank. "C'mon, Frank, pull it together. We've got to get these kids out of here. Maybe they know where Lucy is." That faint ray of hope knocked Frank out of his disappointed tirade. He returned to the open doors.

There were eight girls in that nasty place. None of them wanted to get out of that crate or cooperate. Novak understood that. He told Frank to stand back and let Lori convince the terrified girls they meant them no harm.

Lori now took charge. "I got this, Novak. Back away and try not to look so big and intimidating."

For once Novak was glad to have her call the shots. He gave her a quick boost up inside that awful prison. The stink inside was horrendous. Lori ignored the smell and moved back where she could squat down a few feet away from the scared girls. She started talking softly in a soothing voice. Novak couldn't hear what she was saying, but he could see they were listening. After several minutes, a couple of the girls shifted out of their protective circle and whispered answers to her questions. Whatever she was saying was doing the trick. She helped them stand up one at a time and lead them to the door where they allowed Novak to lift them down out of that hellhole. But they all cringed when his hands were on them and stepped back away from him once their bare feet touched the cold concrete floor. They looked weak and sick and starved and dehydrated. They could barely walk on their own without collapsing. He needed to find them drinking water and quick. He sent Frank on that mission. Moments later, he yelled at Novak from the office wing. The girls looked worse outside in the bright light. All of them had dark bruises and cuts and scratches on their bodies, but they obeyed Lori and followed her to the office where they found a small kitchen with a big side-by-side refrigerator. Inside it was a box of stale Subway sandwiches alongside a good stock of bottled water and Cokes. He doled the food out to the girls, who were huddled together on the floor again, like stray puppies trying to keep warm. Shadowed, fear-filled eyes darted from Novak to Lori to Frank, but they gobbled down the food and guzzled the water. It was an awful thing to watch.

After a few minutes and much too long for Novak's nerves, they began to settle down. Most of them had stopped crying. Novak sat atop a desk a good distance away and tried not to look at them. He watched the door instead. Those kids were more comfortable with Lori. She was good with them. All Novak wanted at the moment was to get them the hell out of there. "Lori, we need to get going. More men could come in here any minute."

"I know. Just let them eat first. They're starving."

Novak turned to the girls where they were sitting on the floor. Now they would look at him. "You're going to be okay. We're taking you somewhere safe, and then we'll get your parents to come get you."

They stared at him. By the looks on their faces, none of them believed him. They had been worn down by physical abuse and deprivation and weren't quite able to believe anything good could happen.

"Look, I know how scared you are. You've been through hell, but you've got to answer some questions. You were held here against your will. Why? Who locked you in that container? Please, tell us what we need to know. There may be other girls in other places that need our help."

Nobody answered; most looked away. They weren't going to tell him a damn thing.

He tried again. "Please talk to us. We're not the ones who locked you in here. We're their worst enemy. We want to stop them from doing this, so please, help us do that."

Sitting silently, they watched him but avoided eye contact.

"Did they make you go with men?"

Not a peep.

Lori took over. "He's okay, girls. Tell him so we can get out of here before they come back."

That did it. She had a golden tongue. One of them spoke very softly. "They told us we had to be with men, but we fought and screamed, so they beat us. Then they brought us in here and locked us in that thing and told us we couldn't come out until we did what they said."

Novak could feel his muscles tensing. He wanted to take Hennessey down himself, preferably up close and personal and with extreme prejudice. He would enjoy it. The man was a monster. All of them were monsters.

Lori continued to comfort the girls, putting her arms around them, and that did appear to calm them down. Frank had been watching from the door, but he moved up closer. Novak decided he needed to contact Leslie and turn these poor girls over to her, but first things first. He needed answers. Frank beat him to the pertinent questions.

"Did they keep you all together the whole time? Were there other girls around?"

They didn't answer him.

Novak hesitated, and then he took the picture of Lucy out of his billfold, held it up in front of them. "This is important. That man over there." He pointed at Frank. "This is his daughter, and they've still got her. Did you see her anywhere? Her name's Lucy. They kidnapped her out of her own house in Galveston. She's just thirteen, even younger than most of you."

One of them leaned up and peered at the photograph. She shook her head. Then another girl took a look and said, "I saw her once. She was inside a van with me when they brought us to this town. She was tied up, but the rest of us weren't. They had tape over her mouth so she couldn't talk to us."

A third girl spoke up. "Where are we? Are we still in Alabama?"

"No, you're in Houston, Texas, but we're going to get you back home as soon as we can."

Frank couldn't contain his excitement. It was the first time anybody had seen or known anything about Lucy that entire night. "Do you know where she is now? Any of you? Please, please tell me, if you know anything that'll help me find her."

Most of them shook their heads, but only one girl answered him. "I know they took her away. But she's okay cause they wouldn't let the guards touch her or anything. They kept her separate from all of us." Her voice broke on her next words. "But they let them hurt us. They said nobody could hurt her." She sobbed, and several of the other girls joined in.

Novak glanced at Frank. His face had relaxed some. He was relieved, but Novak wasn't. Hennessey could use Lucy for payback. They had to find her before he made an example out of her, because he was pretty sure that was going to happen. Novak had miscalculated. He had counted on finding her in one of Hennessey's drug houses. Now, wherever Lucy was, Hennessey would move her to a secure place or just kill her.

Outright blackmail was the only option Novak had. Maybe he could ask Hennessey to hand Lucy over in return for the stolen cocaine and cash they'd taken from him. They might get her back unharmed if the crime boss wanted his profit more than he wanted to hurt Frank's kid. Novak needed to contact Hennessey. Then he had to convince him that if Lucy got hurt, Novak would burn every single dollar of his drug money, one hundred-dollar bill at a time.

He walked a short distance away and dialed Leslie Taylor's number. When she picked up, he told her he had more potential witnesses who could testify against Timothy Hennessey and his men. He told her the kids needed immediate FBI protection and an escort home to their families, most of which were probably out of state. Leslie wasted no time agreeing and gave him directions to the nearest safe house.

"You are definitely exceeding my expectations this time, Novak," Leslie told him. "Maybe you should consider joining the Bureau."

"I got my fill of following orders in the military."

"Yeah, tell me about it. Well, I am impressed, that is, if you don't end up dead or tortured to death before sunrise. Hennessey's going to be gunning for you with everything he's got, and he's got a lot. You do realize that, right?"

"He doesn't have as much as he had this afternoon."

She laughed but immediately cut off her amusement. "You are alive with your head still attached. That's saying something with the guys we're dealing with. Just get those girls over to that address ASAP. What are you driving? I'll alert the guy there to be waiting for you. Will they cooperate with us? Are you sure?"

Novak described the white van. "I think so, given time to settle down and get over their trauma. They've been beaten and abused and starved, and they're worn down. They'll need kindness, and I mean a very soft touch. Can you do that?"

"Of course."

"Are you staying there with them?

"Maybe for a little while, but they'll be fine. I'm staying at the safe house with Judith and her kids for the next few days. She and I have a lot to talk about and get down in writing. Any luck with Lucy?"

"She wasn't here, but we'll find her."

A short pause ensued, then she asked, "Have they pimped her out yet?"

Novak flinched at the cold bluntness of the question. "Doesn't sound like it. One girl said Lucy was treated better and kept apart from them. That is helping Frank cope, at least right now."

"Thank God. So Caloroso's under control?"

"He's doing all right."

"I feel for him. I know you'll find Lucy, sooner or later. I take it you're planning to blackmail Hennessey."

If nothing else, Leslie had always been astute. "You're better off not knowing what I'm doing next."

"Better not get me fired or demoted again, Novak. I knew you were trouble when you walked up to my door."

"Hope not. I'm gonna owe you big-time for what you're doing."

"Yes, you are, but I'll collect those favors when we get Lucy back and indict Locke and Hennessey, and if and when my promotion goes through."

Novak clicked off, a bit concerned with what she expected in return. However, that was the least of his worries at the moment. After that, they wasted no more time. They herded the girls outside and into one of the white vans in the parking lot. Novak had taken keys off a dead guard, and once Frank and Lori had the girls in the van, he ran to the front gate and pried the lock off with his crowbar. Lori stopped the van and picked him up.

Novak was well aware that the FBI had safe houses scattered all across Texas and every other state as well. This one happened to be situated in a suburb called Sugar Land, a neighborhood where median incomes were substantial, and so were the homes, yards, pools, trees, and garages. All was kept nice and neat and hunky dory and safe from crime, or so they thought. Lots of yuppies surrounded by chic designer decor and bottles of imported French wine. Most residents would be shocked to know what went on in one pale yellow house inside a small forest grove and a surrounding wall dripping with ivy.

Vehicles were admitted through a motorized iron gate affixed with cameras, not particularly unusual in the neighborhood. It conveniently opened on its own when Novak stopped in front of it. He drove the van inside and took the driveway around to the back. Leslie Taylor and three other agents met them, two men and one other woman. A few girls still believed they were being moved out of that shipping container to be prostituted. A few started crying. Lori tried to reassure them, but they weren't buying it.

The minute they pulled to a stop, Leslie came forward and took charge, which was one of her good qualities. She was efficient, if nothing else. She was dressed in a black pantsuit and a light blue blouse with a buttoned down collar. She quickly assigned the girls to the waiting agents, after which they were hustled into the house through a back door. No one said a word, just hurried along, no sound anywhere except for shuffling footsteps on the concrete patio. Muted traffic sounds echoed in the distance, but there were no bird calls, no cricket cheeps, nothing but dead silence. It was a quiet place to live or to hide.

Leslie looked up at Novak. "We need to talk."

"Yeah, I figured."

Novak retrieved the packet he'd taken from Judge Locke's office and followed her back across the yard to what appeared to be a large guesthouse. Inside, it looked like a NASA control center for a 1960s moon launch. He glanced at Leslie.

"Yes, we do use this place a lot," she answered without his asking the question. "I trust you, or you wouldn't have gotten through that gate. What's in that packet? More evidence, I hope?"

"Everything you need to take down Judge Locke. I'm still working on Hennessey. I think the judge will turn evidence against him once you get him behind bars and sweat him."

Leslie appeared dubious. "Yeah? Show me. Better yet, tell me how you got this stuff?"

"I stole it when I took Judith out. How's she doing?"

"She's fine. We're still sorting through the documents she turned over. She and the children are settled in a house similar to this one in a location that will remain undisclosed to you or to anybody else. My agents are telling me that all of them are doing all right. Nervous, maybe. Now, time to answer my questions."

"You'll find that journal has some interesting facts about his association with some of the criminal networks he does business with. He names names. That should be helpful in your other cases."

Leslie took the packet from him, opened the clasp, and pulled out the papers. She spread them out across the table. She took several minutes to examine them, and then she turned to Novak. "This will put those guys away for good."

"That's what you wanted, right?"

"Exactly. How can I use this in court if you stole it?"

"You'll think of a way. Say Judith took it out to prove her case. Or tell them it came to you anonymously or somebody left it in your car. That usually does the trick. I'll testify once we get Lucy out of their hands. They'll kill her if they know we involved the Feds. They might, anyway. They're going to figure out who we are, sooner or later."

Leslie didn't look all that happy with his suggestions, but Novak knew she would find a way to get the evidence into court. She always did. "Okay, Novak, but it would be better if you get Lucy to testify alongside these girls. That would put the last nail in Locke's coffin for kidnapping a minor. You need to let me know as soon as you get word on her location. We can help you go in. I'm fond of that girl. I want to help."

"Maybe. We'll see."

"You don't trust anybody, do you?"

"I trust Frank."

Ten minutes later, Novak was on his way back to Frank's cabin. When they left the safe house, the rescued girls were already being bathed and dressed in clean clothes and set up with dinner and a cellphone with which to call their families. Once back at the cabin, the three of them sat around the table once more, pretty much silent and exhausted. All of the cell phones, money, and records they'd confiscated sat on the table in front of them. Novak was thinking about what the children held by Hennessey, now and in the past, had been forced to do. He thought about the girls they hadn't found yet and what was being done to them. The mental images were hideous. He was now willing to do whatever it took to smash the trafficking ring.

One of the confiscated phones rang just before dawn. All three of them sat up straighter. Novak found the phone and clicked on but said nothing. He listened.

An angry voice came from the other end. The Irish brogue was so thick Novak could barely understand him. "What the hell's going on? Is everything okay out there? Somebody's been hitting us hard all over the place."

"Yes, we did hit you hard, and we enjoyed the hell out of it."

Dead silence. "Who is this?"

"You are Timothy Hennessey, I presume?"

"Who are you? What do you want?"

"Not too awfully bright, are you, Hennessey?"

"Who the fuck are you? You're a dead man, you hear me?"

"I'm a guy who doesn't like you or your line of work."

"You are going to regret this night for the rest of your life. I swear to God I'm going to find you."

"I doubt that. Know what? I've got a huge pile of your cash just sitting right here, all bundled up in nice neat stacks, not to mention most of your cocaine. You want it back? You're gonna do exactly what I tell you to."

Hennessey's voice got tight. He was so angry his voice shook. "You are dead. We will find you and take your head and put it on a spike, along with anyone who helped you rob me."

"I don't scare as easily as little girls do, Hennessey. How about I send you my favorite video of me burning all your cash, one bill at a time? Or maybe I could film it when I turn all your cocaine and pills and documents over to FBI agents."

He sounded taken aback. He got quiet, real quick. "What the hell do you want?"

"I want Lucy Caloroso back, untouched and unharmed. I mean not a scratch on her, not a chipped fingernail. I want you to tell your buddy, Judge Locke, to rescind his warrant on Frank Caloroso. You do both of those things, you just might see your money again. Deliver the girl to the Houston FBI office by tomorrow morning, or you'll get to watch that video and see your money going up in smoke. After that, we'll talk about the children you're selling for sex."

"And if I don't?"

"Then you can kiss this cash goodbye. I don't know how much I have, maybe three mil and fifty kilos of coke. No skin off my nose. I've already burned some of it, just because I can and want to put the screws to you. I can do that again. Or, lots of charities around here will love that kind of money if I decide not to burn it. Your choice. Not much of one, though."

Hennessey couldn't get any words out. His voice was shaking with rage. "I'm gonna find you and every single person with you and anybody you've ever loved. I'm going to enjoy slicing their skin off, strip by strip, inch by inch. And then I'm going to dig your guts out with my knife while you scream for mercy."

"That's scary talk, but I'm pretty sure you won't do any of that. What you're going to do is exactly what I said, or face the consequences. Oh, and by the way, in case you don't know it, the judge is double-crossing you big-time. I've got the evidence to prove it."

Novak hung up on him. Lori and Frank stared at him. Frank looked hopeful for the first time.

Lori looked skeptical. "You think he'll go for it?"

"He better, or we'll start making videos so he can watch us burn up a small fortune. He's too greedy to chance it. You two need to get some sleep, because this thing is just starting. I'll take first watch, just in case they track us here somehow. I disabled the phones, but we can't take any chances, not after tonight."

They talked a bit longer, and then Lori and Frank collapsed into bed. Novak walked outside and down to the river dock. He sat down in the stern of his boat and kept an AR rifle lying across his lap. He was waiting for all hell to break loose, because he knew it would sooner or later. No doubt about it. He hoped a gang war would break out and the bad guys would kill each other off. Problem was, hell didn't break loose the way he wanted.

Chapter 19

Somewhere in his mind, Novak knew he was dreaming. It was the same dream he had every night. He was back in New York, working his NOPD shift, standing and staring up at a burning skyscraper until it started to collapse with his wife and children trapped inside. All around him, there was pandemonium in the streets; everyone was screaming and running for their lives, shrieks of terror and horror filled the air. Then the agony hit him and twisted up his heart until he felt he would die. That's when the dream shifted to Bonne Terre, and he was sitting on the porch swing with his beautiful Sarah, holding her hand and watching their children play. He felt himself relax until somebody grabbed his arm. Awake instantly, he shot up, fists balled and ready to fight. But it was only Lori Garner standing beside his bed. She was shocked at his violent reaction, and Novak didn't want to explain, so he looked away.

"You need to see this, Novak. It's terrible," she said.

He looked back at her, his heart still racing as he tried to shake off the effects of the nightmare. That's when he heard Frank in the other room, sobbing. He stood. "What happened?"

"They got Judith." Lori's voice sounded shaky. "It's all over the news."

Novak couldn't quite comprehend what she was getting at. "What do you mean they got her?"

"Local news isn't reporting Judith's dead, but I recognized her. There's no mention of little girls, so I'm hoping they're all right. I think one of the victims is your FBI friend, Leslie Taylor. Hennessey or Locke must've found the safe house. Frank's terrified Lucy's dead, too."

"What victims? How many?" Novak stood up and walked out into the living room where Frank stood in front of the television set. There was a grisly scene on the screen. It wasn't the yellow house where they'd left those abused young girls last night. He'd never seen this house before, but it looked similar in size and was also walled off from the street. The filming looked to have been done around sunrise. Police cars were parked everywhere on the street, flashing lights rotating, cops milling around. Three ambulances and a fire truck were lined up inside a security barricade blocking off the street several houses away. The newscaster was reporting that they were about to air a disturbing video they had obtained from a freelance photographer who got to the scene before the cops arrived. They issued a solemn parent advisory and started the gory clip.

Novak stepped closer as the guy's camera zoomed in on the front gate. His stomach muscles clenched when he realized the victims' decapitated heads were displayed on the fence spikes. The news station had blurred the faces, but Novak could recognize one head by the short and distinctive spiked-up white hair. Just like Judith Locke's. It had to be. He tasted bile, burning at the back of his throat. He couldn't believe his eyes at first. Timothy Hennessey had somehow found her; he felt positive he was the one behind these murders. He looked for Leslie Taylor's long black hair, because she was probably dead, too, and he found it. He could see that silver clip she wore in her hair, despite the blurred focus. The other victim appeared to be man, probably another FBI agent. That was confirmed a minute later when the television returned to the shaken, excited voice of the first reporter to arrive on scene. Novak forced down a swallow. "But they didn't find Susie and Sammi?"

Lori shook her head. "They haven't said anything about little kids, but they probably wouldn't, not yet. They did say the victims had been disfigured with acid, and there were decapitated bodies inside the house with other victims, but they aren't releasing names until they're identified and their families notified. More FBI agents showed up a while ago and took over the investigation from HPD. They haven't given out much information except that there's another decapitated female body on the driveway. Apparently, they haven't found her head. They think the killers took it with them for some reason. Quantico's all over this, and more agents are en route. Hennessey's gone too far this time. Reporters are mentioning his name as having the same method of murder. They think it's the act of several perpetrators who somehow caught the agents off guard. The killers left one of their own behind, and the police hope that once they identify him, that will lead them to the others."

Novak turned away when the newscast went to commercial. He felt sick inside. It couldn't be; not Leslie. He didn't want to believe it. How could this have gone so wrong? "This doesn't make sense. Hennessey wouldn't do something this stupid until he gets his drug money back. We haven't even had time to negotiate terms. This whole thing stinks to high heaven."

Caloroso's face was ashen. "Lucy could be dead inside that house. They said there were victims inside. He killed her because you threatened him. That's why he did it."

Novak knew that. His threatening phone call had caused Hennessey's atrocities, all of them. He hadn't expected that outcome. He should have. Hennessey was a sick and cruel man, crazy and unpredictable. He routinely perpetrated horrendous crimes, but this? So many innocent people dead? Leslie had helped Novak, and she had paid the price with her life. Judith had trusted him, and now she was dead, too. All his fault, every person in that house had died because of his decision to bait Hennessey. His fault and his alone. Surging pain and regret hit him so hard for a moment that he couldn't deal with it. He forced the emotion down, not willing to believe Lucy was among the dead. She couldn't be; he couldn't live with that. There was no proof of her death, not yet. "No, Lucy wasn't there. It makes no sense for him to kill her, anyway. Think about it, Frank. Why would she even be in that safe house with Judith and Leslie? She was never there, never with the Feds. She has no connection to Judith's family at all. She wasn't a part of my trade off with Leslie, either. They've got her somewhere else: she's probably being held by Judge Locke. Don't give up yet. We will find her."

"She can identify them and testify to their crimes. They won't risk that." Frank looked up at him, his eyes defeated. He had already given up.

Novak felt the first nibble of doubt about Lucy's being alive. He thrust that dark thought from his mind and tried to figure out why Hennessey had done it. He was already suspected of the murders because it was his known M.O. Was it just a kneejerk, violent reaction to Novak's threats? It was a truly gruesome scene designed to horrify and frighten. He turned back to the television as a news bulletin popped up and showed a second video of a wide tan beach with waves rolling up onto the sand. He listened, fearing whatever was coming at them next.

"A gruesome discovery was made today at Galveston's East Beach when an early-morning beachcomber happened upon a decapitated body that had washed ashore. Police believe the victim is connected to the bloody massacre before dawn this morning that left up to six people dead, including several Houston-based FBI agents. No word yet as to the identity of this latest victim, but it is believed to be a white female of slight height and build. The body was clad in a black pantsuit and blue blouse. That's all we have for you at this time. If anyone has information on the identity of this latest victim or recognizes the clothing, please call the number at the bottom of the screen."

"That's what Leslie had on last night," Lori said.

Novak had personally delivered Judith and her little girls into Leslie's hands, trusting her to be safe and to keep them safe. Now the two women were dead. Still, he couldn't let himself believe those beautiful little girls would be among the victims. "The judge wouldn't have done this. He's not going to kill his own daughter, and he wanted his grandchildren back with him. That's why he took them away from Judith in the first place. If they're dead, he didn't have anything to do with it. They're already blaming Hennessey. Locke's going to go after him for this."

Lori stared at him a moment and then said something he didn't want to hear. "Don't be naïve, Novak. The judge is capable of anything."

That brought him back to the moment. Maybe she was right. Calvin Locke was capable of terrible things, but Hennessey had been enraged when Novak had taunted him. He had accused the judge pointblank of betraying Hennessey's trust. Maybe he killed his daughter in retribution. But how would he find her and where were her children? "Something's very wrong here. None of this adds up. How would either of them find Judith? How did they know she was there? She hadn't been there all that long. Leslie took every precaution. She always does."

"Obviously they've got somebody feeding them inside information," she answered, thinking more clearly than him and Frank at the moment. She seemed almost too calm. Judith had been her best friend. Lori had taken a severe beating while protecting Judith Locke.

Lori was frowning now. "That means they might have info on us, too. I'd say somebody inside the Houston FBI office clued them in. Could Leslie have been double-crossed by a fellow agent? Did she have an enemy inside that she was feuding with?"

Novak considered that idea. "She told me the new SAC in her office sometimes looked the other way, let her do things that weren't exactly up to FBI standards. She's had problems in the past with her performance, but she was hanging in there and hoping that bringing in Judith Locke would put her back in the Bureau's good graces. Damn it, I want to know who betrayed them. Somebody had to."

"Maybe there's something on the videos you took from Locke's safe. You kept them and some of the other stuff, right? Like that derringer you kept. We need to watch them." Lori picked up Novak's backpack and swung it atop the table. She pulled out the surveillance discs and started sorting them by date. Frank stood behind them at the table. She opened her laptop, inserted them, and hit the play button.

The videos were from a security camera atop Locke's garage. After watching for several minutes, Frank leaned close when the film showed two men leaving out of the open doors. They were dragging a young girl between them. As one man stopped to put down the door, their prisoner jerked out of their grasps and sent a quick hard jab to one man's face. They could see the blood spurt out, and he staggered back a bit, grabbing his nose. She took off running, but he was right behind her. He grabbed her under a lamppost, and they grappled in the circle of light it cast down on the pavement.

"Oh my God, that's her!" Frank cried out.

Novak recognized Lucy, too. She was putting up one hell of a struggle, but the two big men easily subdued her. The one she'd slugged shoved her down on the ground, but she kicked at him until they grabbed her legs. They weren't exactly roughing her up, not as much as they could have. All Novak felt was relief. That probably meant they had been ordered not to hurt her under any circumstances. This was the first good news they'd had, but it didn't last long. The taller man slapped her hard across the face, enough that she stumbled to one side and would have fallen if the second guy hadn't grabbed hold of her.

"That bastard, I'm going to kill him, I swear to God, I'm going to kill him," Frank got out through gritted teeth.

Now the other guy was taping her wrists and ankles together. He picked her up bodily and hoisted her over one shoulder. They watched as he carried her to a waiting black Mercedes sitting out on the driveway. One man threw her inside the back seat and got in with her. The other guy, the one who'd hit her, rounded the car and climbed into the driver's seat. That's when Lori got a good look at his face.

"That's Stephen Locke driving that car." Lori hit a button, and they watched it again. "I don't know the guy in the back seat, but it's probably Stephen's bodyguard. I know he has one with him sometimes when he travels."

Frank was just relieved that his daughter was alive and well. "Where did he take her, Lori?"

"I don't know."

Novak said, "Now you know she was okay then, Frank, you saw her yourself. She strong and still has the guts to fight back, even up against Stephen Locke. She's going to keep fighting just like you taught her until she finds a way to escape. They didn't beat her, even after she slugged that guy. Just that one slap was all they did. That means they can't; it's against the judge's orders. That's the best news you could get, Frank. What's the date on that video cam, Lori?"

"Four days ago."

"That doesn't mean she's alive now." Frank could not be consoled, but he was right. Novak feared for her, too.

"It means she was at the judge's mansion at that point but taken somewhere else by his son. She's being given the royal treatment, all right. They're probably keeping her on the move from one location to another so we can't get a bead on her. Chances are she's still with him, wherever he is."

"Well, I know where he's working out of." Lori looked from one man to the other. "He's doing an action movie called *Trapped in Hell*, as pathetic a title as that is. He was filming there when Judith contacted me, so he's probably still out there." She suddenly frowned. "I can't believe Judith's dead. I can't wrap my head around it yet. I thought she was safe and stopped worrying about her. All of this is my fault."

Novak was still thinking about Lucy. "If he took her there, she wasn't in that safe house with the other victims."

"I hope you're right about that," Lori said.

The two men said nothing.

Lori walked away from the table and over to the front window. She stared down at the boat, taking deep breaths to quell her emotions, and then she turned back and faced them. "I read that the film he's on is having all sorts of trouble and is way behind schedule. That means he'll be out in Scottsdale several more months, at least."

"You know him, Lori. You think he'd bother with taking Lucy to Arizona?"

"He would if the judge told him to. When he comes home to Galveston, he flies in and drives that Mercedes you saw. Locke's got a private jet. Sometimes Stephen uses it to fly back and forth. They might use it to move the girls they traffic, too, or drive them in all those panel vans. Either way, no one would be the wiser. Maybe they've got a private airstrip where the owners don't ask questions or are too enamored with Stephen's celebrity to thwart him. He's got a ton of fans. Most of them are crazy young girls that think he's a god."

Once he saw that Lucy was alive only a few days ago and listened to Novak and Lori's optimism, Frank had calmed down considerably. His rage had dissipated into cold, hard determination. "Driving is safer, though. Put them inside one of those vans and nobody sees anything. They could stop at rest stops along the highway and buy them fast food. Either way, Lucy would be alive and unharmed."

"Yeah, and she's still being treated well. Calvin Locke's put her in Stephen's hands. Why would he do that?" Novak considered what that meant. He looked at Lori. "Is she better off with him?"

"He's no angel, but I'd say that means she's off limits to him, too. They've got something in mind for her, probably to barter her for the money, if they know Frank's involved with you. But Judith's dead and so are the FBI agents, so that means they've got the evidence they were going to use to hang them. I hope to hell they don't have it."

"We've got no way of knowing that he took Lucy out of state," Frank said. "She still could be right here in Houston or maybe down in Galveston."

Novak didn't think so. "She's their pawn to control you. It isn't working right now, but she's all they've got. I'd have moved her out of state a long time ago if I had you two coming after me. Locke didn't want her on the estate in case a Federal search warrant came down."

They were quiet a moment, all probably thinking the same thing. They were all in big trouble. But Novak kept thinking about Leslie, about their past together, about how she'd died in such an awful way. He couldn't shake the guilt and remorse that was eating at him. They had been close once, lovers and friends. He cared about her, and his actions had ended her life, one that was just beginning to bloom again. He couldn't stand to think about what they'd done to her and how scared she must have been. The visual image made his stomach twist up in knots. And Judith, poor Judith, who had thought she was finally free to be with her children, only to be betrayed again.

"What now?" Lori asked Novak.

Novak tried to shake off his grief at what he'd done and think about what had to come next. "We go get Lucy. I got Judith out and Leslie involved, and now they're both dead. That's on me, not you," Novak told her. "I don't think the judge would have Susie and Sammi killed, but he could have ordered Judith's death because she was betraying him to the FBI. This is what Calvin Locke wanted, Judith out of the picture and his complete control over her girls. Hennessey would kill them all for little reason. This is personal for me now. I handed Judith over to Leslie, and Leslie was a good friend. She trusted me. They both trusted me, and I failed them. I signed both their death warrants. Somebody's going to pay for this...."

After his admission of guilt, Novak's voice thickened and faltered. He stopped speaking and looked away.

Lori appeared to understand his pain and picked up where he'd left off. "There's nothing else we can do here," she told them. "It's a hot zone now. If Stephen took Lucy to Phoenix to keep us from finding her, maybe Susie and Sammi are out there, too. Stephen's their uncle, after all, and he's got money and influence and probably his own little estate where he can stash them with a nanny until things cool off here."

"Yeah," said Frank. "We've got dead Feds. This town's going to be crawling with FBI agents, and they'll step on us if we get in the way. Stephen does whatever his father tells him, just like Judith did until she wanted out. They'll take Lucy out of state."

Novak realized that Frank was eager to do something, anything. "So let's go out of state. If Stephen's in Phoenix, he won't be expecting us to come after him there. He'll be hanging loose and overconfident, and that works to our advantage."

Frank had already made up his mind. "If Locke ordered his own daughter murdered, he'll eventually get rid of Lucy. We need to go get her now. No more waiting, no more being patient. I'll go by myself, if I have to. I'm not sitting around and doing nothing anymore."

"We've got a DVD with Lucy on Locke's estate getting into a car with Stephen Locke. It came out of his safe so Locke knows we've got it. Killing her would finger him for her murder. He's not that stupid." Novak wasn't sure about what he'd just said, because Locke was unpredictable. On the other hand, Frank needed something to hold on to. More likely a scenario was that Stephen meant to sell Lucy off to some sex trafficker. Besides her being a threat and eyewitness, Lucy was a valuable commodity because of her innocence and red hair and blue eyes, all traits valued in Asia and the Middle East. Lucy had to be his top priority right now. Hopefully, Judith's children were alive and well somewhere in the hands of the FBI. Another option was that the judge had ordered the hits and had the little girls again, hidden away until the heat was off. That's what Novak wanted to believe. He had to.

Chapter 20

Three hours later they were on the first plane out to Phoenix, which happened to be a red-eye deal on a no-name budget airline. The flight was uneventful and bumpy and crowded, especially for Novak's bulk squeezed into the cramped seat. They put down at a small airport in Mesa that was about a twenty-minute drive into Scottsdale. Novak rented a nondescript black van, and they headed off to AZ-101 Loop N and drove through miles of sunny desert with shadowy purple mountains rising up in dark smudges against an amazing blue sky that domed over the vast desert basin. Businesses and corporate high-rises lined parts of the highway, but the traffic was light so they made good time.

A few miles outside Scottsdale, they found a nondescript motel just off the highway. It was no Trump Tower or Ritz-Carlton. It wasn't even up to Holiday Inn Express standards, but it did have beds and a complimentary breakfast. They checked into adjoining double-king rooms. They had no trouble digging out information on where Stephen Locke was filming his new movie. An angsty, black-uniformed teenager behind the check-in counter was obsessed with the guy. She had a tattoo of his face on her arm and said all her friends had matching ones. Then she said the actor was sick, and it was sweet he was in her town. Lori translated that slang-speak because she was on Twitter and used it sometimes, too. It turned out the girl meant Stephen Locke was just super great and she was excited he was filming in Scottsdale. Novak could've figured that out by himself. Too bad she didn't just speak plain English. Her plastic nameplate identified a Ms. Delilah Percy, but she said they could call her Lah for short. She wore her hair in stiff fluorescent waves in a color that sort of resembled magenta. It hung straight to her shoulders in front in a blunt cut but all the way to her waist in back. There was a lot of hair involved. Novak hoped it was a wig, but the roots were black so he didn't think so. She chewed the hell out of a stick of Juicy Fruit gum as they conversed. Her uniform smelled like marijuana, even from across the desk. Her eyes looked weed bleary, too. Novak was pretty sure she was almost as high as a Boeing 757. She was chock-full of information and excitement about Pretty Boy Locke, uttered in a slow, languorous voice.

"Oh, dudes, it's dope. He's smokin' hot and got that scruff goin' on. He takes off that black T-shirt, all I see is that six-pack. Dayum."

Novak wasn't certain her eyes were tracking the way they should. Neither were her brain synapses, it seemed. He worried about the millennials sometimes, couldn't help but be concerned.

"Holy hell, that dude's lit as shit," Lori told Lah.

Novak turned and looked at her.

Delilah beamed a thousand-watt smile back at Lori. They chatted a moment, after which the kid said that Lori could join her and her besties and watch the filming the next afternoon if she hung around that long. Even Novak could figure that meant best friends. Lori was pretty good at the schmoozing fangirl thing. Novak wasn't surprised. He didn't understand half the internet lingo that Lori came up with. He was glad she didn't use it all the time. But they were wasting time.

"So where's he shooting today, Ms. Percy?"

Ms. Percy looked up at him and then at Lori. They laughed at him, having a good time at his expense. Frank had been frowning through the whole conversation. The expression deepened. He wasn't as cool as them, either.

"I gotta see that hotness in person," Lori told the girl, leaning up against the counter. "That jawline with that scruff. I'm with you, girl. I told these dudes I'd die if I didn't get to scope him out while we were here. He's just so freakin' hot." She leaned closer. So did Delilah. "You know how I can crash that set and see him up close?"

Delilah lowered her voice some, looked around for the manager, real serious when it came to Locke. "Don't tell nobody I told you, okay? He's got some guys bodyguardin' him so you can't get in his space, but those dudes will let you go in and watch Stephen act sometimes. Better to go out on the night shoots, though. Stephen does lots of that night stuff. I got to watch him downtown a coupla nights ago, filmin' up on a roof. It was awesome cause he was way up high, running and jumping over stuff and tackling all these bad dudes. He really didn't do that big jump down to the next building, though. The producers won't let him do stuff that messes him up, so he's got this dude who does it for him."

"What? You mean a stunt double?" Novak asked.

She glanced at him. "Sure, anybody knows that." She dismissed him and turned back to Lori. "That stunt double, he's hot as hell, too. He does the car chases and shit. That's when they block off streets and it's easy peasy to sneak in. Best bet, tell them you live behind those set barriers, and they'll motion you right on in. Me and Aimee's done that a bunch of times."

"Wow, awesome. You know where he's at today?"

Delilah rattled off an address and told them in way too much detail how to find it and where to sneak in and the best vantage point to glimpse her hero's dimples and/or awesome abs. The girl came off as a borderline moron. Novak wouldn't find that hard to believe, but she was young. Maybe she'd grow out of it. They took time to drop off their backpacks inside the rooms, and then stopped at McDonald's for coffee and sausage egg biscuits that they ate on their way into Scottsdale. Lots of traffic once they got into the city. They took a left on E. Thomas Road and then a right onto N. Scottsdale Road. The shoot was being done at a steak house/sports bar kind of place called The Tavern. It was located off Via Linda, and its parking lot was taped off, with cops stationed everywhere to protect the star. It looked as if they were expecting the arrival of a presidential motorcade.

Novak found the parking garage Delilah had recommended for a cool bird's-eye view of the action. Once up on the top level, they figured out fairly fast that the action was currently filming inside the eatery so there was nothing yet to see. There were plenty of rubbernecking fans hanging around up there along the wall overlooking the place. A loitering group of teenagers informed Lori that the outside scene was slated to begin soon and that's what they were waiting for. Below, all around the restaurant, throngs of overeager spectators had been herded behind rope lines along the street. Some pushy guy with a bullhorn was ordering them to keep quiet when the cast and crew showed up outside. The roof level was open air with a great vantage point, just like Delilah had promised, but it was also hot as hell and the sun wasn't even high yet. More important to Novak, the parking garage wasn't busy and they could get out fast if things went south.

The world-famous movie star had still not shown up by eleven o'clock. They were standing under a scraggly tree that was crying out for water. The sun burned down on their heads and gleamed off cars in eye-blinding glare. The wind was warm and dry but better than nothing. There were other people up top with them, standing on either side of them, which made Novak distinctly nervous. They kept to themselves except for a few guys who tried to come on to Lori but went away when she ignored them. Finally, after what seemed like hours, a great din arose from below.

Then, lo and behold, the great Stephen Locke decided to make his entrance by roaring up to the restaurant in a jazzy red Jaguar convertible, its top down, his Hollywood coiffure blowing in the wind. He drove with his right hand and held up two fingers in a casual peace sign. Cool, man, cool. He was full of himself, oh yeah. If his fans only knew what he did behind closed doors, this place would be deserted.

Locke the Younger had been born into privilege, albeit with a disgusting pervert of a father and no mother. His fortunes had only gotten better as he jumped into sin and depravity with both feet. No one was in the car with him to steal his thunder at that triumphant entrance. He drove around to a reserved spot at the front of the restaurant, parked, and swung out of the car with easy athletic grace. Maybe the stunt man taught him how to do it without looking stupid. The teenage girls behind the rope instantly went berserk, crying and laughing and calling out his name. The big man grinned and swaggered over to the closest admirers. Novak watched him a moment and loathed him instantly.

"His teeth are blinding me," Frank muttered, sweating profusely in the heat. He wiped off his brow with a forearm.

"They're dental implants," Lori informed them. "I remember the day he got them. He was sick in bed for a week. Cried and cried from the pain like a big baby. He's nothing but quivering Jell-O under all those muscles and fake machismo."

Stephen was laughing at the hubbub he caused and the efforts to get close to him. He proceeded to blind onlookers with those laser-bright teeth while he took about fifty selfies with pretty young girls. He pulled one lucky girl into his arms and bent her back, and he kissed her on the mouth. Then he posed with her, his chiseled jaw held in mirror-studied effect. Novak wondered how that jaw would look after Novak broke it. He wouldn't feel like taking a selfie, Novak knew that much.

"If that preening peacock bastard hurt my daughter, if he touched one hair on her head, I'm going to murder him with my bare hands. I'm going to break every tooth out of his jaw." Frank's voice promised Stephen Locke would go down with some serious suffering. Okay by Novak. He'd help.

"Stephen's a self-centered prick, and always has been. I haven't told you this, but he sneaked into my bedroom one night at the mansion. I was asleep, but I had to fight him off."

Novak jerked his attention to Lori.

"Don't worry, he didn't get anywhere. He's so unbelievably phony, and he's a misogynist of the worse kind, and Judith told me he's mean and likes to hurt people." She stopped, and they all thought about Lucy. "He seduced a fifteen-year-old babysitter and slapped her face when she struggled to get away."

"Did he hit you?"

"Didn't have the chance. I gave him a nice hard knee where it does the most damage. Funniest thing, once he limped out of my bedroom, he never came near me again. Hope to do that this time, too, or something worse. Yeah, something worse would be better."

"Take a number," Novak told her. Lori's self-defense technique was age-old and had worked for women since time eternal. Still did. "You'll get payback for Judith."

"Yeah, I will. I hope her kids are okay."

"I think they are, and we're going to find them." They were too late for Judith and Leslie, though. Again, Novak's heart twisted with grief for Leslie. She hadn't deserved to die. Stephen and his father had to pay for those crimes, too. And Hennessey.

The movie action eventually spilled out into the parking lot in an overambitious phony fistfight. Dialogue ensued in short pauses between the aforementioned peacock actor and what was supposed to be a couple of bad guys, judging from their black outfits. Probably extras who borrowed their wardrobes right out of Daddy's criminal gang, no doubt, maybe some of Judge Locke's employees moonlighting for sonny boy. The crew took forever setting up cameras and boom mikes while Stephen lounged about in the shade, his assistant hovered around nervously, meeting his needs while the actor waved desultorily at his swooning fans. The big fight finale was coming up. When everything was set up, the director called for action, and who should jump up but Stephen's stuntman, who proceeded to knock the holy hell out of anyone who ventured near, one combatant at a time, of course, as rumbles always went down in movieland. Novak scoffed at that idea. Any bad guys worth their salt would attack from all sides at once and overwhelm a single guy, but he supposed that didn't translate into good cinema.

Meanwhile Stephen drank copious cups of ice water and Diet Coke brought out by several awestruck production assistants while he sat on his name-embossed camp chair and blew kisses to the girls. Everyone else busied around doing that scrawny jerk's work for him. Novak was eager to find out how Stephen performed in a real live fight with actual fists and hard stomps to fragile kneecaps, and/or brass knuckles to handsome noses. Hell, Stephen Locke wouldn't even last two minutes against Lori, bum arm or not.

The choreography of the fight took forever. The stunt guys practiced a bunch of times, lots of run-throughs and multiple takes, over and over again. Stephen was finally called to action, took a couple of swings that didn't come within a mile of his targets, ducked a few blows, and that was it for the day. He went back and sat in the shade in that special tall canvas star chair. Sweat rolled down Novak's face and into his collar. Three hours dragged by, some of which they spent sitting in the air-conditioned van with the motor running.

At long last Locke was done watching people doing his job and leapt athletically back into the driver's seat and drove out slowly through the crowd of his screaming fans. They lined both sides of the street, shouting his name. His sunshades poked back on, his shirt unbuttoned to the waist, Locke gunned the car and sped off down the street. One weeping teenybopper ducked under the rope and ran after him. All in all, it was the stupidest damn spectacle Novak had ever seen in his life.

Within minutes, they were in the van down at street level and on Locke's tail. Novak sped through the traffic until he gained about a four-vehicle length behind the red Jag. He slowed down and shadowed him. Stephen whipped through traffic among BMWs and Cadillacs and Porsches, palm fronds designing lacy patterns of sunlight and shadow on top of his head. Scottsdale appeared to be a prosperous community, a nice secure roost for Stephen to cat about in his shiny automobile while overseeing cruel and inhumane child trafficking in his secret life. Citizens strolled along well-kept sidewalks with well-groomed dogs on fancy leashes, well-mannered rich folks who didn't have a clue what Stephen Locke was doing right under their noses.

Locke finally hung a left into some connecting affluent neighborhoods, streets lined with beautiful homes, most sporting red-tiled Spanish roofs and tall majestic palms and mist-cooled patios and tiny emerald yards behind tall tan stucco walls. Eventually they passed through streets that boasted a big lake colored artificially to a rich deep sapphire blue. Lori called it Lake Serena at Scottsdale Ranch. It was a lovely place to live, no doubt about it. Beautiful homes were built along its shoreline on lots of private inlets that acted like cul-de-sacs but were made of water. Tall walls between the houses gave privacy from too-close neighbors and hid sparkling pools, hot tubs, and lush beds of climbing bougainvillea and every other sort of flower imaginable. Every kind of palm tree was represented, and each lakeside residence sported its own private boat dock where party barges awaited their owner's pleasure. All in all, it was a veritable lush and splendid Garden of

Eden smack-dab in the middle of a giant, hot, arid desert ringed by those blue humps of low scrub mountains.

Novak remained about a block behind Locke, sometimes pulling over to the curb or waiting a few minutes longer at a stop sign. He did not want the actor to realize he was being followed. They needed the element of surprise to hold up. Locke didn't seem to notice anything, probably too busy staring at his face in the mirror. He drove blithely along until he hung a right off Lakeview Drive into a gated driveway and pulled to a stop in front of a security box. As they passed, he was scanning a security card, and the barred gate was slowly opening. Inside was a real cul-de-sac with maybe five or six houses, the backs of which faced the big lake. All were made of stucco and beautiful, with the garages out front and walled patios guarding the front doors, in case intruders got past that vehicle gate. Sidewalks led up to fancy oversized front doors.

All in all, it appeared to be a safe, affluent, and spotlessly clean place in which to live. No fallen palm fronds or McDonald's boxes could be found littering those curbs, that was for damn sure. Novak wondered if all those nice normal folks living around Locke's house realized he was neck-deep in the sex trafficking of underage girls. Probably way too smitten with Locke's good looks and celebrity status to consider what depravities he might enjoy in his spare time. Privacy was the name of the game nowadays. Maybe that's why Stephen had chosen the lake life.

They drove on and spent some time meandering through the surrounding streets until they found the one that gave them a good view of Locke's backyard. Novak pulled over to the curb and stopped. Across from them, the watery inlet was lined on both sides with lovely homes. There were no empty lots; this lake community was no doubt a coveted place in such an arid landscape. Across the street from the van, a waterfall gushed down into the lake but there were no walls or fences discouraging entry into all those backyards. A short walk across the street, a stroll along the shoreline, and they were behind Stephen Locke's house.

Frank was raring to go, probably this very minute if he had his way. "No problem getting inside his house, but you can bet these homes have top-notch alarm systems, so we've got to be careful."

"I can disarm them, Frank," Lori told him. "I learned to do that when I was sixteen. Super easy."

"So did I," Frank told her.

Me, too, thought Novak. *So getting inside is not going to be a problem.*

Surprisingly, no one stirred inside this lovely Shangri-La in the desert. Nobody sat on any of the outdoor patios, nobody sailed about on the plethora of available party barges, and no one swam in the water. That was probably not allowed. Besides that, they all had pools. Then again, it was winter and late afternoon in Phoenix and hot. Probably not as hot as in the summer, but hot enough for Novak. But it was dry heat, not the humid misery of the Louisiana bayous. Blinds were drawn tight across the windows against the sun, and the air conditioners were trying to keep up. Maybe everyone was at work.

Or, maybe these people didn't have to work, already retired or too stinking rich to have to do anything. Maybe it was basically a retirement community or a conclave for Canadian snowbirds. The lake shimmered with that dark indigo sheen. The lawns behind the houses were miniscule and would take maybe ten minutes to mow. It took Novak four full days to mow the grounds at Bonne Terre, and he had a tractor.

"OMG, look—there he is," Lori said softly, sinking down a bit in the seat.

Novak and Caloroso slouched down, too. Locke had exited his home by a glass slider and was standing on the flagstone patio. He wore some kind of short white terrycloth robe. His place was on the right side of this arm of the lake. While they watched, he slipped off the robe and stepped butt naked into a hot tub at the back edge of his pool. Novak wondered how the residents opposite his place liked that spectacle. Maybe they did. He was a celebrity. Maybe they sold his nude pictures to the *National Enquirer*.

"Nobody lounges around in a hot tub on a hot day in Scottsdale, Arizona," Lori remarked. "Is he stupid, or what?"

"Maybe his muscles ache from watching his stuntman do his work," Frank replied, and yes, it was sarcastic as hell. "Or he puts ice cubes in the water."

They waited a few moments to see if anyone else came outside to join him. Nothing happened. Instead, what they observed was movement at the house next door. A sliding glass door opened, and a man appeared. He had a young woman in tow.

"Lori, you need to snap some pictures of them. I think they're headed over to see our man Steve."

"Better yet, I'll get us a video."

The girl looked plagued by anorexia, her body so skinny it was almost skeletal, but she had long dark hair and a pretty face. She looked around sixteen years old at the most. She wore a black string bikini, but no robe, and her bathing suit had less material involved than one of Novak's bath cloths. The man gripped her elbow in a nasty kind of way and jerked her along with him, but she continued to try to resist, which eventually earned her a slap across her face. He pulled her down to the back wall, and Novak lost sight of them momentarily until they appeared again outside the back gate. Novak lifted his binoculars and focused on the guy. He had never seen him before. They came out onto a grassy area just above the lake and walked next door to Locke's gate. Then they climbed the steps to Locke's patio. The two men spoke for a couple of minutes before the girl was shoved toward the tub. She stepped into the water and sat down beside Locke. He immediately had his hands all over her. Her escort turned away and walked back next door.

Lori was incensed. "My God, what's he going to do to her? Molest her right there in broad daylight in front of the neighbors? No way is she doing this of her own accord. They're forcing her. This is disgusting. We need to do something right now."

Novak agreed with most of that. "Yeah, we do, but we can't intervene yet. We can't prove anything against Stephen. Not with credible evidence. We get that tonight."

"We've got this video."

"Which means nothing if the girl says she's willing, and she will because she's scared of them."

"Meanwhile that girl is left helpless in that tub with him," Lori said, angry.

"We'll get her out, don't worry. Tonight. We just can't do it right now."

Frank was more interested in the setup. "He's got two houses right there, side by side. He must keep girls next door. Lucy might be in there, too. She was last seen with him. I'm not waiting until tonight. Let's go in and knock down his front door. He can't go up against us without his body double to fight us."

Novak became annoyed. His companions lacked something important to him. Patience. Reckless haste ended up with somebody dead. "So you want to barge in right now in the light of day with all the neighbors watching? Do that, and we end up in jail. We don't know how many men he's got in there or in the house next door. For all we know, he may have people in the house on the other side of him, too. We can't be stupid here. We make our plans and hit him at night when he least expects it. We can't stay parked here, either, but we've seen enough to get in there."

His companions lapsed into silence but weren't satisfied with his decision. Novak took off and drove around the lake some more, figuring out the best exit routes if things went sour and working out a plan to rescue any girls they found inside. They'd been lucky so far, but that kind of good fortune never lasted long. After they'd reconnoitered, Novak drove straight back to the hotel. They needed to arm themselves, relax a bit, and wait for dark. After that, Stephen Locke was dead meat.

Chapter 21

Around ten o'clock that night they drove back into Scottsdale proper and cruised around the Lake Serena area. Some homes were dark, but more houses had lights on. Both houses abutting Stephen Locke's place looked deserted, no visible lamps or outside lights to be seen, but the shutters were closed tight, and they were pretty sure the young girl and the goon who'd pushed her around were still inside. It seemed that Stephen Locke was at home. The people living across the inlet from his place had their drapes pulled tight. It was unlikely they were peeking out the windows. Stephen Locke was the only pervert in this kind of neighborhood.

Novak had no qualms about breaking into the house where they were holding the girl. Located right beside the through street, the gushing waterfall would blunt any sounds they made. He'd done similar infiltrations before and under more difficult conditions. This place was tailor-made for intruders with ill intent. There were walls behind which they could conceal themselves if Locke decided to sit outside on his patio. They were good to go and wasted no time getting on with it. They drove the van to a busy community center just down the road and parked among the other cars in the parking lot. Then they walked back as if out on a late-night stroll under the stars. Lori entwined her fingers with Novak's, which he didn't mind in the least. Despite the set of handguns hidden inside the pocket of her hoodie, she played the part of his lover rather well. Novak realized that he was beginning to like her a lot, probably more than he should. She was young and impetuous at times, and there was the ridiculous slang, but she was standup. She'd proved herself to him and to Frank.

Frank walked a couple of yards behind them, armed for bear. He meant business tonight, but they all did. Something about watching that girl forced into that tub with that abusive cretin stuck in Novak's craw. He carried his .45 in a shoulder holster under a navy windbreaker and wore a backpack with four handguns, a ton of ammo, duct tape, and Novak's well-worn lock pick kit. He couldn't wait to get his hands on that snotty little actor. Both his colleagues looked intense and pretty much had bloodlust in their eyes. Novak would not want to be Stephen Locke when they got their hands on him.

Careful to keep within the deep shadows hugging the back wall, they crept along in single file. The first house's gate wasn't locked, so making it to the back patio was a breeze. Frank took his penlight and disconnected the security system in about a minute flat. Novak jimmied the sliding door.

Inside, they were met with pitch black. Utter silence. They cleared the first floor within minutes. No cars were in the garage or outside parked on the street. When they moved up the stairs, they found all the bedroom doors secured with padlocks. That meant these guys were holding multiple prisoners. The rest of the house was clear, so that meant the guards had gone off somewhere. Novak listened a few seconds and then tapped a knuckle softly on the first door. Nobody answered. Not a sound.

"Police, open up," Lori belted out, never known for her patience.

That did the trick. Female voices started yelling inside and beating on the doors. Novak waited for a minute. If guards were there and hidden somewhere, this was when they'd show up. Nothing happened, which was surprising and worrisome. They could come in at any time. Frank was in a hurry. He knocked off the lock with his rifle butt. Inside the first room, they switched on the lights and found three teenage girls who looked well underage. There were two girls in both the other bedrooms. Lucy Caloroso was not among them. They were scared and hungry and crying with relief and edging up on to hysteria, just like the girls in the warehouse had been. Two of them sported black eyes. One had been beaten about the face and neck. Lori herded them into the large master bedroom that stretched across the back of the house, made sure the shutters were closed tight, and turned on a bedside lamp. She stayed there with them, calming them down and telling them they were safe, they were going home as soon as they could get them there.

Frank and Novak left her to that task, more interested in taking out Stephen Locke. They found an upstairs window that looked directly down into Locke's master bedroom. He'd conveniently left the shutters wide open. They could see him well. This guy didn't understand the word modesty. He was primping in the master bath, butt naked, prettying himself up for a night out on the town, no doubt. Fifteen minutes later, he was fully dressed in tight gray pants and a loose white silk shirt and backing the Jag out of the double garage. They waited until he was out of sight and then went outside and through the back gate onto his property.

His patio door had been left unlocked, too, no unwanted violent company expected. All the shutters stood wide open in every room. For a hardened criminal, Locke was either stupid or felt invincible. Probably the latter. They didn't have that luxury, so they snapped the shutters shut and switched off most of the lights. Not long after that, they got some beer out of his fridge and settled down to wait for him to return, where an extremely painful lesson awaited him. They sat in the family room and watched a football game with the sound turned off until they heard a car pull up next door where Lori was still with the girls. Novak put down his beer and stood. "That's the guards. Stay here, Frank, in case Locke comes home. Lori's going to need some help."

As it turned out, Lori did need his help but not as much as he'd anticipated. When he got inside the kitchen and flipped on the light, he could see that she had one guy down on the floor in the front foyer, unconscious and bleeding from the head. The second man was down on his knees, arms up and palms planted on the wall. He looked up at Novak. He was bleeding from his nose and saturating the floor. Spilled fountain sodas and McDonald's sacks were scattered all over the place. Bad news was that Lori sat propped against the opposite wall with blood coloring her arm wound and trickling out of the hairline at her temple. It looked as if she'd been slammed against the wall and then slid down to the floor. But she had her Glock beaded on the conscious guy, and she had his weapon in her other hand. He knelt beside her and took the guy's gun out of her hand. "You okay?"

"Been better. They surprised me. Stitches busted when I hit the wall. How about securing this jerk so I can patch up my arm?" She was clutching her shoulder now, and he could see blood seeping through her fingers. She wasn't finished talking. "The girls upstairs? They're freaking out. They want to get out of here, Novak, because they say more bad guys are going to show up. We need to get them somewhere safe."

"Yeah, I figured that. Hang on while I tape him up, and then we'll take care of that wound."

"Well, hurry it up, Novak. I'm bleeding to death."

That was hyperbole. Novak moved up behind the man facing the wall and clubbed him in the back of the head with his gun butt. The guy crumbled to the ground.

Lori scoffed. "Well, I guess that's one way. I thought I'd question him first, but that's out now."

"I can wake him up if I want to talk." Novak tore off some tape and secured the man's wrists and ankles and mouth. He squatted down beside her again. "Can you stand up?"

"A little help wouldn't hurt."

Novak supported her upstairs to the hall bathroom, found gauze and tape in the cabinet, and cleaned her up as best he could. The wound looked bad; it needed to be sutured again. Lori was pretending it was nothing, but that was an act. A recent surgery incision torn asunder was no scratch and couldn't be taken lightly.

"Take it easy for once and just keep an eye on the girls while I go introduce myself to that guy. Chances are nobody else will show up any time soon. They must do this in shifts."

"They told me these two guys bring them food every night. They said they keep them here to—get this, Novak—to accommodate Stephen's *needs*. That makes me sick to my stomach. He likes to slap them around, too. They said the guards aren't much better. They're using them as personal sex slaves."

Novak didn't answer, but he didn't like anything she'd said. In fact, it made him livid. He left her propped on the bed pillows with the girls gathered around her, all thanking her and trying to make her more comfortable. They were really young kids. He went back downstairs, dragged the two men into the kitchen, and gathered up the spilled food and took it upstairs to the girls. They grabbed the food as if they hadn't eaten in days. "Okay, I'm gonna have a little chat with the guy who knocked you up against that wall. Wait here."

"Aw, you're such a sweetheart, Novak, but don't kill him. We're all civilized at the moment."

"I'm not going to kill him. Frank might, though. Would you stop him?"

"Nope, I wouldn't."

Minutes later, Novak was back in the kitchen. He checked their IDs and found them to be residents of Galveston. From Judge Locke's personal goon army, all right, provided with their own little prison condo in which to exploit innocent young women. He didn't feel sorry for them. He checked outside for movement, front and back, found all quiet and dark. Then he went into the downstairs bathroom and filled the tub with cold water. After that, he sat down at the kitchen table and drank a bottle of water.

The guy Novak put down was the one who'd slapped the girl around the day before. He was covered with vulgar tattoos and body hair. He smelled bad, and his hair was greasy. After a while, he woke up slowly, twitching and moaning under the tape. It took a couple of minutes for him to open his eyes and get his bearings. That's when he remembered Novak. After that, he panicked and tried to wriggle out of his bindings, but Novak kicked him over onto his back and stomped him once in his gut. The guy wheezed under his taped mouth and sucked in air through his nose. Novak squatted down beside him. "Okay, here's what's going to happen now. I'm gonna ask you some questions and you're gonna answer them. That's simple enough, isn't it? Do you understand me?"

The guy growled something unintelligible; it didn't sound the least bit friendly. Novak slugged him hard on the temple, dragged him to the bathroom, and hoisted him bodily into the tub. It revived the guy right off.

Novak ripped the tape off his mouth. "Okay, here's the deal. I'm going to hold your head under until you're ready to tell me what I want to know. Let me know when you decide to talk."

Novak pushed him down and held him under for a while. When he started thrashing around in earnest, Novak grabbed his hair and brought his head up. "Ready to talk?"

The guy spit out water followed by some really unpleasant suggestions as to what Novak could do to himself. Novak plunged him back under and left him there until he went into a complete leg-kicking panic. Novak happened to know precisely how long it took to drown someone in a bathtub, and the guy wasn't even to his limit yet. He pulled him back up. It only took three more dunks to loosen his tongue.

The guy came up coughing and strangling. "Stephen'll kill me if I tell you anything! He's crazy. He'll kill me!"

"Yeah, I figured that out all by myself. Where are you taking these little girls?"

The guy cast his eyes around for help that wasn't there, but he didn't answer Novak's question.

Novak thrust him under again. He held him longer this time.

Unsurprisingly, the guy came out talkative. He let him gulp in some air. "Some guy, they call him the Turk, he's supposed to come by and pick them up."

"When?"

"Two days."

"I'm looking for a girl, thirteen years old. Name is Lucy Caloroso. Red curly hair, blue eyes, probably gave you more trouble than you could handle."

His eyes reacted to the name. He knew Lucy, all right. He shook his head as if he didn't. Novak grabbed a handful of hair again, and the man cooperated quickly enough.

"Okay, okay, I'll tell you. Just stop it." Panting, he heaved in deep sucking breaths, and Novak put up with it for less than a minute. He moved to push his head under again, and the guy's answer came in rasping, halting words. "All I know...is she's somebody special. Judge says...he's got something in mind, don't know what, I swear...I don't know what. I just do what I'm told, man. Maybe the judge wants her for his own, I don't know, I swear to God." He was getting his breath back now. Novak let go of his hair. "Stephen brought her out here from Galveston, that's all I know."

"Then where is she?"

"I don't know. He took her off somewhere alone, just the two of them. I don't know where he took her, I'm tellin' you I don't know."

"Think harder. I need answers."

The guy tried to calm down, didn't manage it so well. "He drove her out here himself. Only time he's ever done that." Breathless, wet hair stringing down over his face, he started begging. "I don't know where she is, I don't know! One day we came in with the food and she was gone. Ask the girls upstairs, ask them, I don't know nothin' else, I swear, I swear on the Holy Virgin."

Novak held him under some more, just to make sure he wasn't holding back, but got nothing else out of him. He slapped duct tape back over his mouth and left him bound and struggling in the tub. He wouldn't drown, but he couldn't get out of that tub, either. He walked back over to Stephen Locke's house. Frank had spent his time searching through the actor's stuff. The master bedroom looked as if a windstorm had whirled through.

"Find anything we can use?"

"No. Those guys know where Lucy is?"

"No, but the one who can still talk said she's special and they treated her that way. That's good news. They want her alive and healthy, Frank, so she will be when we find her. We're getting close now, I can feel it. He said Stephen took her somewhere, the guy said he didn't know where they went or why."

"You believe that?"

"I was really encouraging him to tell the truth."

"So the Locke kid can tell me where she is?"

"He might, alongside some serious urging. It worked on that jerk next door."

"I'm gonna get it out of him, then I'm going to kill him."

Frank probably wouldn't. He was prone to exaggeration when riled up so hard. Then again, he might go through with it.

"Well, get the info out of him that we need first before you do something you can't undo."

If Frank had enough self-control not to end the guy for good, Novak just might. It would be a blessing to the world. His only mourners would be those spacey teenyboppers such as Motel Delilah and her equally obtuse besties. Now all they had to do was sit and wait for the cocky little actor punk to come along home.

Chapter 22

They waited for a long time. The Locke kid must be having a binge somewhere, perhaps for the last time. His death would not be a tragedy from which the world could not recover. Novak checked on Lori periodically and found her still propped up on the pillows with young girls around her and butterfly bandages patching her gunshot wound back together. She had two guns in her lap and her eyes fixed on the door. More hired guns were incoming sooner rather than later, and she knew it. So did Novak.

The frightened teens had already called their parents on Lori's cell and were waiting for them to show up in Phoenix. All of them lived in the Midwest or down on the coast, so their arrivals wouldn't be any time soon. So they watched *Riverdale* on TV and ate fast food and were surprisingly calm. Some slept, but no one cried any more. They had learned about survival under the worst conditions known to women since they'd been under Locke's control. Lessons they would never be able to forget.

Novak rejoined Caloroso in Locke's family room and ate the gourmet food in the fridge and watched his big-screen HD TV over the fireplace. Four o'clock in the morning rolled around before they heard the garage door go up at the front of the house. They looked at each other and then both got up and moved past the divider bookshelf into the living room. Spotless white furniture sat around invitingly, and a magnificent metal sculpture stood on a table, but Novak went into the back hallway where the kid would have to enter out of the garage. A utility room was built behind the garage door, so he stepped inside and waited. Frank pressed his back against the living room wall beside a white love seat that hid him from the hall. They both got ready, poised to move fast.

The door opened and then clicked shut. Novak burst out right behind him and hit him hard at the center of his spine. Stephen Locke yelled as he was shoved forward where he fell hard on his knees about two yards from the front door. That's when Frank stepped out from behind the wall and met Locke with a brutal kick in his back that knocked him flat on his belly. The breath was knocked out of him, and Frank took a knee beside his head and placed his SIG Sauer tight against his right temple.

"Hello, big shot," Frank muttered through his teeth. "Know what? You're gonna die tonight. But first, you're gonna tell me where my daughter is."

The actor stared at Frank, still gasping for breath, but he managed to come up with what sounded like a line from his gangster script. "Go to hell, pig," he spit out, all mean and tough-like. Dumb, dumb kid. Not so wise a move, not when it was Frank Caloroso you were dealing with. Lucy's father was not in the mood for anything but shedding blood, but Stephen didn't know that. He thought he was still in a movie where he got to beat the shit out of the extras.

"You first," gritted out Frank. He straddled the guy and grabbed his throat with his left hand. He put the gun up close to Stephen's face. "Open your fucking mouth."

Stephen's eyes bulged a bit, but he was used to calling the shots and having a stunt double take the hard blows. Maybe he was just too damn drunk to make good decisions. Maybe he was a stupid idiot. His bravado was not going to get it done this time. "You know who I am, asshole?" he decided to say next. "You know who my father is? He's the guy who's gonna flay your skin off inch by inch if you touch one hair on my head."

Unceremoniously, Frank grabbed a hunk of said hair and jammed the gun barrel into Stephen Locke's big mouth. He lifted up his forefinger and made sure Stephen watched him place it on the trigger. He gave it a little tug that didn't quite fire the gun, but it came close enough to make Novak tense up. Time to stand down, buddy.

"Better hold up a bit, Frank. You want answers from this guy, don't you?"

Frank's hazel eyes looked cold, and calm as death. He pulled the gun out of Locke's mouth. "Now, one last time. Where is my daughter?"

Locke began to see the light. He was now sweating profusely. "Who are you? I don't know who you're talking about. What daughter? Who?"

"I'm talking about Lucy Caloroso, you miserable excuse of a human being. You tell me where she is or you're gonna die right here, right now, and in the worst way I can think of. Do you understand what I'm saying?"

"I don't know...."

For one heart-stopping instant, Novak believed that Frank was going to pull that trigger and blow the guy's face off. But Frank had returned to his senses and tamped down some of the bloodlust, having always been a fairly reasonable man. Instead of shooting him, he brought the gun barrel down in a hard blow against the bridge of Locke's nose. He, like Novak, had always found that extremely effective when forcing somebody to talk. Red mist exploded outward, followed by a gush of bright red blood that coated Frank's face and hair and the front of his black T-shirt. Locke screamed in absolute agony, twisting and choking on the blood pouring down his throat. His nostrils and lips were all split wide open. That kind of wound was not so good for Locke's pretty boy image. Frank held him down so tight to the floor that the kid couldn't move a muscle. So the highly acclaimed action actor could only lie there immobile, strangling on his blood and struggling to breathe through his butchered nose.

Novak decided to intervene. "Believe me, Frank, I'm not trying to talk you out of anything, but I will say that maybe you shouldn't kill him just yet. Give in to your frustration all you want. You know, give him some of what he likes to dole out to those poor girls next door. Mess up his pretty face some more, if you like, and crack those snowy white tooth implants, fine with me. But a dead man can't tell us anything."

Frank considered Novak's advice, climbed off the guy, and wiped the blood off his face with the tail of his shirt. Then he got out a pair of leather gloves from his jacket pocket. He tugged them on, jerked Locke up to standing by the front of his wet and bloody shirt, doubled his fist, drew back his arm, and hit him square in his broken nose again and about as hard as Novak had ever seen a blow thrown. The force alone propelled Stephen backward onto that crisp white loveseat that didn't stay white very long. His nose looked as if it was smashed to the bone, and blood ran down his throat into his collar. Now he was woozy and couldn't stand up when Frank jerked him to his feet again. Frank held him up by his shirt.

"I saw you slap my girl in the face," Frank ground out, down close to Locke's face. "Like this."

Frank didn't seem capable of stopping once he started slapping Lucy's abuser. Novak had to step in again, not because he wanted to but because enough was enough, even for an enraged father. "Let him catch his breath and answer your questions, Frank. You kill him and we've got zero idea where they're stashing Lucy. He's got to be able to talk. His mouth is already cut to ribbons."

Frank stood up and stepped away from the weeping, gagging film star. "Not such a tough guy anymore, are you, you sniveling little bastard coward."

Stephen rolled off the blood-spattered couch onto his hands and knees on the floor. Blood poured down onto the shiny hardwood floor. He attempted to crawl away.

Frank kicked him in the side hard enough to knock him onto his back. "Where's Lucy?"

"I don't know...."

Frank gave him another shot to the mouth, and that loosened his tongue, in more ways than one. Novak sat down on the matching white chair across the coffee table from their conversation, ready to step in if Frank got trigger-happy again. Stephen needed to live in an eight feet by eight feet jail cell for the final humiliation along with the destruction of his career, and that would happen as soon as his arrest hit the front page of *Variety* and every other Los Angeles newspaper. Novak could give them the scoop himself.

"She's in L.A. I'm telling you the truth. She's out there with Mickey. That's where we take the good ones...."

Wrong thing to say, you dumbass, thought Novak.

"You little punk." Frank grabbed him back up to sitting. "Who's Mickey?"

"Mike Mickey, the famous producer. You've heard of him. Everybody knows who he is." That came out garbled as he lolled his head around, still spitting out blood. "Head of Southern Skies Studios. He does my films. He's got her. I sent her out there to him."

"For what, you bastard?"

Locke's eyes were not focusing anymore, his lower face pretty much ground beef. All he got out was "Virgin."

Stephen Locke is suicidal, Novak thought.

Roaring with rage, Frank went at him again. Novak jumped up. He had to stop him or Frank was going to kill the guy. He didn't have time to intervene. The big front door was kicked wide with a shattering of glass, and half a dozen Scottsdale police officers rushed into the room, service weapons drawn. Within seconds, the three of them were surrounded.

"Show us your hands! Now! Both of you!"

"Get on the floor, get down, now!"

Not stupid, Novak raised his hands high. Frank put his own bloody hands up, too, the SIG dangling off his thumb. Stephen Locke lay on the floor, sobbing and half-conscious.

The cops quickly got Frank down on the floor and disarmed and cuffed him.

Novak was polite. "I've got a .45 in a shoulder holster and a conceal carry permit in my wallet. So does my friend. We're private investigators." As Novak spoke, he went slowly down onto his knees, hands still up. One cop frisked him in expert fashion and retrieved his weapon. Then he pushed him down on his stomach beside the other two men. "My P.I. and C.C. licenses are in my wallet," Novak told them again.

"Shut up and don't move," the cop yelled.

They were all shouting, trying to intimidate them, and Novak knew why. He'd done the same thing. They had burst into a room where a brutal beating was going on. They would assume the blood-covered, unconscious guy on the floor was the victim and the other two were the bad guys. This was not going to end well for him and Frank. The cops were well trained and efficient and had them subdued and handcuffed and an ambulance called for Locke within minutes. The actor was out for the count, barely able to breathe, and no longer of a cocky bent, needless to say.

"We can explain everything." Novak tried to reason with the officers again, once the pandemonium had died down. Not true, but he could wing it a bit, maybe, once they found the girls next door and heard their stories of abduction and forced prostitution.

"You'll get that chance downtown. Stand up and don't try anything, big guy."

Novak was determined to be heard. "You need to listen to me, officer. That guy lying there, he's been holding underage girls captive next door. One of their victims is that other man's thirteen-year-old daughter." He nodded his head at Frank's prone figure. "Frank's trying to find her before it's too late. They're selling these kids for sex. Check it out, if you don't believe me. Go next door, right over there, and ask them. Our friend is in there protecting them in case this guy's guards show back up. A woman named Lori Garner; she's a former military cop. I'm telling you the truth. They'll back me up. Just talk to them."

"Your friend practically killed this guy. He's gonna get charged with felony battery or worse, so you better hope he doesn't die. You're going down with aiding and abetting."

"That guy is no victim. He's a child trafficker, and I can prove it. Please, check out the house next door. We tracked these guys down and rescued those girls over there. Go find them. They've all been kidnapped and sold to somebody in Los Angeles. They'll tell you, they'll corroborate every word I'm saying. We were trying to find out where Frank's kid is, and then we planned to turn Locke over to you."

"Yeah, turn him over to us dead. The neighbors saved you the trouble by calling us." The cop turned around and ordered a couple of men to check out the houses on either side. "Get up, both of you. We're taking you in."

Novak tried to reason some more but to no avail. Stephen was in bad shape, and Frank gave new meaning to the term caught red-handed. This night had gone from bad to worse. Novak went along with the cops peacefully, but he was angry. The cops were simply doing their job. He couldn't blame them. If they were good cops and once they had questioned the girls, they'd either let them go and charge Locke or charge all of them. He hoped the arresting officer wasn't on the Locke payroll.

They were escorted out through the front door and across the walled patio to a wrought-iron gate and then shoved into the back seat of separate patrol cars. All the lights were now on next door. He hoped Lori came up with the right explanation. He was pretty sure she would and might find enough camaraderie with the policemen to make a difference. The girls would be happy to tell them the truth. They would be believed because all they wanted was to go home with their parents. They'd be pleased to have police protection.

All the neighbors in the cul-de-sac stood around outside their homes, attired in bathrobes and slippers, watching the excitement, most of them talking on cell phones and looking scared but fascinated while the revolving lights from multiple police cars and ambulances colored their faces with alternating flashes of blue and white. As Novak was driven off in the first car, he could see Lori being rolled out on a gurney. She was on her way to the hospital instead of jail, and that was the only good thing that had happened. No sign of the girls. That couldn't be good. They should be taken to a hospital, too.

After processing him and taking down his information at the station, the cops stuck him in an interrogation room and cuffed him to an iron ring on the table. Frank was probably in the next room, receiving similar accommodations. They made him wait for over an hour. He couldn't hear anything; the room was soundproofed. No food or drink or last cigarette was offered. Nope, but his interrogators were definitely behind that large two-way mirror in front of him, watching his every move for psycho tendencies. It took some effort not to display his growing anxiety.

Good things: the girls were safe and Lori was being treated for her reopened wound, and Stephen Locke was out of commission, at least for a time but probably for good. He hoped that by now the judge and Hennessey were blaming each other for their losses of drugs and property, enough to put out mob hits on each other. That would be grand but probably was not going to happen. Right now, he just wanted out of that stifling hot room. He wanted to find this guy named Mike Mickey and beat the shit out of him. Lucy was in the producer's hands now, but she would be moved somewhere else the minute word of Stephen Locke's assault got back to him.

Novak had used his one phone call to get in touch with Claire Morgan. She hadn't picked up at her end, but he'd left a message asking her to arrange bail for Frank and him and Lori, if they charged her. She'd come through with that request, he had no doubt. She always had his back, no matter what. At the moment, he wished she and Nicholas Black were in town to help them finish this thing. They needed the cavalry to ride in. Things were at a standstill, and it couldn't be a worse time to do nothing. Frank would be the hardest to bail out. He had beaten a rich and famous actor to within an inch of his life. On the other hand, he was trying to find his daughter and save those girls from a life in sexual slavery. That had to rate a few brownie points. Maybe the cops would be merciful. Maybe the judge would have a preteen daughter. Novak wasn't counting on either.

Another hour passed. They were probably saving him for last, making him sweat it out. That turned out to be true. Finally, after three long hours, a guy dressed in plain clothes sauntered in, wearing black sweatpants and a T-shirt emblazoned with POLICE, all smiley and fake and courteous of Novak's needs. "Hello, sir. I'm Antonio Puryear. Detective lieutenant here at SPD. Sorry to keep you waiting."

Yeah, right, Novak thought, *and I'm a turkey hawk.* "Will Novak."

The detective sat down across from him. He placed a manila file on the table, opened it, and looked through its contents with great interest that was strictly for show. He knew what was in that file before he stepped foot into the room. Then he looked up and met Novak's steady regard. "You're an interesting man, now aren't you?"

"You think so?"

Puryear nodded. "Served your country honorably for many years. At ground zero on 9/11. Decorated Navy SEAL. Why'd a man like you end up in this mess?"

"You know why. You've already talked to my colleagues, I assume. Both of them also served honorably in the military. We're the good guys in this thing."

"That's funny. Stephen Locke's face doesn't bear that out."

"He's lucky he doesn't look a lot worse. He's a brutal abuser and sex trafficker of children. As is his father, the Honorable Calvin Locke of Galveston, Texas."

"So I've been told, twice already. Okay, now let's talk about the crimes you perpetrated inside our fair city."

"We rescued seven young girls being forced into a life that equates with hell on earth and degradation and physical and sexual abuse. Then we roughed up their abuser a little in order to find my partner's abducted kid. You got a problem with any of that?"

"Not so much, maybe. You'll be glad to hear that all those girls backed up everything you and your friends told us. They say they were approached and seduced by young men who took them by force once they were liquored up. Most are still here at the station, waiting for their parents that you guys so kindly called for them."

"Frank Caloroso's little girl isn't waiting here for him."

"No, she is not. If I release you and your buddy, will you stop with this vigilante crap?"

"Sure. I straight-out promise you." He faked sincerity.

Puryear wasn't fooled. He grinned. "Smartass, aren't you?"

"Tonight's been rather trying."

"You've somehow managed to worm yourself out of some serious shit, Novak. Lori Garner is now undergoing emergency surgery, if you're interested. Caloroso's going to be released, too. I had to pull some major strings to get his charges dropped. But I believe you're telling me the truth. It's a good thing those girls backed you up."

"Good, we appreciate it."

"You also had some important people putting in calls on your behalf to the chief and district attorney. Nicholas Black is the one who tipped the scale for me personally. I assume you know he's a forensic psychologist. He called us himself and offered to put up bail for the three of you. We worked with him on a double murder a few years back, so we know he's a standup guy and wouldn't vouch for you if you weren't okay. He testified for the department at a big trial, which pretty much nailed the accused. He says you work in private investigation with his wife. Any or all of that true?"

"All true. We're one big happy family most of the time."

Puryear sighed. "Want to know the truth? I've got a sixteen-year-old daughter. I'd probably have done worse than Caloroso if I found the guy who subjected her to what those girls have suffered." Frowning, he paused. "Do I need to warn you that things won't go down so well next time if you end up down here again?"

"No, sir, I get it."

"We're charging Caloroso with misdemeanor battery but letting him go on Black's bond. That's a stretch. That guy's face will never look the same again. Your friend's gonna have to show up here for a hearing someday, too. Will that be a problem?"

"No, sir. We'll be there."

"You keep his nose clean, understand?"

They stared solemnly at each other, taking good measure. Both knew that Novak and Frank would do whatever it took to get Lucy back unharmed. Puryear slapped the folder shut. "Okay, you're free to go. Good luck, man. You're going to need it if you keep pulling this kind of stuff."

Novak stood up as Puryear unlocked the cuffs and followed him out into the hallway. He saw Frank waiting with another cop at the outside door. Nobody else was in sight.

"Watch where you go next and what you do there," Puryear warned again. "The next cop may not be as understanding as we are."

"Thanks. We owe you."

"Just get the hell out of here. Don't come back to my city except for the court hearing."

They obliged in a hurry.

Outside the station, they found reporters congregated at the front of the building, drawn, no doubt, by Stephen Locke's fame. All had cameras and microphones ready to annoy and pursue. Puryear showed them out a side door that led to the police parking lot.

"What, no ride provided back to our vehicle?" Novak asked Puryear.

"Fat chance. Call an Uber."

The two of them stepped out into the cool early-morning air. Puryear shut and locked the door behind them. They stood there together a moment, breathing in the damp desert smell. It had been raining, believe it or not. Unusual for Phoenix. The tarmac in the deserted lot glittered with silver droplets. The streetlamps were engulfed in pale auras that looked surreal. Thunder growled somewhere behind the dark outline of the mountains.

"You okay?" Novak asked Frank. "I see they bandaged your knuckles."

"I cannot believe they just let us go." They stood silently, and then Frank sighed. "What now?"

"Now we go to Los Angeles and find us one sleazy producer named Mike Mickey. We can sleep on the plane. You think you can keep going with that busted hand?"

"Hell, yeah."

Unfortunately, things didn't turn out so easy. They walked out a gate in the parking lot to a deserted one-way street where Novak dialed up Uber. While they waited for the car to show up, a green Suburban with smoked windows pulled in. It was not the Uber; no obsequious driver got out and opened the door for them. Instead, two burly guys with gigantic biceps jumped out and pointed some serious weapons in their faces. One kept his gun on them while the other guy frisked them and relieved them of their handguns. Right outside a police station. Well, shit. This just wasn't their day.

Chapter 23

After about twenty minutes of dead silence on the road with guns pointed at their heads, Frank asked the obvious question. "Where the hell are you taking us?"

"Shut up, bitch."

"That's rude," Novak told the mouthy guy. "How about we start with something simple, like 'Who the hell are you and want do you want with us?'"

Silence.

These guys weren't smart, either, Novak thought. Guess it was hard to get good hoodlums nowadays. Most weren't required to graduate high school: kill somebody and you're in. Novak made several oral assumptions. "Okay, we're headed west out of Phoenix. That would make one think we're headed out to L.A. You happen to know a producer there by the name of Mike Mickey, perchance?"

In the front seat, the two guys exchanged startled looks that pretty much equated with "uh oh." They knew him all right.

"Well, great, we were headed out there to see him anyway. You saved us plane fare." That was Frank.

"Shut up or I'll shut you up."

Frank wasn't put off by the threat. "Please don't scare me like this. I've already hurt my hand beating a guy's face off. You're gonna make me cry."

That smartass remark earned Frank a hard cuff to the side of his jaw from the guy behind them. After that, nobody seemed to have much else to add. These guys possessed hair-trigger tempers; Novak's guess was that they were Tinsel Town enforcers working for the idle rich and famous. They did not speak with Texan or Arizonan accents. More like Southern

California surfer boys with guns. With nothing else to do, Frank propped his head on the window and dozed off. Novak sat there for a while and worried about Lori's condition. She was being taken care of by doctors now, which was a good thing, but she was probably handcuffed to the bed, which wasn't a good thing. Maybe not, since they were bounced out, she would be, too. Claire and Black would make sure of it. He would feel better if she was with them. He'd grown accustomed to her grit, and Judge Locke's people were still after her.

With Judith dead, the three of them were on the kill list, too. They'd attempted to assassinate Lori inside a hospital once before; they might try it again. Yep, the girl was beginning to grow on him. Then he thought about Leslie Taylor, and it hurt him to think about what she'd suffered and how it was his fault, so he tried to push the image of her head on that spike out of his mind. That didn't come easy and never would.

They didn't reach the outer limits of Los Angeles until the next afternoon. The crazy interlocking mass of freeways, cloverleafs, and eight-lane highways were clogged with thousands of cars all commuting into and out of the city. Novak had been in L.A. plenty of times, so he knew they were headed in the general direction of the Hollywood Hills. An hour later and much too long fighting inching traffic, they pulled up in front of a fancy gate that heralded *Southern Skies Studios* in shiny brass script. Novak was pretty sure they had been summoned to town by the big cheese himself. Why? That was a good question, and most likely the answer was dangerous to their health. They'd know soon enough, and they weren't yet somewhere out in the Arizona desert digging their own graves. That was always a plus. Inside the hectic environs of the studio grounds, the driver dropped them off at a large single-story bungalow painted maroon, though most of the walls consisted of dark plate-glass windows. A fancy sign out front said: Michael Mickey, Owner/CEO/Executive Producer.

They were herded inside like a couple of mangy mutts jerked into a dog pound and commanded to sit in the waiting room with their two inconsiderate guards standing on both sides and watching them like hunting hawks. They had guns out and everything, and in front of Mickey's elderly secretary, too. Her nameplate said she was Imogene McClure. She had hair just going gray, dyed black with swaths of silver like Lily Munster. She had sharp eyes and sharper pale blue fingernails and a superior attitude. She eyed them with unveiled suspicion, told them to take their seats, and went about typing with those weaponized nails and answering the phone, which never stopped ringing.

Novak sat down and gauged his chances of taking down the two guards without Imogene getting hurt or killed, and dismissed the idea as less than feasible. He had to wait. Be patient. He had always been calm and non-reactionary in dangerous situations, so no problem. On the other hand, Caloroso was not the serene type. He politely asked Imogene where the men's bathroom was located and set off with one of their guards. Novak half expected the other guy to come back in a body bag. That didn't happen, but Frank returned looking more awake and ready to face whatever came next.

After twenty minutes of dead silence except for the tap-tap of Mickey's executive assistant's nimble fingers on the keyboard, the studio head strolled in. Novak recognized him at once. He was a handsome man, maybe in his sixties. Snow-white hair and a short well-groomed beard. Friendly face. Big smile. Polite. He seemed pretty damn happy to see them. He carried a cocktail glass in one hand, and because of the salted rim Novak surmised it to be a margarita. He hoped he offered them a drink. Novak could use one. He did not. Instead, Mickey walked straight over to him and stretched out his hand. Mr. Friendly. He better enjoy that wide smile while he still had teeth. "Hey, big guy. Thank you so much for coming. Hope you had an enjoyable journey."

"Might've been better without all those guns stuck in our faces," Frank interjected. "So, what's up with that, anyway? In other words, where the hell do you get off forcing us out here at gunpoint?"

Mickey just beamed at the both of them. "You two really ought to be extras in my movies. You look like tough guys; you know, the real ones, just raring to murder somebody."

"You're a mind reader," Frank told him.

Novak had had it with the small talk. "Oh yeah, we sure are, just raring to get a kill," Novak said. He stood up and towered about eight inches over the bigwig producer. "And just so you know, we've got people, meaning cops, who know where we are and who you are. If I were you, I'd be careful with what you order these guys to do to us."

His face adopted an incredulous expression. Mickey glanced at his armed guards. "Were you rude to these gentlemen, Paco?"

"No, sir. We just picked them up as you directed and brought them here. Just following your orders, sir."

"Well, that's splendid. Please, gentlemen, join me inside my private office. We've got a lot to talk about, I believe."

Imogene stopped typing and watched to see what might happen next. She seemed very interested in their fate. Maybe she'd seen guys go in and come out in brown paper bags. Frank remained his usual shade of livid, clenching and unclenching his teeth and fists, half an inch from showing them what he was feeling, up close and personal with Mike Mickey's face. Novak had a similar desire, a relentless tug on his willpower. They were both sleep deprived, hungry, thirsty, and angry. They hadn't even had coffee.

They followed Mickey into a gigantic office that took up the length of the rear of the bungalow. A red and white kitchen sat at one end, and an ultra-modern office setup was on the other end. White fuzzy couches, black leather uncomfortable chairs, and a round granite table sat out in the middle. All quite lavish and modern and expensive, Beverly Hills style. The walls were hung with life-size movie posters, most with Stephen Locke caught frozen in midair while leaping between rooftops or hanging off a mountain by a rope as he mowed down thugs with a machine gun. It appeared the producer and star were best buddies. That didn't bode well for Mike Mickey. He hadn't seen the post-beatdown Stevie.

"Your money-maker star in that poster over there? He doesn't look much like that anymore. I rearranged his face," Frank told him. His voice had risen and was belligerent in tone.

"Yes, I know, I heard about that. That's precisely why I've asked you to visit me here. I'm very curious as to why you'd want to damage the face of a multi-million-dollar franchise. Not cool, mister."

Not cool, mister? Novak took up the conversation. "Okay, I'll spill the beans. Your star is a low-life, dirtbag creep pervert who abuses women and children and sells them as sex slaves. I think you already know that, Mr. Mickey. I think you are, too. I think you're part of that movie franchise, right? That means you're party to the criminal activities as well."

Mickey should have been the actor. He looked hit by shock and awe. Then he actually laughed at the notion. He took a moment to drain his glass. Then he returned his amused gaze to Novak. "I don't have a clue what you're talking about. I've never heard anything about any criminal activities that Stephen's involved with. All I know is that you've ruined poor Stephen's career, and I'm going to sue you to kingdom come for damages to my star property. And you can trust me when I say that I've got the best attorneys in Southern California."

Novak was damn sick of him. They needed to get to Lucy soon, or they might never find her. "Listen to me and listen good. We want Lucy Caloroso. We want her right now. We know you've got her hidden somewhere. Stephen Locke told us you did. So tell us where she is, and you won't get hurt."

"I've never heard of any girl by that name. Lucy who? Is that Italian? Is she some young actress who came to me looking for a break?"

"Is that how you whitewash this stuff?" Frank demanded. "The junior high girls we found with your star in Scottsdale didn't call it that. They called it abduction and abuse and forced prostitution."

For the first time, Mickey's good nature seemed strained. "Who the hell are you to come into my studio and accuse me of something so perverted?"

"I'm Lucy's father. I'm giving you one more chance. Where is she?"

Novak decided it was time to end the conversation. Only one guard had come inside the office with them, and he was standing too close to Novak for the guy's own good. Novak had ten inches on him and was double his size. Nobody was watching Novak anymore, not even his guard. Novak moved quickly, disarmed the man in a matter of seconds, and grabbed him back against his chest. He placed the gun barrel in his ear. The guard was smart enough not to move a muscle. Frank stepped back, fearing blood spatter. Mike Mickey assumed a shocked expression and reached for his desk phone. Frank grabbed it away from him and jerked out the cord. Then he patted down Mickey and came up with a Luger 9mm. He racked it and held it at Mickey's ear. Novak dropped his guy to the floor and kicked him in the head. Paco groaned once and passed out. After that, the room became very quiet.

"Did you just murder Paco?" Mickey asked Novak, seemingly astounded by the violence he witnessed even if he witnessed worse in every movie he made. "I can't believe you just kicked him like that. Right in the head. I believe he might be hurt rather extensively."

"He should wake up eventually, maybe. He deserved some payback; he wouldn't let us stop for bathroom breaks," Frank told him. "He was rude during the entire ride."

Mickey looked a tad less confident now. In fact, he looked scared out of his gourd. He tried to walk around them toward the front office. Frank shoved him back. Then he slapped him hard in the face, followed by a backhand that drew blood at the corner of his mouth. Frank was good at drawing blood.

"Wait, now wait just a minute," Mickey said, holding his mouth. He took out a snowy white handkerchief and dabbed away the blood. "What do you want from me? I don't know what you're talking about. I swear it. You've come to the wrong person."

"We didn't come anywhere. You brought us here. I want my daughter back. But first, I want you dead for taking her."

Mickey still played his dumb-as-a-stump card. "I don't know what you're talking about. I have no connection with sex trafficking or anything remotely close to that. I make movies and build movie stars. I'm not a criminal."

Frank searched his desk and came up with a file full of photographs of young women in skimpy attire. None pictured Lucy, though.

"Are these the girls you're selling?"

"No, of course not." Mickey gave a nervous little laugh. "Those are aspiring actresses who want to screen test for Stephen's new film. Are you crazy?"

Novak had pussyfooted around enough. He grabbed Mickey by the front of his gray linen tropical shirt and jerked him up on his toes. "Listen up, Mickey, you're going to tell us where Lucy is or we're gonna kill you. That's two clear alternatives. Be smart with your choices."

Mickey looked confused, followed closely by terrified. "I don't know anybody named Lucy or anybody who is abusing girls. I'd never be involved in something like that."

"Hold him down, Frank."

Frank obliged with pleasure.

Novak held Mickey's right hand down on the shiny mahogany desk and picked up a heavy gold statuette, otherwise known as an Oscar. He stared into Mickey's wide blue eyes, which were not nearly so merry now. "Last chance. Tell us or I'm going to hurt you a lot. Then I'm turning you over to Frank so he can bloody you up some more and destroy your nice neat office. Got that, Mike? You are going to die right here and now. But first, I'm going to give you a chance to do the right thing."

"Security will be here any minute. Imogene's already called them. She listens in on all my meetings."

Novak handed the Oscar to Frank. Frank took it and wasted no time. He raised it up high over Mickey's hand as Mickey struggled desperately to pull his arm out of Novak's grip.

"Stop, stop it, don't you hurt him! I'll tell you what you want to know!"

They all turned and stared at little Imogene where she stood in the doorway.

"I'm the one you're looking for, not him. Michael has no part of this. He doesn't know anything about it. Let him go, I said."

"What are you talking about, Genie?" Mickey said, still in the dark as to what was going on.

Novak wasn't. He let go of the producer. Mickey staggered away.

Imogene ignored her boss's questions. "Michael's got nothing to do with any of this. I work with Locke. I'm his contact out here. I move the girls. Michael is not involved in any way."

Mike Mickey sank down on a couch. His expression told Novak that she was telling the truth. He just sat there and stared disbelievingly at her.

"So you know where my daughter is?" Frank walked up closer to the little woman.

"I work for the judge. I have for years. He got me this job out here with Mr. Mickey. He threatened me with my grandchildren. I'm glad it's over now. I'm glad you found me out." She turned to her boss. "I'm sorry, Mike. Stephen's not who you think he is. None of us are."

"Where's Lucy?" Frank asked, impatient.

"I can tell you where you can find her."

"No, you'll show us. We're all going out that back door, and you're taking us straight to where she is. Where are your car keys?"

"In my purse," she said. She was calm, her voice quiet. "I drive the white Cadillac."

"Go get the car, Frank, and bring it around to the back door."

Frank took off in a hurry. Novak watched him run across the back parking lot and climb into the car, and then he looked at Mickey and Imogene.

"Come on, you're both going with us."

They obeyed without argument, and Novak took them out through a pair of French doors and past a small rectangular lap pool with a hot tub at the end. Frank circled around and rolled to a stop in front of them. Novak could smell the pots of roses and gardenias sitting around everywhere. Novak put the woman in the front seat and pushed the producer into the back seat. Mike Mickey was asking his assistant all kinds of questions now, still flabbergasted at what was going down, but she didn't answer him or turn around. She just sat in silence, staring straight ahead, unable to face her boss.

"She's down in Malibu," she finally said. "Stephen's got a house down there. Nobody knows about it except for me and a few of his men."

"Is she all right? Did he hurt her?" Frank kept glancing across at her as he drove.

"Nobody's hurt her that I know of. The judge told Stephen she was fragile cargo. So we treated her that way. She's staying in a lovely house overlooking the ocean."

They had reached the front gate, and Frank stopped at the cross bar. The guy in the booth recognized Imogene and let them through without question. Frank turned out onto Wilshire and headed for the freeway.

"Is she in danger? Tell me what they're doing to her." Frank was not done questioning; he had to know. Novak hoped the answers were not the ones he was afraid of.

"She was fine until now. Then Stephen called the other night and said there was a change of plans. That he intended to sell her abroad because you were after them and getting too close. He said he wanted her out of the country so we wouldn't be tied to her disappearance."

"Did he hurt her?"

"Nobody touched her in the way that you mean. Like I said, she was off limits. I hope she's still out there. I know you don't believe that, but I do."

"You're going to jail, lady, as soon as she's safe with us," Novak said. "How would you feel if your granddaughter was in the hands of these animals?"

"She was. I bargained for her release by working for them and keeping Mike in the dark. Stephen didn't want him to know what we were into. The studio was a good cover for what he was doing."

"Who bought her?" Frank's words came out tight but controlled.

"I don't know things like that. I don't handle that end of the agreements. I just get the girls out there, and they take care of the rest. The ones that come for them are from Turkey. They come in on a big yacht and pick up the cargo. That's all I know, I swear. I just do what they tell me. They've threatened my family for years."

"What are they planning to do with her?" Frank's voice was low.

Imogene hesitated. "They sell them overseas as slaves. Her red hair made her a lucrative commodity. That's what they called her: a lucrative commodity."

Frank's face had blanched. Novak feared he was going to snap, but he didn't. He knew the stakes.

Frank knew Southern California well and got them to the Pacific Coast Highway, but traffic was terrible and held them up. When he finally hit the road to Malibu, he pressed down on the gas pedal. Nobody felt much like chitchatting. It had been a trying day, so it was dead silent inside that car for the entire drive. Novak just hoped to God that Lucy was still there and not on a boat sailing for the Middle East.

Chapter 24

Novak had worked a case in Malibu about three years ago, right along the same stretch of beach that held addresses for many of Hollywood's elite. The houses were constructed side by side at some points, all sporting lots of glass and weathered wood, the gigantic windows opening for vast views overlooking the silver-blue Pacific Ocean. Sunsets were gorgeous out there, and lots of exclusive people in lots of exclusive homes enjoyed it every day of the year. Most homes were modern and sleek, with the beaches close to their patios and decks, always alive with the roaring, rolling surf. Imogene was scared and cooperating fully and maybe relieved, not such a great mastermind when held by fear. Mike Mickey still seemed in shock, or maybe he was turning the whole thing into a movie plot inside his head. His sweet little secretary had been running a sex trafficking ring right under his nose, and he, a famous Hollywood producer, hadn't had a clue. Yeah, he was probably thinking it could be a hit.

The home they sought was not down close to the beach but among houses that sat high on the cliffs overlooking the sea. The cowed and ashamed granny pointed out the way and readily gave them the password for the privacy gate at the upper end of a paved driveway. They reached the house a minute later. Novak got out and told Mickey to stay put or else. He agreed because he had no choice and he didn't want to get hit again. Then Novak opened Imogene's door and took her by the arm. They followed Frank up to the double front door made of dark inlaid drift wood.

Almost there, they heard a girl scream. That did it for Frank. He stepped back, slammed the door open with one brutal kick, and the sound of screaming intensified. He ran down the hallway and kicked open a locked bedroom door with Novak right behind him, gun drawn. And there they found little Lucy with some big guy lying on top of her and trying to rip off her nightgown. She was fighting him like hell, punching him in the head and kicking and screaming. Just as the door flew wide, her attacker slapped her in the face, hard enough to stun her. That's when her father went absolutely berserk, and Novak didn't even try to stop him. Frank charged the guy from the side, hit him like some kind of runaway bulldozer, and they both went flying off the bed to the floor. The would-be rapist was big, and he easily threw Caloroso off, but Frank was finally releasing all the rage he'd contained for days, and that gave him more than enough edge. He was back at the man in seconds, pummeling him in the face and then grasping him around the throat, trying to throttle the life out of him.

Lucy had fled the bed and backed as far away as she could get, but then she saw Novak and ran to him, sobbing her heart out. She came to herself almost at once, however, and stopped crying. When she saw her attacker slug her daddy in the head, she pulled out of Novak's arms, grabbed a lamp from the bedside table, and swung it as hard as she could against the man's skull. It shattered, and he went down like a felled redwood. Novak ended the last remnant of his fight with a well-placed kick to his head.

Frank was back on his feet instantly and had Lucy in his arms. While they hugged and wept together, Novak got busy binding up the man and dragging him out into the living room for the cops to find when they showed up. Lucy was excited and still crying tears of joy, but she was trying to tell them that other girls were being held down in the lower level. Imogene had been standing in the living room, silent, but stepped forward and poked in numbers on the keypad beside the locked door. She stood back, and the two men followed Lucy down a short flight of steps. That's when Novak placed a call to the Malibu police department as Frank kicked open one bedroom door after another and freed the girls inside. They all appeared to be around Lucy's age, all blondes, all barely into puberty, and all bearing bruises and weeping with joy to find themselves freed from a fate that was surely worse than death.

"Are there others?" Novak asked Lucy.

She nodded, wiping her eyes with the back of her hand. Her face metamorphosed into anger. "They bring in different girls every week, always on different days. They kept me here for a while, so I watched and listened. I knew Daddy would come for me. A boat comes in close and picks up girls and takes them out to a big yacht that comes in after dark and anchors somewhere offshore. I guess about twenty or thirty girls have been taken out there since I got here, Daddy. Usually around ten go out at a time. They kept me separate from them and guarded by that guy who had me down on the bed. He hadn't touched me until today."

"Did they hurt you, baby?" Frank's voice was tight with fear of what her answer would be.

"They hit me a few times, slapped me mostly, but that guy was supposed to protect me. He wasn't supposed to let anybody hurt me, kind of like my bodyguard, I guess. Then he got a phone call today from over in Phoenix, I think, and he told me I'd be going to Kuwait on the next boat but he wanted to teach me some things first. That's when I got past him and tried to escape, but he chased me and dragged me back to the bedroom. Daddy, I'm so glad you came for me. I was afraid they'd put me on that boat and you'd never find me again."

"You're safe now," Novak told her. "This whole trafficking ring is going down, we're gonna make sure of it. The cops are going to be here any minute. You've got to pull yourself together and tell them everything you know about this operation, everywhere you've been, who you've seen, every single detail you can remember about the girls you were with. They'll need their names and descriptions, where they're from, if you know that. Their parents need to know they're still alive."

Her face changed abruptly. Fear bloomed behind her eyes. "They killed some of the girls," she said, practically whispering. "They'd take them outside of the house, right here, in this house, and they'd never come back. My guard told me they cut their throats or locked them up in shipping containers and let them suffocate inside. I don't know if that's true, but none of them ever came back. The girls they took out to that yacht were alive when they left here. I don't even know where we are. Stephen Locke put a pillowcase over my head when we traveled. Are we still in Texas?"

"No. California. Malibu Beach."

"I knew I was near the ocean. They let me go outside once in a while."

"I've been looking for you since the day they took you. I was so scared, baby." Frank hugged her close, couldn't seem to let go of her.

Lucy turned and looked at Novak. She was a pretty girl. Her hair was down around her shoulders, falling in long ringlets. Her blue eyes had an adult look in them now. She'd probably never lose that look. "What happened to that lady named Judith? When I was at this big fancy house somewhere, they kept me locked in a stall in a big garage. She sneaked in and gave me something to eat. She said she was afraid the judge was going to hurt me and that he hurt her. She said she'd come back and get me out if she could, but I never saw her again."

"That happened in Houston. Judith is Judge Locke's daughter. He's the one behind all this. We got her out of there, but she was murdered after we turned her over to the FBI."

"What about that lady named Leslie Taylor? Did you get her, too?"

Shame and regret hit Novak. His grief over Leslie's murder cut him deeply. She'd been a good friend to him, a woman he'd once loved, a trusted colleague that had put herself on the line for him over and over, and he'd let her down in the worst way imaginable. He'd never forgive himself for her death. He looked back at Lucy and shook his head. "No, they killed her a few days ago at a safe house in Houston. She was the FBI agent who tried to help us find you. We think a mobster named Hennessey got her and Judith at one of their safe houses. Several FBI agents died along with her."

Lucy frowned. "No, no way, you're wrong, she's not dead. She's out here with those guys who took me. At first, I thought she'd come to get me because I remembered that she knows you and Daddy. But then I found out that she works for them. She set me up to be taken." Lucy stopped there, her face slowly flushing with anger. "Then she said that you were trying to find me but would probably end up dead, both of you, so I should quit thinking about getting rescued. She said you'd deserve it, too, Mr. Novak, but that Daddy didn't. She told me she hoped they didn't have to kill both of you but that you'd never find me. That was yesterday, but she was here early this morning, too. I was locked in my room, but I heard her voice talking to Jake. That's my guard's name."

Novak's entire body went rigid. He felt his mind lock up and freeze in a way that hadn't happened in years. He could not believe his ears at first. Leslie had betrayed him? Even after their history together, the fact they'd been close friends, and then lovers. Blood was rushing inside his ears, drowning out everything else. Anger was taking over his body, his voice, clogging his throat. If Leslie was involved, she'd been the one who'd gotten Judith killed, maybe even killed her herself. She had willingly helped to send Lucy and countless other young girls into lives of slavery. His words finally came, but he hardly recognized his own voice. "Do you know where she is now?"

"No, but I know she lives somewhere around here. One time when they let me out in the yard, I saw her walking up the beach toward us. I think she must live down that way on the beach somewhere." She pointed south.

As shocked as Novak, Frank turned to him. "What are we gonna do about her?"

Novak swallowed down some of the anger, didn't quite get it done. "You're going to take care of Lucy. I'm going to go find Leslie. She thinks she's in the clear, probably planning a new life with dirty money from selling girls to pedophiles. I'm going to end her before she can enjoy it. I want her behind bars in a Federal prison for the rest of her life."

"I'm coming with you. You're gonna need backup. I doubt if she's alone in this."

"No way. This is my fault and mine alone. I went to her for help. I trusted her, and I handed over Judith and her children. She played me, Frank. Now Judith's dead and her children might be, too. It's all on me. I was a fool."

"No, it's on her. Tell the local cops and the Feds what she did and let them find her. Let the law work for a change. When this comes down on them, they're all going to prison for life."

"I need you to take Lucy home to Galveston and let me finish this by myself. I need to do it alone. Understand?"

"Of course I do. But promise me you'll turn her over to the police. We've got proof on her now. Lucy and the girls can testify."

"Sure, I will," Novak told him, but that was a lie. "I just want to find her and make her admit to my face what she's done. Then I'll turn her in, and she can rot in prison."

Malibu law enforcement showed up exactly twelve minutes later. Novak sat down on a beige couch in the living room and gave a long, detailed statement to the detective in charge. His name was James Hayward, and Novak told him everything that had happened, leaving out no details since the day he'd first spotted Lori Garner running from those men on Bourbon Street. He told him about Hennessey and Calvin Locke and Mike Mickey and Imogene McClure and everybody else remotely involved. The cops appeared skeptical of his story at first and reticent to start accusing a sitting judge, but as he rolled out the evidence and swore he had documents in a safe deposit box in Corpus Christi which would prove his allegations, they began to look interested. They interviewed Lucy and the other girls, and Novak was proud of the way Lucy sat still and answered articulately with Frank close beside her for support. She told an ugly story that actually made Novak want to throw up. Frank had a sick look on his face as she recounted all she'd seen and done, but he had found her unharmed and that was all that mattered to him. The cops called ambulances to transport the girls to a nearby hospital and told Novak that he and his friends could go but that they would be called to testify. Then the questioning process began.

While the cops talked to the girls, Novak took Frank aside. "How about going back to Scottsdale first and making sure Lori's okay and being taken care of. You know, maybe you and Lucy could keep her company until I get back there. I need to contact the Bureau and let them know that Leslie Taylor's alive and dirty. Once I find her, they can handle it from that point."

Frank studied his face, but he knew Novak much too well and too long to buy his lies. "Don't overdo the revenge, Novak. Remember what you told me. She'll do time, no question about it. Look, I want her punished more than anyone, more than you, probably, but that's got to be enough for us to live with. She'll never walk free again, not after this."

"Tell that to Judith's kids, if we ever find them. God only knows where she sent them and to whom. After I deal with her, I'm not stopping until I find them."

"You're blaming yourself for all of this. It's not your fault. You were trying to help me."

"I brought her in. I told her everything I knew, every goddamn stinkin' thing. I delivered Judith and those two little girls right into her hands. I'm to blame for everything that happened to her and to them. She betrayed me. I want my pound of flesh, Frank."

"She's not worth going to prison over."

Maybe it was worth it to Novak.

It took nearly all day for the police to get things sorted out. They let Frank and Lucy leave after hours of questioning. They ended up believing Mike Mickey was innocent and didn't know about the crimes being perpetrated out of his office. Much to his relief, they sent him on his way. He immediately called a limo and headed off to find his scriptwriter to pitch his latest movie idea based on a true crime story. Novak wondered who'd play his part in the film.

The cops questioned Novak the longest. When they finally let him go, he found the serpentine sandy trail in the back that led down to the beach. He made his way to the bottom, and then for a long time, he sat down there on the sun-warmed sand, gazing out to sea until the commotion at the house above dwindled and the night became quiet after the cops had locked up the house, strung the crime scene tape, and drove away.

Then he watched the most magnificent sunset he'd ever seen and night gradually fell over the California coast, and the sea turned to ink with only the uneven foaming lines of breaking waves visible in the darkness. That's when he stood up and started walking down the beach in the direction that Lucy had pointed out. The houses on this stretch of sand weren't so close together. There were about four or five homes sitting high atop the hills above the beach, and maybe a mile or two down the shoreline, another line of homes sat right on the beach, close together, with all those plate-glass windows facing the restless waves.

When it was pitch black, lights on in windows high above him, he started climbing steps up to the first house he came to. It was smaller than the one where they'd found the girls, not as posh, not as many flowers, and little lawn. He stopped on a landing halfway up when he glimpsed the family who owned the place. They were sitting together at a table on a deck jutting out over the rocks. They were eating dinner. He stayed hidden inside shadows. It was a man and a woman and two little kids. It wasn't Leslie Taylor. He descended to the beach again.

The next two homes were no-goes. Both had families watching television or eating dinner; both places had kids playing around outside on the decks. Number four was empty and completely dark. He climbed all the way to the top and peered in the windows to make sure. Doors locked up tight, no furniture inside, only vast, empty rooms. Most likely it was a house for sale for millions of dollars.

So he moved down the steps to the beach again and lucked out at house number five. He headed up the steps, keeping low, and finally caught a glimpse of Leslie Taylor. She wore a bathing suit, not much of one, but it was white and almost glowed in the darkness. She was standing high above him at a deck railing. Behind her, he could see a table set with a dozen tall and flaming white tapers. He felt his teeth clamp together, and his fists clenched into hard balls. Lucy was right. Leslie was alive and well and living the high life, no doubt spending money she'd earned betraying Judith and Novak and, worst of all, a young girl she claimed to care about. Lucy Caloroso.

Novak went down on his haunches and took a few deep breaths in and held them. He needed to remain calm. He was so angry that he wanted her dead. He wanted to kill her; he really did. He hadn't known for sure if that's what he'd do when he found her, but the rage was pulsating and pushing him to his limits. Even now, he wasn't sure he could stop himself if he got the chance.

Her steps rose up to the south side of a large rectangular deck, and he was probably out of her line of vision. She was drinking red wine from a long-stemmed crystal goblet. She was standing still, gazing up at the stars. He wondered what she was thinking. Maybe she was congratulating herself on a job well done. Maybe she would continue to do the same thing to other innocent children and their families. Novak started up the steps, proceeding slowly and stealthily. The surf was wild and loud, and she couldn't hear him. He stopped at the next landing. She didn't have a clue he was anywhere around, and apparently, she didn't know that most of her criminal associates were already dead or in jail. He made it to the top before she seemed to sense him. That's when she suddenly turned around. She went completely rigid for a second, her eyes gleaming in the candlelight as she stared at the gun in his hand. It didn't surprise him that she remained composed and didn't run. She had always claimed her nerves were made of steel.

"Hello, Will. How did you find me?"

"Lucy saw you on the beach. I had a hunch, and here we are. Just the two of us. Together again."

"I should've bought a beach house in Santa Barbara instead."

Novak approached slowly, because he wasn't dumb enough to underestimate her. She was a well-trained, experienced FBI field agent, and his reticence was rewarded when she grabbed a gun off the table and pointed it at him. His gun didn't move from where it pointed at the center of her chest. They stood there, aiming lethal weapons at each other.

"Novak, I like you, even after all this, I do, but I can't let you take me in."

"I won't let you get away with murdering Judith and her children."

"I didn't murder her. I didn't murder Susie and Sammi. What do you take me for? Those little kids are fine. I took them to a safe house up in Dallas. The FBI knows where they are and will pick them up, safe and sound. Call and ask them if you don't believe me. What do you think I am? Some kind of monster? I didn't want Judith killed, either, but Hennessey wanted to teach the judge a lesson. He suspected he was trying to take over his operations. I suspect that was because of something you told him. Maybe it was you he was getting back at."

"What about the woman they found at the safe house, the one you tried to pass off as yourself? The one whose face you disfigured with acid and then cut off her head and put it on that gate? The one dressed in your clothes? Who was she? Somebody you didn't like? Somebody expendable?"

"I don't know who she was. Hennessey handled all that. I haven't killed anyone."

"You might not have done it yourself, but you're just as much a monster. You get other people to do your dirty work so you can keep your hands clean. If you didn't murder Judith, who did?"

"I just told you. Hennessey wanted Judith dead and demanded I give her over to him. I had to. His people did the deed, I suppose. I wasn't there. I didn't ask what they were going to do with her, either. I wanted out. I wanted to disappear, and that's what I did. I almost made it."

"What the hell happened to you? You were instrumental in trafficking little kids, Les. You were putting Frank's kid in a position where she could be raped or murdered. You had those innocent women murdered."

"You happened to me. You ruined my career. You know you did. I did what I had to do to get it back."

"I didn't make you go bad. Greed and resentment did."

"So am I going to have to shoot you?"

"I'm not letting you go. You're going to jail for a long time."

Leslie didn't hesitate. She pulled the trigger. He reacted fast, but the bullet hit him in his right side and felt like a hot iron fist had slammed a hole through his body. He was knocked backward, and that saved him from the second bullet. She fired again, but he lunged at her and grabbed her gun arm and forced it upward. He took her down to the floor, but she kept pulling the trigger, the bullets shattering the plate-glass windows behind them. He grappled for the gun and forced it out of her hand, but she was too agile and twisted away from him and was on her feet and running toward the cliff steps.

Novak went after her, holding his side. It was bleeding heavily. She was thundering down the steps to the beach, her spike heels clacking on the wood. Novak ran down behind her. He was almost to her when she spun around. She was panicked now and whirled back around and ran down the next flight. When she reached the next landing, she swung around the landing post but was moving way too fast. When she stumbled, the forward motion sped up her momentum. She went over in a tumbling somersault and flailed her way down the steps, her scream already muted by the sounds of the sea, but it stopped abruptly when she went headfirst into the concrete retaining wall at the bottom.

Novak made his way slowly down the rest of the way, holding his gun at the ready. He pulled up his shirt, but the bullet had only winged the flesh of his side. He could patch it up himself. He was pretty sure Leslie was dead before he got to her. In the faint moonlight, he could see the position of her head, and it was twisted at an impossible angle as was one of her legs. He squatted down beside her and stared at her face. Then he felt for a pulse on the side of her neck. There wasn't one. She was gone, and then so was he. He walked swiftly away through the deep sucking sand and headed for the beach houses where he knew there was a restaurant called Gladstone. When he was a good distance from her dead body, he strolled more leisurely. She had fallen to her death trying to kill him. She had paid the ultimate price for her sins, and that was enough for him. He would tell her superiors every detail of her betrayal and make sure she had no reputation left among her colleagues except for one that would be reviled, but he wouldn't tell them anything else.

Right now, all he wanted was to get back to Scottsdale and make sure Lori Garner was doing okay. Then he was going to give another long, detailed statement naming names and places and crimes committed by Stephen Locke to the Scottsdale police. Then he was going to Austin and turning over enough dirt to hang both Hennessey and Judge Locke. That would end it. After that, they'd both go to prison and he'd pick up his boat and sail home and try to forget everything that had happened for the last couple of weeks. Maybe he'd take Lori Garner with him. The sea was a good place to come to terms with what had happened to them. Maybe she'd like a holiday at sea as much as he would.

Epilogue

Lori Garner had a private room. Novak pushed the door open and stopped inside the door. She was sleeping. He felt a strong sense of déjà vu for a moment. This was the second time she'd been in a hospital since he'd met her. A lot of bad stuff had happened in that short amount of time, most of it worse than bad. She'd done her part well enough even when injured and in pain. He appreciated her strength. He appreciated her in lots of ways. He liked her a little too much for his own liking. He moved toward the bed but stopped when she suddenly lunged up off the pillows. She had a Glock pointed at him.

Novak grinned. He held up the bouquet of flowers he'd bought downstairs in the gift shop. "Don't shoot. I'm bringing you lilies. You told me you liked them."

Lori relaxed back against the pillow but kept the gun in her lap. "What are you trying to do, Novak? Scare me to death? Give me a heart attack, why don't you, creeping around like that. You know better than to sneak up on a gun-shy woman."

"Nope, just came by to make sure you're going to be all right."

Then they smiled at each other.

"You're dangerous to my health," he told her, stopping beside the bed.

"Right back at you, dude."

Novak smiled again. "How do you feel?"

"I feel like I've been shot, stitched up, knocked around, re-stitched, you know, the regular."

"You're a tough old bird."

"Oh, wow, my first compliment out of you and it's insulting. Do I have to get shot every time to squeeze a pleasantry from your big mouth?"

"Maybe. You aren't known for your praise, either, Garner."

She grew serious. "You are something else, Novak. And a good guy to have around in gunfights."

"Thanks." He looked around the room and then back at her. "How are you really doing?"

"I'm okay. Hope you're here to spring me out of this joint. The food sucks."

"I can do that. Didn't I get you out last time when you were unconscious? This time should be easier. You can walk, can't you?"

"True."

"Have Frank and Lucy been here?"

"Yes, they've been hanging around. Waiting for you to show up and prove you weren't dead. I finally told them to scram and go home."

"I asked them to stay with you until I got here."

"Lucy needs to be at home with Frank. She's shaky now that it's all over. Poor kid went through a lot. She told me all about it. I can relate to some of it. Not fun to be that scared for that long."

"You do just fine."

"So what happened? You kill your friend Leslie, or not?"

"What kind of question is that?"

"An appropriate one, considering that Frank told me you probably had gone off to murder her."

"She's dead, but I didn't kill her. Not directly, anyway."

"What's that supposed to mean?"

He told her about the altercation at the beach, and she listened to the tale then nodded. "You're hit in the side. Was it bad?"

"It's nothing, just a graze. I stitched it up myself and took some of your hydrocodone. I'll pay you back if you like."

"I probably will like." She watched his face. "Well, I'm not going to cry for Leslie Taylor," she told him. "Judith was my friend, and that bitch signed her death warrant."

"Ditto. What about Locke and Hennessey?"

"Two legit FBI agents came in here and interviewed me for three hours before they were satisfied with my sad tale. I gave them the info about Judith's safe deposit box. Apparently, Locke and Hennessey no longer trust each other. Can't think why. I believe we started a Mafia war. They're dropping like flies on both sides. And you do know the FBI have Sammi and Susie at one of their safe houses and they're both just fine. They're trying to place them with their paternal grandparents, somewhere in south Florida. Sounds like a good option for them. I plan to go see them there as soon as you get me out of here." She gave him a look. "So, how about coming with me? They seemed to take to you okay. Especially Susie. Guess it was that hot chocolate and cookie thing."

"How about I take you to Florida on my boat? Then maybe after that, I thought maybe you'd come back to Bonne Terre with me and enjoy the plantation life for a while. You know, recuperate in some peace and quiet."

"Like that other lady you nursed there?"

Novak winced at that remark.

"I'm sorry. I didn't mean to bring back a bad memory."

"A sociopath was after Mariah. Nobody's after you anymore. You'll be safe enough there. Besides, you can take care of yourself. But I do have a proposition for you?"

"I thought the invitation to come home with you was the proposition."

Novak laughed. "I guess it sounded that way. I'm not adverse to it."

"Me, either."

"Okay then."

"Okay."

"I was going to ask you if you might want to work with Claire Morgan and me for a while. She's going to be out having her baby and taking some time off. No pressure, but I thought I'd put it out there and give you time to think about it."

"Sounds interesting. From what you've told me, she's a woman I'd like to get to know."

"You'd like her. You've got some things in common."

They stared at each other.

"I'll take it under consideration, Novak. But right now? I think a nice long sail on your boat sounds like heaven. This time with no bad guys on our tail."

"Let's go."

"Hand me those scrubs the nurse left over there, and let's blow this place."

Novak handed her the scrubs. They left and never looked back.

If you enjoyed *Witness Betrayed,* be sure not to miss all of Linda Ladd's Will Novak series, including

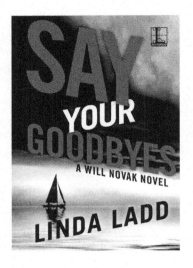

When a scream wakes Will Novak in the middle of the night, at first he puts it down to the nightmares. He's alone on a sailboat in the Caribbean, miles from land. And his demons never leave him. The screams are real, though, coming from another boat just a rifle's night scope away. It only takes seconds for Novak to witness one murder and stop another. But with the killer on the run and a beautiful stranger dripping on his deck, Novak has gotten himself into a new kind of deep water.

A Lyrical Underground e-book on sale now.

Read on for a special excerpt!

Chapter 1

"No, no! Please! Help me!"

Will Novak opened his eyes and stared into utter darkness. He had been drinking earlier that evening before he passed out. He wasn't drunk anymore, maybe hungover some, but he could think straight. He knew who had been calling for help. The same dream had come to him every night. It was Mariah Murray's voice, his beautiful sister-in-law who called to him from the dark corners of his troubled mind. She had died on his doorstep, not a fortnight ago. He had promised to protect her. But he had failed, and now she haunted him, just like his dead wife and his dead children haunted him. All those voices that he loved so much and missed so desperately called out to him, distant and tinny, like static on an old Motorola radio. But he couldn't help any of them. They were gone forever. Sarah and Kelly and Katie had perished when the south tower came down on 9/11. He had watched it happen, unable to help them in that terrible moment, and unable to help them now. He couldn't help Mariah, either. She was dead. Everybody he loved was dead. Those voices calling to him were why he drank himself to oblivion, hoping to stifle the pain and forget his guilt and regret. But it never worked.

Eyes bleary and bloodshot, he sat up and looked around. He was out in the middle of the Caribbean Sea. His sailboat, his prized forty-foot custom-built Jeanneau Sun Odyssey 379, rocked beneath him. The waves were gentle, but the wind was picking up and buffeting the masts and riggings. A gale was probably developing somewhere far away. Maybe it would hit him eventually, but so what? He laid his head on the back of the seat and stared up at the stars above him.

Novak squeezed his eyes shut and felt his heart begin to constrict in upon itself. He dropped his head into his hands. Deep inside his mind, he remembered the day his family died, trapped up so high in the south tower. He had been working the streets of Manhattan in his NYPD cruiser. He'd seen the first plane hit and tried to get to them but couldn't make it through the snarled traffic. He had gotten out of his car and watched the tower, with his family inside, as it began to buckle. He had heard the grinding and snapping of steel beams and breaking glass, the people screaming all around him. And then it had come down, far ahead of him, in clouds of gray dust and fluttering papers and black smoke, with a roar of finality and death.

Will Novak forced that image away. Time to shake it off. Come to terms once again. Pull himself together. But his skin felt clammy in the cool night air, and his hands trembled. The darkness closed in around him, thick and impenetrable, but softly, as if the breeze that touched his face was made of smooth black velvet. It was very quiet, floating out there in the dark ocean. He felt utterly alone, anchored where he was at the edge of a coral reef. He figured he was somewhere off the east coast of the Yucatan Peninsula. The boat's running lights were off. All the lights were off. Around him was nothing but a silent, watery, swaying world.

Novak stretched back out on the padded bench under the dark blue awning. Behind his boat, a billion stars spread out in a spangled canopy, vast and glittering, but also cold and distant and unfathomable. He stared up at the heavens, always awestruck by the clear, impossibly vivid spectacle of the universe when so far out at sea. In the west, a falling star streaked for several seconds and burned itself out. Sometimes Novak felt like that meteorite, like he was burning out. Sometimes he just wanted to burn out, end his mental suffering, end the memories of a life that had been so good, so perfect, but was now dead and gone forever...

Novak cursed his maudlin thoughts and stood up. He leaned down and pulled a cold beer out of the ice. He'd been sailing due south, away from his home deep inside the bayous of Louisiana. Wanting solitude. Wanting to mourn for all he'd lost. He thrust one hand into the cooler and brought up ice to rub over his sunburned face. Then he just froze, with the ice still held against his skin. A woman had just screamed. He'd heard her clearly—far away from the boat, but resonating in the silence around him. Frowning, he put down the beer and peered out over the water. Then she cried out again. A long, hysterical scream.

Novak held on to the gunwale and steadied himself. Those screams were not figments of his imagination. No way. Another scream came. Novak strained his eyes, searching the inky black night. He still saw nothing, just endless, restless water. He rubbed his eyes and scanned every direction. He wished he hadn't drunk so much. He felt a little sick. A full moon was climbing up the sky, easing through the myriad of bright stars and out from a thick cloud bank. Moments later, a glittering trail of white moonlight stretched across the sea. That pale lunar gleam was all he could see. The sky and ocean melded into black nothingness on the horizon. Then he caught sight of a light. Maybe a hundred yards off his port bow. Just a momentary flash. A boat's spotlight, maybe.

Novak grabbed a rifle out of the rack beside the helm, the Colt AR 7.62 NATO. He'd had the gun for years. It felt good when he wrapped his fingers around it. He brought the high-powered scope up to his eye, blinked away some of his grogginess, and adjusted the knob. The dull green night vision screen reacted and slowly pulled the distant lights in close. A large motor yacht was out there. It wasn't running, just floating in the darkness. Predominantly white. One stripe down the side. Sleek, modern, expensive. A honey of a boat, all right, and big, probably sixty, seventy feet, at least. Dim lights glowed softly along the main deck, probably from the staterooms and lounge, illuminating the waterline and the silhouette of the vessel. It looked as if it was anchored, maybe, the captain taking advantage of the coral reef. No screams now. Just quiet.

Novak moved his crosshairs slowly up the length of the boat, up to the bow, where he spotted another light shining in a large plate-glass window. He twisted an adjustment and picked up a couple of dark figures moving around in the bow. One was small; looked like a woman or child. Probably a woman. She was hightailing it back toward the stern, moving at a full run. He could pick up shouting now. This time it sounded like male voices. Loud. Angry. Sounded like they were speaking in Spanish. Novak was fluent in Spanish, but he was still too far away to hear what they were yelling. Then Novak saw a man chasing the woman. He was small, too, didn't look much taller than she did, but he had a gun in his hand and he was almost on her. She screamed shrilly when he grabbed her from the back. She was in big trouble.

Another guy darted out of nowhere, taller, bigger, and thrust the struggling woman behind him, trying to shield her from the little guy. They were all arguing and shouting at each other. Then the little guy raised his arm and fired the handgun at the tall man. Shot him right in the face. Point-blank. That's when the woman went crazy, screaming her head off, her shrieks echoing out over the water to Novak. After that, she put up one hell of a fight with the killer, kicking and scratching and trying to wrestle his gun away. While Novak watched, she twisted loose and made another mad dash down the gangway toward the stern.

Novak shifted his scope down to the waterline and picked up a small Zodiac inflatable boat bobbing at starboard stern. All he could see was the end of it, the rest hidden behind the boat. That's where she was heading, all right, but she only made it a couple of yards. The little guy grabbed the back of her shirt, swung her bodily around to face him, and then slammed his pistol butt hard against her forehead. She went down like a felled tree. Her assailant went down after her.

To Novak, cowards like that guy on that boat were the scum of the earth. Misogynists and bullies and abusers irked the hell out of him. He did not like men who shot unarmed victims in the face for trying to shield a woman, either. Both things he had just witnessed were big triggers for Novak. To him, that kind of behavior labeled them as black hats destined to be put down, and without a doubt. He liked to take them down hard and make it as final as he could. End them. So he calmly and methodically lined up the crosshairs on the little man who was having fun bludgeoning the scared lady. The bully had already jerked the woman back up to her feet. He hit her again, with his fist this time, so hard in the right temple that she went back hard, slammed up against the port rail, and went backwards over the side. The guy followed her movements, leaning against the gunwale above where she was floundering in the choppy swells. When he started taking potshots down at her, Novak shifted his finger to the trigger. Enough's enough, tough guy.

Slowly building anger was coursing through Novak's bloodstream and had been since the first time that guy had hit the woman. Maybe her attacker was a hijacker and was forcibly commandeering the luxury yacht, most likely to sell it on the marine black market. Bulletin alerts from the Coast Guard had been coming in daily about modern-day pirate bands operating in the Gulf and off the Mexican coast. They targeted small and undefended pleasure vessels. He had been on the lookout for them himself. Almost wished they would attack so he could put them down. He was heavily armed and knew how to use weapons. He was going to use one now.

He sat down, held his rifle nice and steady, the barrel propped atop the canopy rigging, gauged the rocking of his hull and the force of the breeze, and set his aim. Slowly, carefully, no hurry, he sighted on the killer and squeezed the trigger. The bullet burst out into the darkness, followed seconds later by a deafening retort that echoed thunderously out across the water. If the killer had not chosen that exact moment to move left, he would have died where he stood, a bullet in his head. But he had moved, bending forward to take another shot down at the girl in the water. The slug might have nicked him; Novak wasn't sure. The guy had disappeared behind the rail and stayed down. So Novak waited for him to stand up again, his finger on the trigger, ready to fire—his version of whack-a-mole.

Novak expected the guy to return fire, be it haphazardly out into the blackness around him, shooting aimlessly at an unspecified target in an unspecified area. No way could he see Novak. No way could he know who was firing at him, or why. Patiently, left eye shut, right eye fastened on the scope, Novak waited for him to pop up again. But nothing happened. Maybe the guy was smarter than Novak thought.

Within moments, a faint whine started up in the distance. Sounded like the man was in the Zodiac. If so, he had wasted no time and crawled back there in a big hurry. Not so stupid after all. He knew when to run. Novak kept the scope focused on the part of the Zodiac that he could see, but he couldn't get off a shot before the guy pulled it back behind the stern. Then Novak heard it roar to full life, and it was retreating at full speed in the opposite direction. The guy didn't know his enemy, couldn't ascertain how many there were or what kind of weaponry they had. He had made the right decision. Under those circumstances, Novak might have retreated. But that didn't mean the little killer wouldn't come back, loaded for bear, and with equally deadly reinforcements.

Novak edged the scope back down to the waves around where the girl had gone into the drink. He couldn't see her anymore, just dark, restless water, spotted with whitecaps as the wind picked up. The guy had just left a seriously injured woman out there to drown. She might be dead already, probably too weak to stay afloat. At best, she was unconscious, or soon to be. Whoever the hell the shooter had been, he was a cold-blooded bastard. Novak wished he'd gotten him with that bullet.

Novak stood up, keeping the rifle gripped tightly in his right fist as he took the helm at stern. If she was still alive, he had to fish her out. In any case, he needed to retrieve her body and take it in to the nearest authorities. She was somebody's wife or mother or daughter. So he weighed anchor, fired up the powerful engines, and steered the *Sweet Sarah* directly at the abandoned yacht. He increased his speed across the deep but kept his eyes glued on the dim light thrown off by the receding Zodiac, now far away to the west. Once he was sure the guy was not circling back, he estimated where the girl had taken the plunge. Wasn't easy, not in the dark, not on choppy seas. Not out in the middle of nowhere at midnight. He didn't have much time to find her, either, before she sank to the bottom and became shark bait.

Once he got closer, the boat's name became legible, painted across the stern escutcheon in big black letters: *Orion's Trident. Cancun, Mexico*. He motored to the port side of the vessel where she'd gone overboard. He cut the engines. He grabbed the laser spotlight and swept it back and forth across the water's surface. The killer's boat was now just a speck of light, heading away as fast as he could make it go. He wasn't coming back. Not now, in any case. It took Novak several more minutes to find the girl—way too long, he feared, but then a big wave crested over her, and he caught sight of her head bobbing in the water. Looked like she might still be alive. Yes, weak as hell, but now she was flailing her arms, trying to keep her face above water. Maybe twenty yards out from him. He focused the spotlight on her. Blood was all over her face. The head injuries were bad—he could tell that from where he stood. She wasn't going to last much longer. He brought the *Sweet Sarah* up as close to her as he safely could, cut the engines, and then tossed out a roped life buoy. She just bobbed up and down and seemed oblivious to it.

"Pull it down over your head!" he shouted to her, his voice reverberating out over the water. He was pretty sure he was going to have to go in and get her. He kicked off his canvas boat shoes, but then, somehow, she seemed to come out of her stupor enough to grab the life ring. She clung to it with both arms for dear life. Relieved, Novak slowly started towing her in, hand over hand on the rope, careful not to jerk it out of her grasp. She was too weak to hold on much longer. When he got her up against the hull, he dropped to his stomach and reached down as far as he could. He managed to grab her shirt, then got up on his knees and hauled her bodily up out of the water and onto his deck. She was conscious, but barely. She was groaning and strangling and coughing and choking. Novak laid her out flat on her back and knelt down beside her. She was bleeding heavily. He found two deep gouges, one at the top of her forehead, the other on her right temple. Her nose was bleeding, too, and the blood kept running down into her mouth and causing her to choke. She kept gasping for air and groaning, but that lasted only seconds before her eyes rolled back into her head, and she was out for the count.

Novak quickly turned her onto her side so she could breathe better. He put his mouth down close to her ear. "I'm not gonna hurt you. I'm trying to help you. Can you hear me? You're safe now. He's gone."

She must have heard his voice because her eyelids fluttered slightly in response. Then they closed again, and she didn't move. Out like a light. Novak stood up and scanned the surrounding water for the killer. He didn't want the guy turning around and flanking him. The guy who beat her up had shown a modicum of smarts. But as far as Novak could tell, the boat was gone for good, completely out of sight now. Her assailant had left her to drown, all right. His plan had been to kill her and the man who had been with her, and dump their bodies out in the middle of the ocean, with nowhere to go but down. No witnesses. Then sail away on a nice new hijacked yacht. But this time, the killer had hit a snag he hadn't expected. He didn't get the yacht he'd boarded or whatever booty was inside. But he probably wasn't acting alone. He probably had cohorts somewhere in the area. Armed men he was calling together right now.

Once Novak was sure the woman's airways were open, he positioned her head so that the blood was draining onto the deck and not down her throat. She was a small girl, looked pretty young, didn't weigh much—really skinny, in fact. Probably not much over a hundred pounds, if that. A buck ten at most. She was bruised up pretty bad, too, and not just from the blows he'd seen her take. There were other bruises, some old, some new, some black and blue and pretty damn awful. She had been beaten, no doubt about that.

Her hair appeared to be dark brown under the dim deck lights, black maybe, and she wore it in a long braid that hung down her back, almost to her waist. Lots of strands had pulled loose during the struggle and were plastered against her cheeks and neck. She had on a white oversize oxford shirt, a man's shirt, it looked like, long sleeves rolled up, dirty, bloody, ripped and torn, most of the buttons gone. She had on tight black nylon shorts and black boat shoes similar to his. She was a lot younger than he had first thought. Just a kid. Maybe even a teenager.

Novak pulled his T-shirt off over his head and wrapped it around her wounds, and then he slid an arm under her shoulders and another under her knees. He scooped her up, and she felt as limp as a boiled egg noodle. He carried her belowdecks to the fore cabin and laid her down on her side. Fetching his first-aid kit from the head, he brought it and a wet cloth back to the bed. She was sopping wet, and blood was still oozing out of the two-inch gash at her hairline. Both wounds were deep and ugly. He cleaned them out with some Betadine, pulled them together with butterfly bandages, and covered them with sterile white gauze. Then he washed a lot of the blood off her face and neck. She did not move a muscle the whole time. Her eyelashes did not twitch. She was not going to wake up anytime soon.

Leaving her lying on the bunk, he climbed the companionway to the aft deck. He took a few minutes to search the horizon with the night scope. Nothing anywhere. No lights. No roaring motors. Just the endless rocking of the boat on the cresting waves. The night was quiet, stars still glittering in their icy white splendor. They were alone. The two of them, two complete strangers, out in the middle of nowhere. He had no idea who she was, why she was with those guys, what the hell was going on. Great, that was just great, damn it. Exactly what he needed. Some helpless girl to worry about.

Once Novak was certain that the killer wasn't coming back, he went below and stood in the threshold and stared at the young woman for a few minutes. Then he went inside, leaned down close, and tried to shake her awake. She did not move. A long slender gold chain hung around her neck. He pulled it out. A beautiful gold crucifix gleamed in the overhead light.

Appeared that she might be a Catholic. He picked up her wrist and felt for a pulse. He found one, slow, but halfway steady. Her skin felt like ice.

So Novak stripped off her wet clothes, down to her underwear, and wrapped her up in some warm blankets. Her body looked wasted, impossibly thin, and sported bruises just about everywhere. After she was settled, he walked to the head and washed his hands and splashed cold water on his face. He was almost completely sober now, the dregs of the booze chased away by the adrenaline of the armed encounter. He needed to shake off the rest of it in a hurry, just in case her captor came back to claim her boat. The spike in his blood pressure was coming down, too, slowly but surely, his heartbeat returning to its normal pace. He stared at his reflection in the mirror. God, he looked like crap. He looked worse than crap. Two weeks of dark beard, bloodshot eyes from the booze, face and chest sunburned from weeks spent alone at sea. He looked like a bum.

Novak was a big man, six inches over six feet, with wide shoulders and thick muscles and a tendency to intimidate most people who met up with him. He was a scary looking guy at the best of times, and he knew it. The girl lying unconscious in that bunk was sure as hell going to wake up and panic when she saw him looking as unkempt and dangerous as he looked right now. That would not be good. Not after what she'd just gone through. On the other hand, she had already been in some very bad company before Novak had come along and saved the day, which might act to make him come off a mite better once she got the story straight.

The big white-and-black yacht was still bobbing nearby, and he went back top decks and brought the *Sweet Sarah* up close, sent a grappling hook across the bow, and tied in to her. He looked at the yacht's name again. *Orion's Trident*. He ought to be able to find its owner on the registry in Cancun. The dead guy was still where he'd breathed his last, on his back, his face and most of his head pretty much gone. Novak sidestepped the blood and brain matter, took a knee, and searched the guy for ID. No luck with that. No driver's license, no wallet, no nothing. After that, Novak went below and tossed the boat slowly and methodically, searching for proof of ownership, a name, mail addressed to the owner, anything, but could find no identifying papers, not even a ship's log.

All of which was highly irregular. That told him that there had probably been some kind of illegal operation going on aboard the *Orion's Trident*. Drug smuggling, maybe. Or something worse. Then he found a torture chamber located down in the bilge and knew it was something worse. Inside, he found steel rings attached to the wall and heavy chains lying unlocked in the shallow water covering the bottom of the hull. The girl had been a captive, all right, and so had the guy who had tried to protect her, it looked like. They must have gotten loose somehow and attempted to run for it, a decision that had turned out badly for both of them.

Novak was careful not to touch anything that he didn't have to. He wiped off his prints when he did touch something. He didn't want any of this illegal operation to come back on him. He found some women's clothes and tennis shoes that looked like they might fit the skinny girl he'd rescued, so he stuffed them into a plastic bag. After that, he took some medical supplies and pain medications he'd found in the head, and then he went topside and leaped back aboard his own boat. He stopped again, carefully searching a full 360 degrees around the horizon. The guy was long gone. On the other hand, hijackers were not wont to give up an expensive boat they'd captured, not without a fight. That was fine by Novak. They could have the *Orion's Trident* and the murdered guy on its deck. They could bring on a fight with him, too, but he wasn't going to hang around and wait for it.

Novak took the controls of the *Sweet Sarah*, maneuvered her away from the yacht's hull, and took off back to the reef where he'd been anchored. He considered heading directly to the nearest hospital but nixed that idea almost at once. They were out in the middle of nowhere. The closest ER would probably be a three- or four-day sail, at the very least. He could call in help on the sat phone, but it would be too long a distance to ask a medical chopper to fly, even if they would even consider coming so far out to sea to pick up one girl with relatively minor injuries. She was in bad shape at the moment, but her wounds were nowhere near catastrophic. The worst-case scenario might be a concussion from the blows to her head. Novak had the training and medical supplies to doctor her himself for a day or two and wait for her to regain consciousness and tell him what had happened, who had attacked her, and where she lived. After that, he could take her home and let her family deal with her. On top of all that, he had a feeling she was involved in something criminal, and he didn't want to get pulled into a legal mess because of her. His course of action now decided, Novak swung the boat east and headed for a protected cove that he had used a couple of nights before. It could act as a temporary stop until she came to and could tell him what the hell had gone on aboard that yacht.

The anchorage he sought was on the far edge of a protected coral reef where nobody could sneak up on him. He had learned to be careful the hard way. He had been a Navy SEAL, and that training had paid off in lots of ways. He was fairly certain that he had stepped into something pretty damn ugly and something that could decrease his chances of living a long and healthy life. Oh yeah, something dark was gonna come back and bite him in the ass for this little Good Samaritan act. Time would tell, but that time was gonna be spent a good long way away from that abandoned yacht. Once Novak brought the injured girl aboard, the die had been cast, whether he liked it or not. And he didn't like it.

On the other hand, Will Novak had never been a man to turn his back on trouble, or on standing up for people who couldn't fight for themselves. Truth was, he liked to fight—especially with dirtbags who deserved to die and die hard. He liked to win too, even better. And he usually did win. That guy who had fled and left the woman to drown was apparently a murderer, a torturer, and a kidnapper. He had turned tail and run like hell when somebody with equal firepower had challenged him. Novak wouldn't mind teaching him a lesson. In fact, he'd get off on it. Maybe he'd go after him when the time was right, hunt him down and let him go up against a man, instead of a weak and injured woman. Right now, he had the unconscious girl to worry about, and that was plenty.

About the Author

Linda Ladd is the bestselling author of over a dozen novels, including the Claire Morgan series and the Will Novak novels. Linda makes her home in Missouri, where she lives with her husband and beloved beagle named Banjo. She loves traveling and spending time with her two adult children, their spouses, and her two grandsons. In addition to writing, Linda enjoys target shooting and is a good markswoman with a Glock 19 similar to Claire Morgan's. She loves to read good books, play tennis and board games, and watch fast-paced action movies. She is currently at work on her next novel. Learn more at lindaladd.com.

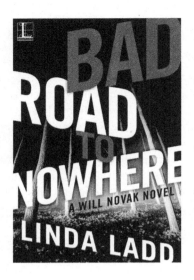

BAD MEMORIES
Not many people know their way through the bayous well enough to find Will Novak's crumbling mansion outside New Orleans. Not that Novak wants to talk to anyone. He keeps his guns close and his guard always up.

BAD SISTER
Mariah Murray is one selfish, reckless, manipulative woman, the kind Novak would never want to get tangled up with. But he can't say no to his dead wife's sister.

BAD VIBES
When Mariah tells him she wants to rescue a childhood friend, another Aussie girl gone conveniently missing in north Georgia, Novak can't turn her down. She's hiding something. But the pretty little town she's targeted screams trouble, too. Novak knows there's a trap waiting. But until he springs it, there's no telling who to trust…

ONE WRONG MOVE
Private detective Claire Morgan has come home from her honeymoon just in time for Christmas at Lake of the Ozarks. And for the sheriff's department, laid low with flu, to hand her a case guaranteed to chill her to the bone.

ONE CHANCE TO DIE
One of the homes in the local Christmas On the Lake House tour—the mansion of an aging rock star trying to turn his life around—has been "decorated" with the body of a young woman, arranged as a bloody angel on the balcony above his Christmas tree. There's a piece from a board game, gift wrapped and left under the tree, a hint that connects this murder to other deaths. With evidence of a gruesome pattern appearing, Claire suspects she's on the hunt for a serial killer.

IN A GAME WITH NO RULES
But the closer she comes, the more certain she is that the killer is playing his game with her, just waiting his turn. The next move might be on Claire herself—or worse, the people she loves…

Made in the USA
Monee, IL
16 August 2022